SHADOWED

OTHER BOOKS AND AUDIO BOOKS
BY STEPHANIE BLACK

The Believer

Fool Me Twice

Methods of Madness

Cold As Ice

Rearview Mirror

SHADOWED

a novel

STEPHANIE BLACK

Covenant Communications, Inc.

Cover image: *Apartments in the Night.NYC* © Lisa-Blue, courtesty istockphoto.com

Cover design copyright © 2012 by Covenant Communications, Inc.

Published by Covenant Communications, Inc.
American Fork, Utah

Printed in the United States of America
First Printing: September 2012

18 17 16 15 14 13 12   10 9 8 7 6 5 4 3 2 1

ISBN-13: 978-1-62108-196-8

To Kirk Shaw, with gratitude.
It was an honor to work with you, and I wish you all the best.

ACKNOWLEDGMENTS

THANK YOU TO MY HARD-WORKING test readers: Megan Anderson, Dianna Hall, Rebecca Hall, Amy McConkie, Sue McConkie, Bonnie Overly, and Jonathan Spell. And thank you to Annette Lyon, who is always so patient in answering the grammatical questions I shoot her way.

As always, thank you to the great people at Covenant Communications, particularly editor Samantha Van Walraven, who did so much to strengthen this book. Samantha has marvelously helpful insights and possibly superpowers, accomplishing more than any human being ought to be able to accomplish.

And finally, a huge heaping of gratitude to my husband, Brian, and my children for all their love and support.

CHAPTER 1

CATHERINE CLAYTON STOOD FOR A moment, resting her oversized portfolio case on the sidewalk as she stared at the two police cars parked in front of Flinders Elementary School. Flashing-light bars reflecting red and blue lights off the darkened school windows made it clear the officers weren't there for a drug prevention assembly or community program. Something was wrong.

She shifted the tote bag on her shoulder, feeling the weight of stacks of glossy flyers. If something had happened to bring the police to Flinders, this was not a good time to breeze into the office to drop off a bunch of flyers and posters. This early in the morning—an hour before school began—it was unlikely that the police were present because of an issue involving a child. Perhaps there had been a burglary.

Drawing a deep breath, she scanned the school grounds. Sunshine brightened the maple trees on the lawn, highlighting leaves beginning to change from deep green to red-orange. The maples were the only attractive touch she could find. She couldn't imagine a burglar desperate enough to think there were valuables in this grubby brick building with its cracked sidewalks and overgrown juniper bushes.

She should come back later rather than bother Danielle now. But considering how precise and organized Danielle was . . . Catherine glanced at her watch. Her appointment was at seven fifteen. Danielle wouldn't forget it, no matter what problems were occurring this morning. She'd be concerned and irritated if Catherine didn't show up, and the last thing Catherine wanted was to appear unreliable on day one. She imagined her father's voice: *You were worried about disturbing her, so you didn't even check in? No one wants to work with a flake, Catherine.*

She could check in, leave the flyers and posters, and come back later to discuss the details for the assembly. She picked up her portfolio case and started toward the front doors of the school.

Rust spots bled through the paint on the dented doors. This school—and most of the rest of Riley, New York—needed to be powerwashed, repaired, and repainted. Catherine pictured the spacious home she'd purchased and upgraded for her studio, with its spotless white siding, gold lettering on the door, wraparound porch, and thick green grass. Bridgeside Music Studio would look like an oasis when students saw it.

Catherine pulled the door open and stepped inside. A faded arrow on a sign pointed left toward the office.

The office door stood propped open, and a police officer with a stocky build and curly hair stood behind the counter, writing on a form. Looking into the office, Catherine saw that the windows facing what must be the back parking lot had been smashed. Glass shards glittered across the counters and floor.

Catherine took a cautious step through the doorway, and the officer glanced up. Without comment, he went back to his writing, but the woman standing behind him moved forward—a heavyset woman with wrinkles around her eyes and red hair nearly the same shade as Catherine's. She gave Catherine a sharp look, scrutinizing her from head to toe. "Unless you want to be murdered too, you'd better get out of here."

Horrified, Catherine started to step backward but froze. *Danielle.* "Who—what *happened*—"

"No one's hurt." The officer glared at the woman before giving Catherine a fleeting smile. "Don't panic, ma'am. Can I help you?"

Heart still hammering, Catherine swallowed and tried to make her voice calm. "I'm sorry to interrupt. My name is Catherine Clayton. I had an appointment with Ms. Knight this morning, but obviously this isn't a good time. I'll come back later—"

The click of heels and a firm voice interrupted her. "Catherine!" Danielle Knight strode out of her office and came around the edge of the counter. On autopilot, Catherine moved to embrace her but stopped herself in time and offered her hand. Danielle wasn't the type to greet a friend with a hug, even an old college friend who'd just moved to town.

"Welcome to Riley." Danielle grasped her hand. "We were out of confetti, so we scattered glass."

Hoping Danielle wouldn't notice that her hand was cold and a little shaky, Catherine drew it away and looked up into Danielle's face. At five foot six, Catherine didn't think of herself as short, but Danielle had three inches on her and added another three with the heels she wore.

"You look fantastic. I love your hair," Catherine said, then felt goofy for gushing compliments in the middle of a crime scene.

Danielle smiled slightly. "Too short?"

"No. It flatters you. As if those cheekbones needed any flattering."

Danielle scrubbed her fingers through her dark-chocolate hair, mussing it. "I don't know about cheekbones, but I like the hair because I can do *this* when I'm frustrated and call it windblown elegance."

"So what happened?" Catherine asked, gesturing at the broken windows. "A burglary?"

"No. Nothing's missing. Vandalism. We've had a few problems lately."

The woman who'd spoken of murder stepped forward. "Other windows broken," she said angrily. "And someone broke into the gym and left big gashes in the floor—"

"Thanks, Renee," Danielle cut her off. "She gets the drift."

"I'm sorry," Catherine said. The last thing this decrepit building needed was someone deliberately destroying it. But if vandalism was all they were dealing with, why had Renee acted so dramatic and talked as though someone had been killed? "Do you have any suspects?"

Danielle shook her head. "Not yet. But we'll nail them. Assuming we have any nails left after hammering this old haunt back together. Got your posters and flyers for me?"

"I do, but we can talk later. You have enough to deal with right now. May I help you clean up? Or do you need to wait for the police to—"

"Forget the mess. It's not your concern." The tightness in Danielle's expression made her angular face sharp and intimidating. Catherine figured that expression must come in handy when Principal Danielle was dealing with troublemakers. "Let's see the posters."

"I don't mind coming back another time, Dani."

"Are you kidding me? We need good news right now, and you're bringing good news." Danielle snatched the portfolio case out of Catherine's hand, set it on the counter, and unlatched it.

"Nice." She held up one of the glossy black-and-gold posters. "*Bridgeside Music Studio.* Snappy. But what happens when you relocate from that place by the bridge?"

"People can contemplate the mystery of how the studio got its name."

"Or you can rename it the Harold Hill School of Music."

Catherine smiled. "The difference being that I actually *know* how to lead a band."

"Beginning bands all sound about the same, whether or not they're using the Think System," Danielle remarked. At the blank look on Renee's face, she asked, "Haven't you ever seen *The Music Man*?"

"Missed it."

"I'll lend you the DVD so you'll know what to expect from this one." She pointed at Catherine and winked.

"Thanks a lot," Catherine said dryly. "Maybe I'd better add a footnote to the posters explaining I'm not a con artist."

"This is Renee Endicott, by the way." Danielle introduced the woman. "Secretary. Keeps us on task."

Catherine couldn't imagine Danielle Knight had ever needed anyone to keep her on task. "It's always good to meet a fellow redhead," she addressed Renee.

"I'm not," Renee said shortly. "Dye job."

The age showing in Renee's face had already proven her hair color was artificial; making a point of it struck Catherine as a cold response—as though Renee didn't want Catherine creating a commonality between them.

"These are the flyers." Catherine drew them out of her silver tote bag. Renee's curtness made her feel even more awkward to be advertising her music studio while a cop was standing a few feet away filling out a report and shards of glass were poking at the soles of Catherine's shoes. Glass had flown so far from the windows that she shuddered to imagine how savagely the vandal must have struck the panes. From where she stood, she could see dents and cracks in the window frames as though the vandal hadn't been content with breaking the glass but had continued pounding even after the windows were rubble.

Struggling to refocus her thoughts, she set the flyers on the counter. "Dani, I'll call you later, and you can let me know if there's anything else I need to do before the assembly—"

"Ms. Knight? We need you back here."

Danielle turned and hurried toward a blond officer who had emerged from the hallway leading to her office. "Cate, leave all your stuff with Renee, along with your card."

"Thanks." Catherine reached into her bag and removed her card case.

Renee raised an eyebrow at the matching silver card case and tote bag embossed with musical notes. "*That's* an eye-catching combo."

Catherine pretended not to notice the disdain in Renee's voice. "Yes, it is. I was going to get dignified black leather, but when I saw these shiny things, I couldn't resist. I'm like a magpie."

"Shiny things, huh? That explains the diamond explosion."

Catherine glanced at the row of chunky cubic zirconia bracelets around her wrist. Apparently Renee was determined to be unfriendly no matter how Catherine tried to be pleasant. Fine—at least snarky remarks were better than her creepy warning when Catherine had walked into the office. "My card has all my contact information. The flyers are already divided into stacks of thirty-five. I didn't know how many children were in each classroom."

Renee said nothing, clearly not interested in letting Catherine know if thirty-five had been a good guess. The officer at the counter turned and walked toward Danielle's office, speaking into his radio as he went.

"Thanks for your help." Catherine gave friendliness another try. "And I'm sorry about the vandalism."

"Yeah, as if this place isn't already falling down." Renee lowered her voice. "And we don't need people wasting our time with touchy-feely do-goodism either. A music studio. Where do you think you are? Boston? Greenwich, Connecticut?"

Catherine flushed. "If you're not interested, don't sign up."

"You're wanting a hobby to keep you busy between tennis dates at the country club. If you really want to do some good, do something that matters. You think kids whose parents have been out of work for a year and a half are going to care about screeching some strings or blatting a horn? Not that I think you'll stick around for long."

"If I weren't planning to stick around, why would I have come at all?"

"I'm sure you have good intentions." Renee made the words caustic. "But talk to me in six months when you're bored out of your mind and decide you'd rather be worshipped by handsome men on a Mediterranean beach than by a bunch of ratty children in Riley, New York."

"I'm in Riley to teach music, not to be worshipped," Catherine said coolly. "I think you misread the flyer."

Renee glanced over her shoulder, probably making sure Danielle wasn't returning.

"We have enough on our plates trying to hold this school together. We don't need your silly program taking up our attention."

"I won't be taking up your attention. This is not a school program. I'm running an independent studio, intended partly to fill the gap left by the cancellation of school music programs."

"So what are you doing *here*, plotting to distract the kids from their work with some flashy assembly while you hawk your wares?"

"Principal Knight feels the program has value and wants the school community to know about it." Catherine started to turn away.

"You might want to leave a guard next time you park your Porsche in the school lot," Renee said. "Unless you like people scratching their names in the paint and using your hubcaps as Frisbees."

"I don't have a car here. I walked. But thanks for the warning."

"You *walked?*"

"It's a beautiful morning."

Renee's expression went darker, and she glanced at the shattered windows. "Hope you can walk fast."

"Why do you keep talking like I'm in danger?" Catherine snapped. "You're dealing with vandalism, not murder."

"*Look* at this." Renee flapped her hand toward the windows. "You think this is some bored teenager whacking windows with a hammer just for kicks? That's *hate* there. Rage. And that was where *she* sat. Near those windows."

Jolted, Catherine asked warily, "Who?"

"One of the other secretaries here. She was murdered."

Catherine gaped at Renee. "When?"

"About two years ago. Pretty girl like you. Just about your age." Renee tried to sound harsh, but her eyes glistened with tears. "They never caught the killer."

"I'm so sorry," Catherine said. "Were you close to her?"

Renee turned away and started picking up papers from a desk and shaking glass shards off of them.

Not knowing what else to do, Catherine walked out the door, glass crunching under her shoes.

CHAPTER 2

"Nice, very nice." Danielle circled the main room, originally designed to be the living room in the spacious home Catherine was using as a studio. "You could put a track in here and make your students run laps between arpeggios."

"It's not *that* big," Catherine said. "It's just empty." A piano took up one corner, shelves filled with instrument cases lined one wall, and a couch provided a place for students or parents to wait, but other than that, the room was just a polished hardwood floor. Twilight showed through two huge skylights in the vaulted ceiling, and outside the windows, a pinkish sunset backlit the trees in the yard.

Danielle stopped at Catherine's side. "Where do you sit if you have non-music-related visitors? Or is this a Greek mythology sort of place—if you step through the door, you're trapped into playing an instrument for eternity unless you can talk someone into taking over for you?"

Catherine laughed. "Yep. And you're trapped now. See that violin case? Go get it."

"Give it up, Harold. I'm too old of a dog to learn new tricks."

"Old? Please."

"Older than you."

"Not by much." At thirty-one, Danielle was three years older than Catherine. Catherine had to concede that she *seemed* older but not due to any physical aging; Danielle's skin was smooth, her chic, short hair a lustrous brown, her figure slim. Her sharp features and narrow face weren't Hollywood pretty, but she had an attractive, powerful aura about her that made Catherine feel childish with her long red hair, heart-shaped face, and sprinkling of freckles.

"If you're not dead, you're not too old to learn to play an instrument," Catherine said. "I'll sign you up for after-school lessons. How about learning the clarinet?"

"Thanks, but I'll pass."

"Come on. I'll finish the tour, and then we can eat." Catherine showed Danielle the office where a receptionist would handle scheduling and other organizational work. The next room, furnished with several music stands, a few chairs, and a whiteboard, would serve as a private or small-group lesson room. The other downstairs bedroom would serve as a practice/warm-up room; couches and chairs arranged around the perimeter of the room provided additional waiting space for parents or students.

"Did you have to do much to get this place ready?" Danielle lightly ran her fingers along the glass sculpture of a violin that stood on a table in the hall.

"Not too much. I had the floors refinished, those shelves installed in the main room, new window coverings placed, new kitchen countertops put in, new landscaping, a few other things."

"That's what you call 'not too much'?" Danielle shook her head. "Do you still plan to someday build a full-sized music studio and hire a staff of teachers?"

"Yes. Think big." Catherine didn't feel like sharing the doubts that gnawed at her. What if this didn't unfold like she'd imagined it? What if people were indifferent to what she was offering—or even antagonistic, like the school secretary, Renee, had been? What if a month from now she was sitting in a silent house with zero students while she tried to keep her chin up and pretend she loved living in this grungy little industrial town?

"My bedroom and a couple of rooms I'm not using right now are upstairs, but I'm guessing you don't care about seeing those." Catherine led Danielle toward the back of the house into the family room adjoining the kitchen. "And finally, a place that looks like a real house. I hope you don't mind if we eat in the kitchen. The dining room is full of boxes of music stands and folding chairs that I still need to unpack."

"I think we can squeeze in here." Danielle walked toward the roomy breakfast nook with its oak table.

"Help yourself." Catherine gestured at the platter of cheese, olives, and sliced baguette. "The pasta's almost ready. What can I get you to drink? Perrier? Lemonade? Juice? Water?"

"Perrier, thanks."

Catherine poured chilled sparkling water into a goblet, added a slice of lime, and offered the drink to Danielle. "Any leads on the vandalism?"

Danielle sat at the table. "No. The police are checking out staff members who've been laid off in the last year or two—which, unfortunately, isn't a short list." She stabbed an almond-stuffed olive with a fork. "We're hurting. But you know that."

"I'm sorry."

"If you're sorry, you'll need a lot of sorry to go around. We're far from being the only school district in trouble. But, frankly, this wasn't a model district to begin with, or they wouldn't have hired a newbie like me."

"You had a few years of teaching experience before you got your master's degree." Catherine opened the oven. "Besides, experience isn't the only mark of competence. You have the brains and guts to fix whatever needs fixing. They recognized that."

"Thanks for the flattery. You've always been a pro at dishing out praise, whether the recipient deserves it or not."

"You deserve it." Catherine took out a foil-covered pan. "Vermicelli with lobster sauce. I hope you're in the mood for seafood."

"You know I am."

Catherine grinned, thinking of the night she and Danielle and a couple of other grad-school friends had gone to a seafood buffet. They'd all been astonished at how many shrimp and clams wiry Danielle could devour.

"It's hard to believe a teacher would want to lash out at the school like that." Catherine set a heaping plate of pasta in front of Danielle. "Surely they know the economic problems aren't rooted at Flinders, and there's no point in blaming the school."

"What kind of idyllic bubble were you raised in if you think people are always rational?"

Catherine smiled sheepishly as a feeling of foolishness and naiveté made her feel like a clueless kid compared to Danielle.

"Do you keep in touch with anyone else from school?" Danielle asked as Catherine sat down.

"A few people." Catherine picked up her fork. "You're much better than I am at keeping in touch. Oh—I got a message from Allie Grigsby earlier this week."

"How is she?"

"She's doing great. Her second baby's due any day. Crazy, huh?"

"Not really. Considering how eager she was to ditch school and become a mother, I'm surprised she's only on number two."

Catherine studied Danielle. Was she in a bad mood, or had she grown harder and harsher in the three years she'd been in Riley? "Not everyone wants a graduate degree. I don't think advanced degrees are required to make you a good person."

"Sorry." Danielle lifted a piece of lobster on her fork. "That was rude. I'm tired tonight. I'm glad Allie's doing well. I envy her."

"Me too. If you know any nice single guys, send them my way."

"I'm surprised *you* aren't married yet. After what happened with Robert, were you too shaken to hunt for another man? I can see how you *would* have trouble moving on after that."

Catherine's cheeks went hot, and she had no idea what to say. Did Danielle think Robert's death had devastated her to the point that she'd never gotten over it? It had been heart wrenching, but . . . had Danielle forgotten that Catherine had broken up with Robert before his accident? "Robert and I weren't . . . together anymore when he . . . You've probably forgotten."

"I'm sorry, Cate." Danielle rested her slim fingers on Catherine's arm. "From the color of your face, I can tell my comment was inappropriate. That's twice in a row I've been a jerk tonight."

"Don't worry about it." It surprised Catherine how shaken she *did* feel. Danielle's comment had caught her with her defenses down and stirred up old pain, old guilt, old longing.

"I think being together again has skewed my time sense," Danielle said. "It makes it seem like everything that happened in school was last week or last month, not four years ago."

"I know what you mean. Where does the time go?" Wanting to pull the conversation away from the past, Catherine poured more Perrier into Danielle's goblet and asked, "So besides the vandalism, what else is going on here?"

For the rest of dinner, Danielle talked about the state of the school and the city, and none of what she said was positive. "Riley's dying, candidly. Half the city is out of work, or it seems that way. We lost a semiconductor fab a few years back—there went a ton of jobs. Then a furniture and cabinet factory closed. There's not much left here, and it's not as though the state has extra money to pour into Riley. The city doesn't have enough money for anything. We keep having to lay teachers off and cut programs, and our classrooms are so crowded now that the remaining teachers are barely keeping themselves from drowning."

"But you stay." Catherine stood to clear Danielle's and her empty plates off the table.

"I stay and you *came*. Which of us is more in need of psychiatric help?"

"Riley is exactly the kind of community I was looking for. When you told me about it, I was so excited I danced all over the house like a kid."

"I'm glad you're here. Your music program brings some sunshine, pardon the cheesy metaphor."

"I hope people feel that way about it." Catherine opened the freezer and took out a carton of pistachio gelato.

"Why wouldn't they feel that way? You're offering a usually very expensive service for free. What's not to like?"

"Your secretary didn't think much of it . . . or of me."

"Renee? Ignore her. She's crabby these days and thinks anything that's not math and English is a waste of money."

Catherine scooped a serving of gelato into a bowl. "Music can help develop—"

"You don't have to defend what you're doing. Obviously, if I didn't think your program was worthwhile, I wouldn't have suggested you use Flinders as a jumping-off point, and I wouldn't let you pass out flyers or take up school time with your assembly. Trust me, I wouldn't give you and your financial backers this opportunity just to be nice."

Catherine handed Danielle a bowl of the dessert, relieved at this reference to her "backers." After Renee's gibes, Catherine had worried that Danielle suspected the source of the money and had tipped off Renee.

When their bowls were empty, Catherine suggested, "Let's go sit in the family room. Might as well find comfortable chairs."

Taking her purse with her, Danielle settled onto the brown leather sofa. "How are you holding up? Has it been hard for you with your father gone?"

"Yes." Catherine sat in the big recliner she'd taken from home with Ava's blessing—the chair that, more than any other item, reminded her of her father.

"So you cope by doing things he'd be proud of. Living up to his memory."

"He did like the idea of my music program . . . though by the time it was really coming together in my head, it was . . . hard for him to focus much on what I was saying. But I know he approved. He loved giving people the opportunity to develop new skills and talents, to better themselves and increase joy in their lives."

"You still get along well with your stepmother?"

"Ava is marvelous, and I adore her. Besides being a wonderful woman, she takes care of all the details I don't want to worry about—like dealing long distance with real estate agents and contractors when we were getting this house ready."

"Ah. So Ava back in Virginia is the one truly managing things. That explains how a right-brained musician who can't get her library books back on time can run a music studio."

Catherine laughed. "Guilty. *You* are the rare breed—the creative mind *and* the super-organized mind all in one woman. Do you still write? Please tell me you still write."

"I write . . . memos. And uplifting go-get-'em thoughts for the school newsletter."

"You haven't given up fiction, have you?"

"I don't have a lot of spare time."

"You have a lot of talent."

"Talent doesn't necessarily equal income. I need an income."

"You need to keep writing. You have a gift, and you certainly have the drive to accomplish anything you want."

"Back off. If I wanted an inspirational 'you can be anything you want' quote, I'd write it myself and e-mail it out to the school."

Catherine smiled. "Fine, I'll back off for now. So how are *you* doing, Dani? How's your—" She stopped herself. It was tactless to ask about Danielle's family. How likely was it that Danielle's alcoholic father had finally gone into treatment or her absent mother had miraculously returned, free of her drug addiction? "How's Esther doing?" Catherine amended. Danielle's younger sister was a safer topic.

"She's okay. You know she's living with me here, right?"

"Yes, you told me. Is she going to school?"

"Not right now. She did take some computer classes though. She's brilliant with computers, numbers, anything like that."

"That's fantastic."

"It would be more fantastic if she'd develop those skills further instead of dabbling. I pushed her to go to college full time for a business degree, but she says she'd rather work right now. Of course, she can't find a full-time job, so working means a few hours a week washing dishes and mopping floors at a fish and chips place. Foolish kid."

"Maybe she'll be more interested in school later. She's . . . what, twenty-one?"

"Twenty-two. And I hope so. Right now she's more focused on dyeing green streaks in her hair and running around with losers." Danielle opened the purse she'd set on the floor next to her. She withdrew a thick envelope and tossed it to Catherine.

Catherine caught it, surprised at how heavy it was. "What is it?" Danielle said nothing.

Puzzled, Catherine tore the envelope open. Heat shot along her nerves as she looked at the bundles of money. This must be thousands of dollars!

"Is this a donation to the studio?" The thought made her wince—she'd made it clear to Danielle that all costs were covered and she didn't need donations. Had Danielle gathered donations for her anyway, from people who really couldn't afford to give? "Danielle—"

"It's not a donation." Danielle's brown eyes held Catherine's gaze. "It's a repayment. With interest. Far overdue."

Oh no. Caught off guard, Catherine tried to look confused but knew she was blushing. "What are you talking about?"

"Oh, please, Cate. To you, ten thousand dollars might be pocket change, so if it landed on your doorstep—or in your mailbox—you'd call it a gift from heaven and wouldn't do much digging to figure out where it came from. But for me, it was a devouring question. It didn't take much research to figure out which of my friends had deep—very deep—pockets."

"So my family has money. That doesn't explain *this*." Catherine tapped the envelope.

"You have a decent poker face, except for the blush. We're square now. I don't want to be in debt to you any longer."

Catherine knew if she kept feigning ignorance she'd look like an idiot *and* irritate Danielle. "How long have you known?"

"Since about a week after a big envelope of cash showed up in my mailbox five years ago. It wouldn't have taken me that long to figure it out, except at first, I didn't think it could be a student, so I was looking in the wrong direction. I'll give you credit for not flaunting your wealth."

Danielle had known for years but had never let on? In the matter of poker faces, she was the winner. "Dani—"

"I should have returned it to you immediately, but it was . . ." Danielle ran her thumbnail along the arm of the couch, and Catherine knew what she was thinking: the money had allowed her to support Esther while finishing up her graduate program. Without it, she might have had to drop out. "The account is closed now," she said. "I'm out of debt."

"I never meant for you to be *in* debt. The money was a gift, not a loan. I don't want repayment. And I won't accept it."

"Yes, you will. I'm not taking it home with me. I knew better than to bring you a check. You wouldn't have deposited it. But cash? You won't let it go to waste. I don't care what you do with it. Buy music stands. Donate it to a homeless shelter. Mail it anonymously to someone else. What counts is that I paid you back."

"I wish you wouldn't do this. You need . . ." She trailed off. Telling Danielle she needed the money more than Catherine herself sounded so condescending, no matter how true it was. "Give it to the school. It can help cover repairs."

"You give it to the school if you want. It's your money. I owe you thanks as well, so thank you."

Catherine didn't know what to say. *You're welcome* felt awkward, especially with the businesslike—almost brusque—tone to Danielle's voice, as though she were going down a list and *thank you* was one more item needing a check mark. *This is hard for her*, Catherine realized. Someone as strong, as proud as Danielle . . . No wonder she sounded edgy discussing this. If Catherine had any compassion, she wouldn't drag this out by arguing with Danielle.

"Well . . . I'm . . . glad things worked out with your degree." The fact that Danielle had known the source of the money for years while Catherine had thought herself anonymous left her embarrassed and disconcerted. "And thank you for helping me get established in Riley."

Danielle shrugged, her expression relaxing a bit. "You were looking for a community that could use your Harold Hill gig. Riley fit the bill."

Catherine wanted to steer the subject completely away from money, but her encounter with Renee Endicott was still troubling her. "You . . . didn't tell Renee that I . . ."

"That you're rolling in so much cash that you can afford to come here, fund this whole program yourself, and give everything away for free because your father was filthy-rich computer guru Jeremy Clayton?"

Catherine tried to smile. "Something like that."

"No, I didn't tell her. I didn't tell anyone. I told Renee exactly what you told me—that the program is funded by private donations. I never told her you were the only one donating, though I assumed that was true. What did Renee say to you?"

"It doesn't matter." The last thing Catherine wanted was to get Renee in trouble with her boss.

"She didn't learn anything from me except your name, the basics of your program, and that we were grad-school roommates. I'm bright enough to catch on to the fact that if you wanted the world to know your bank balance, you'd announce it yourself. But if Renee got curious and did her own research on you, I can't control that."

Wonderful, Catherine thought. *Thanks a lot, Google.* Time to shift the conversation away from herself. "Renee mentioned that a secretary at Flinders was murdered."

Sadness clouded Danielle's eyes before anger turned her face to marble. "Yes. Olivia Perry."

"I'm so sorry. What . . . happened?"

"She was bludgeoned to death in her apartment. The killer was never found."

Catherine shuddered. "Renee seemed very shaken. She talked about the murder as soon as I walked into the office. I think being in the middle of a crime scene with the police around must have . . . reminded her."

"I'm not surprised. Renee's scared because there was some vandalism around Riley not long before Olivia died. Not at Flinders but in other places."

Catherine sat up straight in the soft recliner. "Is there a connection?"

"Why on earth would there be? None of us even remembered that the previous vandalism had occurred around the time Olivia died until Renee got a bee in her bonnet and started talking as though broken windows at Flinders meant the killer is back."

"She made a point that the smashed windows were near where Olivia used to sit."

"Olivia's computer station was near the windows. If a vandal wanted to smash windows in the office, they'd inevitably be near where Olivia sat." Danielle sighed and ran her fingers through her short hair. "Renee had a hard time after Olivia died. She and Olivia were good friends. Olivia was a sweet person and a beautiful girl. Did well connecting with the parents and the kids. It was heartbreaking for the whole community." She frowned at Catherine. "Renee didn't scare you, did she, talking about Olivia? Renee can be melodramatic. This was a couple of years ago, and nothing like her murder has happened since. Why did Renee bring it up with you?"

"Just . . . letting me know Riley isn't paradise, I guess."

"Good thing she cleared that up," Danielle said. "It's an easy mistake to make."

CHAPTER 3

As SHE JOINED THE PEOPLE exiting the chapel, Catherine covertly scanned the faces around her. She was determined that before church ended, she would speak to at least five people and have at least two new phone numbers in her contacts list. These goals made her feel slightly junior high-ish—*make a friend*—but she knew from experience that the best way to cope with a lonely outsider feeling was to set a concrete goal for how to overcome it. *Don't wallow in a problem. Fix it.* Her father's voice rumbled in memory. Now was a perfect time to approach someone—she could start a natural conversation by asking where Sunday School was held.

Catherine zeroed in on her first target: a woman with blonde hair cut in a short A-line and who was wearing a silky orange shirt. She hastened to catch up with her.

The woman glanced at her. She had a square jaw and thick eyeliner too dark for her fair coloring.

"Hi," Catherine said. "I'm new in the ward. Could you tell me where Sunday School is?"

"Well, welcome!" The woman stood to the side to allow people to pass her. "It's great to have you here. I'm Jan Peralta."

The size of Jan's smile relieved Catherine's nervousness by a few notches. *Friendly person. Good choice for a first contact.* "I'm Catherine Clayton."

"Great to meet you. Those are my kids—" She gestured at some teenagers heading toward the hallway. "Gina is seventeen, Matt is fourteen, and Kelly is twelve. And that hunk over there is mine too. Lewis." She waved toward a young man with broad, muscled shoulders. "Just turned twenty-three, and he could *really* use a job, so if you hear of anything, let me know. I'll accept it for him without even asking his opinion. Gospel Doctrine is in the Relief Society room—right down that corridor, back of the building. I'll show you; it's on my way. I teach the sixteen-year-olds."

"Thanks." Catherine walked beside Jan.

"Did you just move to Riley?"

"Yes. From Virginia, near DC."

"I'm jealous. I visited that area once, and it was so gorgeous it made it hard to come home—no offense to home sweet Riley. Got any family with you, or are you on your own?"

Catherine forced herself to smile, even as she pictured her father's casket. "On my own."

"What brings you here?"

"Work," Catherine said. "I teach music."

"Really? That's wonderful. Who are you working for? I thought the schools didn't have music programs anymore—no budget for them. Which is a huge shame, but around here, we're lucky to keep our heads above water."

"I'm running an independent program. Private and group lessons, ensembles. Everyone's welcome, all ages. It's supported by donations, so no fees." Catherine stopped herself from launching into a longer pitch. Church wasn't the time to advertise her studio.

"Wow, really? Sounds like a great program! Listen, I've got to go teach, but I'd love to talk more about this. I think Gina has some real musical ability."

"Here, this has my phone number on it." Catherine pulled a card out of her purse. "We can talk later."

"I'd love that. Thanks. Your stop is right there." Jan gestured toward the Relief Society room. "In fact, let me snag a handsome young man to escort you—hey, Adam!"

A blond man walking past them stopped and turned. Catherine felt squirmy at the way Jan had flagged him down to escort her to a destination she'd almost arrived at—the lack of a ring on his finger made her suspect Jan was jumping immediately into the cause of matching the ward singles.

"Hi, Jan." The man *was* handsome but forgettably handsome—nice, regular features but somehow bland, with no spark in his eyes.

"We have a new ward member," Jan said. "This is Catherine . . ." She paused. "Heck, I've forgotten your last name."

"Clayton." Maybe not bland, Catherine thought as she looked at him. More . . . reserved. Guarded, as though he didn't want to give anything away until he knew more about the situation.

"Catherine Clayton," Jan said. "From Virginia."

"Welcome. Good to grow in numbers. Usually, we're shrinking." He held out his hand. "Adam Becket." His smile surprised Catherine. It was markedly crooked, with one side of his mouth going up and one side staying down.

"Show Catherine to Gospel Doctrine," Jan said. "I need to go teach."

"Let me get your number, Jan." Catherine hastily pulled out her phone before Jan could depart. "Would you mind if I called if I have any Riley-related questions?"

"Please do. I know moving is a royal pain in the neck, and I'm happy to recommend doctors or help unpack boxes or whatever." Jan recited her number, and Catherine entered it into her contacts list.

That's one potential friend, Catherine thought, slipping her phone into her purse as Jan hurried away. *See? You're not a total loner now. You met Jan. One more phone number and you get your prize.*

Adam led the way toward Sunday School. Did she get extra credit on her goals if one of the phone numbers belonged to a single guy? Ava would be thrilled. She'd worried that Riley would have few eligible bachelors, and was Catherine *sure* she wanted to make it that much harder to find someone?

She'd better be careful though. Seeking Adam's number would send a different message than seeking Jan's number, and right now, she didn't want to send any messages beyond *I'm new and want to get to know people.*

"Did you . . . just arrive in town?" Adam's words sounded a little stiff, as though he knew he needed to start a conversation but wasn't sure how best to go about it. Catherine assessed him out of the corner of her eye. Was he nervous—or annoyed with Jan for pushing him at Catherine?

Never mind that phone number; he probably wouldn't want to give it to you anyway.

"Yes, I moved in earlier this week." After he'd walked her into the room, it seemed tacky to go sit somewhere else, so she followed him to a middle row and sat next to him, hoping he wasn't plotting revenge against Jan for making him her momentary companion.

"You're running a music program?" he asked.

"Yes." Glad for a topic of conversation, Catherine explained what she was doing in Riley. Adam looked interested—or at least he pretended to be interested. He got points for that, even if he was faking. She noticed a few narrow white scars near the right corner of his mouth, the side that barely moved when he smiled. He must have some type of nerve damage. It wasn't obvious when his expression was serious but was very noticeable when he smiled.

When the teacher began the lesson with the introduction of visitors or new people, Catherine was thrilled at how many people reacted with smiles and murmurs of welcome to the announcement that she'd moved into the ward. She received the same warm reception in Relief Society, and by the time church had ended, she'd tripled her goal—she had six numbers in her contacts list and had smiled at and greeted so many people she'd lost count. And she had to admit, she was pleased at the way one of the sisters in Relief Society (*Heather Boswell, the one with short black hair and pink-framed glasses,* Catherine reminded herself, determined to remember as many names and faces as she could) had remarked that she was glad to see Catherine had met Adam Becket—there were so few single young people in the area. It had seemed an offhand, guileless comment, but Catherine was glad for this confirmation that Adam was unattached.

Not that she knew if she was interested in him or if he had the slightest interest in her. How could she know that in one brief conversation? But she certainly wasn't *un*interested. Adam seemed nice—on the shy side, not particularly outgoing or smooth. It made her smile to think of how he had paused after giving her a one-word answer, shifted in his seat, and added a few sentences as though he'd realized he was being too brief and was determined to hold up his end of their conversation. She wondered if his mother had lectured him about this when he was a teenager going on his first date: *No one-syllable answers when chatting with a girl.*

Feeling more lighthearted than she had in months, Catherine headed for her minivan. The sight of her super-practical vehicle made her grin. *Not quite the Porsche Renee Endicott assumed you drove.*

Clouds had filled the sky, and raindrops were beginning to fall. A rainy afternoon sounded perfect. She'd settle in her father's armchair near the fireplace with the treat she'd promised herself if she hit her goals—a toasted baguette loaded with fresh mozzarella, sliced tomatoes, and shredded basil, followed by Godiva dark chocolate truffles. Then she'd spend the afternoon with her cello, playing some of her favorite music while rain pelted against the windows. Cozy and relaxing.

She reached for the rhinestone-covered G-clef that hooked over the side of her purse so she could hang her keys there and keep them from getting swallowed. A folded piece of paper poked out from under the key hook—a paper she didn't remember putting there. Puzzled, she slid it out and unfolded it.

In unfamiliar handwriting, the note read, *Since you're new to Riley, there are a few things you need to know. I saw you with Adam Becket, and I need to warn you—Adam is bad news. Call me, and I'll explain.*

The note was signed *Trent Perry*, followed by a phone number.

Rain pattered on her head. Hastily, she clicked the button to unlock her car and slid inside.

Instead of driving away, she reread the note several times. Who was Trent Perry? Had she met him? She didn't think so.

Adam was bad news?

Creeped out both by the warning and by the fact that this Trent person had decided to communicate by sticking a note in her purse, Catherine finally drove away from the church, her cheerful mood sinking and her sense of isolation beginning to regrow. *How do I deal with this one, Dad?*

* * *

The rain had stopped and the sky was clearing by the time Catherine wiped the rosin off her cello and returned it to its case. She'd hoped the music would relax her and wipe away her anxiety about Trent Perry's note. Trent sounded like a nut. A reasonable person would have pulled her aside after church if he had important information to give her, not stuck a note in her purse when she wasn't looking. If she called Trent—whoever he was—she would only feed his nuttiness. This whole thing was ridiculous. She was *not* going to call Trent. If he had something to say to her about Adam, he could do it in person.

She needed to go for a walk. She hadn't set foot out of doors all day, except to climb into her minivan. No wonder she felt fidgety.

She pared a couple of curls of parmesan cheese from the block in the fridge and ate them with a cluster of grapes for a quick snack then headed upstairs to change her shoes.

The phone rang. The sound pleased her—her landline had only rung a couple of times since she'd moved in, and she liked the thought that someone wanted to get in touch with her. One shoe on, she jumped toward the phone on her nightstand. The caller ID read *Becket, Adam.*

Adrenaline tickled her nerves as she stared at the ringing phone and thought of Trent's words: *Adam is bad news. Call me, and I'll explain.*

"This is idiotic," she said, but still, she couldn't bring herself to pick up the phone. What warning had Trent wanted to give her? She hadn't expected Adam to contact her so soon . . . but he seemed like a decent . . . she *did* want to talk to . . . but if Trent *did* have important information about him . . .

"Oh, for heaven's sake," she hissed as her confusion made the decision for her and the call went to voice mail. A moment later, the message light began to blink.

She picked up the phone and listened to the message: "Hello, Catherine. This is, uh, Adam Becket. We—um—met at . . . church." Adam seemed to be one of those people whose tongues got clumsy at the *leave a message* beep. "Just wanted to welcome you to Riley and let you know if you have any questions, I'm glad to help." He recited his number. A beep signaled the end of the message.

How had he gotten her number? From Jan? Why hadn't she answered the phone when he'd called instead of hovering over it while it rang then listening to his message the instant he hung up? Was she thirteen years old? She kicked off her one walking shoe, stalked downstairs, and snatched Trent's note from where she'd left it on the kitchen counter. Gritting her teeth, she stabbed his number into the keypad.

"Hello?"

"Is this Trent Perry?"

"Yes."

"This is Catherine Clayton from church." Catherine drew a deep breath. Her voice was too curt. No sense in starting this off by barking at Trent. "You left me a note."

"Yeah. Thanks for calling. You probably thought the note was weird."

"I did, because it *was* weird. Why didn't you talk to me?"

"Because it's awkward in that setting. But I couldn't risk waiting too long. I saw you sitting with Becket, and I worried that . . ." He paused. "Look, would you be okay meeting with me?"

When dealing with people from church, Catherine's knee-jerk instinct was to be polite and accommodating, but Trent gave her the creeps. "Why can't you tell me whatever you want to tell me over the phone?"

"I'd rather be face-to-face. How about this? My family owns the Leonardi Fitness Center, the gym on Seneca Street. Could you come by sometime tomorrow during the day? We could talk there."

"So church is an awkward place to bring up whatever you want to say but work isn't?"

"You'll understand after we talk."

"Fine." She'd be edgy and restless until she found out what Trent wanted to tell her, so she might as well meet with him. A public place sounded like a good venue for the meeting. "I could come in the morning. Around nine?"

"Ask for me at the front desk—it'll be my wife working there. Her name is Kelsey."

"Fine." Trent was married? At least one person in the world didn't think he was a kook, so that might be a good sign. Unless his wife was kooky too.

"Sorry to bother you," Trent said. "But there are things about Adam you need to know."

"See you tomorrow," Catherine said shortly and hung up.

CHAPTER 4

CATHERINE LOOKED UP THE ADDRESS of the Leonardi Fitness Center and found it was two and a half miles from home. Perfect. An invigorating walk was a good way to prepare herself to meet with Trent.

She'd been tempted to call Jan Peralta to get her opinion on both Adam and Trent but had decided against it. Clearly, Jan didn't think Adam was "bad news," or she wouldn't have hailed him to walk Catherine to class. Until Catherine understood the situation, she didn't want to potentially embarrass either Adam or Trent by telling Jan, or anyone else, about Trent's note—though chances were, if Trent had issues with Adam, Catherine wasn't the first person in the ward to find out about it.

The morning was damp and fresh from the previous night's rain, and the darkness of the clouds signaled more rain coming. Catherine grabbed her ancient raincoat out of the closet—a royal-blue slicker decorated with a red lobster pattern and lobster-shaped buttons. It was colorful and quirky to the point of tackiness, but she loved it and loved remembering how her mother had laughed when she'd seen Catherine buying it in that gift shop in Maine. *Those lobsters clash with your hair, kiddo.* Catherine had planned to buy the same coat for her red-haired mother for her next birthday as a practical joke.

But Catherine and her father had celebrated that birthday at her mother's graveside.

Ten years. She'd had this coat for ten years. Other raincoats came and went, but this one stayed in her closet. Wearing it today cheered her up. *Still as bright as ever. Still clashing with my hair. Love you, Mom.*

Catherine enjoyed her brisk walk to the gym, despite her apprehension about what Trent wanted to say to her. She had a stack of flyers and a couple of rolled-up posters in her waterproof backpack—she didn't know whether or not Trent would be willing to tack her poster to the gym bulletin board, but it couldn't hurt to ask. She just hoped he wouldn't expect her to join the gym in exchange for advertising her program. She hated exercising indoors.

The woman behind the reception desk had light brown hair pulled back in a ponytail and—appropriately enough for a gym employee—a lean, athletic-looking figure. Catherine recalled seeing her playing the piano in Relief Society yesterday. This was obviously Kelsey Perry.

"Can I help you? Oh, you're Catherine Clayton. Trent told me you were coming. I'm Kelsey, Trent's wife."

"It's good to meet you." Did Kelsey know why Trent had called her? Kelsey's expression looked tight, and she seemed to be avoiding eye contact.

"Go on back to his office," Kelsey said. "Around the corner, first door on the right."

"Thank you."

The door to Trent's office stood open. Catherine paused in the doorway, and Trent looked up. He appeared to be in his late twenties or early thirties, with glossy dark hair cut short and spiked upward. She didn't recognize him, so if he'd seen her with Adam, he must have been sitting behind them.

"Catherine." He rose to his feet. He wasn't much taller than she was, but the muscles bulging beneath the sleeves of his polo shirt made Catherine feel small and wimpy. "Thanks for coming. May I take your coat?"

"Thanks." She handed it to him.

"Whew, colorful." Trent hung the coat on a coat tree in the corner.

"A souvenir of Maine."

"Wish I could go there. I could use a vacation. Would you mind closing the door?"

She closed it. With people around—besides Kelsey at the desk, she'd seen another employee, and there were several cars parked out front—she felt safe, even if Trent was a little strange.

"Sit down." He gestured toward one of the chairs facing his desk. The office, like the foyer, was neither large nor elegant, but it was bright, clean, and organized.

Catherine sat.

"Sorry about this." Trent settled back in his chair. "I know you think I'm a weirdo, but here's the situation." He leaned his elbows on the desk and looked into Catherine's eyes. "Adam Becket murdered my sister."

Catherine goggled at him. The most she'd expected to hear was that Adam was a womanizer or a controlling, jealous man. "He . . . if he . . . why isn't he in prison?"

"Why do you think? Because the police couldn't prove it. Adam was either careful or lucky, but they couldn't pin anything on him."

"He was never arrested?"

"No. But he killed Olivia."

Olivia . . . Olivia Perry. Olivia Perry! Because she'd encountered the name Perry in two such different contexts, she hadn't made a connection. "The secretary at Flinders Elementary," Catherine exclaimed.

Trent's dark eyebrows rose. "You know about her?"

"The principal at Flinders, Danielle Knight, is a friend of mine from grad school. I visited there the other day, and Renee—another secretary—told me Olivia had been murdered."

"Renee Endicott. I know her."

Catherine thought of Adam's handsome face and lopsided smile. Had she been chatting with a murderer? "Why do you say Adam killed Olivia? Was he involved with her?"

Trent nodded. "They dated for a year or so. Then Olivia got interested in someone else, an instructor here at the gym—she worked here a few evenings a week—and started seeing him secretly. She was afraid to tell Adam, afraid he'd be angry . . . she wasn't sure how she felt about Adam, or about this other guy, and wasn't ready to burn bridges . . ." Trent swallowed. "I kept telling her she was being stupid. Finally, Adam saw them together. That night Olivia came here crying, saying Adam had said it was over. The next day—" He swallowed again. "Renee called the cops when Olivia didn't show up to work and she couldn't get her on the phone. They went to her apartment and found her—" His voice cracked.

"I'm sorry," Catherine said quietly.

Trent wiped his eyes. "She'd been hit on the head. They never found the weapon, but . . . she had a vase, a wrought-iron vase . . . big, heavy vase, a couple of feet tall, with all these twining metal vines . . . my grandmother brought it from Italy . . ." His voice broke again. He leaned back in his chair, breathing deeply, face tilted toward the ceiling.

Catherine tried to think of something comforting to say, but her tongue felt numb.

"Sorry," he said. "It's still hard to talk about it. That vase was missing, and the . . . the wounds . . . were consistent with . . . he used her own *vase*. Killed her with the vase my grandmother had given her."

Catherine felt sick. He must not have planned to hurt her, but in a moment of overwhelming anger, he'd grabbed the vase and . . . "I'm so sorry. I can't imagine how terrible that must have been for your family."

"It's the kind of thing that happens to strangers you read about in the newspaper, not to anyone you know. Especially not your own family. And *I'm* the one who first encouraged Olivia to date Adam. I told her he was a good guy!"

"You can't blame yourself." Catherine spoke carefully. She couldn't even begin to wrap her brain around the grief and guilt Trent must be feeling. It seemed tasteless to press for more facts; Trent could easily be right in his suspicions. Death at the hands of an angry, jealous boyfriend was a horrific but common scenario.

But Trent hadn't given her any evidence. Adam had never been convicted of this crime—or even arrested for it. Did Trent have only suspicions, or was there more to this?

"Because Olivia had cheated on Adam. . . that's the reason you're certain he killed her?" Catherine asked.

Trent's jaw clenched. "Who else could it have been? Her door hadn't been forced open, so she let the murderer in. Olivia didn't open her door to strangers. No one else had a reason to be angry with her. Nothing besides the vase was missing from her apartment, so it wasn't a robbery. And don't give me some crazy story about a random killer running around Riley, because the only murders since then have been a couple of gang-related shootings."

"Did you find out later that Adam had a criminal record? Or did someone report that he had a violent temper?"

Trent sat silent, staring through Catherine.

Appalled as she realized how insensitive her questions sounded, Catherine said, "I'm sorry. It's painful for you to talk about this." She shouldn't interrogate Trent—she should ask someone else for details, someone less emotionally involved.

"It makes me crazy," he said hollowly. "The things I should have noticed but didn't."

Catherine's pulse raced. If Trent was offering information, she wasn't going to turn it down. "What things?"

"She'd text Kelsey about him. Kelsey was on her case, pushing her to tell Adam the truth before he found out from someone else."

"What did she say to Kelsey?"

"She'd text things like 'I'm scared,' 'I can't do it,' 'This is going to blow up.'" Trent moistened his lips. "A couple of days before she died, she texted, 'I can't tell him, he'll kill me.'"

Catherine gripped the arms of her chair, her fingers clammy with sweat.

"All these signs, over and over, that she was afraid of Adam." Trent folded his arms, his powerful biceps tight. "And none of us saw it. We were *so stupid*—thought Adam was Mr. Good Guy."

Reeling, Catherine tried to organize her thoughts. Had Olivia *really* meant that she feared harm at Adam's hands—or had Trent inserted ominous meaning into the texts after the fact? Any woman might be scared to tell her boyfriend she was seeing another man, knowing the news would hurt and anger him and probably end their relationship. But that wasn't the same as being scared that the boyfriend would physically harm her.

"Other than the texts, did you ever see signs that Adam could be violent?" Catherine asked. "Or possessive or controlling?"

Trent picked up a water bottle with the gym logo on the side and took a couple of gulps. "He's a smart guy—smart enough not to let me see him act that way. He knew I'd rip his head off."

"The only evidence that Adam is dangerous is those texts?"

Anger blazed in Trent's face. "You don't *want* him to be guilty, do you? You spend a few minutes flirting with him at church, and already you're sure he's innocent."

This accusatory response startled Catherine, and her cheeks went hot. "We weren't flirting," she said evenly. Only sympathy for Trent's grief over his sister kept her from showing her anger. "We spoke for a few minutes. That's all. Trent, look at it from my point of view. I'm trying to get the story straight. I don't know either you or Adam. Please don't question my objectivity just because I'm not instantly ready to view someone as a murderer solely because you assume he's guilty—even when there wasn't enough evidence for the police to arrest him."

Trent grunted. "Fine. Fair enough. I just got worried when I saw you sitting with him. He'll try to get to know you, and I'm warning you, you don't want that to happen."

By this point, Catherine didn't want to get to know Adam Becket *or* Trent Perry—she wanted to avoid both of them. Maybe Adam was guilty, or maybe Trent had convinced himself of that because he was frantic for someone to blame. Any objective information about Adam was clearly not going to come from angry, grief-wracked Trent.

"I appreciate you being frank with me." Catherine rose to her feet. "I'm so sorry about your sister. I'll be very careful around Adam." She knew this promise was vague. Right now *she* wasn't even sure what she meant by *careful*.

Trent stood. "You think I'm crazy. Fine. Makes no difference to me. I warned you."

"I'm taking your warning seriously."

"You're not. It's obvious. Well, I tried." He turned to retrieve her coat. "When you end up on your living room floor in a pool of blood, it's not on my conscience."

* * *

As Catherine walked home in a sprinkling of rain, she found it difficult to appreciate the things she'd enjoyed on the walk to the gym—the freshness of the cool air, the shimmering droplets of water on crimson leaves, the deep, soft gray of the sky. Now, grubby-but-endearingly-needy Riley felt grim and threatening. Her posters and flyers were still in her backpack. It hadn't been a good time to ask Trent if she could leave them at Leonardi Fitness.

When she heard footsteps approaching, she fought the urge to look over her shoulder, but whoever was approaching was gaining ground, and Catherine finally checked behind her. A woman in a rain-spattered T-shirt and baggy shorts jogged past, ignoring her.

Catherine shook her head. *Stop giving yourself the willies.* The situation was crazy. She should ignore it and focus on what she came to Riley to accomplish. If Adam tried to contact her again, she could respond politely but distantly enough that Adam would get the hint that she wasn't interested. That would be the end of that. Olivia's death was a heartbreaking tragedy, but none of this needed to be Catherine's problem.

What if Adam was persistent? He'd moved fast, tracking down her phone number and calling her Sunday evening after meeting her that day. What if he didn't back off? What if he'd targeted her already?

"Targeted you?" Catherine whispered, a twig snapping beneath her shoe as her steps got faster and harder. Trent didn't have any solid evidence against Adam. Every one of Olivia's texts he'd quoted could have an innocent interpretation. How often had Catherine said things like, "I can't be late to rehearsal; he'll kill me," when what she'd meant by *kill* was "criticize me in front of the rest of the orchestra"?

What if Adam was innocent?

Did most people familiar with Olivia's death assume Adam was the killer? Did other people at church think so? Yet Adam sat there in church in his white shirt and tie, dutifully looking up scriptures on his phone as they discussed 1 Corinthians—okay, she *had* stolen a few looks at him during the lesson. Why wouldn't she? Nice, single LDS men weren't exactly abundant in her life. Why wouldn't she want to give Adam a little thought?

Now what was she supposed to do? She didn't want to take stupid chances, but she wasn't ready to regard Trent's words as infallible and shun Adam as dangerous. Trent had seemed more angry than rational about Adam. She needed advice from someone not so consumed by Olivia's death. Danielle had known Olivia, and she was usually a good resource for clear-minded, objective advice, but Catherine couldn't bother her in the middle of a school day.

She took out her phone and dialed Jan Peralta.

* * *

"Thanks for letting me crash your afternoon." Catherine took a peanut butter cookie from the plate Jan had set on the coffee table.

"Are you kidding? I'm delighted to have you here. I was going to call you and plan a time to get together, but you beat me to it."

"Your home is beautiful," Catherine said, looking around the living room.

"Hey, thanks." Jan sounded surprised. "I'm not much of a decorator, and who can afford to do much these days anyway?"

"I like it." The cream-colored couch was a little old and a little worn, and the paisley-patterned drapes were outdated, but everything was comfortable and clean—clean but not *so* clean that it looked as though Jan spent all her time scrubbing walls and squirting disinfectant. Catherine smiled at the fingerprints on the wall near the light switch. This was an easy place to relax.

"I'm glad you called me." Jan took a cookie. "I heard Trent was eyeballing you and Adam during Sunday School, and I wondered if he'd say something to you."

Someone else had noticed? Catherine wondered if she'd been the only person in the room oblivious to the drama. "He left a note in my purse telling me to call him. I don't know why he didn't just pull me aside after church."

"I can tell you that. Because the bishop asked Trent not to bring it up at church anymore. It was causing strain and contention, as you can imagine, and you can guess how hard it was on Adam. Not that there were any loud public arguments or anything—I've never seen Adam engage like that. He's quiet about it, but he stands his ground. If I were him, I'd have run away long ago rather than put up with this." She sighed. "Crazy to get this thrown in your lap the first week you're here, Catherine. Welcome to Riley, huh?"

"Do most people think Adam is guilty?"

"No. Good heavens, no. Do you think I would have introduced him to you if I had any doubts about him? He's a great guy. A few people looked at him funny right after Olivia died, when we were all in shock, but I think the rumors started with Trent, and nobody but Trent believes them now."

"It seems so strange . . . the whole story. Olivia's death. Trent's blaming Adam . . ."

"Yeah." Jan took another cookie and nudged the plate toward Catherine. "Olivia Perry was a sweet girl. Very pretty—she had this shiny dark hair that I'd stare at and covet. She should have been a shampoo model." Jan smiled. "We all loved her, but she . . . was a little flaky sometimes. She—"

Footsteps thudded on the stairs. Jan stopped talking and sat nibbling her cookie.

A muscular young man strode into the room. Jan's oldest son—Catherine couldn't remember his name. Friendly face, trimmed brown hair, a dimple in his right cheek.

"I assume you want the car?" Jan asked.

"Yeah."

"I need it back by six."

"'Kay."

"This is Catherine Clayton." Jan gestured toward Catherine. "She's new in the ward. Catherine, this is Lewis."

"Hey." Lewis grinned at Catherine.

"Good to meet you," Catherine said.

"Yeah, likewise. Thanks, Mom. See ya." Lewis hurried out.

Jan kept eating her cookie until they heard a door slam. "Sorry about the interruption. I don't like to talk about Olivia in front of him if I can help it. They were friends, and her death hit him hard."

"I'm so sorry." Catherine had thought of Lewis as a kid, not realizing he was old enough to move in the same circle as Olivia.

"Anyway . . . what was I saying?"

"You said Olivia was a little flaky."

"Oh yeah. I'm not saying she was unreliable, but she didn't always show good sense."

"She *must* have been reliable, or she never would have kept that job at Flinders," Catherine remarked. "I can't imagine Danielle Knight putting up with someone who flaked out on her."

"True. Ms. Knight runs a tight ship, I hear. Anyway, Olivia . . . okay, I'm not sure how to describe her. I hope this isn't bad, being so candid about the dead, but if you don't know what Olivia was like, it's hard to understand the situation. Olivia was darling—I'm not surprised Adam fell for her—but she was immature sometimes. Oblivious. This is how I heard the story, and I heard it from Lewis. He and Olivia talked a lot. Olivia was a couple of years older, but they'd been buddies for a long time. Truth is, I suspect Lewis had a crush on her—*don't* tell anyone I told you that."

"I won't."

"Lewis was working security for an electronics store near Leonardi's—that's the Perrys' gym—so Olivia would sometimes meet him on break to grab a snack. That's how he found out so much about everything. Olivia would spill her boy troubles while they ate. She boggled Lewis—he couldn't figure out why she made things so hard for herself." Jan swallowed the last bite of her cookie. "I shouldn't bake these darn things. I can't leave them alone."

"They're delicious."

"No more for me." Jan wadded up her napkin. "Anyway, one of the trainers at the gym started chasing her, and after awhile, she decided it wasn't a problem seeing both him and Adam. She and Adam weren't married or even engaged—she figured she was still free. Never mind that when she was with Adam, she acted like his girlfriend and she never told him she was seeing this other guy."

"I see what you mean about immature."

"Yep. Lewis said Adam finally saw them together somewhere, so Olivia fessed up. That's why Trent thinks Adam killed her—because Olivia died only a day or two after that. Now the rest of this is rumor, because it's not like the police reported everything to us, but from what I gather, Adam didn't have an alibi, so the police investigated him pretty extensively. But as far as I know, they never found even a speck of evidence that he'd done it."

"Trent mentioned some texts that Olivia had sent to Kelsey."

"Yeah, I know about those. 'He'll kill me.' That's the way Olivia talked—dramatic, exaggerating things. We all say stuff like that. I threaten to strangle my kids half a dozen times a week, but I've never done more than swat them on the rear, even when Lewis glued the piano keys together. Naturally, Olivia was scared to tell Adam about this other guy, and naturally, she was moaning to Kelsey about it. Olivia knew Adam wouldn't put up with what she was doing, and if he found out, it was over between them. But she couldn't possibly have believed he'd really *hurt* her. He's too good of a guy."

Trent's anguished comment about his telling Olivia that Adam was a "good guy" played in Catherine's thoughts, along with wondering how often people were shocked to learn that supposedly good neighbors and friends were perpetrators of domestic violence. "The police never found out who killed her."

"No. Unfortunately."

Catherine absently fingered the multicolored crystal beads around her neck. "What about the other man Olivia was seeing?"

"Will Conti, at the gym. I know they questioned him after Olivia's death, but they must not have found anything. I know him only a little— Gina took piano lessons from his aunt a few years back." Jan brushed a cookie crumb off a couch cushion. "I'm sure Trent meant well talking to you, but he's not thinking straight. Hasn't been since Olivia died. I think he needs so badly to see someone convicted for her murder that he's fixated on Adam and can't let go."

"I feel sorry for both of them."

"Yeah . . . sad situation. But accusing Adam is absurd. You don't turn from solid, upstanding guy to murderer overnight just because your girlfriend cheats on you. I'm sorry, Catherine. I feel horrible that this is how you got welcomed to town, but please don't let Trent poison things for you. Adam is a great guy. Don't be afraid to get to know him."

Catherine gave a half smile, the most noncommittal response she could think of. On the one hand, she felt better finding out that Trent's suspicions were far from universal. On the other hand, Jan couldn't offer proof of her opinion of Adam any more than Trent could, and with the stakes so high, making a mistake as to Adam's character seemed like a spectacularly rotten idea.

CHAPTER 5

"You did well, Cate. I'm impressed." Danielle closed her office door behind them. "You're a natural with kids."

"Thanks. That means a lot coming from you." Catherine had always admired—and been amazed by—the skillful way Danielle dealt with young children. She would have guessed that Danielle's no-nonsense personality would scare kids off, but Danielle knew how to connect with them and how to lead them, and they loved her. Maybe it was a skill she'd acquired through caring for her younger sister. "I can't help thinking it's a shame having you stuck in this office when you're so good in the classroom," Catherine added.

Danielle grinned. "It pays better."

Catherine pushed up her sleeves, wishing she'd thought to wear a short-sleeved blouse. Excitement, nervousness, and moving around the stage during the assembly had left her sweating. The kids had seemed riveted by her demonstration of various musical instruments and had laughed like crazy when she'd created dying-cow or tortured-cat noises to demonstrate how it sounded when you first began to play an instrument. And she'd heard *oohs* and clapping when she'd demonstrated how each instrument should be played. There had been so much excitement and shrieking when she'd asked for volunteers to come try out instruments that she'd felt like a rock star. Now if only the children could hold on to that enthusiasm long enough to take the flyer home and show it to their parents, and if only the other school visits would go that well. She had three more lined up for next week, thanks to Danielle's influence.

"I'm interested to see how many kids sign up." Danielle sat behind her desk. "If all the kids who were squealing sign up, you'll have far more students than you can handle, even before you make any other school visits."

Catherine lifted her hair off her neck in hopes of a breeze hitting her sweaty skin. "Trust me, the ranks will thin fast when parents read the fine print and realize this involves commitment."

"A problem all single women can relate to."

Catherine laughed. "Amen."

Danielle tilted back in her chair and propped her stocking feet on her desk. She looked beautiful today in a red silk blouse that complimented her olive skin and dark hair. That cropped hair looked so chic, and Catherine wondered if she should consider cutting her own long hair.

"I have a question for you," Catherine said. "I want to hire an assistant, mostly to do secretarial and receptionist work. The hours would be flexible at first—maybe ten to twenty hours a week. Within a couple of months, I hope it will be a full-time position. You mentioned that Esther is good with numbers and computers and that her job situation right now is lousy. Do you think she'd be a good match for a position like that? Answering the phone, keeping track of records, contacting parents, and so on?"

Danielle arched an eyebrow. "She *has* done secretarial work before, and she's good at it. Strangely enough, for a girl who aspires to look like she fished her clothes out of a Dumpster, she's a good detail person. Notices little things, keeps things organized."

"The hours could fit around her other job."

"What are your thoughts on green-streaked hair, ripped jeans, purple nails, and eight sets of earrings?"

Catherine hesitated. She hadn't seen Esther since the girl was a teenager visiting Danielle in grad school. She remembered her as a tall, skinny girl—even taller than Danielle—who had looked a little extreme with her hair dyed half black and half blonde and her clothes too short and too shredded. Apparently she was trying for an even more extreme appearance now. "If she does good work, I can handle some . . . uniqueness in appearance. It's a music studio, not a bank or a law firm. But she'd need to make sure her clothes are modest, and I'd appreciate it if she'd tone it down while at work. Not to sound narrow-minded, but she *would* be representing the studio. Would that bother her?"

"As long as you're the one telling her to tone it down, it won't bother her. If I told her to do it, she'd do the opposite."

"She likes to bug you, I take it."

"She wore extremely long acrylic nails for a while—spent hours grooming them. I heard her complaining to a friend about how hard it was to do anything with them, and the friend asked why she didn't take them off. She said, 'Because they annoy Dani.'"

Catherine laughed then wished she hadn't—Danielle wasn't smiling. "So rebelling against you is more important than being able to use her hands."

"Apparently."

"I'm sorry," Catherine said. "I shouldn't have mentioned this."

"Don't worry about it." Danielle's tone turned businesslike. "But as to your question—I know Adam only superficially, and I don't remember much that Olivia said about him. Renee would know more. She and Olivia talked a lot. I *do* know I never heard Olivia say anything indicating Adam was possessive or abusive or cruel in any way. If I'd heard that, I would have remembered it, and so help me, he would have regretted it."

Catherine could easily picture Danielle on the attack if one of her cubs was in danger.

Danielle gave a small smile. "If you're looking for a character recommendation for Adam, I take it this means you're interested in him?"

"I'm not looking for a character recommendation. I just wondered what really happened . . ." The look Danielle was giving her—an eye-roll look, minus the roll—made her voice fade. "Okay. I'm looking for a character recommendation."

"Thanks for not going all mush-mouthed on me. There's nothing wrong with wanting to know if you should take Becket's next call or change your number and hide."

"Something like that." Catherine did appreciate Danielle's forthrightness; her candor reminded Catherine of her father. Danielle jarred her at times, but at least Catherine didn't have to be afraid to say what she thought. "I feel foolish even asking you about this. For goodness sake, Adam probably just called to be neighborly, and here I am freaking out."

"It doesn't hurt to do your homework, no matter what. If you want my two cents, I'd say Olivia's brother is whacked-out. A mysterious note in your purse? That's either creepy or juvenile."

"It struck me that way too."

"I wouldn't get your hopes up though. Adam has been through a lot, and with Olivia's murder unsolved, I bet he's still suffering. I doubt he's looking to get involved with anyone."

"Don't read so much into this." Catherine hoped her face wasn't too red. "I just met him. I don't have any 'hopes' yet."

"Sorry. I'm accustomed to playing parent. I just don't want you to build expectations for something that'll never happen."

"I know you want what's best for me," Catherine deadpanned.

Danielle smiled and tapped her fingernail on one of Catherine's flyers that lay on her desk. "I *do* want you to be content here. If you pack up and head back to Virginia, how will I explain it to your screaming fans?"

* * *

Nibbling a square of Muenster cheese on a sesame cracker, Catherine stood on her back patio and watched leaves flutter in the rising wind. More rain would hit later tonight, but right now, the cool breeze against her face was pleasant.

It had been a wonderful day. The excitement of the kids at Flinders—the thrill in their eyes at the thought of making music—had left her tingling with optimism. If she could give this joyful gift to children who otherwise wouldn't have had it, she was definitely doing something good, something her father would have applauded. She wished she could call and tell him about the assembly. He'd have been thrilled for her. Of course, he'd have also reminded her that it was easy to cheer for an idea but harder to commit to it and follow through, so she shouldn't get *too* giddy over her success when she didn't yet have a single student on her roster.

Catherine grinned. She would stay giddy tonight anyway, harvesting every last molecule of cheer before getting practical again.

Her talk with Danielle had also lifted her morale. Danielle's matter-of-fact dismissal of Trent as "whacked-out" and her assurance that she'd never heard Olivia say anything negative about Adam had gone a long way in helping Catherine relax over this bizarre situation with Trent and Adam—though not far enough to relax her entirely. She felt slightly guilty over the fact that four days had passed and she hadn't returned Adam's call but not guilty enough to pick up the phone. Better not to send any signals until she knew what signals she wanted to send.

Though avoiding calling him back *was* sending a signal.

The phone rang, and Catherine jumped, dropping the last fragment of cheese and cracker. She raced through the open sliding door and snatched the phone in the kitchen. Not recognizing the name on the caller ID, she offered her cheerful, professional greeting.

"Hello, this is Catherine at Bridgeside Music Studio."

"Yes, hello . . . uh . . . my name is Maren Gates." The woman sounded hesitant. "I heard about your program. My niece . . . I babysit my niece, and she goes to Flinders, and I saw your flyer . . . um . . ."

"That's wonderful," Catherine said. Maren Gates was clearly nervous, and Catherine wanted to put her at ease. "What grade is your niece in?"

"Third, but that's not why I'm calling. She's not interested in learning a musical instrument. Soccer and softball . . . she's all about the sports . . . but I . . . well, I noticed your flyer said your lessons were open to all ages.

Does that—" She gave a tremulous chuckle. "Does that mean adults too, or am I reading too much into it?"

"Absolutely, it includes adults. All ages. You're never too old to learn something new and to take joy in creating music."

"I . . . don't know a thing about music. I can't read music at all. Would that be a problem?"

Catherine could feel Maren gaining confidence. "No, of course not. We'd start at the beginning. What instrument are you most interested in?"

"Well . . . when I was a kid, I thought it would be fun to play the flute. I had this book, a fairytale, with a picture of this princess with long blonde hair, and she was playing the flute, sitting in a meadow . . . I used to love that picture. It was so pretty, all peaceful and . . . sorry." She giggled nervously. "Dumb story. I don't know why I brought it up. Anyway, I figured I'd lost my chance to learn, but when I saw your flyer . . . anyway, it's . . . are . . ." She drew an audible breath. "Are the lessons really free? Totally free?"

"That's right."

"And you have the instruments? I don't need to own a flute or rent one or anything?"

"That's right. We'll lend you the instrument at no charge. All you need is the desire to learn and the commitment to practice and regularly attend lessons. If you like, I can give you the details over the phone, or we can meet and go over them. I do require a certain level of commitment from my students, and I require them to sign an agreement indicating they understand my expectations."

"Not a problem. I wouldn't have called if I didn't really want to do this. Could I . . . come over sometime during the day and sign that paper or whatever?"

"That would be fine." Catherine picked up her cell phone and opened her calendar. "What days work best for you?"

"I could come in the morning any day this week."

"Do you mind coming early? Say, eight thirty tomorrow?"

"That works great. My husband has to leave at seven thirty, and it's better if he doesn't . . . anyway, yes, eight thirty."

"Perfect. Do you need directions?"

"No, I have your address on the flyer. I can find it. Thanks! I'll see you tomorrow!"

"I'm looking forward to it." Smiling, Catherine hung up. She'd never expected her first student would be an adult, but she was delighted to think she might be able to help Maren Gates fulfill a long-deferred dream. She'd put Maren in a private slot; an adult would prefer not to study in a group with a bunch of kids.

Before sunset, the phone rang four more times, and Catherine's excitement rose higher. Two children were interested in the cello—Catherine's snippet from the Dvořák cello concerto had impressed a few kids—one was interested in the violin, and one in the clarinet. She also received a bonus interrogation from the father of the potential clarinetist, who had apparently seen *The Music Man* too many times: could Catherine *really* teach all these instruments, or was this a scam? Catherine resisted the urge to either crack jokes about the dangers of pool tables or point out how lame of a scam it must be when she wasn't asking for money. She assured him that, while the cello was her primary instrument and the one she'd played since childhood, she had studied all of the instruments listed on the flyer, had a master's degree in music education, and was perfectly capable of teaching his child to play the clarinet. And parents were always welcome to attend their children's lessons and ask any questions they desired.

At seven thirty, the doorbell rang. Glowing with enthusiasm, Catherine hurried to answer it, wondering if an overeager parent had come to have a look at the studio. She looked through the peephole and saw Adam Becket standing on the porch.

An eruption of surprise, apprehension, and confusion left her standing motionless. It would be plain to Adam that she was home. Though the blinds were pulled over the windows flanking the door, her lights were on, and he must have heard her rapid footsteps on the hardwood floor. In fact, he must know that right now, she was standing in front of the door, hesitating.

She was *not* going to ostracize Adam based on a completely unsubstantiated rumor. Squaring her shoulders, she swung the door open. "Hello!"

"Good evening, Catherine." Adam was holding a plate bearing a small round cake covered in smooth dark chocolate and decorated with white-and dark-chocolate curls. He offered the cake to her. "I wanted to welcome you to Riley."

"Oooh! Best welcome ever!" Catherine took the plate. "You made this?"

He gave his lopsided smile. "I'm a computer software engineer with a secret ambition to become a pastry chef."

"It can't be *that* secret if you just told me."

The mobile corner of Adam's mouth flattened. Wondering what she'd said wrong, Catherine opened her mouth to gush compliments about the cake, but Adam spoke first: "I'm guessing it's probably the least interesting of the secrets you've heard about me."

Caught off guard, Catherine studied the dark-chocolate ganache covering the cake and tried to think how to respond. Should she feign ignorance and pretend she *hadn't* been standing paralyzed in front of the door, unsure whether or not to open it? Should she say something vague and polite? Crack a joke?

"It's all right," Adam said. "Trent Perry talked to you, didn't he?"

Blushing, she made herself look up at Adam. She hadn't expected him to be so blunt, even if he did suspect she'd heard rumors.

"From the look he gave me after he saw me sitting next to you, I figured he would," Adam added.

Catherine steadied herself. If Adam was going to be blunt, she could be blunt too. "I never said I believed what Trent told me."

"But you're nervous," Adam said quietly.

Catherine wanted to deny it but suspected that if she did, Adam might list all the ways in which she'd already exposed her discomfort. "I'm rattled by the whole situation. That doesn't mean I believe Trent's accusation. He had no evidence."

"I apologize for bringing this up." The weariness in Adam's face aged him; he looked older than he had when they were chatting pleasantly on Sunday. "It's not the best way to start a friendly conversation. But after two years, I'm tired of the elephant in the room."

"I understand." Maybe that was a shallow thing to say. She couldn't truly understand what it was like to have people suspect you of murder. "Come inside. We don't have to stand on the porch."

Adam's eyebrows rose. "Thanks for offering, but no. I don't want to make you uncomfortable."

"You offered to answer any questions I have about Riley. I do have a few, if you have time."

"Catherine . . ." Adam shoved his hands into his jacket pockets. "You're not obligated to invite me in. I just wanted to drop off the cake and . . . let you know I'm glad you're here and I hope your music studio is a great success."

"Thank you." Catherine picked a chocolate curl off the cake and put it in her mouth. She thought about repeating her invitation for Adam to come inside, but she wasn't the only one who was uncomfortable—Adam was obviously ill-at-ease, and the thought of sitting on the couch, trying to hold a conversation while Adam wondered if *she* wondered if he was a killer—Catherine winced internally. But the thought of sending him away, leaving him wondering the same thing . . .

"Would you like to go for a walk?" she asked.

"A—walk?"

"Yes. I walk a lot. It's great exercise. And it's not raining yet." She smiled at him. "We can walk downtown, and you can show me the sights. Do you have time?"

"Sure . . . I'd be happy to . . . but there aren't many sights worth seeing here."

"I'll find some. I'll be the newcomer, noticing the beauty the old-timers are too jaded to appreciate."

"Um . . . good luck."

She laughed. "Let me get my walking shoes on. I'll be right back."

"Better grab a raincoat too, just in case."

Leaving Adam on the porch, Catherine put the cake in the kitchen and laced up her shoes. She nearly grabbed the stylish Burberry raincoat she'd bought last fall but changed her mind and put on her kitschy lobster raincoat instead. *Comfort clothes.*

She headed to the porch. Adam was sitting on the carved wooden bench near the door, his posture too straight, as though he were awaiting a nerve-wracking interview.

"I'm ready," she said.

He stood. "Where to?"

"How about the library? That's one place I haven't been."

"That's pretty far, isn't it?"

"Only two-point-four miles. I looked it up earlier."

Adam checked his watch. "It closes at nine."

"I just want to see the outside. We can admire that frog-pond fountain out front. I saw a picture of it on the Riley city website. The concrete frogs looked adorable."

"Must be an old picture. That fountain was destroyed a few years back—a vandal smashed many of the sculptures and took a chunk out of the basin. The city didn't have the money to fix it, so it's been roped off."

"That's awful!" She thought of the vandalism at Flinders and Danielle's comment that there had been vandalism in Riley a few years earlier, before Olivia died. "I'd still like to see the library."

He started down the stairs. "Do you have a route picked out, or do you want me to lead the way?"

"You're the native. You lead. If you get us lost, I'll make fun of you and then rescue us." Catherine held up her phone. "GPS."

Adam laughed. "I think I can make it to the library without needing a rescue party. So you're a walker, huh?" he asked as they headed toward the bridge.

"Yes, I love it. I have to exercise a lot because I love to eat. I have this terrible addiction to cheese."

"Cheese?"

"Yes. And I can't stand exercising indoors. Getting on a machine and doing the same motion over and over again—snore! Give me fresh air and changing scenery that isn't on a TV screen."

"What do you do in winter?"

"If there's a bad storm, I'll stay inside, but other than that, I still like walking. If you dress for the weather, you're fine, no matter how cold it is."

"You may need some expedition-grade gear for Riley's winters."

"I looked up your average winter temperatures. You won't give Minnesota a run for its money."

"It gets miserable though."

"I'll be prepared." Catherine stopped on the bridge and peered over the rusty railing at the river below. "I love the way the streetlights reflect on the water."

Adam rested his hands on the railing and stood with her, looking at the river.

"Thanks for coming with me." Catherine glanced at his profile, wondering what he thought of her impulsive invitation. "You're a good sport. Most guys would think I was nuts, suggesting a walk to the library."

"I'm happy to join you. I enjoy walking. Don't do it much though. Mountain biking is more my thing. That's how I—" He touched the corner of his mouth that remained flat when he smiled. "Took a spill and landed on my face."

"Ouch!"

"It's amazing what plastic surgeons and dentists can do, but there was some nerve damage nobody could fix."

"Do you still bike?"

"Yes. I'm not quitting because of an accident. Catherine . . . thanks for talking to me. You're very kind."

"You make it sound like I'm doing a service project. You're the one doing me a favor, helping me feel at home here."

He tapped his fingers against the railing nervously. "You . . . probably thought I was pushy when I left you that message Sunday night."

"Not at all." Catherine was glad he didn't know how she'd hovered over the phone, too rattled to pick it up.

"I . . . to be honest, I was hoping to get to know you a little bit before Trent went on the attack. Not that I . . . Listen, I don't want you to get the wrong idea. I just wanted a few minutes of friendship with someone who didn't have any preconceived notions about me."

"I understand."

"I hoped that if I could get to know you, then by the time Trent talked to you, you'd already have formed some of your own opinions about me. But I apologize if my tracking down your number and calling you made you feel pressured."

"You're fine. Where did you find my number?"

"Called Information."

"I'm sorry I didn't return your call." She didn't try to explain why she hadn't; Adam would know anyway. "And I'm sorry for what you've been through."

"Thanks." Adam resumed walking across the bridge, and Catherine fell in step with him.

"It must be hard for you here," Catherine said.

"Are you wondering why I haven't left Riley?"

"Yes, actually." Catherine thought of what Jan had said about not knowing how Adam endured it. "I think I'd move away—get away from the memories, and people who . . . people like Trent."

"I thought about leaving. But moving away—running away—seems like something a guilty man would do."

"You want to stay until your name is cleared."

"Yes."

"But it's been two years, and no one's been arrested."

"Then I guess I'm not going anywhere."

"Have you . . . figured anything out? Do you have any suspects—you personally, I mean, not necessarily official police suspects?"

He shook his head.

Embarrassed, Catherine realized that had been a nosy question. He would have avoided answering it even if he *had* suspected someone. "So you just have to hunker down and wait, hoping they'll catch the guy eventually."

"Pretty much."

"That would drive me crazy. I'm not that patient."

"What can I do?" His voice was edgy—not sharp enough to be rude but enough to tell Catherine her comment had been thoughtless. "I have no idea who killed Olivia. I told the police everything I could think of that might help them. They've investigated everything. It's all come to nothing. I can be patient and hope something eventually turns up, implicating the murderer, or I can drive myself insane and stir up turmoil in Riley playing futile detective games I'm not qualified to play."

"I'm sorry. I didn't mean to offend you. Patience is definitely better than insanity."

"Don't apologize. I'm not offended. I just wish this were resolved."

For a few moments, they walked in silence. The wind blew wisps of hair into Catherine's face. She reached into the pocket of her jeans and pulled out the hair elastic she'd shoved there earlier when she was straightening up her bedroom and found the elastic on the floor.

"*I* apologize," he said. "I'm making you uncomfortable, talking about this. It's just . . ." In the dimness, Catherine could see his jaw muscles clench. "People don't move here too often. The flow in Riley goes outward, not inward, and it's rare to have someone new in the ward. And the instant you show up, Trent tries to poison—" Adam inhaled deeply, his shoulders lifting. "I'm sorry."

Catherine pulled her blowing hair into a ponytail and looped the elastic around it. It *did* unnerve her, the tension and pain she could read in Adam's face and voice. She was glad they weren't trying to dodge this elephant-sized subject, but it was an uneasy topic for two people who hardly knew each other. "As you might have guessed, I like to make up my own mind about things. Besides, Trent's suspicions aren't exactly universal."

Adam glanced at her, and Catherine realized she'd hinted that she'd talked to other people about him. *Oops.*

"True," he said. "Fortunately, Trent's opinion is in the minority."

"Have you tried talking directly to Trent about his accusations?"

"Yes. It was useless. We avoid each other now."

Catherine tried to steer the subject in a less awkward direction. "Do you have family here?"

"My father lives here." Adam sounded relieved at this new topic. "My mother died several years ago, and my dad's health is failing. I'm the only kid left in the area, but my brothers visit whenever they can."

"Does your dad live with you?"

"Nope. I tried to get him to move in with me, but he refused—said he was stuck with me for the first eighteen years of my life and he doesn't plan to be stuck with me for the last year of *his* life." From the humor in Adam's voice, it was clear his father's words hadn't stung him. "He likes his own space. He has an aide who checks on him a couple of times during the day while I'm at work and a nurse who visits regularly as well."

"I'm sorry he's ill."

"Cancer. Sometimes he rallies, and I think he'll be around a long time, and other times I think I could lose him any day. That's the other reason I'm staying in Riley for now. The last thing I want to do is bail out on him or insist he move—not that I could *make* him do anything."

"I . . . lost my father to cancer last year. And my mother died ten years ago. It's hard."

"Catherine, I'm sorry."

"Thanks. It's lonely sometimes."

"Do you have any brothers and sisters?"

"No. Only child. My parents didn't marry until they were in their forties, and they felt blessed to have me. Someday, I'd love a house full of kids." Catherine felt herself reddening. Saying she wanted a lot of children was probably not the most tactful statement to make while on a stroll with a single man. "So I'm hoping my music studio is a big success and I get lots of students under my roof soon," she amended quickly.

"I'm sure it'll be successful."

"I've already gotten a few calls." For the next mile, they chatted about the studio. Catherine felt herself relaxing, enjoying the exercise and the brisk autumn air—and Adam's company. He *did* seem like a nice guy.

Of course, that didn't mean there wasn't something awful beneath the surface.

"Why Riley?" Adam asked. "What made you decide to set up shop here, of all places?"

"I was looking for an area that could benefit from the program and would welcome it. Danielle Knight suggested that I consider Riley."

"You know Danielle Knight?"

"We were roommates during grad school. We've kept in touch since then."

"She's Wonder Woman, from what I've heard. Smart, efficient, keeps Flinders running well, even with budget cuts right and left. Olivia admired her a lot."

"Yeah, she's awesome. She worked like crazy in school, trying to get her degree and support her younger sister at the same time. She's definitely part superhero. I told Danielle about my music program, and she told me about Riley; it seemed like a perfect match."

"Don't think I'm dissing my hometown," Adam said, "but I'm surprised you were willing to come to a dying little city like this when you could have gone anywhere."

"But I *wanted* a place like Riley. I wanted a place that *needed* this program, not a place where it would be icing on the cake—to use a pastry chef metaphor you'll appreciate."

"It's our good fortune that you're here. I'll spread the word for you whenever I can."

"Thanks."

They were approaching the library. Catherine stopped in front of the battered fountain that had been shooting out crystalline water in the photograph. Rubble had been cleared away, leaving a cracked concrete basin studded with odd-shaped pieces sticking up from the bottom of the basin. Those pieces must have been frogs and lily pads before the vandal had paid a visit. Weathered-looking barricades and a ragged orange construction fence circled the fountain.

"That's such a shame," Catherine said. "Did you hear there's been vandalism at Flinders?"

"Yes. Infuriating."

"Crazy how people destroy things. What's the point? Does the vandal step back, look at the mess he's made, and think, wow, I am *awesome*?"

"I have no idea why people destroy things. Anger, maybe?"

"Anger at . . . society?"

"Society seems a nebulous thing to be angry at."

"Okay, maybe anger at something specific, but smashing fountains is a way to vent pain when you don't know—or can't smash—what's really hurting you."

"Makes sense. I don't suppose the vandal was angry with the fountain."

Catherine scrutinized fractured concrete. "Well . . . I said I'd find beauty on this walk, so . . . the scalloped edges on the concrete basin—the ones still intact—are lovely. Whoever built this fountain was very skilled. There, I found something good to say."

"That talent will come in handy," Adam said. "Most things in Riley are somewhat damaged."

Catherine almost made a light response, but Adam had a serious note to his voice that made her wonder if he was speaking about himself. She turned away from the fountain. "I'm craving something sweet, and it'll take me two-point-four miles to get home to your cake, so I don't think I can wait that long. How about we grab something downtown? My treat. What do you recommend? I don't suppose anywhere sells chocolate croissants?"

"Best pastries in Riley—best pastries I've had anywhere, in fact—are at the Sunrise Bakery, but unfortunately, it's closed right now. If you'll settle for ice cream, there's a good place a few blocks away."

"I'm always willing to settle for ice cream," Catherine said. "Lead the way."

CHAPTER 6

Given Adam's recommendation, Catherine had high expectations when she went to the Sunrise Bakery four days later. The outside was drab—a faded clapboard facade with chipped paint that must once have been bright salmon pink, and peeling vinyl letters on the window—but when she stepped inside, the aroma of baking cinnamon rolls was enough to make the place a heavenly contrast to the cold, rainy Monday morning outside. Catherine had always liked rain, but enough was enough—she was ready for some sunshine.

"Hi," she said to the balding man at the counter. "Your bakery smells amazing. I'm tempted to roll out my sleeping bag and move in."

"Health department will blow a gasket if I let you do that." His cheerful pink face and rotund shape made her think he'd do well in a Santa suit. "But I'll be happy to sell you something that tastes as good as it smells."

"My name is Catherine Clayton. I have a pastry order to pick up."

"Oh!" He nudged his glasses with his knuckle. "Hang on." He headed into the back and returned a few seconds later carrying two large, white boxes. "Here you go, Catherine."

"I'll take a loaf of your multigrain bread as well." The thought of a ham and swiss on the fresh bakery bread made her salivate.

He slid the bread into a bag. "Anything else?"

"No—oh, actually, yes. How about a piece of that asiago focaccia? And then I'm racing out of here before I get tempted to buy your whole inventory. But I'll be back."

He rang up her purchases. "Tomorrow's special is peach cobbler. You ought to try it."

"Ooh. I'll definitely be back. I'm new in Riley—just moved here."

"I didn't think I'd seen you before. I'm Dennis Ivan, the fat old guy who owns this place. What brings you to Riley?"

"I'm opening a music studio." Catherine reached into her bag and took out one of the smaller posters. "In fact, I see you have some advertisements on your window for local activities. Would you mind if I hang this here for a couple of weeks?"

The jingle of a bell over the door accompanied footsteps entering the bakery. Dennis smiled at whoever had entered before taking the poster from Catherine's hand. "Bridgeside Music Studio. Violin, viola, cello, bass, flute, clarinet, blah, blah, blah—gonna start yourself an orchestra, huh?"

"Yep."

"Guess we can use some more culture around here. Sure, I'll hang this for you." He bent and stowed it under the counter. "Your total comes to—"

"*You're* the music studio lady?" The new customer spoke behind Catherine. Startled by the hostility in her voice, Catherine turned to see a short woman with wrinkled cheeks, narrow glasses, and curly dark hair that was gray at the roots.

"Yes, I'm Catherine Clayton."

"Then let me say thank you *so much* for marching into town and ruining the livelihood of every music teacher in Riley."

"Whoa, Francie." Dennis Ivan spoke before Catherine could. "Let's keep it friendly. What can I get you this morning?"

The woman marched up to the counter. "You're advertising for her? Then maybe I don't want anything from your bakery this morning. Or ever."

"Ma'am, I'm not trying to put anyone out of business." Catherine wished she could stop herself from blushing. It was hard to feign self-possession when her face was as red as her hair. "My hope is that I can work with local music teachers, and we can—"

"Who else is ever going to get any business when you're offering *freebies*?" She glared at Catherine. "That is the ugliest raincoat I've ever seen in my life. Whoever thought of putting lobsters on a raincoat?"

"Ma'am, may I ask what instruments you teach?"

"She teaches piano," Dennis supplied.

Catherine smiled. "Well, there's definitely room for both of us. Piano is one thing I *don't* teach."

"You don't play the piano? You're teaching everything from the violin to the kazoo, and you don't play piano? What kind of hack are you?"

"I play," Catherine said, getting the feeling that no matter what she said to this woman, it would make her angrier. "But I'm not teaching it right now. I'm hoping to provide an alternative to school orchestra and band programs that were canceled due to lack of funding. Oh, your name is Francie—are you Frances Randolph?"

She nodded curtly.

"Hey, you're good, kid," Dennis remarked.

"I remember Ms. Randolph's name from when I sent an introductory letter to all of the music teachers whose names we could track down. Ms. Randolph, I apologize if I worded my letter so poorly that you thought I was trying to run you out of business. That's not my intention at all. In fact, if there's enough interest in my program, I'll be looking to hire additional teachers."

"What makes you think anyone would want to work for you? People like their independence, and here you think you can carry off some kind of takeover—"

"Takeover?" Dennis gave a belly laugh. "Francie, how about you give the girl a break? Are you even teaching anymore? Last you told me, you were retiring."

"I haven't retired. I still teach."

"How often?" Dennis asked. "Once a month?"

Frances frowned, but she didn't answer.

"Here." Dennis took a blueberry muffin, slid it into a bag, and held it out to Frances. "On the house. You need something to put a smile on your face."

"You can't afford to give away food," Frances snapped.

Dennis patted his round stomach. "Guess you're right. Look at me—on the verge of starving to death. Take the muffin, Francie, and play nice."

Scowling, she accepted the bag.

Catherine made another attempt at civility. "If you have any cards with you, Ms. Randolph, I'd be happy to take some and make them available at the studio in case anyone is looking for a piano teacher."

"Cards!" Frances snapped. "When did I ever need *cards*? I taught as a labor of love, not as some soulless *business*."

Catherine bit the inside of her cheek to keep herself from pointing out that Frances had started by accusing Catherine of ruining her livelihood and was now offended at the suggestion that she'd been running a business at all.

Frances tapped the display case. "Give me a raspberry scone and a caramel latte."

"Gotcha," Dennis said.

Doubting there was anything she could say to Frances to soften her, Catherine turned to leave. "Thanks, Mr. Ivan."

"Anytime, Cathy. If you have any openings for kazoo lessons, sign me up. I always wanted to learn."

* * *

Carrying her boxes of pastries, Catherine walked slowly up the sidewalk toward Flinders Elementary. It bothered her how much she didn't want to face Renee Endicott this morning. The clash with Frances Randolph at the bakery had been more than enough "welcome" for the day. It hurt to find a music teacher so hostile toward her arrival—and rude enough to hiss and claw at her in public. How could Frances think she was trying to steal her students when Catherine wasn't even teaching piano? Hadn't she read the letter Catherine had sent, emphasizing that she would work cooperatively with other music teachers to ensure this program benefited all of them and her focus was on group lessons and ensemble playing to replace canceled band and orchestra programs? Not that there were a lot of music teachers in Riley—Ava, in her research, had only found five local teachers: three piano teachers, one violin teacher, and one flute teacher.

Thank heavens there hadn't been anyone else in the bakery to overhear Frances's spiteful words. And at least Dennis Ivan had been a sweetheart. She'd make sure to go back for that peach cobbler tomorrow.

Steeling herself, she walked into the office. No matter what Renee said, Catherine wouldn't let it annoy her—or scare her.

Renee was at the front desk, head bent, and eyes on her computer screen.

"Good morning," Catherine said.

"Ms. Knight isn't here," Renee said curtly. "She's at a meeting at the district offices."

"That's all right." Catherine set the bakery boxes on the counter. "I just wanted to thank the staff for helping me get the Bridgeside Music Studio off the ground. I appreciate the help. I'll leave one of these here and one in the teachers' lounge if that's all right."

Renee glanced at the boxes. "What are they?"

"Pastries—scones, muffins, cinnamon rolls, croissants."

"Bought your thank yous from Dennis Ivan, huh? I guess girls like you don't do their own baking."

The comment was so over the top that it veered from stinging into silly. "Oh no, I could never bake," Catherine said. "Besides, in my position, I have a responsibility to support local businesses. Help the common man. Noblesse oblige."

Renee glared at her.

"You're not obligated to condone this aristocratic largesse," Catherine added sweetly. "Take a stand; don't eat the pastries, and be proud of yourself. I hope the joy of disdaining me is worth missing Dennis's almond croissants."

The corners of Renee's mouth flicked upward then flattened. "It's not," she said. "Hand one over."

At the touch of dry humor in Renee's voice, Catherine grinned. She unfastened the sticker holding the top box closed, took out an almond croissant, and handed it to Renee on a napkin.

"Good stuff," Renee said. "Dennis knows what he's doing."

Renee's tone was a half step away from being pleasant. *Progress*, Catherine thought. More progress than she'd expected to make with Renee. "He told me tomorrow's special is peach cobbler. I'm planning to camp out overnight so I can be at the head of the line."

"It'd be worth it." Renee's eyes were a little bloodshot, and she looked pale. Catherine wondered if she was sick but didn't dare ask; the wisp of truce between them was too fragile to make personal questions about health a safe topic.

"Make sure you try his blueberry turnovers too," Renee said.

"I will." Catherine picked up the second box. "I'll take this to the teachers' lounge."

"Wait."

Catherine paused, mentally bracing herself in case Renee was preparing to reopen hostilities.

"You'd better be careful," Renee said. "Very careful. There's been more trouble."

"Oh no! *More* vandalism?"

"The old multipurpose room. The vandal came in through a broken window and painted messages on the walls."

"What did they say?" Realizing she was probably asking Renee to repeat a string of profanity, she amended, "Did the messages give the police any hints about the vandal?"

"Just that he . . . wants to kill."

"To kill!" No wonder Renee looked haggard. "The messages threatened someone?"

"They just said, 'Kill.' Again and again."

Horrified, Catherine stood gripping the cardboard box of pastries and trying to collect her thoughts. "Do the police think anyone is truly in danger? A coward who breaks windows when no one is here doesn't seem like the type to actually attack someone."

"Tell it to Olivia." Renee spoke through gritted teeth. "The secretary who was murdered. Maybe after two years, her killer is ready again."

"The . . . vandalism around the time that Olivia died. Was it like this? With threats?"

Renee reached for a tissue but missed and knocked her hand against the box, pushing it away from her. "There weren't any threats. And it wasn't the school. It was different places around town. City offices. The library."

"No one connected it with her murder."

"No. But when new stuff started happening, here where Olivia worked . . . and now . . . the death threats . . . It's the killer, obsessed with Olivia, trying to punish her, even after her death. That's why he's come to Flinders. Because we were her friends, he hates us too." Tears welled in her eyes. "Maybe we're the targets now, and he's getting tired of just breaking windows."

Catherine wanted to suggest that a person angry at losing a job was a more logical explanation for the vandalism than a serial killer, but Renee would think Catherine was dismissing her fears. "I'm sorry. No wonder you're worried."

"You should be too. You're young and pretty like Olivia was. You're all intertwined with Flinders now—your name is all over the place on those posters. The room that got attacked—you know that room; it's the old music room, the one Ms. Knight was going to let you use if you ever got that interschool orchestra off the ground."

Catherine went icy from her scalp to her feet. "I can't imagine . . . It's absurd . . ." Trent's harsh words blared in her head: *If you end up on your living room floor in a pool of blood, it's not on my conscience.*

"If you have any sense, you'll get out of here," Renee whispered. "There's a murderer loose, and he's ready to kill again."

* * *

"You're doing great." Catherine smiled at Maren Gates.

"I can make noise, anyway." Maren clicked her case shut with soft, careful motions, as though afraid she might damage the latches.

"Noise is excellent progress." Catherine tried to sound extra friendly and positive—Maren had done very well during her lesson, concentrating intently and listening to everything Catherine said, but she was trying *so* hard that it was plain she was still nervous. With her rounded cheeks, blonde hair brushed back into a ponytail, and sky blue eyes, Maren looked so young that Catherine had been surprised when she'd said she was twenty-four. Perhaps it was the way she treated Catherine that made her seem younger—or made Catherine feel older. Maren was so respectful and deferential that Catherine felt like an honored great-grandmother.

Maybe Catherine would have done a better job of helping Maren relax if she could have relaxed herself. She'd been glad that she'd driven to Flinders this morning and not walked—walking home after what Renee had told her would have felt like strolling through a minefield. *There's a killer on the loose.* From the look in Renee's eyes, she hadn't been exaggerating to maliciously spook Catherine. Renee was terrified. And every time Catherine tried to dismiss Renee's fear as an overreaction, she thought of Olivia Perry.

Calm down. What kind of killer goes around trashing an elementary school? The vandalism and Olivia's death are unlikely to be related. Renee is drawing a far-too-hasty conclusion.

But Flinders is where Olivia worked. There is *a connection. It might not be relevant, but what if it is?*

"Same time next week?" Catherine rose to her feet. "Oh—no, I'm sorry. I actually have a school visit next Monday afternoon. Where's my brain? Would you like to meet Monday morning?"

"I can't. I'm sorry. Could we . . . do a different day?"

"That's fine. I apologize for the disruption to the schedule; this usually won't happen. What would work for you?"

"Um . . . I could do next Friday."

"Friday?" Catherine checked her calendar. "I can do next Friday, but it'll be in the evening. Eight fifteen? Is that too late?"

"That's fine." Maren giggled nervously. "I hope I'll . . . get up the guts to tell my husband by then."

"Your husband doesn't know you're taking lessons?"

Maren's cheeks went pink. She picked up her music book and tucked it into the folder Catherine had given her. "He's not much of a music guy, right? Unless it's rock or country."

"He doesn't have to be a flute fan to appreciate that *you* like it and want to learn to play."

"Yeah, that's true."

Maren's bright tone was so clearly faked that Catherine sat down again, scrutinizing Maren. "Do you think he won't be happy that you're taking lessons?"

Maren shrugged. "Who knows?"

Catherine touched Maren's knee. "You look worried."

"It's nothing . . . not a big deal. I just . . . you know, sometimes Dylan—my husband—doesn't have a lot of patience with . . . stuff. He's been out of work for a year now—all he can find are temp jobs, a few weeks here or there. It's tough on him. He's a hard worker, and it drives him nuts that he can't support . . . well, he's cranky these days." Her lips quivered, as though she wanted to smile but was having trouble making her mouth cooperate. "Hard to talk to."

"I'm sorry. Would he be angry if he found out you were taking flute lessons?"

Maren pushed at a clump of hair that had come loose from her ponytail. "I . . . tried to tell him about your music program, but he just . . . thought it was a waste of time. I didn't dare tell him I'd signed up."

What kind of husband was this guy if Maren was afraid to tell him something as harmless as the fact that she was learning the flute for free? "If it would help, I'd be happy to talk to him and explain the benefits of studying music and the goals of the program."

"Oh no, don't do that. He'd just . . . it wouldn't help. Like I said, he's cranky these days."

"What kind of work does he do?"

"Well, he worked at Parker—that furniture factory that shut down a few years ago—and then he did construction for a while, but no one's building, so he lost that job too. So many people are hurting for work—it's crazy hard trying to find something. I had a good cleaning job, but they had to let me go—didn't have the money to keep me. I looked all over the place and couldn't find a new job, but I bring in a little cash babysitting my niece."

"Has he looked outside of Riley?"

Maren sighed. "Not really. His whole family is here, and I don't know—it's like the world outside of Riley doesn't exist. Gotta stay within a couple of miles of each other so they can get together and yell at each other on Christmas, I guess." She stood up. "It'll work out. I'll keep the flute out of sight for a while. I'll practice when he's out at interviews or with his brothers. No reason he needs to find out about it, as long as the neighbors don't complain about the weird squeaky noises."

Catherine smiled, but the anxiety in Maren's eyes troubled her. She didn't want to foment conflict between a husband and wife, but she wasn't going to tell an adult woman she shouldn't take flute lessons because her husband thought they were a waste of time.

"I'll see you next Friday." Maren started toward the door. "I'll be the one wearing a wig and sunglasses."

"Maybe we should arrange to meet after dark in an abandoned warehouse," Catherine joked.

"Good plan. There are plenty of those around. Bye, Catherine." Maren headed out the door, clutching her flute case.

As she watched Maren walk away, Catherine's annoyance at Maren's husband swelled. She could understand being grouchy and stressed by prolonged unemployment, but to create an atmosphere where your wife felt she could only develop her talents under the radar—even when there was no financial cost whatsoever—

Catherine sighed and closed the door. Music was supposed to bring joy and a sense of accomplishment, not marital conflict. But maybe Maren was overreacting, taking her own shyness and embarrassment at trying something new and conjuring up disapproval where little or none existed.

Or maybe Dylan Gates was a jerk.

She had hoped her lesson with eager-to-learn Maren would be enough to revitalize her spirits and renew the feeling that coming to Riley had been the right choice, but now she felt worse. *Get a grip. So you had a bad day. Poor you. Give the place a chance. You knew before you came here that Riley would be an acquired taste.*

But she'd also expected that *she* would be the one who'd struggle to adjust—not that people like Frances and Dylan would struggle to welcome her.

And not that a serial killer might be on the loose.

She sank into her armchair, pulled out her phone, and texted Danielle, expressing her sympathy for the new round of vandalism and saying she'd call later.

To her surprise, Danielle promptly called her. "Hey, Cate. Sorry I missed seeing you this morning. Thanks for the pastries. One bright spot in a dark day."

"A very small bright spot," Catherine said.

"Did you meet Dennis Ivan at the bakery?"

"Yes. He's great."

"One of the nicest guys in town. I'm glad you discovered his bakery. Spend lots of money there; he could use the help."

"Trust me, I will. And he was a lot nicer than the other person I met there."

"Who was that?"

"I ran into a piano teacher who thinks I'm out to ruin her livelihood."

"Who?"

"Frances Randolph. Know her?"

"I know of her. But you don't teach piano."

"That didn't seem to matter to her. Never mind; I'm not going to waste your time whining about my day. How are *you* holding up?"

"We sealed off the damaged room at Flinders, and the kids have no idea what happened. Could have been a lot worse. But I'm afraid the room won't be available for your use anytime soon. I'll talk to some people and see about getting you a new place to make your base camp for your school group."

"Thank you, but I don't want you to have to worry about—"

"It's not hard to make a couple of calls, and you'll have better luck if I pave the way for you."

Catherine wanted to protest, but it was better to let Danielle run with things in her own way. "Renee said there were threats this time. Death threats."

"I wish she hadn't told you that, though I suppose asking her to keep it quiet is pointless—it'll be in the paper, I'm sure."

Catherine looked into the empty stone fireplace, thinking of switching the gas flames on. The house felt chilly. "She seemed very shaken."

"I know. She's afraid Olivia's killer is back, but that's a completely irrational fear. There is no reason to think this has anything to do with Olivia."

"The vandalism before Olivia's death—"

"Catherine, why would there be a connection between Olivia's death and a shattered fountain at the library or some broken windows? Was her killer also responsible for any hit-and-run accidents in the weeks before her death? Any shoplifting? Any cases of tax evasion? It's possible to have more than one criminal in town." Though Danielle's words were sarcastic, her tone was melancholy, and Catherine had the feeling she felt sorry for Renee.

"Since the newest vandalism included death threats, I'm sure Renee can't help connecting it with Olivia," Catherine said.

"I understand. But spray painting vicious words on a wall does not constitute a confession for Olivia's murder—even when the vandalism took place where Olivia worked. It's far more likely we're dealing with an angry person who lost his or her job recently. The police are investigating any possibilities."

"Dani, let me help. I'd be happy to hire a security guard to watch the school at night."

"It's not your worry," Danielle said shortly. "We'll deal with it. The superintendent and the police are discussing options."

"Parents must be freaking out."

Danielle groaned softly. "They are, Cate. Thanks for reminding me."

"Sorry." Catherine rotated her wrist, watching the late afternoon sunlight glitter on her bracelets as she tried to think of what to say. She knew Danielle wouldn't welcome further offers of help. "I hope Renee is okay."

"Renee is still struggling with Olivia's death, and this is bringing back too many memories. She's had a rough time—her husband left her awhile back, and her kids are grown and moved away. I don't think she has much of a relationship with them. She loved Olivia like a daughter."

"No wonder she's hurting."

"They were neighbors as well as colleagues—lived in the same apartment complex, did things together after work sometimes. She misses Olivia, and having *Kill* painted on the school walls isn't helping."

"That's awful."

"Gotta run, but I wanted to check in. I'll let you know what I find out about locations for your orchestra." Danielle hung up.

Catherine laid her phone on the table and sat trying to figure out if there was anything she could do that would help settle her churning emotions and shift her thoughts to more positive tracks.

She needed to do something for someone else. Renee Endicott was lonely and scared and missing a dear friend. Maybe she'd appreciate it if someone reached out to her—even a rich do-gooder she despised.

CHAPTER 7

WITH A FOIL-COVERED PAN of macaroni and cheese resting on the seat beside her, Catherine drove to the address she'd looked up online—an apartment complex a mile from Flinders. She tried to focus only on the desire to do good and not on any hopes of getting a good reception from Renee. It wasn't easy—her nerves were so shot that she feared she'd have trouble responding graciously if Renee started firing insults. *Keep it together. Squashing a pan of macaroni and cheese in Renee's face won't make you feel better.*

For long.

Catherine fought a giggle. If she was in *that* kind of mood, she should have stayed home. No matter what happened tonight, she would remain polite and in control of herself. If Renee did give Catherine a chance to talk, maybe Catherine could help convince her of what Danielle had said—that it was highly unlikely Olivia's killer was responsible for the vandalism.

The apartment complex was a worn-looking cluster of redbrick buildings, but the sunshine-yellow birches, red maples, and blue-green spruces on the lawn helped mellow the building. With a little squinting, it looked charming and antique instead of flat-out old. Catherine parked near the entrance, studied the directory, and headed toward Renee's apartment.

Worst case, she won't touch your mac and cheese—and then you can eat it yourself, so it's still a win.

The stairs clanged beneath Catherine's feet as she headed up to number 503. No matter how rude Renee was, visiting her was better than sitting at home looking at pictures of Virginia—and pictures of her parents. Her father would approve of this trip to Renee's: *Don't wallow. Act.*

Drawing a deep breath, she knocked on the door.

Footsteps approached. A long silence followed. Renee must be peering through the peephole and trying to decide whether to open the door or wait until Catherine went away. *Now you know how Adam Becket felt when he came to see you.*

A jingling sound, a clicking sound, another clicking sound—locks being opened. Catherine straightened her spine and smoothed the corner of the foil covering the casserole.

"What do you want?" Renee was scowling but looked more puzzled than angry. "What are you doing here?"

"I wanted to say I'm sorry for what you've been through. Danielle Knight told me you and Olivia were close and that this vandalism is bringing back a lot of bad memories. I wanted to say I'm thinking of you." *Wince. How Hallmark can you get?* Catherine held out the foil pan. "I thought you might use this on a night when you don't feel like cooking. It's my mother's recipe. Macaroni and cheese."

Renee stared at her. "You brought me macaroni and cheese?"

"It's one of my favorites. Four kinds of cheese. I'm a cheese addict."

"You *cooked* it?"

"You do know I was joking earlier when I said I never bake, right? I do own a stove. And an apron."

"Why the heck would you cook for me?"

"I knew you'd had a rough day." Renee looked so suspicious that Catherine added, "No ulterior motives."

"You decided out of the blue to bring me a casserole."

"Cooking instructions are on the top. You can freeze it if you don't want to eat it soon. Just make sure to hold your hand under it when you carry it; those foil pans bend if you don't support them."

"You're weird," Renee said, but she took the casserole. "Last person who brought me anything like this was Olivia. She brought me lasagna a couple of times. And that Italian dessert. Can't remember what it's called . . . the tube things with stuff in the middle."

"Cannoli?"

"Yeah, that's it." She poked at the foil. "Funny you'd bring pasta. Like Olivia."

"We both have good taste."

"I haven't had homemade macaroni and cheese in years. Used to make it for my boys but not fancy jazz like this—just one kind of cheese."

"That kind's good too. Anything with cheese, and I'm there."

Renee picked at the baking instructions taped to the foil. "Thanks." She sounded more uncomfortable than grateful, but any word of thanks was huge progress.

"You're welcome. Are you doing all right?"

"Yeah, I . . . guess. Trying to watch TV, but . . . hard to concentrate."

"I can imagine."

"Has anyone *you* cared about ever been murdered?" Renee asked sharply.

"No. But I've had loved ones die, so I know how much that hurts. I imagine it must be worse when your loved one is taken violently."

"Who've you lost?" Renee sounded as though she were challenging Catherine to enter her grief in a contest. Before Catherine could answer, Renee said, "Oh yeah. Your dad died not too long ago, right? Cancer. I saw some articles about that when I was trying to figure out who the heck you were."

"Yes." Catherine tried not to feel uncomfortable at this confirmation that Renee had researched her. "My mother died ten years ago. Brain aneurysm." Robert Fields also flashed into her mind, but she didn't want to bring up his death; that subject was too complicated.

"Both parents, and you with no brothers or sisters." Renee's tone softened. "That's too bad."

"It's a little lonely."

"Guess it makes things easier when you don't have to earn a living and can go traipsing around making music."

"Money doesn't buy off grief."

"Yeah. I guess not."

"I do have a stepmother, and we're close," Catherine said briskly, not wanting to give Renee the impression that she was seeking sympathy.

"That's nice that you get along with your stepmom. Some kids resent it. My sons keep their distance from my ex's wife. 'Course, they keep their distance from me too." She looked down at the casserole. "Nice of you to bring me this."

"I hope you like it."

"I will. Comfort food." She sighed. "When you knocked on the door, I jumped so high I about smacked into the ceiling. I was afraid it was the cops, coming to tell me something bad had happened to . . . I don't know. To Danielle, maybe. Or one of the teachers."

"I don't blame you for being jumpy. I'm jumpy myself."

"Yeah . . . listen . . . you . . . if you want to come in for a minute, I could get you a drink. A Sprite or something, I mean. I know you're a Mormon."

"Thank you. I'd enjoy that. Honestly, my house is way too empty tonight."

"I hear you." Renee stepped back, and Catherine walked into the apartment.

The beige carpet looked as though it had been cleaned too many times, with faint, permanent stains lingering below the surface. The couch had a faded red slipcover, and the glass coffee table had a couple of chips near the edge, but everything was tidy, and a series of black-and-white photographs formed an artistic arrangement on the wall.

"Are you a photographer?" Catherine asked, admiring a close-up of a weathered wood fence.

"I mess around with the camera. I did take a couple of photography classes at RCC—the community college."

Catherine moved from picture to picture. "These are gorgeous."

"Thanks." Renee sounded surprised. "I don't know any darkroom stuff—where would I put a darkroom?—so it's all digital."

Catherine looked at a photograph of glistening, ice-encrusted branches. "You're good."

"I like nature pictures. Or inanimate objects. An old fence might fall down from weather and age, but it won't walk away. Won't stab you in the back either."

Catherine scanned the wall and realized there were no pictures of people.

"What do you want to drink?" Renee asked. "I've got Sprite, Coke, milk, or water. Ice water. I could throw a slice of lemon in there."

"Lemon water sounds great."

"Have you . . . eaten yet? I could put this in the oven." She held up the casserole. "Unless you don't want to stay that long," she added, the edge reappearing on her voice.

Renee was inviting her to share a meal? That was more than progress—it was a miracle. "I haven't eaten yet. I'd love to join you. I know for a fact that that macaroni and cheese is delicious."

"I'll stick it in the oven. Have a seat." Renee headed into the kitchen area.

Catherine settled on the couch, optimism beginning to bloom again. She hadn't thought she and Renee Endicott could end up as friends, but why not? This had been a good idea to come here—far better than sitting at home feeling bad about everything and sorry for herself.

Renee brought Catherine the lemon water and sat in a frayed, plaid, wingback chair. "You regret coming to Riley yet?"

Figuring Renee would respect her more if she was forthright rather than sweet and diplomatic, Catherine said, "Not regretting it, no. But it's not easy."

"I can't figure you out. You must have had better places to go than *this*."

"I wanted a place that . . ." Catherine held back the words *needed me*. She could already hear Renee shooting them down.

"A pathetic place you could save." Renee filled in the blank.

"That's not fair."

Renee looked into her glass. "You're right." She picked the lemon slice off the rim and squeezed it into her Coke. "I know I owe you an apology. I just don't like apologizing."

"You don't have to apologize. I'd be happy if you'd just stop snarking at me. I'm trying to do something worthwhile, and I don't appreciate your treating me like some flaky princess type."

"You're right. Maybe you aren't flaky."

It was almost *half* an apology. "Tell me about yourself," Catherine said. "Have you lived in Riley all your life?"

"Born in Utica. Moved here after I married my jerk of a husband. Stupid choice, marrying him. He was no prize, but neither was I, and I figured he was as good as I could get. I should have stayed single. He walked out on me ten years ago. I'd have stuck with him forever, never mind the garbage he gave me, but he left. Who cares about marriage vows anymore?"

"I'm sorry."

"Easy for you to say. 'I'm sorry.' What do you care? You ever been dumped by someone you loved? Someone you gave your life to?"

"I haven't given my life to anyone yet."

"Don't bother. You'll end up regretting it. You think someone will stand by you, and then they get bored and dump you. Even my boys—nice when they were little then turned out like their dad. Sided with him when he left. I don't hear from them much."

"Where do they live?"

"Sean's in Pittsburgh. Lee's in Oregon. Neither of them is married. Whatever. I'd be a lousy grandma anyway. You won't catch me baking cookies with a batch of noisy kids."

"You don't have to bake cookies to enjoy being a grandmother. I can't remember ever baking with my grandmothers, but I adored both of them."

"Good for you, Miss Perfect Life."

"You work hard to be offended by everything I say, don't you?"

Renee looked startled. Catherine expected a nasty comeback, but humor began to twinkle in Renee's eyes. "Yeah, I do. Why do you put up with it?"

"Because I'm hungry, and there's macaroni and cheese in the oven."

Renee grinned. For the next half hour, while the macaroni and cheese baked, they chatted about Renee's family, her job, her sons, her divorce, her desire to leave Riley but fear that she was too old to start over somewhere else. It surprised Catherine how open Renee was, and though she still shot barbs at Catherine, Catherine was learning not to let them sting.

When they sat at the table to eat, Renee turned the conversation to Catherine. "What gave you this idea in the first place?" she asked, sprinkling pepper on her macaroni and cheese. "You could do anything with your life, go anywhere, but instead you came to this dump to teach music."

"I've always been passionate about music. My original plan was to play the cello professionally, but I discovered that what I really love is teaching. Maybe it sounds corny, but I get so much joy out of making music that I want other people to feel that too. I decided I wanted to offer this opportunity to people who wouldn't have the chance otherwise."

"If you really feel that way, I guess you mean well."

"Thanks. If I ever need an endorsement to post on my website, may I use that one?"

Renee chuckled—the first time Catherine had heard her laugh. "Yeah, go ahead."

"When Danielle told me about Riley, it sounded like the perfect place," Catherine continued. "And having Danielle help me get things off the ground has been great."

"Yeah, if you've got Danielle Knight on your side, you'll do okay. Sorry I don't sound gung ho about this. I'm not that into music—can't sing, never wanted to learn an instrument. Now that my boys are gone, I never even turn on the stereo."

Catherine smiled. "I'll try to convert you."

"Back off, sister." Renee lifted a forkful of macaroni. "This is good. What kind of cheese is in it?"

"Parmesan, cheddar, gruyère, and fontina."

"Never heard of half of those. So who are the people backing your program?"

"They prefer to remain anonymous."

Renee picked up the serving spoon and scooped more macaroni onto her plate. "It's all you, isn't it?"

Catherine hesitated. Her plan had been to stay vague about her "backers," not to outright lie. "What makes you say that?"

"Obviously you come from a rich family. Very rich family. And it's the way you talk about things—it's all *I, I, I—I* wanted to do this, *I* wanted to come here. Never any talk of having to charm people into supporting this harebrained idea, which would have been a huge part of your planning if you weren't financing it yourself."

"Why did you research me anyway?"

"I wanted to know who this Pied Piper was, marching into Flinders to recruit kids."

"Okay, that's fair. But I'd appreciate it if you'd keep what you learned to yourself."

"I get it. You don't want people beating down your door and asking for money. No matter how much gold you've got in the bank, you can't support the whole world. I can keep my mouth shut."

"Thank you."

The conversation lapsed. Renee kept her gaze focused on her plate while she ate, and Catherine toyed with her fork and tried to resist the urge to take a second helping.

"Thanks for staying for dinner," Renee muttered. "It's . . . nice to have company. Especially tonight."

"My pleasure."

"I doubt it's a pleasure being with me." Her voice stiffened. "You like doing the 'good' thing no matter what, don't you? Do you get heavenly points for bringing me a casserole?"

Catherine sighed. "Are your porcupine quills on a timer? If you say something nice to me, does that reset the clock so the quills spring out thirty seconds later?"

"I just can't figure out why you'd visit me."

"I'm here because I want to be here. I'm here because I'm having a hard time right now, and I need to think of someone besides myself and I thought you could use company too."

After a few more mouthfuls of pasta, Renee said softly, "Olivia used to come over sometimes when she didn't have a date. We'd watch movies—she loved sci-fi stuff, would you believe it? She knew all the *Star Trek* trivia. Or sometimes we'd just talk. She'd tell me about her guy problems or whatever."

Guy problems? Interest tingled through Catherine. She hadn't talked to Adam since their walk to the library—beyond a smile and a hello at church yesterday—but she'd enjoyed his company and had been wondering how to respond if he contacted her again.

She thought of asking offhandedly what kind of guy problems Olivia had talked about, but attempting to sound casual was a lousy strategy. Renee would hate verbal games, and trying to find out about Adam while pretending she wasn't asking specifically about him was silly. "I've met Adam Becket, her boyfriend," Catherine said.

"At your church, right? I figured you would have met him. Did he say anything about Olivia?"

"Not until someone else brought her up first."

"Olivia's brother?"

"Yes."

Renee removed her glasses and rubbed her eyes, smudging the remnants of the day's make-up. "He told you Adam killed Olivia."

"Yes. But I know not everyone thinks that. Having met him, I don't believe it."

Moisture glistened in Renee's eyes. She picked up her napkin, dabbed her eyes, and replaced her glasses. "I hoped things would work out between Olivia and Adam. He was sweet to her. Good-looking, mostly—too bad about that injury that makes him smile funny."

"Was Olivia in love with him?"

"She was, but then Will Conti started after her."

"What's Will like?"

"Mr. Charm. Mr. Flirt. Eye candy. Olivia started to get interested, but she didn't want to dump Adam. I told her she was playing a stupid game. She was going to lose Adam over a womanizer who wouldn't last a month. Adam was much better husband material, but Olivia said she wasn't ready to get married anyway—she just wanted some fun, and it wasn't like she and Adam were engaged or anything. Will makes pottery—pretty stuff, sells it online—and he gave Olivia this beautiful red pitcher filled with white roses. She showed it to me and chattered about how hot Will was and how talented and romantic. Made me sick! Couldn't she tell he was good at flirting because he flirted with every woman he met? Lots of practice! She didn't say it, but I could tell she thought Adam was dull compared to Will."

"But she didn't want to break up with Adam?"

"She wasn't as stupid as she was acting . . . Guess that doesn't make sense, but what I mean is, she liked Will's attention, but in the part of her brain that hadn't melted, she knew Will wouldn't last. She claimed Adam wouldn't get upset over a little flirting, but I could tell she was nervous about what she was doing. No matter how she rationalized it, she was cheating."

Renee poured herself some water, her hand unsteady. Water splashed onto the table. "It made me *furious.*" Her voice rose. "What was she thinking, betraying him like that?

Renee's anger surprised Catherine. "That's maddening, to watch someone you love make stupid mistakes."

"She wasn't my daughter. What could I do?" Renee gulped water. "I saw Adam the day Olivia died."

"You saw him!"

"He brought me a cake—did you know he bakes? I was supposed to take a cake to school for a raffle, and Adam had volunteered to make it for me—I'm not much of a baker. Wouldn't let me pay him either. I was home sick that day—had an awful sore throat and fever. I remember dragging myself off the couch when he rang the doorbell."

Catherine wiped up the spilled water with her napkin. "Did he say anything about Olivia that day?"

"Not until I asked. I could tell he wasn't happy, and when I mentioned Olivia, the way he looked . . . it didn't take ESP to figure out he'd learned about Will, so I asked him flat out. He'd seen Will and Olivia coming out of a movie all snuggly with their arms around each other."

Ouch, Catherine thought. "Did he confront her?"

"No, not right then. *I* would have—would have made it loud and made it public—but Adam's not that way. He called her later, and she confessed to seeing Will but tried to tell Adam that Will didn't mean anything to her, and he was only a friend."

"And Adam didn't buy it?" Catherine said.

"Nope. He told her it was over. He was calm about it when he talked to me and said maybe it was better this way, that he and Olivia weren't right for each other. I can't believe he would be that calm—and even remember to bring me that cake!—and then that night go kill her in a rage. Just can't believe it would happen." Renee looked haunted. "Could someone be *that* furious—*that* filled with hate—and hide it so well?"

Catherine thought of Adam's kind voice and crooked smile. "I don't know."

"I don't think Adam would have hurt her." Tears welled again in Renee's eyes. "She always told me what a gentleman he was, how he treated her with respect and even opened doors for her. How many guys these days will do that for a girlfriend? Then Olivia fell for that snake Will Conti . . . Silly girl . . ."

"Do you think Will—?"

"Don't know. I didn't know Will personally—just know about him from what Olivia told me and from gossip I've heard here and there. I have no idea who killed her, but it rips me up knowing some sicko smashed her head and got away with it."

"And you're afraid the killer is back now?" Catherine asked gently.

Renee wadded up her napkin. "They never caught him. He's around somewhere."

"But the vandalism could be the work of someone angry at losing a job. It probably has nothing to do with Olivia."

"You've been talking to Danielle, haven't you?"

"Yes," Catherine admitted, hoping this wouldn't annoy Renee.

"Maybe she's right," Renee said. "But did she tell you the vandalism a couple of years ago stopped with Olivia's death?"

"What do you mean it stopped with her death?"

"I mean there were problems for a while—different places getting smashed up. Then she got killed, and boom—no more vandalism."

"But . . . why would there be a connection?"

"Don't you get it? Maybe the killer has some anger or hate that builds up, so he breaks things. Then, finally, that's not enough, so he commits murder. Then he feels better for a while—until it builds up again."

Catherine felt both chilled and dubious. "You think the new vandalism means the killer is building up to a new victim?"

"There were death threats today. Painted on the walls."

"You told me the vandalism before Olivia died didn't include threats."

"That doesn't mean there's no pattern here."

"But, Renee, maybe the fact that the vandalism stopped with Olivia's death only means that the vandal—along with everyone else in Riley—was so shaken by her murder that . . . well . . . maybe whatever was leading him to run around breaking stuff didn't seem so important anymore, so he quit."

Renee's expression was remote, her gaze on the darkening sky outside the kitchen window. "Maybe you're right. But I think you're closing your eyes because you don't *want* to see a connection. The murderer is *still out there*, and if you're a nut who can brutally murder a woman, I don't think you can go back to being a good citizen forever. I think sooner or later you crack again."

The thought made Catherine shudder. "Maybe the murderer left town long ago. Or never lived here in the first place. Maybe he was passing through."

"Get real. Someone is passing through, so they randomly knock on Olivia's door and she opens right up to a stranger and he kills her? Uh-huh."

"Okay. But I still can't believe the vandal is the killer. Anyone who sneaks around breaking windows at a school doesn't sound like a person who'll follow through on confronting someone."

"Keep hoping that." Renee took her empty plate and set it in the sink. "Maybe you could hope Olivia back to life while you're at it."

With her back to Catherine, Renee straightened a row of blue-flowered canisters then brushed her hand over the counter as though hunting for crumbs. Catherine had the feeling she was looking for excuses not to turn around and face Catherine. Wanting to give her time to get her emotions under control, Catherine quietly served herself another spoonful of macaroni.

"Sometimes I leave flowers at Olivia's apartment," Renee said.

"At her apartment?"

"It's still unoccupied." Renee opened a cupboard and aligned some spice canisters. "They cleaned it up, but no one's rented it. With all the other vacancies, who'd want to live where someone was murdered?"

It *would* be unnerving, Catherine thought, walking across a floor and knowing a woman had died violently on that spot.

"I think she knows I leave the flowers." Renee spoke softly. "Do you believe in ghosts?"

"I believe we have spirits that live on after our bodies die."

"Yes. That's right; that's what I believe too. I think Olivia is aware of us." Renee swung around and glared at Catherine. Catherine steeled herself for a fresh porcupine quill.

"You think that's strange, don't you, leaving flowers at her apartment?" Renee snapped.

"Not at all. You're mourning the loss of a close friend. If it comforts you to leave flowers where she lived, I think that's beautiful."

Renee's rigid shoulders relaxed. "I bought some flowers." She pointed to a pot of yellow chrysanthemums. "I was going to take them over, but . . . I . . . wasn't sure I wanted to go out there alone tonight, not after what happened at Flinders."

"Would you like me to go with you?"

"You'd go with me?"

"If I wouldn't be intruding. Sometimes it's nice to have company."

"She had a ground-floor apartment. There's an enclosed patio in front. I leave the flowers there. Sometimes I . . . sit for a few minutes. I hate cemeteries—they give me the creepy crawlies, so I never visit her grave. I'd rather remember her here."

Catherine rose and picked up her empty plate. "Let's go over there."

"You didn't even know her. Why would you want to bother?"

"It's not a bother."

Renee's eyes revealed both hope and suspicion. "If you can spare the time, I guess I could show you where she lived."

Catherine replaced the foil over the remaining macaroni and cheese. "Do you want this in the fridge?"

Within a few minutes, they'd cleaned up and were heading out the door, with Renee holding the pot of flowers and telling a story about a time she'd gone bowling with Olivia and Olivia had rolled eight gutter balls in a row and couldn't stop laughing at herself. Catherine listened intently, wondering how long it had been since Renee had had someone to confide in about how much she missed Olivia.

"Right here." Renee stopped and gestured at a darkened apartment. She unlatched the gate to the small courtyard. Not sure why she felt apprehensive, Catherine followed her inside.

The patio consisted of a bare square of concrete ringed by a strip of dirt crowded with weeds. A couple of mildew-stained Adirondack chairs sat in the center.

"Those were here when Olivia moved in," Renee whispered.

Catherine didn't know if she spoke quietly out of respect for Olivia's memory or because she didn't want to be overheard by neighbors.

"Her family left the chairs when they moved her stuff out."

Catherine nodded, not sure what to say.

"She had petunias planted all around the edges there. She'd plant them and forget about them, but we get enough rain that they survived." Renee chuckled. "Barely."

Figuring Renee would want to linger for a few minutes, Catherine sat in one of the chairs. It felt cold and damp.

Renee walked to the sliding-glass door and carefully set the chrysan-themums down. "I suppose one of these days they'll rent this place, and I—" She stopped and leaned closer to the door.

"Are you all right?" Catherine asked.

Renee reached forward. Her voice went suddenly loud and sharp. "The glass! There's a hole—the glass has been—"

"Don't touch it!" Catherine jumped to her feet and reached into her purse. She dug a mini flashlight out and shone the beam on the door. A circle had been cut from the glass, near the handle.

"Someone broke in. Someone cut the glass and broke into Olivia's place," Renee said hoarsely.

"Why would—"

Renee wrenched the flashlight out of Catherine's hand and aimed the beam through the hole. She moved the beam along the walls, illuminating painted words: Olivia's name, over and over in red paint, and in the center of the wall, the phrase, "I didn't want to kill her."

CHAPTER 8

CATHERINE TWISTED THE LID OFF the bottle of Tylenol and swallowed two capsules. From the pounding in her head, the medicine she'd taken at lunchtime had long since worn off. Thank heavens the day was over. She'd never imagined she'd be anything but excited to meet with new students and their parents, but she'd found it difficult to present a cheerful, businesslike demeanor, and it was nearly impossible to concentrate.

Getting only a couple of hours of sleep last night hadn't helped. She'd waited with Renee for the police to arrive then had lingered at Renee's apartment until nearly midnight, trying to calm and comfort Renee. Renee had insisted on seeing the inside of Olivia's apartment, and in addition to the spray-painted message, they'd found holes and scrapes in the walls and cabinets, as though the vandal had gone after the place with a butcher knife.

It now seemed Renee was right. The vandalism at Flinders *was* the work of Olivia's murderer.

Catherine had never been as scared in her life as she had when she'd left Renee's apartment and hurried to her car in the darkness. Renee had offered to call a neighbor to escort Catherine, but Catherine hadn't wanted to disturb someone she didn't know at such a late hour. She'd sprinted to her minivan.

She stared listlessly at the fridge. She ought to do something about dinner—hunger was making her headache worse—but at the moment, she wanted to lie down on the couch more than she wanted to eat.

The phone rang. Trying to summon any remaining enthusiasm and professionalism, she reached for it. Ava. Thank goodness—someone for whom she didn't have to put on a cheerful front.

"Hello, Ava."

"Catherine." Her stepmother's warm voice loosened some of the tightness in Catherine's neck muscles. "Are you all right? You sounded so shaken in your message."

Catherine walked toward the couch. "I'm sorry if I made you worry. It's been crazy here." She flopped on the couch. "Remember how you warned me I had an overly idealistic view of how things would be in Riley?"

"I wanted you to be realistic."

"I'm feeling a lot more realistic than idealistic now." Catherine positioned a gold throw pillow under her head and updated Ava on the new round of vandalism at the school and at Olivia's apartment—evidence that her murderer was back and growing more angry and agitated.

"That's a terrible and terrifying thing to happen." Ava's tone was grim. "But my first inclination is to wonder if this is really the work of a killer growing hungry for another victim or if someone is simply taking advantage of the fear associated with Olivia Perry's death and using it to stir things up."

Catherine focused on the recessed lights dotting the vaulted ceiling and tried to let Ava's smooth voice guide her into more logical thinking. "That's possible."

"If someone is angry and bitter and wants to lash out—but doesn't actually want to hurt anyone—think how powerful they would feel, knowing they could stir terror in Riley just by painting a message on a wall that reminds people of Olivia's murder."

"Good point." After spending so much time with Renee, and after the chilling walk through Olivia's damaged apartment, she'd been so rattled that she'd believed Renee was right. Maybe she'd panicked too quickly.

"Last night was so spooky that I came home in a cold sweat," Catherine said. "I checked every door and window about ten times and checked my security system three times to make sure it was armed."

"I'll wager that's exactly the reaction the vandal wanted to get. By connecting spiteful, petty destruction to Olivia's name, the vandal has you—and everyone else in Riley—panicking and locking their doors and checking over their shoulders. What a rush of power for some sad person who has lost their ability to cope with tough reality."

"You're probably right." Catherine massaged her aching forehead. "I wish you were here to keep me grounded. I don't know what's wrong with me."

"Dear child, you're under tremendous stress trying to get your program started and adjusting to a new area. While you're going through that transition, everywhere you turn, people are telling you about a young woman who was murdered and pointing out that her murderer was never caught—with the implication that you might be next. That's absurd. To assume there's a serial killer out there because a vandal decided to invoke Olivia's death is pure overreaction. Let the police find their vandal. *You* stop worrying, and instead, bring some music and joy to that stressed-out town."

Catherine managed to smile. Lying down and listening to Ava's calming words was doing more for her than the Tylenol. "Good advice. And things *are* going well. I had five new students sign up today."

"Excellent. E-mail me the info."

"Will do. In other good news, my name didn't end up in the paper. A couple of reporters showed up last night, but when they tried to talk to me, Renee shoved her way in front of me, said I was a friend of hers, I didn't need my name connected with this, and the only way they were getting an interview with her was if they left me out of it completely."

"Good for her!"

"Yes, I appreciated it. I don't want the studio linked with Olivia's murder in people's minds. But . . . it did freak me out, because afterward, when we were alone, Renee said the reason she'd been so adamant about keeping me anonymous was because if my name was in the news, the killer would notice and might get . . . interested in me."

"Oh, Catherine. It was good of Renee to intervene, but she's worrying far too much and scaring you in the process. Get some rest and stop letting paranoid people make you think you've walked into a horror movie. Someone in Riley is trying to cope with their own pain by scaring others. Don't let it work on you."

"Thanks, Ava."

"Tell me about your students. Give me all the updates. Did Esther Knight accept the job?"

"Oh! Yes, she did. I'm sorry; I was going to fax you her job application so you could get everything set."

"Don't worry about it tonight. Do it tomorrow when you get a chance. Did she seem excited about it?"

"She did." Catherine pictured the way Esther had looked when she showed up to the interview: button-up shirt, khakis, her short, green-streaked hair brushed smooth, her make-up subtle, and only one pair of small hoop earrings, despite multiple piercings in each ear. Esther wanted the job—a lot—or she wouldn't have gone to so much effort to look businesslike.

"She seemed very excited about it," Catherine said. "With Danielle's recommendation, I feel good about hiring her. Danielle doesn't gush about anyone unless they deserve it, and she recommended Esther."

"Excellent. I'm not surprised Esther's excited. I imagine a secretarial job with a good hourly wage isn't an easy thing to find in Riley."

"I'll be glad to have her here."

After another half hour of answering Ava's questions about the studio, Catherine hung up feeling much better. Her headache had faded, and Ava's reassuring words had pulled her fears into perspective. She'd never thought of herself as melodramatic or susceptible to her imagination, but she'd certainly been acting that way lately. Ava was right—she wouldn't be overreacting like this if she weren't already stressed.

She wasn't going to buckle to paranoia and cower here. It wasn't even dark outside yet. She'd walk to that little pizza place a mile away and get dinner.

The fresh evening air and the brightness of changing leaves made the walk rejuvenating. Catherine lingered at the bridge. Running her fingers along the rusty railing, she watched the water shimmering below, carrying leaves scattered by recent rain and wind. Riley *did* have beauty.

Maria's Pizza was an aged stucco building that had probably last been painted before Catherine was born, but the reviews she'd read said the pizza was top-notch. Her hunger peaking, she stepped inside. Warm air scented with tomato, garlic, and sizzling sausage swept over her. *Thank you, Ava.* If not for that phone call, she'd still be holed up in her house, eating whatever she could find in the fridge, too scared to set foot outside. Instead, she'd get a refreshing walk, a great meal, and proof that she wasn't letting words painted on a wall turn her into a prisoner.

She studied the menu board above the counter. The restaurant was about half full—busy but not crowded—and the chatter of voices was a pleasant background. Catherine stepped forward. "I'll have a small pizza with sausage, artichokes, red onions, olives, and extra cheese. And a root beer."

The teenage boy at the counter took a bottle of root beer from the refrigerator behind him and handed it to Catherine, along with a plastic number card. "Put this number on your table. We'll bring the pizza out."

"Thanks." Catherine handed him her money. "I'm looking forward to it. I've heard good things about this place."

The kid grinned. "Yeah, we were rated best pizza joint in Riley. Want to try our parmesan-stuffed breadsticks?"

"Tempting. Next time. Thanks."

Catherine turned and scanned the room for a table. There were a few empty ones near the windows. She walked toward them.

"Catherine."

She looked toward the voice. Adam was sitting at a table near the back wall.

"Adam, hi." She moved toward him. "How are you?"

"Enjoying the best meal I've had all week." He gestured at the massive, partially eaten calzone on his plate.

"Looks delicious. I didn't realize how hungry I was until I got a whiff of the air in here."

Adam smiled his crooked smile. "How are things going?"

"They're . . . actually, that's a complicated question, but overall, things are fine. You?"

"*Complicated* is a good word. I'll borrow it. So . . . uh . . ." He glanced around the room. "I'd better let you go; you must be meeting someone."

"Nope. I'm solo. It felt like a good night to get out of the house." She noted that there was no other plate and glass at Adam's table. He'd come alone as well.

"Would you . . . like to join me?" Adam asked. "No pressure. If you need alone time, I don't want to interrupt."

Uncertainty and apprehension stirred briefly then quieted. "I'd like to join you."

Relief flashed in Adam's face before his polite expression covered it. Catherine reached for a chair; Adam sprang to his feet and pulled it out for her.

"Thank you." She sat and placed her number on the edge of the table.

Adam returned to his seat. "How's the studio? I've seen your posters all over town."

"It's good. Getting people interested is a slower process than I'd anticipated, but give me time."

"I can't imagine you'll be anything but hugely successful."

"I hope it works out. Go ahead and eat." Catherine waved at his plate. "I didn't mean to interrupt your meal."

"I'm fine. This thing is so huge it's good to take a break midway."

"How's your father doing?"

"Not too bad. Thanks for asking. He's stubborn—he exercises every day, doing circuits around the kitchen table, since that's all he can manage. I know he's in pain, but I can't get him to stay still. He says the day he can't manage laps around the table is the day he quits and dies."

"It must be hard to watch him suffer. And he's adamant about living on his own?"

"Yes. I want someone there all night at least, but he says if anyone else is there—including me—he'll go sleep on the sidewalk. So I stop in at bedtime and help him get settled. And I keep my phone close at all times. It's frustrating that he won't let me do more."

"Is he . . . thinking straight?"

Adam grinned. "Yes, he's of sound mind. He's always been like this. And it's his life. If this is how he wants to spend the . . . end . . . of it, it's his decision."

"Does he ever accept visitors? I'd love to meet him."

The surprise on Adam's face made Catherine blush. Maybe that had sounded pushy—telling a man who was still a new acquaintance that she wanted to meet his family. She tried to clarify her intentions. "I thought he might feel isolated since he probably can't get out much."

"He does love visitors when he's feeling well enough. But it's hard to plan visits since there's no telling how he'll be feeling at any given moment."

"If a good time comes, give me a call. If I'm free, I'll come over."

"Thank you. I know he'd appreciate it. I always spend Sunday afternoons with him. Maybe . . . sometime if he's doing well after church, I'll give you a call."

"That sounds great. But if he's not up to it, no problem. The last thing I want to do is impose."

"You're not imposing. Thank you for thinking of him. He gets lonely, though he denies it." Adam's gray eyes were pensive. "Will it be hard for you though—after your own father?"

"Will it remind me too much of when he was ill, you mean?"

"Yes."

"He's never far from my thoughts. It won't make things worse. But he went very quickly—just over two months from the diagnosis to when he passed."

Adam absently pushed at a shaker filled with red pepper flakes. "That must have been traumatic, having him go so quickly."

"It was hard, but at least he didn't have to suffer long. How long has your father been ill?"

"He was diagnosed almost three years ago. Went through a couple of rounds of chemo and radiation and went into remission for a while, but the cancer came back. They tried another round of chemo, but it kept spreading.

He decided he didn't want any more treatments—he'd rather wring what he can out of life and go when it's time."

A server set Catherine's pizza on the table, along with a plate and silverware.

"Thanks. Ooh, this looks delicious." She lifted a piece onto her plate, glad for the distraction. Memories of her father's last weeks had left her eyes stinging. She blinked quickly. "Adam, would you like a slice?"

"Thanks, but I'm in over my head with this calzone."

"If you change your mind, help yourself." Catherine took a few bites of pizza while Adam resumed work on his calzone. The pause in the conversation was friendly at first, but it grew awkward—or maybe *she* was the one growing awkward as thoughts of the break-in and vandalism at Olivia's apartment returned. Did Adam know what had happened? Had he heard it on the news? If he hadn't, someone must have told him.

Or had the police questioned him? The thought of the police interrogating Adam left Catherine off balance.

In the silence, Adam's expression had gone grim. Was he thinking about his father's illness, or was he thinking about the break-in? She didn't want to bring it up, but Adam *must* be aware of it—and he was probably wondering if *she* knew about it.

Did he wonder if she suspected him?

Catherine grabbed the parmesan shaker, sprinkled cheese on her pizza, and jumped off the high dive. "I went to visit Renee Endicott last night."

Adam swallowed his bite of calzone. "I didn't realize you were friends with Renee."

"I wasn't until last night." Catherine told him about Renee's cold response to what she was doing in Riley and how she'd decided to take Renee dinner to help both of them cheer up after the vandalism at the school.

"Did you hear that Olivia's old apartment was vandalized as well?" Adam asked.

"I was with Renee when she discovered the vandalism. We'd gone over to Olivia's apartment so she could leave flowers by the door. She does that occasionally."

Adam leaned toward her in a jerky motion, reaching for her arm. Before he touched her, he withdrew his hand and settled back. "You were *with* her? The news mentioned Renee but not you."

"Renee told the reporters that if they wanted an interview with her, they wouldn't mention me except as a 'friend.' Renee's terrified. She's sure Olivia's killer is back and . . . wants to kill again."

His jaw tightened. "A lot of people will be worried about that."

Fears about Olivia's killer being on the move would awaken any dormant suspicions people held about Adam. "I'm sorry," Catherine said. "This will stir Trent up again, won't it?"

Half of Adam's mouth lifted in a bleak smile. "He doesn't require stirring."

"Has anyone else given you a hard time? Have the police talked to you?"

"Yes. Last night. Problem is, the police don't know when the vandalism occurred. The best they could do was ask if I've been anywhere in the vicinity of Olivia's apartment—or Flinders Elementary—in the past couple of weeks. I haven't been, but there's no way to prove it."

Two years after Olivia's death, Adam was still a suspect. "Frustrating," Catherine said, fighting another wave of uneasiness. *Of course he's still a suspect. They don't know who the killer is. They have to question everyone associated with Olivia's death.*

In silence, Adam finished his meal, and Catherine started on a second slice of pizza.

"You must be sorry you came to Riley." Adam folded his napkin and set it on his empty plate.

"Everywhere has problems."

"But you're not usually in the middle of problems like *this*, I'm guessing."

"I'm not in—" Catherine's words stalled. She *was* in the middle of this. Danielle's school was the one being vandalized. She'd been with Renee when she'd discovered the vandalism at Olivia's apartment. Now she was eating dinner with the man the victim's brother insisted had killed her. "I'm definitely not used to these types of problems," Catherine said instead then felt ridiculous. Who *would* be used to these types of problems? A cop, maybe. "But there's no point in panicking. I'm here. Things will work out." More silliness. If someone else got murdered, that didn't qualify as things "working out."

That's not going to happen. Ava's right.

"I'm sorry." Adam sounded tired. "I shouldn't have called out to you when I saw you here tonight. I'm adding to your stress."

"Talking to you doesn't add to my stress." Catherine glanced out the windows at the twilight sky. "But I do need to head home. I don't want to be out too late." The confidence she'd felt when she walked over here was ebbing. She should have driven. "I'm going to ask for a box for the rest of this."

When she returned with the box, Adam had risen to his feet and was waiting near the table. "May I walk you to your car?"

"It would involve a mile or so."

"You walked?"

"I did." Catherine slid the leftover pizza into the box.

"Good exercise," Adam said, but he looked troubled. "May I give you a ride home?"

Catherine hesitated. Three minutes in the car versus fifteen minutes on the street worrying who was going to jump out from behind a bush . . . but that was ludicrous. It wasn't even dark yet. "That's kind of you, but I'm fine. I'll walk you to *your* car." She started toward the exit.

In the parking lot, Adam stopped next to a blue VW. "Thanks again for joining me for dinner. Are you . . . sure you don't want a ride?"

"Really, I'm fine. It was good to talk to you." Was it her imagination, or did the sky seem darker than it should for this time of evening? Was another storm blowing in?

Get a grip.

Adam stood fingering the remote but not unlocking his car. "Catherine . . . I'd feel a lot better if you'd let me give you a ride. It's getting dark."

Not sure what to do, Catherine smiled at him. His expression had changed—had closed—his eyes taking on the guarded look they'd shown when Jan had first introduced him to Catherine.

Adam Becket. Olivia Perry's former boyfriend. The man Trent Perry insisted had murdered her.

Renee's words: *Could someone be that furious—that filled with hate— and hide it so well?*

Her skin prickled. "I'll be fine. I walk fast. See you Sunday." With rapid strides, she hurried away.

* * *

Catherine finally loosened the hair on her bow and returned it to her cello case. An hour of scales, etudes, and sonatas had relieved some of the confusion and fear she'd felt on the walk home from Maria's Pizza, but she still felt bad about the way she'd rushed off.

What had happened to her? For a moment, Trent's warning about Adam had dominated her mind, and she'd doubted Adam. The fear of getting in the car with him had outweighed the fear of walking home alone in the dusk.

And Adam knew it.

She wanted to hope that Adam had perceived her exit simply as evidence of her love of walking, but he was too familiar with having people doubt him. She was certain he'd noticed the anxiety in her eyes—her hesitation—her too-upbeat rejection of his offer and too-hasty departure.

She set her cello in the case and latched it. She hadn't *really* been afraid that Adam would strangle her on the one-mile journey to her studio. What murderer would be stupid enough to let people see him walking out of a restaurant with a woman then kill her on the way home—especially when he was already known to the police?

What *had* she been afraid of? That she was showing too much interest in Adam, doing too much to encourage him? That if she accepted the ride, he would interpret it as permission to call her again?

That she was getting entangled with a man who might be dangerous? What *did* she think about Adam Becket?

She liked him. But beneath her positive impression of his kindness, courtesy, and friendliness—beneath the positive words spoken by Jan and Renee, beneath the fact that Trent had no solid evidence against Adam—she *still* couldn't eradicate her fears. Shaken by the words painted on Olivia's wall and Renee's certainty that the killer was ready for another victim, she'd found herself more affected by Trent's suspicions than she wanted to be.

What was she going to do? Poll everyone in town about Adam, tabulate the results, and *then* make up her mind as to whether or not she wanted to get to know him? She'd prayed about Adam several times but had felt nothing in the way of either warning or confirmation. Maybe she needed to do more work on her own to figure out how to proceed.

She did want to get to know Adam better. Why else would she be feeling this panicky need to make a decision? If she thought their interaction would never go beyond a casual greeting at church, then there was nothing much to decide. But if she thought she might want more than that . . .

Of course, right now, he was probably deleting her phone number from his contacts list. The last thing he needed was another person acting skittish around him.

If you doubt him, then leave him alone. He doesn't need you sending mixed signals and making him feel like you're a friend in his corner one minute and you're off trading rumors with Trent the next.

Catherine wandered into the master bathroom and turned on the faucet in the oversized jetted tub. She needed a long, hot soak. It wouldn't help her make up her mind about anything, but it might help her sleep tonight.

This was incredibly ridiculous. She'd finally found a man she wanted to get to know better—in Riley, New York, of all places—and she was tying herself in knots over *gossip*. Weren't her instincts better than that when it came to trusting someone?

But Olivia had unlocked the door to admit her murderer. Apparently, Olivia's instincts about whom she could trust had failed her—and cost her her life.

CHAPTER 9

CATHERINE TOOK HER TIME MAKING her way to Sunday School. She paused to talk to a woman she'd met the previous week, making sure to use her name so it would get more deeply imbedded in her mind. She stopped at the drinking fountain and then lingered in the restroom, brushing her hair and touching up her lipstick. The later she arrived in class, the more natural it would seem if she slipped in and took the first seat available rather than sitting by—or openly avoiding—Adam. It appalled her to know how wishy-washy she was being—her father would be horrified—but since her clumsy departure from Adam on Tuesday, it had been easier to focus her energy and attention on the studio and try not to think about Adam or anything connected with Olivia Perry.

Now, here she was at church with no idea how to act around Adam. The uncertainty and uneasiness she'd experienced the other night seemed embarrassingly exaggerated now—she did *not* believe Adam was a murderer, but she still didn't know what to say to him.

She stepped into the hallway. It was almost clear of people; only one woman was approaching. She was slim and toned, with her hair in a long braid, and Catherine smiled at her. She looked familiar. Catherine ought to be able to call her by name—Kelsey Perry. Trent's wife.

Kelsey fell into step with her. "Catherine."

"Hello, Kelsey. How are you?"

"I'm fine. You?"

"Doing well."

Kelsey spoke quietly. "I heard you were with Renee Endicott when she found the message at Olivia's apartment."

Surprised, Catherine nodded. "Who told you that?"

"Trent talked to Renee."

So much for assuming that Renee's wanting to keep her name out of the news meant Renee wouldn't talk about her to anyone. "I'm sorry. What a shock for your family."

"Thank you. Yes, it's hard." Kelsey's expression was so controlled that it was impossible to discern her feelings. "I didn't realize you knew Renee."

"I met her at Flinders. The principal there, Danielle Knight, is a friend of mine from school."

"So Renee . . . invited you over?"

The question seemed oddly nosy. "No. It was a spontaneous visit on my part."

"You're friends with Renee?"

"We're . . . becoming friends." Kelsey's cordial but unreadable demeanor was unnerving. Why was she asking about this? "If Trent has already talked to Renee, I'm sure he can answer any questions you have." Catherine was careful to keep her tone polite. She didn't want to come off as rude, but this was none of Kelsey's business.

"I apologize." Kelsey stopped walking, so Catherine stopped too. "I didn't mean to make you uncomfortable. Renee didn't say much to Trent, and I was curious what you were doing there when the vandalism was discovered."

"Renee seemed like someone who could use a friend, so I stopped by. We ended up eating together, and when she went to leave the flowers for Olivia, I went with her."

"So she didn't know you were coming. You hadn't planned it earlier."

"No, it wasn't planned. Why does this matter?"

"I was just curious."

"Why?"

"We'd better hurry. We're late to class." Kelsey started toward the doors of the Relief Society room, which someone was swinging shut.

Nonplussed, Catherine followed her. Kelsey took an empty seat on the back row; Catherine chose a seat on the opposite side of the room, two rows behind Adam.

What had *that* been about?

Catherine opened her scriptures and found the correct chapter, but she felt too unsettled to concentrate. She didn't know why Kelsey's questions bothered her so much. Who cared if Kelsey knew the whole story of her effort to reach out to Renee?

But why was Kelsey so curious about it?

And where was Trent today? Kelsey was sitting alone.

When Sunday School ended, Catherine stayed in her seat and opened her Relief Society manual as the men streamed out of the room. She kept her eyes down as though she'd had a sudden guilty urge to cram for the lesson before Relief Society began. Today, she wasn't going to make any progress on her quest to meet people, but that was fine—she'd worry about that when she wasn't feeling so edgy.

Someone paused by her chair. Out of the corner of her eye, Catherine could see a charcoal-gray suit. She looked up.

Adam. She smiled, her face instantly hot. Should she apologize for the way she'd run off Tuesday night, or was it better to pretend it wasn't a big deal? "Hey."

Small, crooked smile. "You mentioned you wanted to meet my father. Are you still interested?"

Catherine had nearly forgotten that part of their conversation. What had she been thinking when she'd made that impulsive request? "Yes, of course I'd love to meet him," she fibbed. "How's he doing?"

"Not too bad. I told him you'd like to visit him, and he was thrilled."

"Was he?" Catherine kept a smile on her face.

"If you're free anytime this afternoon, he'd love the company."

More interaction with Adam while her thoughts about him were still a mess. *Great job, Catherine.* His father probably thought she was chasing Adam. But she wasn't going to back out now and disappoint a dying man who was delighted at the thought of a visitor.

"I'm free," she said. "Name the time."

"How about if we say four o'clock? I'll call you if that changes."

"That works great. Give me his address." Catherine pulled out her phone, figuring that asking for the address would make it clear she preferred to drive herself rather than have Adam pick her up.

He gave her the address, along with his cell phone number. Catherine entered the information. She should probably give him her cell number in case he needed to get in touch with her at the last minute, but she felt reluctant to offer it, and he didn't ask for it.

"See you later." As Adam walked out of the room, Catherine returned her gaze to her manual and wondered if Kelsey Perry had witnessed that conversation—and what Trent would think when he found out.

* * *

Her hands sweaty on the steering wheel, Catherine parked across the street from the condos where Adam's father lived. When she'd told Adam she wanted to meet his father, it had seemed a casual, friendly thing to say, but now it seemed so problematic.

It's only problematic in your imagination. Aren't we supposed to visit the sick? You're here to uplift Brother Becket with some cheerful company. This is about him, not you. And it's not about Adam either.

Dad would have appreciated a visit.

Catherine wiped her hands on her skirt. If Adam was inviting her to visit his father, at least she knew he hadn't completely scratched her off the friendship list after the way she'd fled from him at Maria's Pizza.

Maybe she could learn a little more about Adam through visiting with his father. *But that's not why you're here, so whatever you do, don't start interrogating him. This isn't about you.*

Still, if she could get a fuller picture of Adam *while* providing pleasant company for Brother Becket, that would be a nice bonus.

In the lobby, she found the buzzer for 216, but before she could press it, the interior security door swung open.

"Hello, Catherine." Adam had changed out of his suit and tie, but he was still dressed up in Dockers and an oxford shirt. Catherine was glad she hadn't opted for jeans. "I saw you drive up and thought I'd come be your official escort."

"Since I *am* a visiting dignitary." Catherine hoped her smile looked natural.

"You more than qualify." Adam held the door open for her. "Dad's looking forward to this."

"Did you warn him I'm not that exciting of a person to talk to?"

"I told him he's in for the most thrilling afternoon of his life. Don't disappoint him."

"No pressure."

Adam grinned. "Don't worry. You could sit and smile at him, and it'd make his day." He gestured toward the stairwell door. "I'm guessing you're a stair person, not an elevator person."

"I have to be to work off the clam chowder I had for lunch."

The paint on the stairwell walls was so pristine that it couldn't have been more than a few months since it had been redone, and there was no dust or debris anywhere on the stairs. Adam led the way to the second-floor corridor. The crimson hallway carpeting was a little worn in the center, but it had been recently vacuumed, and watercolor paintings decorated the cream-colored walls.

"This is very nice," Catherine said.

"Yeah, not a bad place. Dad sold the house a couple of years ago."

Adam opened the door to number 216, and Catherine stepped inside. The aroma of chocolate welcomed her. "You've been baking."

"Just a Texas sheet cake. One of Dad's favorites." Adam led her into the living room, where an older man stood in front of an armchair. He was gaunt, his cheeks hollow and his eyes sunken. A fuzz of white hair covered his skull. But once she looked past the illness, she could see the resemblance to Adam— the gray eyes, the shape of a face that must have once been boyishly handsome. He stood very straight, and the tightness in his jaw told her he was in pain.

Her father's pain-drawn face flashed in her thoughts.

"Dad, this is Catherine Clayton. Catherine, my father, Dale Becket."

Dale moved toward her and held out his hand. "Catherine." His voice was deep and slightly raspy. "It's a pleasure to meet you."

Catherine smiled and shook his cool hand, hoping the knot in her throat would relax. She'd feel like an idiot and upset both Adam and Dale if she greeted Dale by bursting into tears. "Thanks for letting me stop by."

"I never turn down visitors, unless they're selling something." He grinned widely, and Catherine could see what Adam's smile would look like if not for the nerve damage. "Have a seat." He waved toward the couch. "We'll let Adam bring us some cake."

Catherine sat on the couch, and Dale settled gingerly into the armchair.

"That's a wonderful photo gallery." Catherine gestured toward the upright piano. Covering the wall above the piano were dozens of framed photographs.

"Have a closer look," Dale invited. Catherine stood and went to look at the photos. In the center was a large family portrait. Dale and the blonde woman next to him looked to be in their mid- to late sixties; they were surrounded by what must be their children, children's spouses, and grandchildren. Catherine recognized Adam. A couple of the other men in the picture resembled Adam; they must be his brothers.

"Four sons," Dale said. "Jeffrey, Paul, Adam, and Scott. Three daughters-in-law: Hannah, Chelsea, and Leah. Eleven grandkids, but I won't bore you with their names. Adam's the only one not married, but we'll get him there."

"Thanks, Dad," Adam said dryly as he walked into the room carrying two plates of cake. He set one on the lamp table next to Dale.

"Claire—my wife—passed away only seven months after that family portrait was taken," Dale said. "Heart attack. Very sudden. Three years ago."

"I'm so sorry."

"I'll be with her soon. No need to be sorry now."

"That's what my father used to tell me near . . ." Catherine's voice trailed off. She'd been about to say "near the end," but that sounded callous. It was one thing for Dale to state that he was dying; it would sound different for Catherine to imply that he was in his final months.

"Adam told me your father passed last year. I'm sorry to hear that."

"Thank you." Catherine looked at a photo of Dale and Claire in ski gear. "I know he was happy to rejoin my mother—she died nine years before he did—but it was hard for me to let him go." She drew a deep breath and blinked, fighting the stinging in her eyes.

"It's hard on the kids, no question," Dale said. "Even when you know you'll see each other again, it only goes so far in comforting you at the moment."

"Very true." Catherine looked at a picture of Adam sitting next to one of his brothers and holding a fishing pole. The picture looked fairly recent, but he was smiling with both sides of his mouth, so it was before the biking accident. She would have liked to stand there much longer, studying the photos and learning everything the pictures had to tell her about Adam and his family, but she decided to sit down instead of making Dale hold a conversation while she had her back to him.

She returned to the couch. A piece of cake waited on the other lamp table near where she'd been sitting. Adam had seated himself at the opposite end of the couch.

"Adam told me about your music studio." Dale lifted a tiny fragment of cake on his fork. "You're doing a good thing for Riley. Claire would have loved it. She played piano and organ. Loved all kinds of music. She taught all the boys piano."

"You play?" Catherine asked, looking at Adam.

He nodded.

"He's good," Dale said.

"Only by comparison to my brothers."

For over an hour, the conversation moved from family member to family member—Adam's brothers, their wives and children, Catherine's parents and Ava, Adam's deceased mother—then shifted to the topic of Catherine's music studio again. It was light, friendly conversation, and Dale was either enjoying it, or he was putting on an excellent front; he looked happy and intently interested in everything Catherine said. He ate very little—not much more than a forkful of cake—and Catherine suspected that Adam's giving him a piece had been more courteous ritual than expectation that he would eat it.

Dale finally glanced at his watch. "You'd better get a move on, son. Don't you have a home teaching appointment at five thirty?"

"I do." Adam checked his watch.

"I'd better get home." Catherine took her cue. "I've enjoyed—"

"Don't run out yet," Dale interrupted. "Just because Adam's leaving doesn't mean you have to go. Stick around a little longer if you can."

Catherine glanced at Adam.

"Dad, you must be getting tired," Adam said.

"I'm fine. Go do your home teaching. I'd like to have Catherine to myself for a while."

Adam's brows drew together, and his mouth opened. Catherine expected him to say something, but instead, he closed his mouth and shot Dale a look of . . . suspicion? Warning? "I'm sure Catherine has things she needs to do," he said after a moment.

Dale smiled. "I'm hoping she'll spare a few more minutes for me."

"Dad—"

"It's fine. I can stay." Catherine hoped that was the right response. She was pleased that Dale wanted her company but disconcerted at the expression on Adam's face. He didn't look anxious for his father's health so much as he looked wary.

"Get moving, Adam," Dale said. "You don't want to be late."

Adam rose slowly to his feet. "Catherine . . . I'll . . . talk to you later."

She smiled at him, wanting to reassure him but not sure what she was reassuring him about. "Thanks for the cake."

As soon as Adam had closed the door behind him, Dale chuckled. "I'm in trouble now," he said. "Naive kid didn't suspect a thing when I told him we'd be done for sure by four forty-five and go on and make his appointments. But he has me nailed now."

Puzzled, Catherine could only smile wordlessly in response.

Dale shifted in his seat, his breath becoming uneven when he moved. "I wanted to talk to you alone."

"That's fine, but are you sure you don't need to go lie down? I can come back another time."

"I can last a few more minutes." Dale studied her, his expression keen. "Catherine, I know Trent told you my son murdered Olivia."

Startled at such a jarring leap from pleasant into painful, Catherine said awkwardly, "He told me that, but I didn't believe him."

"But you're still a bit afraid, aren't you?"

Jolted again by his candor, Catherine had no idea how to respond. Clearly, the reason Dale had maneuvered to talk to her alone was so he could say things he didn't want to say in Adam's presence. "I wouldn't have sat here eating cake with Adam if I thought he was a murderer."

"But would you sit here if you didn't *want* to believe Trent's accusation and were *almost* positive it wasn't true—but you still weren't 100 percent certain Adam was innocent?"

The instinct for politeness made Catherine want to declare that of course she didn't doubt Adam's innocence even a smidgen. She held the words back; she had the feeling that courteous dissembling wouldn't fool Dale Becket. On the other hand, how could she admit to doubting . . . This was crazy to try to discuss this with—

"You're having trouble answering," Dale said. "That's good. I was afraid you'd give the easy response."

"The easy response?"

"Phony statements about how such a nice man could never be a killer. Catherine, do you like my son?"

Catherine's cheeks burned.

Dale smiled. "Dear, you can turn redder than Claire, and she could turn the color of bing cherries. I don't mean 'like' in a kissy-kissy sense or in anything beyond the straightforward meaning of the word. Do you like him?"

"Of course I like him. He seems like a nice guy." Sweat trickled down her back. *Seems like a nice guy* sounded like he *appeared* nice but who knew what evil seethed in his soul.

"You'd like to get to know him better?"

"I . . . yes, it would be nice . . . making friends is good . . ."

Dale lifted a hand. "But you feel a little scared, a little in over your head, given the gossip about him?"

Catherine steadied herself mentally. *Stop cringing and blushing. You spent your whole life dealing with this type of straightforward approach—this is just the way Dad would have handled this. No dancing around it. Get to the point.*

"It *is* disconcerting," she said. "Did Adam tell you I felt this way?"

"Adam has become adept at reading people. After you see enough people react with discomfort, you learn to recognize when someone is squirming."

Adam had obviously told his father how she'd fled from the parking lot. "I'm sorry. I wish I . . . I wish . . . I don't think . . ." So much for straightforward. "This must sound terrible to you, that I could . . ."

"Why should it sound terrible? You just moved here. You just met Adam. I'm not offended that you're struggling to make a judgment about whether my son is what he seems or what Trent says he is. You'd be a nitwit if you weren't concerned, and you're clearly not a nitwit."

"I do feel bad that I've been sending mixed signals. I just don't know what to do. Ever since I moved here, Olivia's death has been shadowing me. I walked into Flinders Elementary, and Renee, the secretary, promptly warned me that another young woman like me was murdered here and I'd better be careful. Then I had Trent telling me Adam killed Olivia and to stay away from him. Now this vandalism—I was with Renee when she found the messages in Olivia's apartment, as I'm sure Adam told you. Some people think Olivia's killer is back; other people think a vandal is using Olivia's name to try to scare people. My head's a mess. I've never dealt with anything like this before."

Dale's pale lips lifted in a melancholy smile. "I'm sorry this was your welcome to Riley. You shouldn't have to deal with this at all—Olivia's tragic death happened two years before you arrived here. But with the killer still at large, Riley hasn't done much healing." Dale closed his eyes and fell silent, breathing shallowly.

"Brother Becket, you should rest. I can come back later . . ."

He opened his eyes. "For me, there might not be a later, so I don't like to waste time. Let me tell you something you might find interesting. The day Adam met you, he came here as miserable and discouraged as I've ever seen him."

"Miserable! Why?"

"Because a nice young lady who seemed fun and intelligent had moved into the ward. And he enjoyed a few minutes talking with you and then turned around and saw Trent glaring at him—and he knew Trent was going to poison you against him, and there was nothing he could do to stop it. Ten uncontaminated minutes of conversation was all he was going to get before Trent planted dark doubts in your mind."

Dale brushed the back of his hand across a sheen of sweat on his forehead. The pain must be worsening.

"Can I get you something?" Catherine asked, yearning to help him. "Is it time for your medication?"

"You can listen to me. That's all I want. After church the day Adam met you, he came over here and sat and stared out the window. Would hardly talk to me beyond giving me the bare bones of what had happened. I tried to give him some fatherly encouragement, but I knew he was right—Trent *was* going to talk to you because Trent can't let go of the need to blame Adam, and infecting the new girl with suspicion was a way to hurt him."

Catherine didn't know what to say.

"You're not a parent yet, but someday you'll learn that there's nothing worse than watching your child suffer. It cuts Adam to the core, knowing there are people who think he killed Olivia. He's dealt with this for two years, and he's handled it with dignity, but it wears on him, and with my illness, he's already under too much stress. When he saw Trent ready to pounce and turn you against him, he wanted to fold."

"But he didn't give up on making friends with me. He came to visit me. He brought me a delicious chocolate cake."

Dale chuckled. "Yes. I'm still strong enough to twist an arm."

"*You* told him to do that?"

"After you didn't return his first call, he was, frankly, scared to contact you again. So I grabbed the kid by the collar, threw him out my door, and told him not to come back until he'd visited you, that the longer he waited, the more time Trent's warning would have to marinate."

"Thank you for doing that."

"Adam is not an outgoing man. It's hard enough to put yourself out there when you fear rejection, but when you're afraid a potential friend will be outright terrified to see your face through the peephole, wondering if you're planning to sink a knife into her chest—that makes him reluctant to reach out. Thank you for giving him a chance."

Catherine thought guiltily of her confusion and hesitation when Adam had rung the bell. "I'm glad I did. Isn't Trent worried that Adam might sue him for slander or something like that?"

"The last thing Adam wants is to turn gossip and accusations into a legal battle. Publicly stirring it up like that would only multiply rumors a thousandfold. Fact is, Adam can't prove he's innocent any more than Trent can prove he's guilty. And Trent is smart enough not to spread rumors in a way that would openly harm Adam's job, for instance. He prefers the personal touch, like targeting you. I'm sorry for Trent. I suppose in his own mind, he thinks he's seeking justice, but he's let grief blind him."

Dale gripped the arms of his chair, and Catherine wondered if he was bracing himself against collapse. "Two more important things, Catherine.

The first is that in telling you how much it mattered to Adam that you give him a chance, I don't want to scare you away with the impression that he's in hot romantic pursuit. That's not how Adam works. Right now, as far as I can see, he's hoping for a friend. First things first."

"I understand." Catherine hoped Dale didn't assume she was vain enough to think Adam was infatuated with her.

"Second thing." Dale straightened up in his chair and looked directly into Catherine's eyes. "Conventional wisdom has always been that we're blind to faults in those we love, but that's baloney. If people don't see the flaws in their children, it's because they refuse to look. I know my son. He's not perfect. He can be stubborn. He struggles with pride at times—can't imagine where he inherited *that* from. But I will tell you this with absolute certainty: Adam did not kill Olivia Perry or harm her in any way."

Trying to figure out how to phrase a response, Catherine drew breath to speak, but Dale shook his head. "You don't have to say anything. I want you to listen. I want you to know that as the person who raised Adam and has stayed close to him into adulthood—and I see a lot of him now; he's over here every day making a pest of himself trying to take care of me—I know without question that he's innocent of Trent's accusations."

"Thank you," Catherine said quietly.

Dale settled back in his chair, his posture slackening. "There," he said. "Never expected *that* out of a Sunday afternoon visit to the sick and afflicted, did you?"

"I guess not."

"Adam didn't expect it either, so how about we keep this between us? I didn't used to interfere in his life like this, and he won't appreciate it, but as I said, I'm short on time. How about now I show you my bowling trophies so if Adam asks what we talked about, you can tell him bowling. Do you bowl, Catherine?"

"I'm pretty good at bumper bowling," Catherine said.

* * *

Sunset oranges and pinks tinted the sky as Catherine sat on her patio contemplating the day. The evening was surprisingly warm, and the gentle breeze soothed her. A lounge chair was a good place to relax and think about Dale Becket's words.

She'd hoped to glean more knowledge of Adam from visiting his father, but she'd never expected Dale to be so blunt. She wondered if Adam suspected what his father had wanted to say to her. He probably did—he'd looked so uneasy when he realized he'd been tricked into leaving Catherine alone with Dale.

It was more than Dale's faith in Adam that had affected her. It was watching Adam with his father—the concern and respect Adam showed him, the affection in his words and actions, affection and respect that Dale, in turn, showed his son. If Adam was a psychopath who could maintain a stellar front while being a conscienceless killer underneath, she couldn't believe Dale Becket wouldn't have seen evidence of that. If Dale did suspect something, she couldn't believe he'd lie to her about it.

Dale had reminded her so much of her father—his warmth, his candor, his humor. And his illness. She knew how it felt watching a parent die. Adam was hurting.

She also knew how it felt to lose someone you'd once loved—*still* loved in many ways, even though you knew the future you'd dreamed of would never happen. Maybe it was a stretch to compare the loss of Robert to the loss of Olivia—Robert hadn't cheated on her like Olivia had on Adam, and Robert had died in an accident, not at the hands of a killer—but she did have *some* inkling of the shock, grief, and confusion Adam must have felt at Olivia's sudden death.

Adam could use a friend.

So could she.

The landline phone rang. She reached for the stone-mosaic-topped table where she'd set it. The number wasn't familiar. "Hello, this is Catherine at Bridgeside Studio."

"Hi, Catherine," a friendly male voice said. "You still have openings for lessons?"

"I do."

"Your flyer says you teach all ages. Does that include adults?"

"Yes, it does."

"I might be interested. I'm hoping for a tour, a demo, something to help me make up my mind."

"You're welcome to visit the studio."

"That would be great. Got any time tonight?"

Catherine felt simultaneously pleased and cautious. The enthusiasm in his voice almost sounded flirtatious. She'd definitely need to put him in a time slot when Esther Knight would be around so Catherine wouldn't be one-on-one with him. "Unfortunately, I'm not available tonight. Let me check my calendar." She picked up her cell phone and opened the calendar. "Do evenings work best for you?"

"Depends. I could do tomorrow morning if you have an opening then. The earlier the better."

Perfect. Esther was scheduled to come from eight to eleven. "Would eight thirty work for you?"

"Sounds great. I'll bring breakfast."

Catherine laughed. "Not required. What's your name?"

"Will Conti."

Frozen, Catherine stared blankly at the calendar. "Will Conti?"

"Yep. That's *C-O-N-T-I*."

Will Conti. The man who had flirted his way into Olivia's heart right before her death. Will Conti wanted to take music lessons? Mechanically, Catherine typed his name into the calendar for Monday morning. "All right, Mr. Conti." She tried to keep her voice smooth. "Do you need directions to the studio?"

"Nope. Got the address here on the flyer I grabbed at the library. I'm looking forward to meeting you, Catherine. See you in the morning."

Catherine lowered the phone. Will Conti. She didn't want to meet Will, but what was she supposed to do? Tell him music lessons were open to everyone in town except him?

Was she afraid of him? Jan had said Will had also been questioned after Olivia's death.

No, she wasn't afraid of him—not under the circumstances of introducing him to the music studio and not with Esther present. But why did Will have to call her?

Will Conti. One more connection to Olivia Perry. Riley was a small city, but it wasn't *that* small. Was it pure coincidence that Will Conti, of all people, would pick up a flyer and become interested in her studio?

Did Will still work at Trent's gym? Had Trent said something about Catherine? What?

With the anxious feeling that she was blundering into a situation she knew nothing about, Catherine closed the calendar on her phone and thought about her first encounter with Renee, when Renee had taunted her that after six months, she'd be so bored she'd want to flee to a Mediterranean beach. Renee had guessed the timing wrong and the motivation wrong—Catherine was anything but bored—but catching a flight to Greece or Italy or France was sounding better and better.

CHAPTER 10

THE FRONT DOOR OPENED SLOWLY. Esther Knight poked her head into the entryway then stepped all the way inside.

"Good morning, Esther." Catherine was sitting on the hardwood floor of the main room of the studio, sorting stacks of music. She'd told Esther to walk in when she arrived at work—no need to ring the doorbell—but considering how tentatively Esther had opened the door, she didn't seem convinced that Catherine had meant it.

"Hi." Esther had relaxed her appearance a little since that first interview—a black knit shirt and metallic purple vest had replaced the button-down shirt, and skinny jeans had replaced the khakis—but Catherine could tell she was still being careful to dress modestly and not overdo the make-up or jewelry. Danielle had texted Catherine the other day with the message, *You're good for her. She's brushing her hair instead of styling it by sleeping on it.*

"Hope you don't mind sitting on the floor," Catherine said. "I promise it's clean."

"Are you kidding?" Esther said. "This place is totally dust free. It's freaky. Did you hire Dani to clean for you or what?"

Catherine laughed. "No, but maybe she secretly runs the housekeeping service I use. Is she gone at odd hours and keeping secrets from you?"

"Probably, but I'm too busy hiding from her to notice."

"I'm trying to get this music sorted." Catherine gestured at the piles of sheet music. "My stepmother has a friend who managed a now-defunct community orchestra, and she had boxes of music in her garage that she passed on to me. But everything looks like it was sorted by hurricane—it's a complete jumble. I'm trying to get it sorted first by piece and then by instrument."

"Let me at it." Esther dropped her purse to the floor.

Catherine climbed to her feet. "I'm also hoping you'll play chaperone this morning. A man is coming over to learn more about the music studio, and he sounded like a flirt on the phone. Let's just say I'm planning to leave the office door ajar." She kept her tone humorous; she didn't want to explain the other reasons why talking to Will Conti made her edgy.

"I'm a chaperoning ninja." Esther took Catherine's spot on the floor. "I've watched Dani do it to me my whole life."

"Thanks, Esther. I'm going to grab some more folders; I didn't bring enough out here. There's even more music than I thought." She headed into the office.

When the doorbell rang half an hour later, Catherine rose from her place on the floor next to Esther and whispered, "Watch my back."

"If he tries anything, he won't know what hit him," Esther said as Catherine headed for the door.

"Good morning, Catherine." Will Conti grinned at her. No question about why Olivia had found him physically appealing—Will was hot. Strong nose and jawline, playful smile, wavy dark hair spilling over his ears and down to his collar. Catherine usually didn't care for longish hair on men, but it gave Will a rugged, swashbuckling look.

Swashbuckling? Is this Talk-Like-a-Pirate Day? Catherine bit the inside of her lip to keep from grinning. Stress was catching up with her.

"Come in, Will," she said. Calling him Mr. Conti would seem stiff.

"Breakfast." He held up a bakery bag. In his other hand were a white cardboard box and a grocery sack. "As promised."

"You brought it? I thought you were joking."

"No way." He stepped inside.

Catherine closed the door. "This is my assistant, Esther Knight." She gestured toward Esther, who sat with a stack of music in her lap.

Esther's eyes widened, and her mouth dropped open.

"Heyyy . . ." Will said. "Hey, Esther. Long time, huh?"

"*You* are interested in music lessons?" Esther's tone was caustic.

"I'd have been interested a lot sooner if I'd known you were here. We miss you at the gym. You ever think of joining up again?"

The fury in Esther's eyes startled Catherine. Clearly, there was some negative history between Esther and Will, and the best thing to do would be to get Will out of the room. "Why don't we sit down in my office, and I'll tell you how the studio works," she said quickly.

"Lead the way."

They sat in Catherine's office—with the door ajar—and Will set the bags and box on the desk.

"Brought some juice, but I thought you might want something nice to drink it from." Will opened the box and drew out a pottery mug. The mug was a deep, rich aqua, drizzled around the rim and handle with an iridescent green glaze.

"That's beautiful," Catherine said, hoping Will didn't intend the mug as a gift.

"Welcome to Riley." Will turned the mug so Catherine could see the bottom of it. Etched into the clay was *To Catherine*, the year, and a signature.

Catherine thought of Renee's describing the pottery pitcher Will had given Olivia. Under the desk, she interlaced her fingers, trying to warm her cold hands.

"Pottery is my hobby." Will set the mug on the desk, took a bottle of orange juice from the grocery sack, and filled the mug for Catherine.

"Cheers." He offered it to her.

Flustered, Catherine took it. She did *not* want a gift from Will Conti, but she couldn't think of a gracious way to reject a handmade, personalized mug filled with orange juice.

Will took a matching pottery plate from the box and set it on the table. He opened the bakery bag and set three muffins on the plate.

"Apple streusel, chocolate chip, or orange-ginger. Take your pick."

Catherine took the orange-ginger muffin. She couldn't help admiring the beauty of the plate and the gloss of the richly colored mug in her hand. Will was certainly a talented potter, but she didn't want to gush over his skill. She was already uncomfortable at what seemed a far-too-personal beginning to what was supposed to be a business meeting.

"Tell me what sparked your interest in music," she said. "Did you take lessons when you were younger?"

Will took the chocolate-chip muffin. "Never did. To tell the truth, Catherine, music was never my thing."

"It's not too late to start. I have a woman who started flute lessons—she's never had any musical training before—and she's making great progress."

"Fascinating. Never too old, huh?"

"That's right."

"Free music lessons, huh? No hidden charges."

"That's right. There's no financial cost to you. However, I do require a certain level of commitment from my students, both in lesson attendance and in practice time. I don't want to waste your time or mine, and learning to play an instrument takes dedication."

"Looking for commitment, huh?"

From the way Will was grinning, he wasn't talking about music lessons. Rather than matching his smile, Catherine said matter-of-factly, "Yes, I am. You'll need to decide up front if you're serious about this."

"I'm serious about listening to everything you say. Tell me about yourself." He took a bite out of his muffin.

"I've always loved music. I studied the cello from the time I was six—"

"Nah, no, not the music education background. Tell me about *you*. Where are you from?"

"Virginia." Catherine tried not to sound too curt. She could read his ego: he expected her to be flattered by his interest in her and drooling over his handsome face and curving biceps. Maybe his charm would work better on her if she could look at him without thinking of Olivia. And had he been romantically involved with Esther?

"Virginia," he said. "Nice. Been there a few times. What brought you to Riley?"

"I came to start this music studio. Mr. Conti, what instruments do you think you might be interested in?"

"Anything you play, Catherine. I'd listen to a concert from you anytime."

Catherine kept her voice brisk. "Let me tell you about the studio. Lessons are usually—"

Will leaned forward, holding her gaze. "I already found out what I need to know. Bridgeside is run by a beautiful woman. A beautiful woman with long, red hair. You have amazing hair. It's killing me to keep my hands to myself, looking at that hair. I want to run my fingers through it."

Catherine set the mug on the desk. "Mr. Conti, are you interested in taking music lessons or not?"

He smiled—the smile that must have sent Olivia's good sense into meltdown. Catherine caught herself comparing that blindingly handsome smile to Adam's damaged, crooked one.

She preferred Adam's.

"Truth is, Catherine, the only music I'll ever make is on an iPod," Will said. "I just wanted to meet you."

Was this how he'd approached Olivia? Flattering her, complimenting her? "I'd have preferred you to be honest about your intentions rather than scheduling a meeting under false pretenses."

His dark eyes were so sweet and contrite that he would have given Bambi a run for his money. "I'm sorry. It was sneaky, but I was intrigued with what I'd heard about you and figured you'd be more likely to meet with a potential student than a plain old stranger."

Catherine took a bite of her orange muffin to give herself time to think. The last thing she needed was to be pursued by Will Conti. What was he up to anyway? It would be nice to believe she was so beautiful that Will and every other eligible male in town would chase after her and bring her gifts, but if she'd wanted to maintain *that* delusion, she shouldn't have bought a mirror.

"Let me take you to lunch today to make up for tricking you," Will said. "I know where to find the best pasta in town."

Catherine wondered at the logic of thinking a lunch date could make up for maneuvering to meet her socially under the pretense of a business consultation. "Thank you, but I'd rather not. If you don't have any questions about the studio, then I have work to do."

"You're mad at me," Will said. "Sorry. I lost my head when I heard about you—and when I caught a glimpse of you at Leonardi Fitness."

"You saw me at the gym?" He must have seen her when she went to visit Trent. She felt eerie knowing Will had been watching her—and had apparently asked Kelsey or Trent who she was.

"Men in Riley are more likely to get kidnapped by aliens than to spot a gorgeous, redheaded newcomer, so you made an impression. Your hair inspired this." He leaned across the desk and ran his finger along the side of the mug he'd given her. "Blues and greens are stunning on redheads. The whole time I was shaping the clay, I pictured you drinking from it."

"I'm flattered," Catherine said, which wasn't true. Imagining Will saying these types of things to Olivia left her more tense than flattered.

"I've been trying to work up the nerve to call you and realized this might be my only shot at getting in the door," Will said. "I hope you can forgive me."

Catherine couldn't imagine that an experienced flirt like Will ever had to "work up the nerve" to call a woman. "You're forgiven. But if you're not interested in the studio, I really do have work to do."

The charismatic smile on Will's face finally flattened. "It's because of Olivia Perry, isn't it?"

Prickling spread over Catherine's skin. How did Will know that *she* knew about Olivia and him? "I don't understand what you mean."

"Don't play dumb. Trent told you I dated her, didn't he? The jerk."

Catherine couldn't remember if Trent had given her Will's name or if she'd heard it first from Jan. "I know you dated her," she said, "but I don't remember who told me. I've heard a lot about Olivia since moving to Riley."

"Whoever told you about Olivia also told you I'm a creep, didn't they? Did Adam Becket tell you that? You know Adam; you go to the same church."

Catherine wrapped up the rest of her muffin in a napkin and pushed it aside. How much did Will know about her? He'd done some homework. "What I've heard is that while Adam was dating Olivia, you started seeing her on the side, and Adam broke off the relationship. That's all I know."

Will's voice was hard. "That and the fact that she was murdered right after that."

"Yes." Catherine took a swallow of orange juice, not out of thirst but to moisten her throat in case she needed to yell for Esther.

"You think I'm a creep," Will said. "You might even think I killed her."

Will's words surprised her. She'd expected him to accuse Adam. "I don't think you killed her. I have no idea who killed her."

"But because my name is linked with hers, I'm scum in your eyes. That's how it is. I sneak a couple of kisses with Olivia, she dies, and I'm damaged goods forever. Everyone looks at me and thinks of her."

Catherine met Will's angry gaze and kept her voice steady. "The reason I don't want to go out with you is not because of Olivia. It's because we're not each other's type."

"Don't make up stupid lies. *No one* turned me down before Olivia died."

"I'm done with this conversation. I want you to leave."

"You're dating that boring geek Becket, aren't you? Admit it."

Catherine rose to her feet. "You need to leave. Now."

"It's getting stirred up again. Just when it was finally going away. Someone's haunting the town now, claiming to be Olivia's killer. You heard about the vandalism, about those threats?"

"Yes."

"It's all back; it's all people can think about." Will jerked to his feet. "You're not getting away from it either."

"Away from what?"

"Away from Olivia, away from what her death did to everyone. She'll destroy you too. Watch and see." Will turned and stomped out the door.

Catherine stood waiting for the sound of the front door slamming. It finally came. She was surprised Will hadn't snatched back his gifts, but then again, what was he going to do with a mug inscribed *To Catherine*?

Knees shaky, she emerged from the office. Esther was arranging stacks of music on the lid of the piano, her back to Catherine.

"Wow," Catherine said. "That was . . . interesting. I'm sorry I didn't warn you who was coming. I didn't realize you knew Will."

"Dani and I used to be members of the gym where Will works." Esther's voice was cold, and she didn't turn to face Catherine.

"He's . . . quite a flirt." Catherine wondered how much of the conversation Esther had overheard. Probably all of it, with the door ajar.

Esther said nothing. Catherine figured she'd better not ask questions. Whatever had gone on between Will and Esther, Esther plainly didn't want to talk about it. "The good news is, we won't be seeing him again," Catherine said.

Esther slapped another stack of music on top of the piano with such a loud *whap* that Catherine flinched. "You won't get rid of Will Conti that easily." Esther snatched another stack. "But his pottery shatters really well if you throw it against concrete."

"Good to know," Catherine said evenly, thinking of what Danielle had said about Esther's temper. "Could you take it easy on that music? Some of it's old and fragile."

Esther set the next stack down gently, but her shoulders were rigid. "I'm hungry," she said. Her voice was as level as Catherine's but stony. "Do you mind if I run to the bagel shop?"

"No problem." Catherine doubted Esther wanted food; she wanted to be alone to calm herself down—which sounded like a good idea to Catherine. "Take whatever time you need."

Esther grabbed her purse and stalked toward the front door. Given her hostile body language, Catherine expected her to slam the door like Will had, but she closed it quietly.

Dazed, Catherine crumpled onto the piano bench.

CHAPTER 11

"Remember, the quarter note gets one count. Like this." Catherine clapped the rhythm. It was the third time she'd demonstrated it.

"Right . . . that's right . . . sorry." Maren Gates lifted the flute to her lips.

Increasingly concerned, Catherine listened to Maren struggle with the rhythm. She'd done so well at her previous lesson that Catherine had been amazed, but tonight she seemed to have trouble remembering anything Catherine told her.

At least Catherine felt more emotionally on keel and capable of helping Maren than she had last time. It had been a surprisingly good week. After Monday's confrontation with Will, she hadn't heard anything more from him. Esther had returned after a short time away, calm and ready to work; they hadn't mentioned Will again, and when Esther came to work on Wednesday, they'd had a great time laughing together as they filed music and swapped Danielle stories. There had been no further vandalism or any other disturbances in town. And eight new students had signed up for lessons.

"Very nice," Catherine said as Maren lowered her flute after a somewhat better attempt. "Maren . . . are you worried about something? You seem distracted tonight."

Maren pushed a wisp of hair back from her face. "I'm sorry. You . . . probably wonder why someone like me is even trying to learn the flute."

Catherine frowned. "What do you mean, 'someone like you'?"

Maren tapped her fingers against a couple of keys, not meeting Catherine's eyes. "I'm . . . not very educated . . . I'm sure you can tell."

"Your level of education has nothing to do with your ability to learn the flute."

"Yeah, but . . . I mean, come on." Maren's rounded cheeks went rosy. "I almost flunked out of high school. I never even thought about going to college."

"So what? You're doing great with the flute. You have a lot of natural ability." Catherine scrutinized the unhappiness in Maren's face. "Did someone give you a hard time about your lessons?"

Maren stared at the polished hardwood floor. "Tonight at dinner I . . . finally told Dylan I was taking flute lessons. He told me to quit."

Catherine figured it wouldn't be diplomatic to show how angry those words made her. "I apologize if he was upset at your having a lesson on Friday night."

"Oh no, that's not it. He always plays video games with his brother on Friday nights. That's why I asked for Friday in the first place."

"He doesn't want you taking lessons at all."

"He . . . thinks getting stuff for free is charity, and he hates charity. He's . . . I mean, he's a good guy, hard worker, really responsible. He doesn't want anyone else taking care of him. He doesn't even like it that I have to work right now, but it's just tending my niece, and he has to live with it, since we need the money."

"Maren . . . obviously it's commendable to be self-reliant, but just because the studio doesn't charge for lessons doesn't mean I don't require commitment and work on your part. You work hard for this."

"I know. But he . . . said I'm making a fool of myself."

Realizing she was clutching her own flute too hard—as though preparing to whack Dylan over the head with it—Catherine laid it on top of the case and tried to speak calmly. "Why is learning an instrument making a fool of yourself?"

"Because I'm too old and too stupid to learn." Maren's voice caught.

"Maren." Catherine scooted her chair closer and rested her hand on Maren's arm. "You're *not* old, and you're far from stupid. Did Dylan tell you those things?"

Maren wiped tears away with the back of her hand. "Well . . . he . . . didn't mean it. He just doesn't understand. He says what am I trying to do—make myself into some hottie musician up on stage in a miniskirt with men throwing hotel room keys at me?"

"*What?*"

"I *tried* to tell him I didn't want to get up on any stage ever, that this is just something for me, but he . . . doesn't get it."

Catherine drew a few slow, deep breaths to keep herself calm. "Maren, you're *not* stupid, and you *can* learn to play, and you *are* learning to play, and you're doing fantastically well. At your first lesson, I was astounded at how quickly you caught on. I thought it would take several lessons for you to learn to make a decent sound, and you're already playing this." She gestured at the workbook.

Maren gave a trembling smile. "I told him I wasn't quitting."

"Good. What did he say to that?"

"He told me I couldn't use the car or spend money on the bus. If I wanted to come, I'd have to walk."

Catherine squeezed her arm. "I'm a walker myself. Do it all the time. It saves me from having to buy a gym membership. How far is it to your house?"

"Oh, I don't know. It took me about an hour. Maybe three miles or something like that?"

That distance wouldn't have bothered Catherine, but if Maren wasn't used to regular walking, her feet would be sore—especially in those flimsy flats she was wearing.

"It was good of you to come tonight, under the circumstances," Catherine said.

"I wasn't going to flake out on you."

"Do you need any Band-Aids? You probably have blisters."

"I'm okay. These shoes are really broken in." She sniffled. "I think Dylan will be okay after awhile. He'll get used to me taking lessons and gripe about something else. I hope."

She sounded doubtful, and Catherine's muscles tightened at the thought of Maren's having to listen to a continuing stream of insults and accusations over her music lessons. Her confidence could erode until she was convinced Dylan was right: she wasn't smart enough to learn to play. Even if he quit criticizing her, she'd certainly never want to share her talent in front of him. His disdain would leach away much of the pleasure Maren could receive from her new skill.

Catherine would have loved to corner Dylan to tell him what she thought of his attitude toward his wife and her budding love of music, but that wouldn't help the situation at all. It would only make Dylan angrier.

Surreptitiously, Catherine scanned Maren's arms and face, checking for bruises. She didn't see any injuries, but if Dylan was jerk enough to call Maren stupid and jealous enough to accuse her of wanting to use her music to attract other men, was he jerk enough to hit her?

"Sorry." Maren mopped her eyes. "Sorry about that. It'll be okay. Oh wow, it's raining." She glanced at the water-spattered glass of the window. "I forgot it was supposed to rain tonight."

"Yes, rain and more rain," Catherine said, reluctantly going along with Maren's clear wish to change the subject.

"We'd better get back to work." Maren lifted her flute. "Should I start at the beginning?"

Catherine tried to cool the steam building inside her. "Yes, let's go over it one more time. Maren . . . if you ever need someone to talk to—not just about music—call me. Seriously. Anytime, day or night."

"Thanks, Catherine. You . . . that's sweet, but I wouldn't want to be a pain."

"You're not a pain. I'm new to Riley. I could use a friend, so if you ever need one, call me."

"I will." Maren smiled at her. "Thanks."

For the remainder of the lesson, Maren's focus was a little better, but Catherine's was worse. She was fuming about Dylan more than she was concentrating on Maren's technique.

As Maren packed up her flute and music at the end of the half hour, Catherine wished she could offer some steel-clad encouragement that could shield Maren against whatever Dylan would throw at her. The best she could offer was, "You're doing great. You learn very quickly. Don't let anyone discourage you. You can do this."

"Thanks." Maren headed toward the door. Catherine walked along with her.

"Call me anytime," Catherine said again. "You have my cell number." Through the windows flanking the door, she could see rain falling, glistening in the lights that lined the walkway. Maren was neither carrying an umbrella nor wearing a raincoat.

"You'll get soaked walking home." Catherine eyed Maren's sweater, a thin cotton one that looked as though it had shrunk in the wash. "It's late, and your feet must be sore."

"I'll be okay." Maren glanced at the windows. "It's not raining that hard."

"I'd love to offer you a ride, but I have some parents coming in ten minutes to talk about lessons for their kids. Why don't you take my car? I'll walk over and pick it up tomorrow. I enjoy stretching my legs."

Maren's blue eyes went huge. "I can't take your car!"

"It's just a Toyota minivan—nothing fancy. I don't need it again tonight."

"Catherine, you're a sweetheart, but no way can I drive off in your car! Besides, Dylan would go nuts if I showed up with it. I'll be fine swimming home." From Maren's too-cheerful tone of trying to joke when something wasn't funny, Catherine could tell she was anything but thrilled at the thought of slogging home through the rain. But pushing her into borrowing the car—or offering her money for the bus—would only make things worse.

"I don't think my appointment with these parents will take long," Catherine said. "Not more than half an hour. If you'd like to relax in the family room and watch TV, I could give you a ride home as soon as my appointment is finished."

Maren bit her lip, hesitating. "No, thank you. I'll be okay. I know it sounds stupid, but I don't want a ride. I'll do this on my own. If I get a ride home, it'll make me look like a wimp, mooching off you."

Catherine wanted to say that was ridiculous, but she knew Maren was anticipating Dylan's criticism. "At least take an umbrella and a raincoat." She opened the closet and took out an umbrella and her new Burberry.

"It's okay. It's not very cold out, and I don't mind getting wet." Maren reached for the doorknob.

"Maren, get real. You'll be soaked and freezing." Catherine looked uneasily at the rain dotting the window. She liked walking in the rain if she was dressed for it, and she didn't mind walking at night—if the neighborhood was safe. She'd thought it *was* safe until . . . But the fact that someone had vandalized the school and Olivia's apartment didn't mean . . . None of those events had happened near Bridgeside . . . but Maren had three miles to walk . . .

"I'd feel better if you'd take the car," Catherine said. "Or I could drive you to the bus stop before my next appointment."

Maren looked grimly at Catherine. "Thanks, but I'm not giving Dylan something new to yell about. I'll be fine."

"Please, at least take the coat and umbrella." Feeling like a worried mother, Catherine held the items out to Maren. "If it will bother Dylan to see you borrowing things, then shove them in a bush before you go inside."

"Well . . . that's sweet of you." Maren half reached for the raincoat then drew her hands back. "I can't take that. That looks like a brand-new raincoat, and I'll bet it was super expensive."

"Here." Catherine shoved the Burberry back in the closet and pulled out her old lobster raincoat. "This thing is ancient. I've had it for ages. Wear it, okay? Or you'll end up with hypothermia."

"Um . . . I guess I'd better, or I really will be swimming home." Maren set her flute down and took the coat. "But I don't need the umbrella. This coat will be more than enough to keep me dry. Thanks, Catherine. I'm sorry to be a pain."

"You're not a pain at all. I wish you'd take the car, but I understand you don't want to upset Dylan. Would you do me one favor?"

"What's that?"

"Would you be able to give me a call when you get home—so I'll know you're fine? Or would that be too hard with Dylan . . ."

"No, I can call," Maren said. "Dylan will still be with his brother. He won't notice if I call you."

"Thanks. I'll see you next week—back to our normal Monday time. Keep up the good work. You're doing great, and it's a pleasure teaching you."

"You . . . enjoy teaching me?"

"What's not to enjoy? You're dedicated, talented, and you're fun to work with. I'm honored to be your teacher."

"Thanks, Catherine." Maren hugged her. "You're the best."

"Stay dry." Catherine thought about offering Maren a pair of more sturdy shoes—their feet looked about the same size—but knew Maren would refuse.

"See you next week." Maren pulled up the hood on the raincoat and headed out the door.

CHAPTER 12

GIVING UP HER ATTEMPT TO concentrate on a biography of Leonard Bernstein, Catherine set the book down and checked her watch again. Even if Maren walked slowly, she should have been home long before now. Catherine had looked up her address in the studio files, and it was three-point-one miles away.

Intellectually, she knew she was worrying too much. Maren could simply have forgotten to call her.

But what if she'd arrived home to an angry Dylan waiting on the doorstep? Dylan was obviously verbally abusive; what if he was physically abusive too?

Catherine rose from her recliner and wandered restlessly around the house. It was eleven fifteen. She'd tried texting Maren twice and had received no answer. She didn't dare call this late for fear of enraging Dylan. Maybe she could drive over, park a block away, and walk past the house to see if things seemed quiet. It wasn't much, but if everything seemed fine, maybe it would calm her nerves enough to allow her to sleep.

That won't help. Even if you don't hear screams or dishes breaking, that doesn't mean she's okay.

The studio phone ringing made her start. She leaped toward the kitchen counter and snatched the receiver. The number on the caller ID wasn't familiar. "Hello, this is Catherine."

"You're the music lady? The teacher?" Instead of Maren's soprano voice, a harsh tenor hit Catherine's eardrum.

"Yes, this is Catherine Clayton. Who is this?"

"This is Dylan Gates. My wife had a lesson with you tonight, and she should have been home hours ago. She still there?"

Icy adrenaline flooded Catherine's veins. "She left two and half hours ago, Mr. Gates. Have you tried calling her?"

"'Course I called her. She's not answering."

Catherine fought a spasm of panic. "If Maren isn't answering her phone, you should check with her friends."

"I *did*. How stupid do you think I am? No one's seen her."

"Is there somewhere she might have gone if she was angry with you? I understand you told her you didn't want her taking music lessons."

"She's still holed up with you, isn't she? *Put her on the phone.*"

"She's *not here*. She left over two hours ago."

"What did you do—cook up a scheme to get her strutting around the stage in some nightclub, telling her it was a musical show?"

Catherine spoke coldly. "If she's not home and you don't think she'd go to a friend, I'm calling the police." She disconnected the call then dialed Maren's number, hoping Maren *was* at a friend's house and would pick up for Catherine even if she wouldn't pick up for Dylan.

No answer.

Catherine hung up, grabbed the phone book, and looked up the non-emergency number for the police department. Maybe Maren *had* decided to delay her return home either to avoid Dylan or to punish him, and this didn't seem like a 911 occasion—yet.

Catherine dialed the police department and explained the situation to the woman who answered the phone; the woman promised to have someone call Catherine back.

Catherine hung up and spent several minutes pacing the house, trying to figure out what to do. What had she gotten herself into, worrying this much about Maren? Maren seemed like a nice person, but Catherine knew very little about her. Maybe she was a passive-aggressive, manipulative woman who'd revel in deliberately scaring both Catherine and Dylan by dropping out of sight for an evening.

But what if something had happened to her on the way home?

The doorbell rang. Heart pounding, Catherine grabbed the phone and edged toward the door. Before she could get there, the doorbell rang twice more. The visitor could ring as many times as he or she wanted, but no way was she opening up unless she could identify the person through the peephole—or see a badge.

A youngish man with wet brown hair and a black sweatshirt stood on the porch. She didn't recognize him, but from the scowl on his face, he was Dylan Gates. Who else would come storming over here at eleven thirty at night?

"What do you want?" Catherine shouted through the door. He was crazy to think she'd let him in after the way he'd talked to her on the phone.

"I want my *wife*," he yelled.

"Maren *isn't here*. I already told you that," she shouted back. "I called the police to tell them she's missing."

"What are *they* going to do about it?"

"I don't know. I'm waiting for them to call me."

A thud rattled the door. "If you're hiding her in there—"

"You have ten seconds to get off my porch, or I'm calling the police again."

Dylan took one step backward. He stood glaring at the door then turned around and sat on the top porch step, just out of the rain.

Warily, Catherine watched him. When he made no move to leave, she lifted the phone, ready to dial—this time it would be a 911 call. The phone rang before she could push a button.

Same number as before. She glanced through the peephole and saw that Dylan had lifted his phone to his ear. After a few beats of hesitation, she answered. "What do you want?"

"Did she say *anything* about where she might be going?" Dylan's voice through the phone was gruff, but he sounded like he was trying to control himself. He must be tired of the shouting match through the door—thank heavens; she hoped the neighbors were heavy sleepers.

"As far as I know, she was planning to go directly home," Catherine said. "You'd know better than I would where she'd be."

"How would I know? She's never done anything like this."

He's genuinely worried, Catherine realized. How much of his aggression was an attempt to manage fear?

"She always answers her phone," he said. "But she's not answering."

"After the way you talked to her, maybe she's not eager to take your call."

His voice heated up. "So she blabbed everything to you?"

"I could tell she was upset. I asked her why."

"It's none of your business!"

"I'm hanging up. Get off my porch."

"Wait! Which—when she was going home, do you have any idea which direction she went?"

"I have no idea. She didn't say—" Catherine's call-waiting beeped. "I have another call coming. It might be the police. If you wait, I'll tell you what they say." She punched the button to switch to the new caller. "Hello, this is Catherine Clayton."

"Ms. Clayton. This is Detective Nancy Burgess with the Riley Police Department. We met the other night when you were with Renee Endicott."

"Yes." Catherine pictured the fortyish woman with hair combed straight back and twisted into a bun. She was relieved to hear a familiar voice. Burgess had been calm and polite at Olivia's apartment, and her matter-of-fact attitude had helped settle frantic Renee down. Plus, Burgess hadn't given Catherine's name to the press.

"I'm at the emergency room at Henderson with a woman who was found unconscious on the street," Burgess said. "She wasn't carrying any ID, but the name and phone number of Bridgeside Music Studio were on the tag of the flute case next to her. We're hoping you can help us figure out who she is."

Catherine stood frozen.

"She's blonde, probably in her twenties—"

"Her name is Maren Gates," Catherine interrupted, feeling sick to her stomach. "What happened to her? Is she okay?"

"Do you know how to contact her family?"

"Yes. Please—she's my student. Will she be all right? Can you tell me anything?"

"She's injured, Ms. Clayton. That's all I can tell you right now. Could you tell me how to contact her family?"

Catherine looked through the peephole at Dylan Gates, still hunched on the top step of the porch. "Yes," she said quietly, unlocking the door.

* * *

Catherine paced around the waiting room of Jamie Henderson Memorial Hospital. She'd followed Dylan here after he'd flung Catherine's phone to the porch and raced off without any explanation as to what Burgess had told him about Maren. She couldn't endure the thought of staying home in ignorance, especially knowing Dylan wouldn't call to give her any information.

The instant he'd seen her walk through the ER doors, Dylan had, in an explosion of profanity, shouted at her to get out. Catherine would have withdrawn rather than disturb the entire ER with further confrontation, but Detective Burgess had approached, flashed a badge at Dylan, and asked Catherine to remain. Burgess had then escorted Dylan away.

Catherine wondered if Burgess was taking Dylan to Maren's bedside— or if she was taking him somewhere so she could question him. Had it occurred to Burgess that Maren's angry husband might be responsible for whatever had happened to her? Had Dylan intercepted Maren partway home, argued with her, attacked her, then panicked and called Catherine, pretending he didn't know where Maren was?

What had *happened* to Maren? Catherine had tried asking the receptionist for information on her condition, but the receptionist claimed she had no information—which probably meant she couldn't give information to Catherine.

Had Maren been attacked, not by her husband but by Oliva Perry's murderer?

Who says she was attacked? Maybe she tripped and hit her head. You're like Renee—paranoid and jumping to conclusions.

But Maren hadn't tripped. Given the grim, guarded expression Detective Burgess had been wearing, Catherine couldn't believe this was an accident.

"Ms. Clayton?"

With a knot in her throat, Catherine turned to face Detective Burgess.

"I have a few questions for you," Burgess said. "If you'd come with me, please."

Catherine followed Burgess into the back of the ER and into an office. A uniformed officer stood near the back wall. Burgess gestured at a chair, and Catherine sat down. Burgess sat as well and pulled out a notebook.

"Can you tell me what happened to Maren?" Catherine asked. "How did she get hurt?"

"Mrs. Gates was taking flute lessons from you?"

"Yes. We'd had to reschedule her lesson because I had a conflict on Monday, the regular day for her lessons. We met at eight fifteen this evening."

"What time did Mrs. Gates leave the studio?"

"At about five to nine. She was walking home—her husband had refused to let her take the car."

"Why had he refused to let her take the car?"

Catherine wondered what story Dylan had told Burgess about why Maren was walking home. "He didn't want her to take flute lessons." Careful to not let her anger at Dylan put words in Maren's mouth, Catherine reported what Maren had said, as well as how angry Dylan had been when he'd hammered on Catherine's door.

"Did Mrs. Gates seem apprehensive at the thought of returning home?"

"A little apprehensive. I offered to let her take my car—I couldn't leave the studio to drive her home because I had an appointment—but she said her husband would be angry if he saw it. Can you *please* tell me what happened to Maren? Is she going to be all right?"

Burgess studied Catherine. "She was hit on the head. The doctors don't know the extent of the damage yet. She's unconscious right now."

Hit on the head. Like Olivia. Catherine felt dizzy as she thought of the graffiti painted on the wall of Olivia's apartment. *I didn't want to kill her.*

But it might have been Dylan who attacked Maren—a domestic incident that had had nothing to do with Olivia. Or maybe it was random—a mugger had hit her and grabbed her purse . . . but she hadn't been carrying a purse.

"This must be very upsetting to you, to have this happen to one of your students," Burgess said. "Did you know Mrs. Gates well?"

"I've only known her for a couple of weeks. As you know, I'm new to Riley. But I like her a lot. She's a nice lady, works hard. She seemed shy—not a lot of self-confidence. Detective, I'm not making any accusations—I know very little about the situation—but I'm assuming you're keeping a close eye on Dylan Gates."

"He's not been permitted to be alone with Mrs. Gates, and we're checking him out." Burgess held out a business card. "Please call me if you think of anything that might be helpful in leading to the arrest of whoever attacked Mrs. Gates."

"I still have the card you gave me the other night." The words made Catherine feel disoriented. Up until a couple of weeks ago, the only interaction she'd ever had with the police was one speeding ticket when she was twenty. Now, since moving to Riley, she'd been interviewed twice by a police detective. "Detective Burgess . . . do you think Olivia Perry's killer is back?"

"I don't know." Burgess's expression was solemn and so intense that it unnerved Catherine more. "Please be careful, and call us immediately if anything alarms you. Keep your doors locked."

Catherine nodded.

"Be aware that the attack took place near your studio," Burgess said. "Just east of the bridge."

CHAPTER 13

FROM THE NORMAL MIX OF cheer and mischievousness in the four budding violinists in Catherine's Saturday morning class—three fifth-grade girls and one fifth-grade boy—it was clear they hadn't heard about Maren Gates being attacked near Bridgeside Studio. Either their parents didn't know, or they'd wisely chosen not to let their children hear the news. Their innocence made it easier for Catherine to keep her mind focused on the lesson; she didn't want them to sense she was upset and wonder why.

The string lesson followed by two clarinets, three flutes, and a lone trumpeter who wanted to blow his trumpet loud enough to shake the roof kept Catherine occupied all morning, but as soon as she had a break, the tension returned. How was Maren doing? She'd tried calling the hospital for an update, but, not to her surprise, they'd refused to give her any information.

This uncertainty, this fear clawing at her—*this* was what the people close to Olivia must have been enduring for the past two years. How could they stand it, not knowing who had killed her? How could they stand knowing the murderer was probably someone who knew Olivia, someone who was still here, going about his—or her—life, maybe even interacting with Olivia's loved ones? How could they stand not knowing whom to trust? For the first time, she felt sympathetic toward Trent's attitude. He'd dealt with his pain and uncertainty by obsessively blaming Adam. He was wrong, but she was beginning to understand why he was so desperate to *know*.

No matter what the truth is, you can't do anything about it. Focus on why you came here. Focus on your students.

The studio seemed so quiet that Catherine started toward her cello with the goal of putting sound in the air, but she stopped partway there. She didn't want music. She wanted a comforting human voice.

She could call Ava. Ava would provide sympathy mingled with practical advice—but she wanted someone here in Riley.

Admit it. You want to talk to Adam.

Catherine toyed with her phone, flipping it over and over in her hands. She hadn't heard from Adam since they'd visited his father last Sunday. She'd hoped he'd call her this week, but considering the confusing signals she'd sent him, she couldn't expect him to risk a negative reaction by calling her. If she wanted to talk to him, she needed to initiate it.

Rallying her nerve, she touched the screen and found his number.

"Catherine." Adam sounded surprised. "How are you doing?"

"Not so great," she admitted. "Have you heard?"

"About Maren Gates?"

"Yes."

"I heard about it last night. Directly from the police."

"Are you—okay?"

"I was with my father at the time Maren was attacked."

Catherine wondered if the police would accept that as an alibi or if they would assume Dale might lie to protect his son.

"I'm sorry about Maren," Adam said bleakly. "You must be very upset."

"I am. Adam . . . are you busy tonight? I could use some company."

Whoa. Wait. What are you doing? You barely managed to scrounge up the courage to call him, and now you're asking him out?

"You . . . want to get together tonight?" Adam sounded strange. Was that surprise in his tone? Or wariness?

"If you're busy, I understand." Catherine's cheeks burned. Dale had made a point that Adam wasn't chasing her. She was pushing things way too fast. "Or if you need to be with your father—"

"No, that's . . . I . . . no, it's fine. Yes, I'm free. My father will be fine. I can . . . What would you—" He stopped and chuckled nervously. "Sorry. I'm free tonight. What would you like to do?"

"I . . ." Catherine hadn't thought it through any further than a desire for Adam's company. "I want to walk. Around Riley."

"You want to walk?"

"Yes. I need to get outside. I'm smothering indoors, but I'm nervous about walking anywhere on my own."

Adam spoke quietly. "And you'd like to . . . walk with me?"

She knew what he was asking: *Have you made up your mind about me? Do you trust me, especially now that another woman has been attacked?*

She *had* made up her mind. Everything she'd seen Adam say or do, along with her own instincts and his father's words, said Adam was a good man. "Yes. I want you to walk with me. Would you mind?"

"It would be my pleasure."

"The weather is gorgeous today. I'm finished teaching at four. Could you—is there anywhere we could have a picnic?"

"A picnic? Sure, yes, there are a couple of parks. Or have you been to Orenda Gorge yet?"

"Not yet, but I've been wanting to go there. I've seen pictures. It looks beautiful."

"It has some good hiking and walking trails. Takes about twenty minutes to drive there . . . if you're okay with that."

"Perfect. I'll bring the food."

"Let me bring dessert."

"Deal. Are you sure your father will be all right?"

"If I *don't* leave him when I have an opportunity like this, *I'm* the one who won't be all right. He'll make sure of that."

Catherine laughed, imagining Dale grabbing his son by the scruff of the neck and tossing him out the door.

"What time should I pick you up?" Adam asked.

"Five? Does that work?"

"Great. I'll see you at five."

"Thanks, Adam."

"My pleasure, Catherine. Thank *you* for calling me."

Smiling—finally feeling a little better—Catherine put her phone down.

CHAPTER 14

"I LOVE IT WHEN THE leaves change." Sitting at the picnic table, Catherine gazed at the early evening sunlight glowing in the crimson leaves of a nearby tree. "It's a shame autumn can't last longer."

"I'd trade January for another September." Adam lifted a Tupperware container out of the bag he'd brought. "In fact, I'd trade January for a piece of used gum."

Catherine laughed. "Not my favorite month either, but snow *is* beautiful, and the cold isn't bad as long as you dress warm."

"You have a good attitude."

"My mother was an optimist. I inherited it from her. My dad was more practical. Analytical."

Adam opened the container and offered it to her. "The ones on the left are a Norwegian walnut cookie. On the right is an almond cookie dipped in chocolate."

"Yum." Catherine took one of each. "Thanks for bringing dessert."

"It's good to have a reason to bake."

Catherine bit into the rich, buttery walnut cookie. She'd enjoyed the picnic. The more she talked with Adam, the more she appreciated his company, and his crooked smile no longer looked odd to her at all.

Still, she had to fight the urge to sneak a look at her phone to see if there was any news of Maren. *Try not to think about it. There's nothing you can do, and I'm sure Adam would appreciate one evening that doesn't include painful subjects.*

"Have you heard any updates on Maren?" Adam took another cookie.

Catherine wondered if her expression had revealed that her thoughts had taken a stressful turn. "No. I called the hospital, but they told me no information was available. And it's not like I can call her husband to ask. He's . . . he doesn't seem easy to get along with."

"Is that a diplomatic way of saying he's a jerk?"

"Do you know him?"

"Not personally. But I know Maren."

"You do?" This startled Catherine, though it made no sense to be surprised—why shouldn't Adam know Maren? They were both Riley natives, and it was a small city.

"I don't know her well, but she worked janitorial at Leonardi's while I was a member," he said. "While I was dating Olivia."

"She worked at Leonardi's?"

"Yes. I'd see her around when I was at the gym. And Olivia enjoyed talking with her."

"Did Olivia ever say anything to you about Maren's husband?"

"She mentioned that Maren was . . . I think Olivia's word was *paranoid* . . . around the male customers and employees." His face hardened. "She said Maren's husband was jealous."

"Paranoid—like too nervous to talk to them, afraid she'd give Dylan the impression she was flirting?"

"Yes. In fact, I remember seeing Will Conti—you know who Will is?"

"Yes."

"I remember seeing Will try to flirt with her, and she avoided eye contact and pretended she didn't hear him. It sticks out in my memory because most women don't ignore Will."

Catherine knew he was thinking of Olivia. She thought of telling Adam about Will's visit to her studio but didn't feel like bringing it up. "Did Dylan come to the gym? Was he a member?"

"Not that I know of."

"Did Olivia know him?"

"I don't know if she ever met him. She didn't say she had."

"He didn't want Maren to take flute lessons," Catherine said.

"Why would he care about that?"

"He thought free lessons were charity, which he detests. He also told her she was too stupid to learn the flute."

Disgust and anger filled Adam's eyes. "I hope the police are looking hard at him with what happened to Maren last night."

"They are. The reason she was walking home is he'd told her if she wanted to take lessons, she couldn't use the car or spend money on the bus. She was determined to come anyway, so she walked."

Adam stared at her. "*That's* why she was out walking last night?"

"Yes."

He drew a deep breath, and Catherine had the feeling he was censoring what he wanted to say about Dylan. "The police had *better* be looking at him. Sounds like a case of domestic violence. Meanwhile, all of Riley is panicking, thinking Olivia's killer is back."

Panicking and looking at you, Catherine thought. "The more I think about it, the more I think things will never be settled here for any of us until the police figure out who killed Olivia."

"I know that," Adam said. "But there's not much we can do about it."

Catherine sat silently, eating another almond cookie, leaning her elbows on the picnic table. "Is it all right if I ask you some questions? I don't want to hurt you, but I'm wondering if there's something we can figure out if we look at this fresh."

Adam's eyebrows rose. "Catherine, for two years, I've wrung my brain dry trying to think of any clue that might lead to the murderer. I just *don't know*. If I've had even the smallest inkling of an idea, I've immediately shared it with the police."

Catherine averted her eyes. "I sound ridiculous. Like I want to play detective."

"Not at all. You're new to Riley, and the story of Olivia's death is new to you. In your shoes, I'd feel the same way—thinking there must be *some* clue as to who killed her and believing we can find it if we look for it."

Catherine appreciated his kind response, but she still felt silly.

"It's good to have someone who *can* view this fresh." Adam sounded thoughtful, but Catherine couldn't tell if he was sincere or still trying to ease her embarrassment. "It doesn't hurt to go over it. Maybe you'll see something I'm too jaded to recognize. What do you want to ask me?"

"I'm sure you've thought of everything. I'm grasping at straws."

"Straw grasping is a good idea. I'm all for it. You'll see things differently than I do. Please. I'm happy to answer your questions."

Catherine swallowed the last bite of cookie. "Okay . . . I've been thinking about how Trent said the killer didn't break into Olivia's apartment. He's sure she kept her door locked at all times and wouldn't have opened the door to someone she didn't know."

"That's true. Olivia *was* careful about keeping her door locked, and she always checked through the peephole to see who was there before she unlocked it."

"So the killer is someone she knew. Maybe someone with a motive so deep no one can see it." Catherine cringed at how melodramatic she sounded. *A motive so deep*—did she think this was an Agatha Christie novel? Real-life crime was probably more straightforward than fictional crime.

A leaf fluttered to the table and settled on top of the cooler. Adam picked it up and folded it in half, creasing it with his fingertips. "I suppose the killer *could* be a stranger who somehow tricked her into trusting him—by impersonating a repairman or a police officer, for instance—but that seems far-fetched."

"There wasn't any evidence that anything else happened that night?"

"Like a robbery? I never heard that anything was taken from her apartment besides . . ." His voice trailed off, and Catherine remembered Trent's describing a heavy wrought-iron vase decorated with twisting vines . . . the vase that had gone missing from her apartment.

Rather than make Adam say it, Catherine said, "Trent Perry told me a vase was missing, the vase the police thought was the murder weapon."

Was it the shadows cast by trees overheard, or did Adam look pale? "Yes. A vase made of wrought iron. Olivia . . . she loved that vase. Her grandmother had bought it in Italy and given it to her for Christmas a couple of years earlier. Big vase, tall and narrow, with leaves and vines and flowers."

He was definitely pale; his lips were bloodless. "I'm so sorry." Catherine didn't know what else to say.

"Nothing else was taken, not that we know of. And no other harm was done to Olivia besides the blows to the head that killed her. As far as hidden motives, yes, that's likely. If we had any idea *why* someone killed her, we'd have a better idea of *who* killed her."

Feeling foolish again at the way she'd stated the obvious as though she were contributing something insightful, Catherine asked, "Did Will Conti have a motive?"

"I don't know."

"Did they fight?"

"I have no idea. They looked happy with each other when I saw them together." Adam's tone was almost matter-of-fact—only a tinge of acidity told Catherine that Olivia's betrayal still stung him.

"I doubt Will can look past his own ego far enough to know what it means to be happy with someone else," Catherine said.

"Have you met him?"

"He came to the studio the other day," she admitted. "He claimed he was interested in taking music lessons."

Adam sat up straight, setting the container of cookies down so abruptly that two cookies bounced onto the red-and-white checkered tablecloth. "Will came to the studio?"

"Yes. It turned out he wasn't interested in music. He wanted to check me out."

The stony look in Adam's eyes made Catherine wish she hadn't mentioned Will. "What did he say to you?"

"He . . . flirted and flattered, asked me out for lunch. I said no thank you."

"How did he respond?"

"He got mad and blamed my standoffishness on Olivia's death—said no one had ever turned him down before she died, but now her death has tainted everything. He warned me it would destroy me too, like it had him."

Mouth twisting, Adam picked up the spilled cookies. He reached for the trash sack, but Catherine held her hand out for the cookies.

"Five-second rule. They're clean."

"It's been more than five seconds."

"They're still clean. They were only on the tablecloth."

He dropped the cookies into her hand. "Will said Olivia's death had destroyed him?"

"He said people associated him with her death or even suspected him of killing her."

"That's interesting." Adam's voice was chilly. "He seemed to jump right back into action after her death, as far as I could see. Not that I hung around Leonardi's after Olivia died, so I didn't see much of him, but according to rumors, he didn't waste any time finding a new woman."

"Do you know if he was ever involved with Danielle Knight's younger sister, Esther?"

"That sounds familiar, but I can't remember where I heard it. I think they were involved a few years back, before he was involved with Olivia."

"Esther was at the studio when Will arrived, and she was sending out hostile vibes. I figured there was a history there but haven't dared ask her about it."

"I don't know any details. Sorry."

"No worries. I was just curious." Any former relationship between Will and Esther was none of her business, and she was embarrassed that she'd mentioned it. *Are you trying to figure out what happened to Olivia, or are you searching for juicy gossip?* "Did Will ever confront you? Accuse you of killing Olivia?"

"No. We stayed away from each other."

Catherine thought about Will's anger when she'd turned him down. What if Olivia had rejected him, telling him she preferred Adam?

"You're wondering if he killed Olivia. Believe me, I've wondered that too," Adam said. "But from what I know of him, I have a hard time believing he cared enough about Olivia to get angry enough to murder her. He strikes me as shallow and narcissistic—a guy who couldn't be bothered to commit a crime of passion when it's too easy to move on to the next girlfriend."

"Maybe. But if Olivia wanted to dump him and go back to you, maybe it wasn't so much that he loved her as that he couldn't stand the rejection."

"Could be. I'm . . . assuming you have some new pottery in your cupboard?"

Catherine blushed. She'd felt odd keeping the gifts Will had brought her, but it was such gorgeous pottery that it had seemed wasteful to toss it in the trash—or onto concrete, as Esther had suggested. "Not in my cupboard, exactly. Sitting on top of the washing machine because I didn't know what to do with custom-made pottery with my name on it after the giver stomped out of my office. I take it that's his usual gift?"

"Olivia had several pieces. It wasn't until after she died that I found out where that handcrafted pitcher on her counter had come from."

Could this conversation get any more uncomfortable? Why had she thought asking Adam about Olivia's death was a good idea?

"He's talented at the potter's wheel," Adam continued, his voice steady. "No denying that. He runs a small online business and does well with it. I'm sorry, Catherine. I didn't mean to imply there was anything wrong with your accepting his gift."

"Oh no, don't worry about it." She knew the redness in her face would undermine any attempt to pretend she wasn't embarrassed, but she tried to sound breezy. "It caught me by surprise when he gave them to me—a mug and a plate—and I didn't know how to react. When he got angry and left, I thought he'd take them back, but . . . I guess he didn't know any other Catherines to give them to. And I hope it doesn't sound like I'm accusing Will of anything." She broke one of the cookies in half. "When I asked you if he had any motive for killing Olivia, I was just thinking out loud."

"I understand."

"I'm sorry I brought this up. We can change the subject now."

He smiled slightly. "Have you run out of questions, or are you worried you're making me uncomfortable?"

"Well . . . this must be hard for you."

"I don't mind answering your questions. Please go on. Is there anything else bothering you?"

"I . . . do have a weird question."

"Ask it."

"Can you think of any reason at all that Trent would have wanted to hurt Olivia?"

Adam remained quiet for a moment, his expression shadowed. "I don't know of any." He stuffed his empty plate into the trash sack. "I wondered about Trent. Wondered if all his accusations were a smokescreen. But I have no idea why he'd kill his own sister. Their relationship had some bumps—Trent was bossy with Olivia, which annoyed her—but as far as I could tell, they were pretty close. I can't think why Trent would kill her."

"Maybe there were problems going on in that family that we don't know about?"

"No idea."

"Do their parents think you killed Olivia?"

"No."

"Are they here in Riley?"

"No. They're divorced—their dad lives in Georgia. Their mother lived in Riley up until about a year ago but moved to California to be near her oldest daughter and the grandkids. At the funeral, their mother apologized to me for Trent and said he was crazy with grief and he'd realize I was innocent." Adam held the cookies out to Catherine. She shook her head, so he snapped the lid onto the container. "Sorry I'm not more help, but as I said, I don't have a clue who killed her."

"Thanks for being willing to talk about it." Adam *had* been helpful—he'd told her there was a connection between Maren and the Perry family. Maybe there was a connection between Dylan and Olivia. Just because Olivia had never mentioned to Adam that she'd met Dylan didn't mean she hadn't.

Catherine had been assuming Maren had been attacked by Dylan *or* by Olivia's killer. What if they were the same person?

"Want to go for that walk before it gets dark?" Adam asked.

Catherine thought of mentioning her newborn suspicion about Dylan but decided to wait. Adam had been patient with her questions, but she needed to give him a break. She'd do a little research on her own before asking Adam about Dylan again.

"A walk sounds great." Catherine rose to her feet.

They stowed the remains of the food in Adam's car and started along the path Adam showed her.

"This path winds up the hill and veers near the edge of the gorge," he said. "It's not in great shape. I used to bike here but don't anymore—too many potholes in the trail—but at this time of year, the autumn leaves make for spectacular scenery."

"I'm all for it."

As they climbed higher, the scenery was even prettier than Catherine had anticipated. Through the vivid reds and yellows in the trees and shrubs, she could see bare, jagged cliffs sloping sharply downward to a river of clear green water that foamed over tiers of rock as it flowed down the hill.

"This is gorgeous." She stepped over a root on the path. "It feels like we're hours away from civilization, not just a few minutes."

"Amazing that such a beautiful place is so near ugly Riley, huh?"

"I didn't say that!"

"It still amazes me that you decided to set up shop here." Adam glanced at her. The evening light made his hair a rich gold and his eyes a deep blue. "It's a strange place to choose. I know you have that connection with Danielle Knight and you wanted a place that needed your program—which we do—but how did you feel personally about moving here?"

Catherine plucked a blood-red leaf off a tree. "I wouldn't have come if I weren't happy with the thought of coming."

"You must have left a lot behind. I know your parents have passed away, but other family? Friends?"

"I do miss Ava, my stepmother, but we're in touch a lot. She takes care of all the business details—I don't enjoy dealing with accounts and spreadsheets. I'd rather leave the numbers to her, and she thrives on it."

"Anyone besides Ava whom it was hard to leave?" Adam's voice was casual, but he had angled his face toward the gorge, away from her.

"I keep in touch with a lot of friends online." From the way Adam was avoiding her eyes, Catherine wondered if his real question was "Are you involved with anyone?" Deciding to get to the point, she said, "I wasn't dating anyone. Haven't for a while . . . Ava's always on my case to be more social."

Adam said nothing, but there was something tense in his silence, and Catherine felt the need to keep talking. "I think she's disappointed that I'm not married yet, though she'd never admit it. I did date a guy for a while in grad school, and it got serious, but . . . it wasn't right. I haven't been involved with anyone since then."

Adam still didn't speak, and Catherine felt like a complete idiot. It was *way* too early in their friendship to start trading romantic histories. What was she thinking?

While she was trying to figure out how to resuscitate the conversation, Adam looked at her and said, "You probably have some regrets."

"Regrets?"

"Wishing you . . . hadn't ended the relationship?"

"We weren't right for each other." Apparently Adam *did* want to discuss romantic histories, and if so, she wanted to push the questions back at him. But asking about previous girlfriends meant bringing up Olivia again, and she didn't want to do that. Time to change the subject. "So how is—"

Before she could complete her question about his father's health, Adam spoke. "It must be difficult to find someone to measure up to him."

This comment baffled Catherine. Where had Adam gotten *that* idea? He knew nothing about Robert or the situation. And why had he assumed *she* had ended the relationship, not Robert? He was right, but that was a risky assumption to make.

"I'm not sure what you mean," Catherine said. "Robert was a nice guy, but . . ." Her voice faded. Adam was keeping his gaze on the trail, but the red blotches on his neck told her he was either nervous or embarrassed or both.

After they'd crossed a dozen yards in silence, Adam said, "I'm sorry. I'm not good at this, as I'm sure you've figured out, and I'm not good at being subtle."

"You don't have to be subtle. I can handle direct. My father was blunt. I'm used to it. I'm not sure what you're asking me, so if you want to know something about my past, say it straight. I don't have anything to hide."

"I'm being a fool. Ignore me."

"Adam, for goodness sake. What is it you want to know?"

"Nothing." His neck and ears were now scarlet. "I'm sorry. Let's change the subject."

Catherine moved in front of him, stopped, and faced him.

He halted rather than step around her. "I'm sorry," he repeated. "I have no right to ask you anything like this. Forget it."

"Why did you assume I was the one who ended the relationship?" She felt a little guilty, as though she was trying to make him feel foolish when he *had* been correct, but his assumption bothered her.

He stared in the direction of the gorge. The rushing water sparkled in the sunlight, but Catherine doubted Adam was appreciating nature.

"I'm the last person who ought to pay attention to hearsay," he said at last. "But I was told you'd had a serious relationship with someone who was perfect for you—perfect in every way, in fact—and everyone thought you'd get married. Then for no reason at all, you broke it off, leaving him devastated, and now no one can ever be good enough for you."

Shocked, Catherine gaped at his reddened face. "Who in the world told you that?"

Adam looked so mortified that it made Catherine want to avert *her* eyes rather than witness that depth of embarrassment. "I . . . uh . . . took some cookies over to Renee at Flinders the other day," he muttered. "I thought she could use cheering up after what happened at Olivia's apartment."

"But . . . I never told Renee anything about—"

"While I was there, Danielle came out, and we talked for a minute. She invited me into her office."

Despite the cool evening breeze, Catherine's face kept getting hotter. "*Danielle* told you about Robert Fields and me?" Of course it had to be Danielle. Who else in Riley knew anything about Robert?

Adam shifted his weight, and Catherine wondered if he was contemplating jumping into the gorge rather than finishing this conversation. "Adam, what did she tell you?"

"I'm sorry. I should never have brought this—"

"Will you stop apologizing and tell me what she said that's left you *this* uncomfortable?"

"I have no right to—"

"Who cares? It doesn't matter. Just tell me what she said!" Realizing she was raising her voice, Catherine forcibly slowed her breathing and let her shoulders go slack. What was wrong with her, getting worked up so quickly? Her nerves were shot after everything that had happened, but she didn't want to vent her stress on Adam—especially not when he looked so miserable. "Let's keep moving." She resumed the walk along the trail. Adam followed, falling in step with her.

"I'll feel better if you level with me," Catherine said. "If Danielle gave you the impression that I'm still hung up on Robert, she's wrong. I can't understand why she'd bring him up at all."

"She was . . . concerned."

"Concerned about me?"

"Concerned about *me*. She . . . uh . . . assumed I might . . . um . . . have some interest in getting to know you, and she . . . wanted to . . . make sure I was fully informed."

"Fully informed about what?" With an effort, Catherine kept her voice calm. If she showed anger, Adam would probably shut down. The fact that he'd brought Robert up meant he wanted to ask her about him, and the easier she made it for him, the quicker they could wade through this horrible conversation. "*Please* be blunt," she said. "I can take it."

"Danielle said you were head over heels in love with Robert, and he was head over heels in love with you. She said Robert was a remarkable man—from the way she described him, he could have given the Olympian gods a run for their money."

Adam hesitated, and Catherine said, "Go on."

"She . . . said you . . . came from a very privileged, moneyed background and were used to being catered to and having everything you wanted, and you took Robert for granted." Adam spoke faster. "She said you invented some flaw in him as a pretext for ending the relationship when nothing was wrong—everyone else could see he was perfect for you, but you couldn't commit to him—and ever since then, no one has even come close to being good enough for you. She apologized for being so candid but said she felt obligated to warn me. She didn't want me getting drawn in, thinking I had a chance with you, when the truth is that no one has a chance with you."

Catherine kept walking, her legs moving mechanically, but her whole body seemed to be burning—her face fiery, her chest smoldering, her lungs scorching with each breath. *You asked him to be blunt*, she mocked herself. *Was that blunt enough for you?*

Danielle had said those things about her? Danielle, her friend? She and Danielle didn't always see things the same way, and heaven knows Danielle could be judgmental. But to actually warn Adam off, describing Catherine as a spoiled, impossible-to-please princess with a commitment phobia? How *dare* she? *That* was what Danielle thought of her?

"Are you okay?" Adam asked.

Catherine couldn't answer. Her legs felt weak and uncoordinated, and sweat rolled down her back. *I thought we were friends.*

"I'm sorry," Adam said. "I shouldn't—"

"No." Catherine pushed the word out. "Thank you for being honest. If you believe her, that's fine. You can leave. I'll summon my coachman to take me home in my jeweled carriage."

"I don't want to leave. If there's one thing I've learned over the past couple of years, it's that people who mean well can have opposite takes on the same situation. I didn't say I believed her. I was foolish to bring it up."

"Why would you bring it up at all if you didn't believe her at least a little bit?"

Adam didn't answer, and the heat of Catherine's humiliation doubled. She jerked her jacket off, veered around, and started heading downhill. This was ridiculous. If he didn't want to leave, *she* would. This date was more than over.

"Wait. Please." He caught up with her. "Here's why I brought this up— besides the fact that I'm an idiot. I have enough stress in my life right now, and I'm short on patience. If we have deep-rooted differences in . . . what we want out of life, I want to know that now, before—" He cut himself off, and Catherine knew he couldn't think of a way to say *before we get involved* without embarrassing himself in case Catherine had never even considered a relationship.

After several paces of silence, Catherine said, "Okay. In that case, I'll be blunt. You wonder what I think about relationships? I'm looking for a husband. And I'm not looking for an Olympian god. I'm looking for a righteous priesthood holder who I enjoy being with. Yes, I *was* in love with Robert, and I tried to tell myself everything would work out, but after a while the doubts got too big. Robert was active in the Church, but he didn't take things as seriously as I did. He was okay with cutting corners here and there—small things, things that would make me sound rigid and judgmental if I started listing them. It all came to a head one Sunday when I was sitting alone in church because there was yet another big ball game Robert wanted to attend and he didn't think skipping out once in a while was a big deal. And you know what? To me it *was* a big deal. I realized I was kidding myself, that we simply didn't see things the same way, and it wasn't going to work. I'm *not* judging him or saying he was bad. I'm saying he wasn't right for *me*, and no matter how handsome and fun he was, I knew he wasn't the man I wanted. I don't know what Danielle's problem is, but I'm not hung up on Robert. I'm not scared of commitment. And I didn't think I was self-centered or spoiled, but maybe I am and I'm too self-centered to know it." Catherine wished she could have kept herself from crying, but the tears came in a gush—a more rapid flood of tears than her hurt and embarrassment should have produced, and she knew accumulated stress was escaping. Just what Adam needed—a bawling, hysterical woman.

"I'll call you later," she choked out. She increased her pace toward the entrance to the path.

"Catherine—"

"You don't want to be around me for a while. I'll call a taxi." Sobs rendered the words squeaky and jerky. "I'm losing it bad. I'll call you when I'm done. I'm not upset with you."

Adam's rapid footsteps told her he was pursuing her. "Catherine." His hand closed on her elbow. "I'm sorry."

"You didn't do anything wrong!" *Shriek at him. Great strategy to prove you're not the spoiled brat Danielle described.* "I need to go." He must think she was a drama queen, sobbing like she wanted everyone within a mile radius to hear, but she couldn't control herself. "I don't know what's wrong with me. I need to go home." She pulled her arm free and started speed walking, stepping rapidly around potholes and roots. Adam kept pace with her.

"Please let me drive you home. It's ridiculous to call a taxi."

Her chest hurt; it was hard to sob and power walk at the same time. In the distance, she could see two people heading up the trail. The park wasn't exactly deserted. Catherine was making a fool of herself in public. *Dad would love to see this—his daughter acting like a hysterical teenager.*

Off to the side of the trail was a knee-high boulder with a flat top. Catherine veered toward it. She sat on it, rested her folded arms on her knees, buried her face in her arms, and struggled to quiet her emotions.

She felt Adam's hand on her back—light, tentative, as though he didn't know whether or not to touch her. She wanted to tell him it was okay, that she *needed* the comfort of human contact, but she couldn't speak.

After a few moments, his touch firmed, and his fingers rested warm and strong against her back as he sat next to her in silence, letting her cry.

CHAPTER 15

FINALLY, CATHERINE LIFTED HER DRENCHED face. "Okay," she said, sniffling. "I think I'm done." The one Kleenex she'd had in her pocket was soaked and shredded, and her jeans were spotted with water.

"Are you feeling better?" Adam asked.

It surprised her to realize the sun was setting. She'd been crying longer than she'd thought.

"Yes." She wiped her eyes on her wet sleeve. "You must think I'm crazy. I don't usually break down like that."

"I don't think you're crazy. I think you needed to vent some stress."

Sitting upright made her feel shaky and light-headed. "Do you mind if I lean on you for a minute?"

"Please. Go ahead."

Catherine slouched, letting Adam's shoulder support the weight of her aching head. "That sounded like a pathetic pick-up line, didn't it? 'May I lean on you?'" Laughter spilled out along with a new wave of tears. "Oh heck, Adam, I'm losing it again."

"It's okay." He wrapped his arm around her shoulders. "It's okay. Take all the time you need."

She inhaled and exhaled deeply, fighting off more hysteria. "You'll never believe me if I tell you I'm usually a calm person."

"I believe you. You cry like you've been saving it up."

Catherine sighed. Adam's arm around her shoulders was comforting. Supportive. She liked the feel of it.

But at best, he must think she was an immature, high-maintenance damsel in distress.

For several minutes, she sat with her eyes closed, appreciating the cool breeze on her swollen eyelids and raw cheeks. "It's getting cold," she murmured. "We should go."

"Whenever you want."

"That Niagara Falls imitation wasn't only because of the things Danielle told you," Catherine said, still not lifting her head from Adam's shoulder. "I hope you don't think I'm so frail that I'd fall apart because a friend bad-mouthed me."

"I know that, Catherine."

"But it does hurt. I'm trying to figure out what I did to make her think . . ." Why *would* Danielle think of her as self-centered and spoiled—so much so that she'd felt the need to warn Adam?

Catherine rose slowly to her feet; after sitting too long on a rock, she was stiff and half numb. *It's the money,* she thought. *The ten thousand dollars. She's proud. She hated accepting your help, but she had to live with it all these years. If she can cast you as a spoiled princess, it gives her a better reason for feeling resentful than admitting she doesn't like owing you gratitude.*

If that's how Danielle felt about Catherine, why had she wanted her in Riley?

"You okay?" Adam asked again.

"Yes. Just stiff, and you must feel the same. Sorry to strand you sitting on a rock for so long."

"It's fine."

Catherine flexed her legs, restoring circulation. *Danielle wanted you here because she loves Flinders and she loves Riley. She wants your program here—even if she resents you sailing into town and spilling money everywhere.*

"I think I get it," Catherine said. "She resents me for something I did that has nothing to do with Robert Fields, but this is the only way she's comfortable striking out. I'll talk to her."

"I'm sorry to bring tension into your friendship."

"Really, if she thinks I'm a selfish princess, the tension was there already. I just wasn't aware of it. I'm glad to get things into the open. Did she . . . mention that Robert died?"

Adam's eyes widened. "No, she didn't tell me that. I'm sorry."

"It was soon after we broke up. A hiking accident—he tripped in the wrong spot on the trail, fell down a rocky incline, and hit his head. By the time his cousin—he was hiking with his cousin—could get help, it was too late."

"That's terrible. I'm sorry."

"It was a shock. Adam . . . thank you for staying with me and putting up with the hysterics. I swear I'm not usually like this."

"Please don't worry about it. I'm glad you were able to get rid of some stress." He touched her arm. "I know how it feels to hold feelings inside until they explode in ways you don't like. You don't have to be embarrassed."

"Thanks. And no pressure at all from me. If you need a friend, you know where to find me, but I totally understand if you need awhile to make up your mind about whether or not you want to get to know me better."

Adam gave her a small grin. "I guess it's only fair."

Catherine laughed. Maybe it was a bleak thing to laugh about, but she appreciated the dry humor in his voice. "Touché," she said.

* * *

"Dad would have been mortified." From where she lay sprawled on the rug, Catherine watched the bright flames reflecting off the fireplace tools. Buying a poker and shovel for a gas fireplace had been pointless, but she loved the gleam of polished brass. "You wouldn't have believed it was me. I couldn't stop crying."

"Tears can be a wonderful release valve." Ava spoke gently. "And if your father wasn't as patient with tears as he could have been, that was *his* problem, bless him. Sometimes a woman needs to cry."

"Poor Adam." Catherine pressed her fingertips against her puffy eyelids. "I'm sure he had no idea what to do with me."

"It sounds like he handled the situation just fine."

"He was so sweet. Poor guy. I think I've scared him away forever."

"I doubt it, honey."

Catherine rolled onto her stomach and rested her cheek against the shaggy area rug with the phone pressed to her other ear. "Ava, what's he supposed to think? First Danielle warns him how spoiled I am, and then when he tries to talk to me about it, I fall apart. I'll never hear from him again. He'll change his phone number. He'll hire a bodyguard. He'll go into the Witness Protection Program."

"If he has the guts—if that's the right word—to tell you to your face what Danielle said about you, he probably has the guts to handle tears without running away in a panic. If he's going to tell you things like that, he'd better be ready to deal with the consequences."

"I *did* ask him to be blunt. I'm glad he told me instead of stewing about it."

"Is this hand-wringing an official confession that you're falling for him?"

"No!" Catherine flipped onto her back. "Don't jump to conclusions. I like him. As a friend. I don't know him well enough to fall for him."

"Are you planning to confront Danielle?"

"Yes. Do you think I'm guessing right? *Was* it the money? Is that why she's holding something against me?"

"Yes, I think you're right. But, honey, it's more than that gift. You had everything she didn't. A loving family—you lost your mother as a teenager, but you lost her knowing she loved you and you would be with her again someday. The same with your father. You've always been loved, always had that safety net. You've never had to worry about money, and she's had to struggle all her life."

Catherine thought of Danielle's family—an absentee, drug-addicted mother, an alcoholic father, and a little sister who clung to Danielle for the support she should have received from her parents. "Very true."

"Perhaps the thought of you netting another thing she doesn't have—a loving husband—brought out the worst in her when she was talking to Adam."

"It's way too early in the game for her to look at Adam as my potential husband!"

"I don't know what's going on inside her head."

"I'll talk to her. I'm dreading it, but if she was criticizing me to Adam, she might be doing it in front of other people, and I don't need that in Riley."

"Be kind when you talk to her, sweetie. She's hurting or she wouldn't have done this."

Catherine sighed. "I know. But it's hard to think of maintaining much of a friendship when she thinks I'm a self-centered brat."

"She knows you're not. She's wrestling with her own insecurities."

"Ava . . . will I sound self-centered if I whine that I've had a hard time lately?"

"You may whine all you like. Get it out of your system with me."

"Thanks. Or maybe I should vent with my pen, Danielle style."

"Danielle style?"

"In college, she used to write things down when she was mad at someone—work out her feelings by creating hilarious fictional revenge fantasies."

"Sounds like a better idea than lashing out at someone."

"They were very funny. People think Danielle is so serious, but she's got this witty, dark sense of humor . . . I remember one story about a boy who was treating Esther like garbage . . . I think it involved fire ants . . . Anyway, I told her she should pursue a degree in creative writing, but she said there was no money in that unless you were Stephen King. It's sad, isn't it, that she didn't feel she could pursue something she was so good at because she didn't think it was practical?"

"What people love to do often doesn't pay the bills," Ava said. "Most people have to take practicality into account in choosing a career."

Most people except me, Catherine thought, suddenly embarrassed as she remembered the blithe way she'd urged Danielle to make a career out of her writing, not bothering to consider that the odds that Danielle could support herself and Esther as a beginning novelist were a million to one. Catherine must have seemed so naive, so oblivious.

So spoiled?

Feeling confused and guilty, Catherine said, "What was I talking about anyway? I've gone off track."

"You were whining about your week."

"Oh . . . yes . . . anyway, I *will* make it work here. The studio *is* doing well. I'm getting a steady flow of new students—I've even had a couple of other adults sign up for lessons. I just wish I knew how Maren is doing."

"I'll be praying for her."

"Me too. Thanks, Ava. I always feel better—" The crash of breaking glass and the blare of her house alarm made Catherine spring to her feet. "Someone's breaking in!" she screamed.

"Call 911! *Now!*"

Catherine fumbled to hit the buttons.

Another crash. Catherine yelled her address at the emergency operator as she ran to grab the nearest weapon she could see—the decorative fireplace poker. "Someone's breaking in!" Catherine shouted at the operator. Loud thuds followed, like the intruder was slamming something against the house. She should hide—where? Frantically, she looked around the family room and kitchen. The pantry—but that hiding place was obvious, and she'd be cornered there.

Mingled with the noise of the alarm, she heard the distant wail of a siren. The police would be here soon. She could hold the intruder off with the poker until—but what if he had a gun?

Another crash and a faint musical note, like something had struck one of the piano keys. The main studio room was full of musical instruments— her *cello*—

Gripping the poker, Catherine charged toward the main room. She slapped the light switch, illuminating the room.

Shards of glass littered the floor, and a chunk of glass lay on the piano keyboard. The curtains on the front and side windows billowed in the wind. Her cello stood undisturbed on its stand, where she'd left it when Ava's call had interrupted her efforts to de-stress herself through a vigorous practice session.

Keeping a firm grip on the poker, Catherine waited in the doorway. If someone tried entering through one of those broken windows, she'd start cracking bones with the poker.

No more thuds or smashing noises followed. The intruder had probably fled, knowing the police were approaching.

The sirens stopped in front of her house, and she could see flashing red and blue lights through the curtains. She scurried to unlock the front door to let the police enter.

I'd better call Ava back and tell her I'm alive, she thought.

CHAPTER 16

"Thank you so much, Jan." Catherine sat at Jan's kitchen table and reached for a box of Cheerios. "I can't tell you how much I appreciate it."

"Good grief, no need to thank me." Jan tossed chopped onions into the Crock-Pot. "You couldn't spend the night at your studio with some lunatic destroying the place! I'm so glad you called me."

"Thanks for the room and board. If I can ever do anything to help you, I'd love to."

"Have you heard from the police?" Jan started peeling a carrot. "Do they have any leads?"

"I haven't heard anything yet."

"I'm betting it's Dylan. From what you said about him, he sounds like a guy who'd take a baseball bat to your windows."

"Could be." Though she suspected Jan was right, she didn't want to be too emphatic. If she was wrong about Dylan, she didn't want it on her conscience that she'd publicly blamed him.

"I can't believe what's been happening lately." Jan chopped the carrot into chunks. "It's insane. I . . . honestly, Catherine, I thought Olivia's murder was a fluke, a lightning-strike horrible thing that would never happen again. But now it feels like Riley is boiling over with danger."

"It does feel that way."

"You must be ready to jump on a plane and get the heck out of here."

"I won't let some nutcase scare me into abandoning my studio. But I do need to be careful, obviously. Jan . . . when we first met, you told me your son Lewis was looking for work."

"Yes." Jan gave her a hopeful look. "Do you know of something?"

"I don't know if he'd be interested," Catherine said. "It's night shift."

"He'd be interested! Of course he'd be interested. Hang on a second; I need to crack the whip." Jan walked out of the kitchen, and Catherine heard her shout, "Kelly! Are you out of bed? We leave for church in forty-five minutes!"

Jan returned to the kitchen. "Lewis is a hard worker, and he's desperate to earn money for school. He's not going anywhere if he can't get some cash."

"Would he be interested in working security? You told me he once worked security at a store. The pay would be good."

"You bet he'd be interested. Who is—oh! For your studio?"

"Yes. I'd like to hire a night security guard." Catherine wasn't worried about being at the studio during the day, but the thought of being alone at night made her shiver. Having a security guard onsite would allow her to sleep easily—and she didn't doubt it would keep Dylan away.

Jan smiled. She looked so pleased that Catherine felt her own spirits lift. "He's your man. I guarantee you he'll want the job, and I guarantee you'll be happy with him. He's conscientious, reliable, all that—and I'd say that even if I weren't his mother."

"Would he be comfortable with the work, with everything that's going on?"

"You mean would he be scared?" Jan snickered. "My ex-linebacker son isn't going to be intimidated by a coward who sneaks around smashing windows—or who sneaks up and attacks a woman. But don't worry. He's a smart kid, not someone looking for a fight. He'll be careful, and if he sees anything, he'll get the cops there immediately. He won't confront someone unless he has to. But if he has to, he can hold his own."

Lewis Peralta sounded like the man she needed. "When would be a good time for me to talk to him? I'll need a day or so to get the legal stuff drawn up."

"If you don't want to talk business at church, then come to dinner, and you can talk to him tonight. In fact, you'd better stay here until you can get him on the job."

"I don't want to impose, Jan. I don't mind going to a hotel."

"Don't you dare go to a hotel! I would never let a friend waste money on a hotel when we have an empty bed right here. Stay as long as you need to."

Declining Jan's offer by saying the money wasn't a problem would sound tacky and ungrateful. "Thank you. I really appreciate it." Catherine poured milk into her glass, less stressed now that she had a plan for keeping her studio—and herself—safe from visits from the window smasher. But she would never feel totally safe and at peace—and neither would anyone else in Riley—until both the person who had attacked Maren and the person who had murdered Olivia were arrested.

Were they the same person? She needed to find out more about Dylan. She already knew he had a tenuous connection to Olivia through Maren's job at the gym, but she didn't know enough to make it worth talking to Detective Burgess. Burgess must already know Maren had worked at Leonardi's; Catherine needed more than that. Who would be the best person to ask about Dylan, Maren, and Olivia?

Will Conti? His giant ego would make him think Catherine was asking questions as an excuse to get herself back into his drop-dead-handsome presence.

Trent Perry? *That* would be a fun conversation, with Trent accusing Adam all over again. Maybe he'd already heard rumors that Catherine and Adam had been spotted together, so he'd know she'd rejected his warning.

What about Kelsey Perry? She also worked at the gym and might have information. Catherine thought of the way Kelsey had questioned her about being with Renee the night they'd discovered the graffiti on Olivia's walls. If she could persuade Kelsey to meet with her, she could not only ask about Dylan but also try to learn why Kelsey had been so strangely curious about her visit with Renee.

Catherine scooped up the last bite of cereal from her bowl. Taking some action to solve her problems and figure things out was a lot better than sitting on a rock and bawling her eyes out.

* * *

"Why didn't you call me?" Adam hurried to intercept Catherine in the hall as she headed toward Sunday School. "I didn't even find out what happened until Craig Peralta told me this morning."

Catherine stepped to the side of the hallway so people could pass her. "I'm sorry. I . . ." She thought about saying she didn't want to bother him or didn't want him to worry, but she decided to be forthright. Speaking softly, she said, "After all the craziness in the park yesterday, I thought I'd better give you a little time. Let you call me if you wanted to."

Adam leaned toward her so he could keep his voice too soft for passersby to easily overhear. "Don't be silly. Something terrible happened—of course I'd want to know, want to help if I could. Are you okay?"

"It scared me to death, but I'm fine. The police are keeping a close watch on the neighborhood today in case the intruder decides to wreak more damage on the studio. I brought my cello with me to Jan's—I stayed with the Peraltas last night, as Craig probably told you. My cello is the only thing I'm worried about. It's a member of the family."

"I'm glad it didn't get damaged. I have to run; I'm subbing for the twelve-year-old class, but I'll call you this afternoon."

"Thanks." Relieved that she hadn't scared Adam off completely, Catherine resumed walking toward her class.

"You're taking your life in your hands," a male voice said behind her.

Catherine whirled around and saw Trent and Kelsey. "I don't agree," she said.

"Yeah, obviously." Trent stepped close to Catherine and whispered, "A woman gets attacked right next to your studio and you *still* can't see you're in danger. Who do you think is next on his list?"

Catherine glanced at Kelsey. Kelsey's expression was unreadable.

If you want to talk about this, let's do it outside," Catherine said. "It doesn't seem appropriate here."

"Fine." Trent turned as though to march toward the exit, but Kelsey grabbed his arm. "Excuse us," she said brusquely and pulled Trent past Catherine.

Uncertain what to do next, Catherine stood waiting until Trent and Kelsey were out of sight, having turned in the opposite direction from the room where Sunday School was being held. Slowly, she resumed walking.

Halfway through the lesson, Kelsey came into the room alone. During the shuffle following the end of the lesson, she walked over and sat next to Catherine.

"I apologize for Trent," she said. "He's having a hard time right now."

Catherine wanted to say that didn't give him the right to accuse Adam of murder, but this wasn't the place for that discussion. "I understand."

Kelsey lowered her voice so it was nearly inaudible. "Do you know about the . . . history between Trent and Adam?"

"The history?" Catherine whispered back.

Kelsey shook her head; clearly she didn't want to talk about it right there. Grabbing this opportunity, Catherine said, "May I come talk to you soon? I have some questions I think you might be able to answer."

"Yeah, okay. Can you meet me for lunch tomorrow? Or Tuesday?"

Catherine pulled out her phone and checked her calendar. "Tuesday works, if it's between noon and two."

"There's a soup and sandwich shop near your studio—the Bowl and Plate. Know where it is?"

"Yes." She'd noticed the sign, with its peeling pictures of a smiling bowl and dancing plate.

"I'll meet you there on Tuesday. One o'clock?"

"Fine."

"See you then." Kelsey rose and exited the room.

* * *

On Sunday afternoon, Catherine rang the doorbell at Danielle's home.

Esther opened the door. "Hey," she said. "I was going to call you. I heard what happened. Do you need help cleaning up?"

"No. But thank you." Seeing Esther in her own territory reminded Catherine of how careful she was being with her appearance at work. Esther's hair was a gelled, tousled mess. She wore a tight black T-shirt full of artful holes and had so much metal in her ears that the weight probably strained her neck muscles. Her face was so pale and the shadows under her eyes so dark that Catherine doubted she'd slept in the past twenty-four hours.

"Are you going to have to shut down next week?" Esther asked.

"No. Business as usual. We'll get the windows fixed as quickly as possible, but we don't need to wait for that in order to continue with lessons."

"Let me know if you need help with anything. I can work extra hours." Esther leaned toward Catherine. "Uh . . . this isn't the best time for you to visit Dani, if that's what you're here for. She's been totally . . . " Esther paused, and Catherine wondered if she was hunting for a description of Danielle's mood that didn't include profanity. "She's grouchy. Driving me crazy."

Wonderful. Had Esther been partying all night and that's what Danielle was grouchy about? The things Catherine wanted to say to her weren't likely to improve her mood. "She's expecting me," Catherine said. "I need to—"

The clack of approaching footsteps interrupted her. "Hello, Catherine," Danielle said. "Come in. Esther, get that mess off the coffee table."

"I will when I'm done," Esther snapped, holding up a hand with half the nails painted.

"Do your nails somewhere else. You're smelling up the living room."

From the anger on Esther's face, Catherine knew she wanted to say something harsh, but she didn't, probably not wanting to argue in front of Catherine. She gathered up her supplies and stalked into the kitchen.

"Have a seat," Danielle invited.

"Let's talk in your study," Catherine said quietly.

Danielle lifted sleek, dark eyebrows. "Whatever you want." She led the way.

Danielle's study was a small, tidy room with a desk, a few chairs upholstered in a black houndstooth fabric, and shelves of books filled with titles on educational theory and other topics related to Danielle's job. No novels, though Catherine knew Danielle loved reading them. Or she *had* loved reading them. Did she feel even her leisure reading needed to be practical now?

Danielle closed the door. "Have you heard any updates on Maren?"

"I can't get any information at all." Catherine chose a seat. "How about you?"

"I've tried but haven't learned much." Danielle sat next to her. "I've had dozens of parents calling me for updates, and all I can tell them is as far as I know, she hasn't woken up. I get the feeling the police are keeping her condition private."

"Maybe she's doing better than we think, but they don't want to tip the attacker off in case he's afraid she can nail him if she wakes up," Catherine said. "I hope."

"I hope so too. The thought of her lingering in a coma or waking up unable to function . . ." The sorrow in Danielle's face softened some of Catherine's anger toward her. "Maren Gates is a good woman. Always willing to support Flinders however she can. She babysits her niece during the day, so she's the one who takes her to school and so on. Helps out in the classroom. I wish we could clone her." Her keen brown eyes focused on Catherine. "It was good of you to give her the chance to take music lessons."

"My pleasure." Would Maren ever pick up her flute again? Catherine blinked at the tears forming in her eyes.

"I was sorry to hear that the vandalism spread to your studio." Danielle leaned back and crossed her long legs. "Have the police arrested anyone?"

"No." She didn't add that they suspected Dylan.

"You're being careful, I hope, in case the culprit decides to do more damage."

"I'm hiring a security guard."

"Good idea. Do you need suggestions? I could talk to people for you."

"I have someone lined up." Here was Danielle being helpful, efficient, concerned for Catherine—normal Danielle. It made it harder for Catherine to open the topic of Danielle's trying to shred her reputation in front of Adam. She'd always thought Danielle was a straightforward person—not someone who'd conceal her negative opinions and then stab a friend in the back.

She was tempted to hope Danielle had simply been in a bad mood when she'd talked to Adam, to let it go, and not confront her. But Catherine knew she'd regret it if she tried to ignore this. She'd always be wondering what Danielle *really* thought of her and what Danielle was saying behind her back. If she wanted to salvage the friendship, she needed to trust Danielle, and if Danielle resented her, they needed to talk this out.

"Are you staying with someone?" Danielle asked. "I can't imagine you'll want to sleep in your studio until everything is fixed and your security guard is there."

"Yes, I'm staying with a friend from church." Catherine straightened her shoulders and held Danielle's gaze. "I went on a picnic with Adam Becket on Saturday evening."

"Fun," Danielle said casually. "Where did you go?"

"Orenda Gorge."

"I take it you've decided to trust him?"

It annoyed Catherine that Danielle didn't look uncomfortable. She'd hoped the mention of Adam's name would make her squirm. "I trust him. But I hope he can trust me after the things you told him about me."

Danielle's gaze dropped for an instant. She didn't look guilty, but at least she looked disconcerted. "What did he tell you?"

"That you tried to warn him away from me. That you told him in essence that I'm a spoiled, self-centered brat, no man is good enough for me, and I'll never commit to anyone."

"That's an exaggeration."

"How much of an exaggeration?"

Danielle's face assumed a calm, professional expression, and Catherine wondered if that was the look she wore when handling angry students or parents. "You can't deny that you have commitment issues."

"I do *not* have commitment issues. I broke up with Robert for solid reasons, not because of some commitment phobia."

"That's not how it looked to the rest of us."

"Then you misinterpreted it. *Here* was the commitment problem: Robert and I had different levels of commitment to our religion, and for me, that's a deal breaker. Maybe you don't understand how important that is to me, but how can you take that one incident and make it into evidence that I'll never be happy with any man? And that any fool who tries to get to know me will get his heart broken? That's *not true*, and I don't appreciate you trying to scare Adam away."

Danielle's voice remained even. "I didn't try to scare him away. I wanted to make sure he was fully informed."

Catherine's anger steamed. She'd expected Danielle to apologize—or at least *pretend* to be apologetic—but instead, she was standing behind what she'd said. "Why would you feel it was your responsibility to 'inform' him? You told me you knew him only superficially."

"Because I don't know him well doesn't mean I don't care what happens to him. He strikes me as a good man who deserves happiness after what he's been through."

That was a lot more of an opinion on his character than Danielle had given her when she'd asked about Adam a couple of weeks ago. "So you warned him I—"

"Cate, you're overreacting. I didn't 'warn' him, and obviously, I didn't scare him away. Didn't you tell me you went on a picnic with him?"

"That's not the point. You painted me as a selfish—"

"I didn't paint you as anything terrible at all. You're a nice person. You're smart. You're talented. You're fun to be with. I value our friendship. But you've never had to be responsible for another person. You've never had to take care of anyone else. You've never had to worry about money or how you'll support yourself and your family. How can you *not* be self-focused with the life you've led? I did *not* insult you when I talked to Adam. I was merely letting him know that you two have very different backgrounds and he might want to be aware of that."

"Is this because of the money I gave you in grad school? Do you resent me because of that—because you had to accept my help to stay in school?"

Danielle looked blank. "What does that have to do with anything? We settled that account."

Embarrassed, Catherine wished she hadn't mentioned the money. Danielle probably thought she was bragging by making the point of how she'd helped her. "I left my home, set aside more glamorous opportunities, and moved to Riley to give the gift of music to people who wouldn't otherwise have it. Would you please explain to me how *that* comes across as self-focused?"

"I never said everything you did was self-focused, and your music program is a wonderful, commendable thing. But I'm guessing you were anticipating plenty of adulation and admiration and plenty of starry-eyed devotees showering you with thanks. Is that correct?"

Too flustered and humiliated to even try to pretend Danielle's blow hadn't landed, Catherine sat speechless.

"Cate, I'm *not* criticizing you, though I know it sounds like I am. You're human. So what if part of your motive in starting this program stemmed from a desire for admiration? We all do things for mixed reasons. And you have a lot to live up to—you need to earn a lot more adulation if you're going to get anywhere near achieving your father's fame."

"I'm not after fame, and neither was my father!" Catherine's face burned; why did she have to blush like that? It made her look childish, while Danielle looked wise and mature. "He was doing what he loved, what he was good at. And so am I."

"You don't care at all if people applaud what you're doing?"

Catherine stared at a row of books on Danielle's shelf and struggled to think of a response. She wanted to lash back that she *didn't* care, but she knew that was a lie. Maybe Danielle was right about her, and that's why this hurt so much. She *had* expected people to love her in Riley. To admire her and be grateful to her.

How would her father have handled it if he'd heard something upsetting that he didn't want to hear but that he knew might have merit?

He would have thanked them, evaluated the information, and acted on it if he decided he agreed with it.

"Thank you for being candid with me," Catherine said stiffly. "But I would appreciate it in the future if you would speak to me *first* if you feel there are deficiencies in my character, rather than alerting people behind my back."

"It wasn't so much deficiencies in your character as differences," Danielle said. "I didn't want Adam getting hurt or you getting hurt either. But you're right. I should have talked to you, not Adam. I apologize. I didn't want to upset you. And, frankly, I didn't think Adam would repeat what I told him."

"I'd better go." Catherine stood. She was too shaken to sit here trying to change the conversation to some fluffy, painless topic.

Danielle rose. "I hope I haven't destroyed our friendship. You know I'm not someone who babies the people around me. I think you have enough strength of character to not *want* babying."

"I don't want it. I'll think about everything you've said. But, Dani, you're wrong about me and Robert Fields."

Danielle opened the door to the study. "Call me if you need any help with the studio," she said. "Assuming you can stand hearing the sound of my voice."

CHAPTER 17

CATHERINE DIDN'T WANT TO RETURN to the Peraltas' home when she felt this agitated. She was still ashamed of last night's breakdown in front of Adam; she didn't need to go all weepy in front of Jan's family too. Dinner would be at six, Jan had told her, so she had about an hour to calm herself.

Good luck.

She braked at a stoplight, futilely blinking at the tears that kept filling her eyes. Was Danielle right? Just because Catherine hadn't had to raise a younger sister like Danielle had didn't automatically make her self-centered. Just because she was an only child didn't automatically make her self-centered. Just because her family had money didn't mean she'd never worked hard. She'd worked hard to become a musician. She'd worked hard to get her graduate degree. She'd worked hard to set up her studio. She worked hard every day teaching her students and promoting the studio.

You were anticipating plenty of adulation and admiration.

A desire for admiration had *not* been the reason she'd come to Riley. But had she wanted it?

Maybe Danielle saw her more clearly than she saw herself. Maybe Danielle genuinely *had* been concerned for Adam's happiness when she'd warned him about Catherine.

Is that how I come across to everyone? Am I that oblivious to what I'm like?

She needed to work off some stress. While she was this upset, it was impossible to think rationally or even attempt to evaluate Danielle's observations. She could go for a walk—she wasn't afraid to walk in daylight—but if she couldn't get her emotions under control, she'd give all of Riley a chance to witness her nervous breakdown in progress. She'd made enough of a scene at Orenda Gorge last night.

She'd go home and practice for a while. Her cello was at Jan's, but it would be good to spend an hour with a different instrument. What would be the best stress reliever? Blasting a trumpet loud enough to shatter her remaining windows might make her feel better, but the neighbors wouldn't consider it a tranquil serenade on a Sunday afternoon. Flute? Catherine flinched. That would remind her of Maren. Bass. The deep, resonant tones of a double bass would help unsnarl the tight feeling in her chest.

She scanned the front of the studio as she drove toward it. It appeared peaceful if you ignored the plywood nailed over the front window. Looking at the studio drew her morale up a little. The birch leaves on the trees in front were turning sunshine yellow—she loved those trees with their white trunks and delicate, droopy branches. Was the gold-lettered calligraphy and scattering of musical notes decorating the front door too ostentatious—too attention seeking?

Don't you dare start ripping apart every decision you've made, looking for selfish motives. You are running a music studio. Putting the name of the studio on the door and trying to catch the eye of potential students is not ostentatious.

The boarded-over windows made the main room of the studio dimmer than usual. Thank heavens for the helpful neighbor who'd offered sheets of plywood out of his basement workshop to cover the windows until Catherine could have them repaired. Catherine switched on the lights and walked to the piano. Last night, she'd looked for damage where the glass had landed, but with her thoughts scattered by fear and fury and her studio chaotic with police officers and neighbors, she might well have missed something.

She couldn't find any scratches on the polished instrument. How bad was the damage to the siding? She ought to take some daylight pictures. Ava would want them immediately; she'd deal with the insurance company. Catherine grabbed her camera and opened the front door.

Dylan was standing on the sidewalk in front of her house.

Catherine jumped backward. She nearly slammed the door, but the thought of letting him inflict more damage on her studio while she hid inside infuriated her. Gripping the doorknob so she could slam and lock the door in an instant if he started up the stairs toward her, she snapped, "What are you doing here?"

Dylan glowered at her. Stubble covered his chin, his hair was a mess, and his T-shirt was stained. "What was Maren really doing when she said she was with you?"

"She was taking flute lessons. You know that. Get out of here, or I'll call the police." She drew her phone out of her pocket.

"Call them. I don't care." Dylan took an unsteady step toward the stairs then backed up. He looked horrible—not just disheveled but haggard, with gray patches under bloodshot eyes. "It don't matter now. You already wrecked everything."

"Get away from here. I don't have anything to say to you."

"Lying there . . . like she's *dead*. It's your fault, you—"

"Enough." Catherine cut him off. She wanted to say that if he hadn't been such a jerk about Maren's taking music lessons—to the point of refusing to let her take the car—Maren would have driven safely home on Friday night instead of walking after dark. But what was the point of striking out at him? If Dylan was the one who'd attacked Maren, his attempt to blame Catherine was only a bluff anyway. If he *hadn't* hurt her and he had any kind of a conscience, then he already felt awful about his role in Maren's condition.

She *hoped* he had that much of a conscience. He did look miserable. Scared. "Go home," Catherine said. "Go get some sleep."

"Was she seeing another guy?"

"Why would you say that?"

"Is that what you do in your fancy studio? Women slip you some cash, and you match them up with—"

"Are you insane or just drunk? This is a music studio! I teach music lessons!"

"Since when do grown-up women take music lessons?"

"There's no age limit on music. If you think Maren was doing anything other than taking flute lessons here, that's your own sick mind trying to find a way to blame *her* for the fact that *you* treated her like garbage."

"I never hurt her! I never hit her!"

"What kind of man calls his wife stupid? What kind of man tells her she's wasting her time developing a new talent?"

"Did *you* tell the cops I hurt her? They won't let me be alone with her."

Good, Catherine thought. "I didn't accuse you of anything. What do you want? If you came to ask if I was running some type of brothel or escort service, you're an idiot—and even if you *are* an idiot, I don't think you're stupid enough to believe Maren was using flute lessons as a front for cheating on you. You just can't face the truth that she was doing something good in her life and you were too selfish to support her."

Dylan swore at Catherine, but the pain in his face was so marked that she couldn't help feeling bad for him. Was he hurting because his wife was critically injured or because he was the one who had injured her?

"You told them I messed up your studio," Dylan said.

"I didn't tell them you did anything. I don't know who broke my windows. But if you don't like getting questioned by the police, maybe you shouldn't come here shouting profanity and making ridiculous accusations."

Dylan stared at her, but he looked so glazed that Catherine wondered how well his eyes were focusing. He was a wreck, and maybe she'd have better luck handling him if she tried a gentle approach.

"Has Maren showed any signs of waking up?" Catherine asked quietly. "What have the doctors said?"

Dylan turned and staggered along the sidewalk toward the road. Catherine watched him until he was out of sight, glad he hadn't driven to her studio. She couldn't tell if he was drunk or not, but even if he was sober, he shouldn't be behind the wheel of a car.

Catherine closed and locked the door. She should have called the police immediately instead of standing there talking to Dylan. But he hadn't seemed aggressive—not physically aggressive anyway. Just angry and hurting and wanting someone to blame.

She headed into the kitchen for a glass of water. Should she call the police now? Dylan hadn't threatened her, but would Detective Burgess want to know he'd been here? They'd questioned him about the vandalism last night, but from the fact that he hadn't been arrested, they plainly didn't have any conclusive evidence against him. Still, she ought to let Burgess know.

She dialed Burgess's number and got voice mail. She left a message.

Sipping her water, Catherine stood near the patio door, looking out at the sunny backyard and hoping Dylan hadn't returned to hide in the bushes. What could Kelsey tell her about Dylan tomorrow? And what had she meant by a connection between Adam and Trent?

Catherine turned away from the door. Adam had called earlier that afternoon, and Catherine had talked to him for a while but hadn't mentioned she was meeting with Kelsey. Despite Adam's polite words about how Catherine's fresh viewpoint and straw grasping might be helpful, he probably thought she was silly or arrogant for thinking she could uncover information about Olivia's death that the police—and Olivia's friends and family—had all overlooked.

Maybe I'm self-centered enough to think I'm the only one who can solve this, Catherine thought caustically, dumping the rest of the water into the sink so savagely that it splashed her blouse.

She walked to the landline phone on the counter to check her messages. Six of them.

"Hi, Catherine. This is Mary Henry, Shelly's mom. Heard what happened ... too bad about ... it's crazy that anyone would ... I think it would be better if Shelly didn't take lessons for a while. Sorry, but I'm sure you understand."

Grimly, Catherine deleted the message and made a note that she was down one aspiring violinist. That was a shame. Fifth-grader Shelly had seemed awed at the thought of learning to play. Hopefully Mary Henry would let her daughter come back when she realized Shelly wasn't in danger.

She played the next message. "Miss Clayton, this is Dan Kemp. Don't know what crazy stuff you have going on there, but my son's not coming anywhere near it. Take him off your list."

Click.

Clenching her teeth, Catherine made another note. After the attack on Maren, followed by the vandalism, she couldn't blame parents for being scared. But pulling out students—who met in group lessons, usually with their parents waiting for them—seemed like a hysterical reaction. Whoever had attacked Maren had either targeted her specifically—in which case the attacker was probably Dylan—or had attacked her on some psychopathic whim when he saw her walking alone at night. Students coming to the studio with parents were in no danger—at least in no more danger than everyone else in Riley with a murderer on the loose.

She didn't want to listen to the rest of the messages, but she might as well get it over with. The next was a hang-up. The fourth soothed a little of her frustration—the mother of one of her trumpet students had called to ask if she was all right and if she needed help.

The next two messages were students dropping out.

Catherine carefully set the phone down. Slamming it in the base would be childish, and the last thing she needed was to lose control again in any way.

Renee had worried about this—that Catherine's name and the studio would be tainted by any connection with the violence in Riley. Renee had been right to be concerned. Four students gone already. How many would she lose tomorrow? If everyone packed up and quit, at least she wouldn't have to feel guilty if she bailed out too.

If she did bail, at least that would give Danielle the satisfaction that she'd been right about Catherine's self-centered motives and inability to work through problems when things got hard.

* * *

"The clam chowder is a specialty here." Kelsey's voice was more businesslike than friendly.

"I was eying the baked potato soup," Catherine said. "I have a hard time resisting bacon and cheddar. Ever tried it?"

"No, but pretty much everything here is good." Kelsey stepped forward to place her order. The soup and sandwich shop had a homey, eclectic decor that Catherine liked, with mismatched glass bud vases filled with fake flowers on the tables and sun-faded gingham curtains on the windows. Tacky but cozy. The aroma of baking bread made her want to linger as long as she could, but she'd asked Kelsey if they could get their meals to go. She didn't want anyone overhearing their conversation.

After Catherine ordered and they stepped back to let other customers approach the counter, Kelsey remarked, "You must think Riley is a horror house. It isn't like that."

"Everywhere has crime. But it *is* stressful dealing with it directly. I've never had to do *that* before." She bit her lip. That was exactly what Danielle would expect her to say—viewing Riley's problems only in light of how they affected *her*.

"What made you come here anyway?"

Catherine couldn't tell if there was hostility in Kelsey's voice—*Go back where you belong*—or if she was honestly curious. "I was looking for a place to start my music program, and I had a personal connection here. I was grad-school roommates with Danielle Knight. Danielle thought Riley was a good match for the program."

"Guess so, since not many people here have money to shell out for music lessons, and all the school programs have been canceled. I forgot you knew Danielle—Trent told me about that. She's well respected in Riley. Good administrator. Olivia always had good things to say about her."

"She's a strong personality." Catherine tried to keep her still-tumultuous emotions about Danielle from coloring her voice.

"The kids like her, I hear."

"Yes, she's good with children. She used to teach." Catherine wanted to get away from the subject of Danielle. To her relief, the cashier called out Kelsey's number, and she stepped forward to pick up her sandwich.

When they'd both been served, they headed out to the parking lot.

"My car or yours?" Kelsey asked.

"I walked."

"So my car. Do you want to sit here and eat, or do you want to go back to your studio?"

"Let's talk here. My studio's a construction zone—they're fixing the windows and the siding."

"Don't you need to be there for that?"

"My assistant is taking care of things."

When they were seated in Kelsey's car, Catherine said, "Thanks for being willing to talk with me."

"No problem." Kelsey unwrapped her turkey sub.

Again, she sounded pleasant but not warm. Catherine was having trouble reading her mood. She watched Kelsey out of the corner of her eye—lean and sleek in her warm-up suit embroidered with the Leonardi's logo, her brown hair brushed back and braided, her expression remote but not cold. Kelsey ate in silence, not attempting to start the discussion of whatever she'd wanted to say about Adam and Trent.

Catherine decided to open with the least emotionally treacherous of the subjects she wanted to discuss with Kelsey. "Why were you asking me about my visit with Renee Endicott?"

Kelsey picked up a fallen shred of lettuce and dropped it onto the sandwich wrapper. "How well do you know Renee?"

"Not well."

"What's your impression of her?"

"At first she came across as prickly. Hostile and judgmental. But the more I get to know her, the more I think she's just lonely and scared."

"Does she talk about Olivia?"

"Yes, she mentioned her the first time we met and . . . every time since, I guess. It's obvious she cared about her a lot."

"It bothered her tremendously that the police weren't still looking hard for Olivia's killer."

"What do you mean?" Catherine stirred her soup. "Why wouldn't they look for him?"

"They *did*. They did everything they could, but it happened two years ago. After two years, the trail is cold. Her case couldn't remain top priority forever, not when no new evidence had come to light. Something new needed to happen to get things moving again."

"Like the killer striking again."

"It didn't need to be that extreme. How about a round of vandalism at the school where Olivia worked? Then a round of vandalism that includes painted death threats? Followed by vandalism at Olivia's apartment?"

"You're suggesting . . . are you suggesting Renee might have done those things? To bring attention to Olivia's case?"

Kelsey swallowed her bite of sandwich. "People can't stay freaked out about something forever. Except among her family and close friends, Olivia had almost been forgotten. The vandal did an effective job of getting Olivia's name into the news again."

"You think that's what Renee wanted."

"I might be wrong. But Renee was devastated when Olivia died. It enraged her that the police couldn't figure out who killed her. She called the family many times after Olivia's death, demanding that we tell her everything we knew, that we must know *something* that could lead the police to Olivia's killer. I felt sorry for her, but she made me nervous. Then when you were conveniently with her when she 'discovered' the vandalism . . . I'm wondering if she was waiting for the right moment to 'find' it, and when you showed up, she decided you'd make a good witness."

"I don't know Renee well enough to have an opinion." Her thoughts spinning, Catherine tried to remember if Renee had said anything suspicious relating to the vandalism. "She seemed genuinely terrified when we saw the message on Olivia's walls. And she seemed genuinely scared when she first told me about the vandalism at Flinders."

"I wonder if the police have questioned her. As a suspect, I mean."

"I have no idea." Catherine hated the thought of Renee being disturbed enough to perpetrate the vandalism herself.

"The whole thing seems too strange to take at face value." The car was heating up in the afternoon sunshine, and Kelsey twisted the key in the ignition and switched on the air conditioning. "If the killer *is* back, why would he advertise himself? He didn't do any of that before killing Olivia. Why do it now?"

"But there *was* vandalism right before Olivia died. Danielle told me that."

"Was that before she died? I remember it was awhile back but can't remember the exact timing. But that was random stuff, like that fountain in front of the library. It wasn't death threats!"

"Maybe the killer decided to ramp it up. Maybe he likes knowing he has the power to scare the whole city."

"Sure, maybe. But it's more likely that Renee—or someone else—is trying to stir people up."

"But the killer—or *a* killer—*is* back. Look what happened to Maren Gates."

"I know. But I don't think that has anything to do with Olivia."

"Who do you think attacked her?"

Kelsey sighed and took another bite of sandwich. Catherine waited, not wanting to lead the witness by bringing up Dylan herself.

"I don't know," Kelsey said at last. "But I hear Maren's husband has a temper, and things were rocky between them."

"I've met her husband," Catherine said. "I wasn't impressed."

"I used to see him at the gym when he'd come to pick up Maren—she used to work at the gym, so I know her. But I never talked to him. He seemed pretty quiet. What's he like?"

"He . . . honestly, he seems like a jerk and a half. Controlling and emotionally abusive. I don't know if he's anything more than that. He didn't want Maren taking flute lessons, and he's come ranting and swearing at me more than once." Catherine ate a few spoonfuls of soup. "Do you know if there was any connection between Dylan and Olivia?"

"Hang on. You're suggesting *Dylan* is Olivia's killer?"

"I'm exploring any angle I can think of."

"Why should it be up to you to explore anything about this? You weren't even here when Olivia died."

"I *don't* think it's up to me. But since I'm involved now, I'm thinking a lot about it."

"I don't know if Dylan knew Olivia. He might have met her at the gym. Olivia was outgoing, good at talking to people."

Catherine scooped up another spoonful of creamy soup laced with cheddar, bacon, and green onions. "I've seen pictures of Olivia. She was beautiful. Do you think Dylan might have noticed her that way?"

"Olivia would have told me if he'd tried to hit on her. She was usually pretty chatty, pretty open."

Catherine felt stupid at how much she'd hoped Kelsey would say, "Now that you mention it . . ." and offer strong new evidence that Dylan might have had a reason to kill Olivia. *Yep, that's likely. Everyone overlooked that obvious possibility until you and your genius brain waltzed into town.*

"Thanks," Catherine said tiredly. "I was just wondering if what happened to Maren might shed new light on what happened to Olivia."

"So you think Dylan got involved with Olivia—or wanted to—she rejected him, and he killed her. Then he got mad at Maren and tried to kill her too. And now he's mad at you, and that's why you're desperate to figure things out." Kelsey shoved the paper sandwich wrapping into the bag. "I'm sorry you're stuck in the middle of this. I wish I knew something, but I don't. I *can* tell you that Olivia wouldn't have gotten involved with

Dylan Gates. For all her . . . um . . . flakiness about Will Conti, she never would have gotten involved with a married man, especially considering she knew and liked Maren. But as to whether Dylan got obsessed with her or something, I don't know. If he did, Olivia didn't know it, because she would have told Trent and me." She eyed Catherine. "At this point, you probably think the whole group of us are crazies in disguise—Trent included."

Catherine resisted the urge to say that if Trent was sticking notes in her purse and giving ominous warnings with no proof to back them up, he wasn't doing a great job of disguising his craziness. "You . . . said there was some history between Trent and Adam."

"Yeah. Give me your word you won't repeat this—well, you can talk to Adam about it; it's not like he doesn't know what happened, and I already know he keeps his mouth shut. But if you repeat anything to anyone else, I'll deny it, and I'll make sure it hurts *your* reputation more than it hurts Trent's."

Astonished, Catherine said coldly, "You don't have to threaten me. If I give you my word that I won't tell anyone, then I won't tell anyone."

Kelsey shifted in her seat and crumpled the bag in her hands. "Sorry. That was out of line. I just don't want anyone bad-mouthing Trent."

"I'm not planning to bad-mouth your husband. I want to know what happened between Adam and him, and since you're the one who brought it up, I assume you want to tell me."

"Okay." Kelsey's expression softened. "I do want to tell you, because I think Adam deserves a break and I don't want Trent driving you away from him. Trent and Adam were friends—never close friends; Trent is intense, and Adam's more laid back, so their personalities never clicked really well, but they'd play basketball together or mountain bike. Trent's in better shape overall, but Adam's a better biker, and that bugged Trent—he's competitive. When they were biking a few years ago, Trent got too aggressive and too competitive, and he crowded Adam. Adam hit a rock and went flying. He broke his arm and tore up his face. That's why he can't smile right—he has nerve damage from the accident."

"He told me. Not what caused the accident but that the damage was from biking."

"He never tells the whole story to anyone. Just says he took a spill. He never openly blamed Trent, but it was Trent's fault."

"Does Trent admit that?"

"He used to. To me. Right after the accident, he felt awful."

"Did he talk to Adam about it?"

"No. Trent panicked, thinking like a lawyer. If he apologized and admitted guilt, he was afraid Adam would sue him or at least demand payment of medical bills. Trent was struggling to keep the gym afloat. The thought of getting sued terrified him."

"Did he truly think Adam would sue him?"

"Adam went through a lot of pain, several surgeries, and ended up with permanent damage. Don't you think Trent had reason to be nervous?"

Catherine couldn't imagine Adam filing a lawsuit over an accident, but in the litigious climate of modern life, she wasn't surprised Trent had worried about that. But if he'd been at fault and had never apologized to Adam or taken responsibility for his actions, that didn't say much for Trent's character. "If Adam knew Trent caused the accident, wasn't Trent worried Adam could sue him without his admitting guilt?"

"Yeah, but Adam never did. If he'd tried, it would have been his word against Trent's." Kelsey crunched her empty water bottle and shoved it into the sandwich bag. "I can tell you're thinking Trent's a loser for not owning up. Go ahead and judge him if you want, but he was doing the best he could to support his family. And he did feel terrible."

Catherine figured she'd better not respond to that.

"He wanted to make it up to Adam somehow, but there wasn't much he could do," Kelsey said. "Then Olivia got home from college and Trent went after her, talking up Adam's virtues like he was the most amazing guy on earth, hounding her to give him a chance. Olivia knew Adam, of course, but hadn't had much to do with him since he was a few years older than she."

"Trent pushed Olivia to date Adam."

"That's right. Olivia finally asked Adam out, and they ended up liking each other. It made Trent feel he'd done something good for Adam— found him this awesome girlfriend who, Trent hoped, would end up as his wife."

What was Trent's rationale? *I tore up his face, but, look, he can still get the girl, so I don't have to feel guilty?* Catherine wanted to say that Trent had a strange way of dealing with guilt, using his sister to ease his conscience, but despite Kelsey's candor, she was obviously inclined to defend Trent, and Catherine didn't want to anger her.

"They dated for a while, but then that whole mess with Will Conti started. Olivia would talk about how she didn't want to get serious with

Adam so soon and how she wasn't ready for marriage. I think part of the problem was that she resented how invested Trent was in the success of her relationship with Adam. Flirting with Will was a way of pushing back—even though she *did* like Adam a lot."

"Did Trent and Olivia have a good relationship?"

"Overall, yeah, but Trent likes to control things, and Olivia was feisty, so they'd butt heads. When she started seeing Will on the side, it drove Trent crazy—he'd rant at her about what an idiot she was to get involved with Will and that Adam was the guy who could go the distance. He wanted to fire Will but didn't dare—he's a big draw at the gym, and Trent knew Olivia would keep seeing him anyway. Then Adam found out, and . . . the next day Olivia was murdered."

Catherine gathered up the trash from her lunch. "If Trent was the one holding Adam up as the ideal husband, how did he end up convinced that Adam killed her?"

"It's . . . partly my fault. I'd been urging Olivia to break things off with Will and come clean with Adam. Riley isn't a big place, and I knew he'd hear about Olivia and Will sooner or later. If Olivia was honest with Adam and told him she'd made a mistake and it was over, maybe she could salvage things, but she . . ." Kelsey wrapped her fingers around the steering wheel, her arms tense. "She didn't want to own up. We exchanged a bunch of texts—me pushing her to tell him, her saying no way, she was scared, he'd be upset, and so on."

Catherine thought of Trent's describing the texts—his so-called evidence against Adam. "Did *you* think she meant she was scared Adam would hurt her?"

"No. It was obvious to me she meant she was afraid he'd dump her, that he wouldn't shrug off her fling with Will. She was being stupid, and deep down, she knew it. She was so infatuated with Will that she wanted to keep playing with him a little longer, hoping she could have her fun with Will but keep Adam in reserve. But when Trent was going through Olivia's phone after she died and saw those texts, he started freaking out and misinterpreting them. Adam *did* have a motive—he was the only person Trent could see who had any reason to hurt Olivia. Trent convinced himself that the accident had warped Adam and that after Olivia's betrayal, his hatred for the whole Perry family had erupted in violence. He . . . thought that not only was Adam furious with Olivia but that he was also striking back at Trent by attacking her."

Catherine shuddered. "I wonder if he was trying to relieve his own guilt at what he did to Adam by accusing him of something much worse."

"That crossed my mind. But in his defense, I think he just *had* to know who killed Olivia, or he'd go crazy. Trent likes to act. He can't *stand* uncertainty. To know someone had murdered his sister and he was helpless to find justice for her . . . he couldn't take it. So he blamed Adam."

"It gave him someone to hate?"

"Trent's a good guy. He really is. But he twists things in his mind sometimes, and it's hard for him to let go. I've been candid with you because after the way you've been drawn into this mess, I think you deserve to know why Trent acts like he does, and I think you deserve to know more of Adam's story. Since it was my text conversation with Olivia that got Trent going in the first place, I wanted to explain things. I hope you'll keep your word and keep your mouth shut."

"If Adam isn't inclined to tell people the full story, I'm not going to share it for him."

"Adam keeps his mouth shut. When Trent started going after him, I thought for sure he'd spread the story of how that bike accident happened, but he didn't." Kelsey shifted the car into gear. "I'll drop you at your studio."

"Thanks."

How angry had Trent been with Olivia when she'd thwarted his plans by getting involved with Will? If Trent was good at rationalizing—if he sometimes twisted things in his mind, if his conscience was already fractured—

Adam had said he couldn't think of any reason why Trent would want to hurt Olivia. But maybe Adam wasn't looking hard enough.

CHAPTER 18

Catherine walked toward Renee's apartment, fingering the ribbon on the box of chocolate-covered almonds she'd picked up at the grocery store. Renee had sounded normal—curt, sarcastic—when Catherine had called to ask if she could visit, but she'd agreed so quickly that Catherine knew she was eager for company.

Could Renee be the vandal? Catherine hoped a friendly talk with Renee might help her get a better handle on Renee's mental state. Even if Renee had been the one to damage the school and Olivia's apartment, Catherine still thought Dylan was likely to be the one who'd gone after her studio with a bat or crowbar.

And maybe in talking to Renee, Catherine could learn more about Olivia's relationship with Trent. It probably *was* futile to think she might be able to notice something crucial that people who were accustomed to Olivia's story didn't think was important, but trying to figure out the truth was better than sitting passively in the studio playing sunshine songs while vandals and murderers closed in. If she ever wanted peace of mind—and safety—she needed resolution to these crimes. If she wanted it, she ought to work for it.

"You must have been bored out of your mind tonight if you're coming to visit me." Renee's wrinkles looked deeper, her skin more slack and pale, her posture droopier. Catherine wondered if stress had doubled the tempo of aging for all of them.

"I'm not bored," Catherine said. "But I do want company." She held out the box to Renee. "I hope you don't have nut allergies."

"What do you think you need to bring me another present for?"

Catherine smiled. "You're welcome."

Renee took the box. "You don't have to bribe your way in." She looked at the label. "Dark chocolate–covered almonds. Let's eat 'em."

They sat on Renee's couch with the open box of chocolates on the table in front of them. "Heard about everything." Renee took an almond. "I'm sorry about Maren Gates. Horrible. But I knew this was coming. I knew someone was going to die."

"She's not dead."

"Someone tried to kill her."

"Do you know Maren?"

"Yeah. She's a sweetheart. Doesn't whine and demand things, and believe me, some parents do. Not that Maren was a parent—she tended her niece."

"Do you know her husband?"

"Yeah. He did some painting at the school. Worked for a local contractor . . . can't remember who."

"What do you think of him?"

"Reliable and all that. I know Danielle was happy with his work." She narrowed her eyes. "Are you wondering if he's the one who clonked Maren on the head? Like he was abusing her and finally did her in?"

"Yes," Catherine admitted. "But it's only a theory."

Renee picked up another almond. "If he was smacking Maren around, I never heard any rumors. I never saw Maren with a black eye or anything."

Catherine thought of Dylan's angry accusation that Catherine was using the studio as a front to help Maren see another man. "Did you . . . ever hear any rumors about Maren? Like that she was . . . involved in anything she didn't want Dylan to know about?"

Renee snorted. "Do you have a dirty mind, girl? Why would you think that?"

Catherine wondered why the color of her face ever bothered to return to normal these days. She was embarrassing herself so constantly that she might as well stick with perpetual crimson. "No good reason."

"Are you asking if she was cheating on him and her boyfriend is the one who tried to kill her? Can't imagine Maren would do something like that—she seemed real nice and responsible. But who knows?"

Who knows. The truth was, Catherine knew very little about Maren. Troubled and embarrassed, she decided to turn the subject away from the Gates family. "How are *you* doing?"

Renee shrugged. "Okay. I walked by Olivia's apartment yesterday. The glass is fixed, and when I peeked inside, I saw that the wall had been repainted."

Catherine's knee-jerk reaction was to label it creepy that Renee had been peering into Olivia's window again, but she probably wouldn't feel that way if Kelsey hadn't suggested Renee might have vandalized the apartment herself. After all, when Renee had originally told her about leaving flowers at Olivia's apartment, she'd thought it was sweet.

"I'm glad it's been repaired," Catherine said, wanting to handle the subject in a way that would lower Renee's guard and build her trust in Catherine. "You must miss Olivia all the time. And it must be even more painful when you see her murder fading out of people's memories . . . the case turning cold at the police department . . . people moving on when Olivia never had justice."

"*Yes.*" Renee grasped Catherine's arm, her fingers pinching. "Yes, *exactly.* It's like people cared for a while, but they couldn't stick with it long enough to punish whoever did this."

"That's so frustrating."

Renee yanked her hand back as though embarrassed at having grabbed Catherine. "During the first year after Olivia died, I'd call the police every few weeks asking for updates, and they'd tell me they didn't know anything. After a while, it was obvious they weren't even looking anymore—they were just trying to get me off the phone."

Catherine decided not to point out that even if the police *did* have information, they weren't likely to give it to everyone who called asking for it.

"Even her family started brushing me off when I asked about any new developments," Renee added.

"Even Trent? He still seems intent on catching the killer."

Renee shook her head. "Trent is intent on catching the killer as long as the killer is Adam Becket. He's not interested in exploring other ideas. Have more chocolate, Catie; you're not eating your share."

Catie. A nickname was a good sign—Renee was feeling a bond with her. Catherine took another almond. "I imagine the only thing that could have generated interest in her case again is the fear that the killer is back." She searched Renee's eyes for a hint of guilt—or triumph—indicating that Kelsey was right in her suspicions.

Renee's eyes were sad. "Yeah, that's how people work, huh? Scared for their own necks, so they finally care about Olivia again. But even with all the garbage that's happened, people don't want to face the truth—like *you,* kiddo, hoping Maren's husband is the one who hurt her, because that's an answer that will let you sleep at night. You know darn well it wasn't Dylan. It was whoever killed Olivia. He's back. I knew this was coming. Once someone started smashing up Flinders, I knew this was coming. But no one wants to believe there's a serial killer in town."

"Did Olivia ever mention Dylan? Is it possible there was a connection between them?"

"You think he killed Olivia? That *he's* the serial killer?"

"They might have met each other at the gym Trent owns."

Renee's eyes gleamed, and her eyebrows arched. She tapped her fingers on her knee. "I can't recall her ever mentioning his name."

"Did she ever talk about getting pursued by a married man?"

"She was a lovely girl. A lot of men tried to flirt with her, but she'd shrug them off. Did Dylan chase her or something? I think she would have told me if he had because she trusted me. I was like her mother."

Appalled to realize she was spreading a 100 percent unfounded rumor, Catherine said, "I have absolutely no reason for accusing Dylan of anything to do with Olivia. I'm trying to figure out who killed her, and obviously Dylan has a connection with the second victim. I wondered if he had a connection with the first."

Renee sighed, the interest in her face dying out. "Olivia would have told me if a married man had started chasing her. She would have thought he was a creep."

Catherine reached for another chocolate-covered almond. "How well did Olivia get along with Trent?"

"You suspect *Trent*?"

"I'm trying to learn as much about the situation as I can. I don't know who to suspect."

"She griped about Trent a lot—how he treated her like a kid and tried to tell her what to do. But she never *really* seemed mad at him—she'd laugh about how he couldn't figure out she wasn't six years old."

If Olivia was laughing about it, were her problems with Trent likely to run deep enough to provoke Trent to murder?

What about the vandalism? If Renee was the vandal, wouldn't she have been shocked when Maren was attacked—shocked that a *real* attempted murder had followed her fake messages? Wouldn't she look more caught by surprise?

Or was she an excellent actress?

"You're scared," Renee said. "That's why you're asking all these questions."

"Of course I'm scared. Everyone in Riley is scared."

"Maren didn't die. The killer won't be satisfied. He'll strike again and do it right."

"Maybe not. Maybe Maren didn't die because he got scared for some reason and didn't finish the attack. Maybe he'll lie low."

"You don't believe that."

"I . . . *want* to believe it."

"I told you from the beginning. I warned you the minute you walked into Flinders, right into the middle of broken glass. Broken windows right where Olivia used to sit. I could sense it right then. I tried to tell myself I was wrong—you're young and pretty, but other than that, you don't look at all like Olivia. She had dark hair. Yours is red. She had olive skin. Yours is pale. Her eyes were hazel. Yours are blue. But next thing I knew, you were involved with Adam Becket. Just like Olivia."

"Wait—I—who told you that?"

"I hear things. You start dating Adam, taking Olivia's place. I thought you were stuck-up and wouldn't waste your time on me, but you showed up at my door, like Olivia. You even brought pasta like Olivia. You *are* Olivia all over again. I think Maren Gates was a mistake. I think the killer thought she was you."

"*What?*"

"She was near your studio, carrying a musical instrument. It was dark and raining, and you and Maren are about the same size, aren't you? And you walk everywhere. People know that; they see you walking. It was supposed to be you. The killer's going to try again. To him, you're Olivia."

Catherine's heart pounded like crazy. Maren . . . walking near the studio . . .

Maren had been wearing Catherine's raincoat. That distinctive bright, red-and-blue lobster raincoat. Catherine had been so upset by the attack on Maren that she'd forgotten about the coat. It hadn't rained since the night of the attack, so she hadn't noticed it missing from her closet.

It was supposed to be you.

The raincoat. She'd worn it all over Riley—and it was memorable. If the killer had seen a woman in that raincoat, hood up, carrying a flute case, walking in the rain—

Catherine felt sick.

Stop it. Why would someone target you? Your coat doesn't have anything to do with it.

How in the world could Renee "sense" you'd be the next victim the moment she saw you? She's trying to spook you—or she's so spooked herself that she's not being rational. And if she is the vandal, she isn't *rational.*

How disturbed *was* Renee?

Are you kidding? Renee Endicott as the murderer? Why would she kill a woman she loved like a daughter?

But if a killer was completely psychotic, she wouldn't need a reason that made sense to anyone else.

Stop it. Hands clammy, Catherine took another chocolate almond, not because she wanted it but because she needed something to give her an excuse not to look at Renee. Was Renee warning her? Or threatening her?

She couldn't have killed Olivia. Or attacked Maren.

Could she? Renee was overweight, and she wasn't young, but a person didn't have to be an agile athlete to sneak up behind someone and club them over the head.

This was the first time in Catherine's life that she'd found chocolate hard to eat. She swallowed hard, pushing the almond down her dry throat. *You can't possibly be this paranoid.*

She didn't know Renee very well. She didn't know Trent very well or Kelsey or Will or even Adam. She'd thought having an outsider's perspective might give her an advantage. Instead, it made her unable to trust anyone. Was she sitting on the couch eating candy with a woman who, beneath her prickly, sarcastic exterior, was murderously insane?

"I shouldn't have said anything." Renee grasped Catherine's wrist. "You're all pale. But I had to warn you. If you want to save your life, get out of Riley fast. Do it secretly. If you tell anyone, you might be tipping off the murderer. You'll never make it to the airport alive."

Renee's fingers curling around Catherine's wrist made Catherine want to shriek and jerk away from her.

"I don't want you to leave. It's nice to have a friend again. Doesn't happen often." The bitterness in her voice overshadowed the sadness. "But I don't want you to die."

Catherine tugged her wrist out of Renee's grip, trying not to reveal how frightened she was. "I'll think about it." She kept her voice even. "You're right. Coming to Riley was a mistake. I should leave."

Renee snickered. "Good thing you're not teaching drama, girl. You stink as an actress. You're not going to leave. You're stubborn, like Olivia. I warned her it was stupid to get involved with Will. I warned her she was betraying a good man who didn't deserve that garbage from her, but she dug in her heels. You dig in your heels too, don't you?"

"I'm only stubborn when I'm being stubborn over a good idea. I'd better head home. It's been a long day." She reached for her purse, hoping she didn't appear to be hurrying—or panicking.

"Don't leave yet." Renee sagged against the faded red couch. "You don't want to be home alone at your studio."

"I've hired a security guard. He'll be keeping a close eye on the place." Catherine didn't specify that she'd only hired him for the night shift. She should hire someone for daytime as well.

"Stay a little longer. I know it's stuffy in here—I've been too nervous to open the windows all day—but we could go for a drive. We could stop by the supermarket and get some carnations. You'd probably like to leave flowers on Olivia's doorstep."

Why would Renee think she would want to leave flowers? Had she cast Catherine so firmly in her mind as Olivia's successor that she'd forgotten Catherine had never even known Olivia? "That's a sweet thought, but I'd better get home." She stood, tense and ready to run if Renee lunged at her.

Renee rose but didn't move toward Catherine. Her eyes were bleary. "Be careful," she said. "Be very careful."

"I will." Without waiting for Renee to show her out, Catherine rushed toward the door, exited Renee's apartment, and ran to her car.

CHAPTER 19

"THANKS FOR LETTING ME COME over," Catherine said softly. "I'm sorry to bother you. I don't want to disturb your father . . . I'm sorry . . . When I called you, I didn't realize you were staying here at night now . . ."

"Catherine." Adam touched her shoulder. Catherine bit the inside of her cheek and stopped babbling. Adam's eyes were bloodshot, his hair was sticking up on one side, and a book lay open on the floor next to the couch. Guiltily, she read the clues: he'd dozed off early until her panicky phone call had awakened him.

"I'm glad you called," Adam said. "Dad is asleep, and with the medication he takes at night, nothing could wake him. I appreciate the company. Please come sit down and tell me what's wrong."

She managed a smile. "I promise not to cry this time."

"It's okay if you do."

"I'm usually a stable person. I swear." How many times had she said that to him? Did she think repetition would make him believe it?

"Did something else happen at the studio?"

Catherine's mouth was so dry that even swallowing didn't do much to moisten it. "No, the studio's fine. Lewis Peralta will be there tonight working security. How . . . is your father doing?" If Dale had consented to let Adam stay with him at night, had his health deteriorated to the point that he was too weak to protest Adam's hovering?

"He's a little more tired," Adam said, and Catherine had the feeling he was soft-pedaling his answer. "My brothers and I ganged up on him and finally convinced him he either needed to let me stay with him at night or hire a nighttime health aide. He chose me—'the devil you know,' I suppose."

"I'm sorry he's doing worse."

"He's not too bad. He'll be annoyed that he missed visiting with you tonight." Adam studied her, his brow creasing. "What's wrong?"

Catherine tried to think where to start. *I'm scared sick? I've never felt so lonely in my life? I keep thinking everyone around me is a potential murderer? I don't know if Renee is warning me or threatening to kill me? A woman I thought was my good friend thinks I'm a selfish brat, and I'm afraid she's right? I want to go back to Virginia, but I can't quit?*

"Let's sit down." Adam's voice was so kind that Catherine knew the maelstrom of fear, confusion, and pain was showing in her face.

"Yes . . . good idea." That was the second time he'd invited her to sit; she shouldn't keep standing nervously by the front door as though planning to flee. Catherine eyed the couch. She should march over there, sit down, rationally present the problems she was dealing with, and seek Adam's advice.

Or maybe she could collapse on the floor and have a complete breakdown.

"Catherine." Adam rested his hands on her shoulders. His mouth was a little crooked even when he wasn't smiling. She hadn't noticed that before.

With a small, hesitant gesture, he tugged very lightly on her shoulders—an invitation, given subtly so she was free to accept it or step away without leaving too much awkwardness between them.

She stepped forward and clung to him.

Adam's arms went around her, one hand on her lower back and one between her shoulders, supporting her. Breathing slowly, fighting to keep her vow not to cry, Catherine closed her eyes and rested her head on his shoulder.

She should back away. She should say something light, joke about needing a hug since the last person to hug her had been Ava the morning she'd left Virginia and she was getting desperate. But she couldn't make herself talk. Or step away from the warmth of his arms.

"If there's anything I can do to help you, I will," Adam said.

Catherine rallied. "Thank you." She stepped back. "I . . . hope I haven't . . . scared you off. Again."

"You haven't scared me off. Have I scared you off?"

"No. We're a skittish pair, aren't we?"

He grinned. "Guess so."

"I . . . Adam . . . I hope you don't think I . . . I know I keep calling you and dumping stress on you, and I don't want you to think that's the only reason . . ." Deciding to skip the dithering and go with forthrightness, she said, "If I didn't have a nervous breakdown as an excuse, I'd be coming up with another reason to call you."

"You don't need an excuse. The only reason I'm not calling *you* constantly is because I don't want to push too hard and scare you away."

"I'm not scared. I mean—I *am* scared of almost everything, hence the nervous breakdown, but I'm not scared of you calling. Call me anytime."

"I will."

Blushing, Catherine tried for a new subject. "It smells wonderful in here. What have you been cooking?"

"Just mulled cider. Dad loves it in the fall. He can't drink much of it, but he still loves the smell in the air. Cinnamon, cloves, orange slices. Would you like some?"

"Please."

Adam walked into the kitchen and returned with two filled mugs. They sat on the couch and Catherine told him about her visit with Renee. "She gave me the chills. I walked in there thinking it was far-fetched to believe she was the vandal and walked out—I fled, actually—wondering if she was . . ."

"The murderer."

"I'm paranoid. I know that. But she seemed to *want* to frighten me. The things she said about my being Olivia all over again were chilling. She was that way when I first met her—she talked about Olivia and how I was about her age and how I'd better be careful. I thought she was trying to scare me because she wasn't happy about my music program—she thought it was some snobbish hobby I was foisting on them. But now, when I thought we'd become friends, she went spooky again, only worse." Catherine took a sip of mulled cider, hoping it could magically calm her down in addition to moistening her dry mouth. "And suggesting the killer thought Maren was me . . . Adam . . . I'd forgotten about the raincoat. I was so shaken over what happened to Maren that I forgot she was wearing my coat. What if the killer *did* think she was me? She *would* look like me in that coat, with her face hidden. If the killer had seen me in that coat, he—or she—would have remembered it. It's not exactly generic looking."

The troubled look on Adam's face chilled her further. She'd hoped he'd say she was overreacting and why would the killer target her? Instead, he said, "Has Renee seen you in that coat?"

"Yes. I remember wearing it to Flinders. I've worn it all over Riley, what with all the rain we've had."

Adam set his mug aside. His worried expression became remote, as though his attention had shifted to thoughts he didn't want to share with Catherine. She waited, hoping he would speak, but he remained quiet.

"You've known Renee for a while," Catherine prompted, unable to stand the silence. "What do you think of her?"

"Good question. I like Renee. Beneath the spiky armor, she's funny. Loyal—stands up for people she cares about, helps them out. Olivia really liked her."

"From what I've heard of Olivia, she seems like a very different personality from Renee."

"Yes, they were different in a lot of ways, but they complemented each other. Balanced each other. Olivia didn't have a close relationship with her parents. Her dad lives out of state, and she had a rocky relationship with her mother and her stepfather, so she didn't visit her mother much. Olivia and Renee seemed to fill each other's needs."

"Olivia wanted a friend and a mother figure, and Renee wanted a friend and a daughter?"

"Yes." Adam picked up a porcelain statue of a fisherman that stood on the lamp table and absently rubbed dust off the statue's hat. "If you're asking if Renee could have killed Olivia herself . . . that's hard to believe. I can believe she's troubled—troubled enough to try to scare you. Maybe even troubled enough to be responsible for the vandalism. But I don't think she's troubled enough to kill anyone, especially Olivia. But sometimes you think you understand a person, and later you find out you misread them. I can't read Renee's mind."

Catherine sipped her cider, debating what to say next. She might as well tell him everything. "I talked to Kelsey Perry. She told me about the history between you and Trent."

Adam set the statue down so abruptly that Catherine feared he'd cracked the porcelain. "What did she tell you?"

"About the bike accident Trent caused."

"Kelsey told you about that?"

"She said Trent didn't dare admit fault and apologize for fear you'd sue him."

Adam touched the scars next to the paralyzed corner of his mouth. "I wouldn't have sued him. What good would that do? It was an accident."

"She did say he felt horrible about it."

"I'm surprised she was that candid with you."

"She wanted me to understand why Trent acts like he does. And she said you deserve a break and she didn't want Trent scaring me away from you."

He raised an eyebrow. "I appreciate that."

"She also said Trent encouraged Olivia to date you—that Trent pushed her into calling you that first time."

Adam's mouth twisted in a melancholy grin. "Yeah, I know that. Olivia told me straight out when she invited me to that first dance."

"She told you?"

"She said she needed a date to the regional Christmas dance and her brother said to call Adam Becket and he wouldn't take no for an answer, so would I please go with her to get him off her case?"

"What kind of approach is *that*?"

"Unusual."

But it worked for Olivia, Catherine thought. She imagined darling Olivia making her invitation in a fun, flirty voice. "You weren't bothered that Trent was behind it?"

"I wanted to go out with Olivia. And I didn't know if she meant that about pressure from Trent or if it was a way for her to feel less nervous in approaching me. Twenty-first century or not, some women are still shy about initiating dates."

"Kelsey said Trent did push her. Kelsey thought Trent was trying to assuage his guilt by making something good happen in your life through Olivia."

Adam fingered the fishing pole in the statue's hand. "Did he keep pushing her?"

Catherine regretted that she hadn't handled this more carefully. Adam wouldn't appreciate the implication that Olivia had gone out with him under pressure. "He was glad when you two hit it off, but it was her choice. He got angry with Olivia when she started seeing Will, furious that she was jeopardizing things with you."

Adam rose to his feet. He walked to the window behind the couch and closed it. "Should have closed that a long time ago," he said. "Once the sun goes down, it gets cold fast."

She'd upset him. "I wasn't implying that Olivia only went out with you because Trent wanted her to. If that's how it sounded, I'm sorry."

Adam lowered the blinds. "No, it makes sense. I'm not saying I think Olivia was gritting her teeth and enduring my company because Trent was twisting her arm. But I can see her dating me partly because it's what Trent wanted. They bickered, but deep down, I think she wanted to please him. Olivia leaned a lot on her big brother. There were no other great options at the moment, and she liked me all right, so why not?"

"You're not giving yourself enough credit."

"The way she acted about Will made it clear she hadn't found what she was looking for in me." The hardness in Adam's voice made Catherine wish she hadn't brought this up at all.

"Trent obviously has issues." She tried to redirect the angle of the conversation. "He felt guilty about what he did to you, but he didn't have the strength of character to own up, and eventually he flipped around and decided you were so warped by anger and jealousy that you murdered Olivia. Maybe he's projecting his own twisted emotions onto you."

Adam still stood near the closed window, facing half away from Catherine, his posture stiff. "The problem with everything we've talked about is that we have no proof and no way of getting proof. The police have asked all these questions already, but they haven't found enough evidence to arrest anyone. Unless someone decides to confess, or whoever attacked Maren made a mistake the police can latch on to, I don't see how we're going to make any progress."

Great job, Catherine. In trying to share what she'd learned, she hadn't offered anything useful. All she'd accomplished was to stir up Adam's pain and make him feel inadequate. Saying bluntly that Trent had "pushed" Olivia to call him . . . asking him if he was bothered about Trent's role . . . she'd been worse than tactless. She'd been callous, oblivious.

"I'm sorry," Catherine said. "You're right. I'm so sorry I brought this up."

"Don't worry about it." Adam turned to face her. "Did you ever talk to Danielle?"

That was *not* where she wanted the conversation to go. "Yes."

"Did you work things out?"

"More or less," Catherine said, not adding, *And I'm afraid she's right about me.*

"What did she say?"

Catherine folded her arms and stared at the large family portrait above the piano, trying to relax the knot in her throat. This was the last thing she wanted to discuss with Adam right now, but exhaustion, discouragement, and guilt were shorting out her brain, leaving her unable to think of a lighthearted way to downplay the tension between her and Danielle. "She's sticking to her opinion that I'm a self-centered princess with commitment phobia," Catherine said flatly. "No offense to me though. She still values our friendship."

Adam sat on the couch. "That's what she told you?"

"She's wrong about the commitment issues, but maybe she's right about everything else. I don't know. Maybe I am what she thinks, and I'm the only one blind to it." *Perfect. Melodrama. Now you can cry again.*

She blinked and stood up. After the thoughtless way she'd talked to Adam tonight, how could he *not* think Danielle was right about her self-centered worldview? "I need to go. I'm stressing both of us out, and I need to get home to meet with Lewis before he starts his shift."

Adam stood. "Don't leave. Please."

Catherine hesitated. She doubted Adam truly wanted her to stay after the tension she'd created. He was being polite. But if she ignored his request and rushed out, she'd leave him thinking she was being dramatic in hopes he'd chase after her. "I'd better go," she said tightly. "Or we're going to have Niagara Falls, part two."

"Do you always run away when you think your emotions are escaping your control?"

"I don't know what's wrong with me. I feel like I'm losing my mind."

"I'm not sure why Danielle thinks you've had such an easy life. You lost your father less than a year ago. And your mother was already gone."

Catherine closed her eyes. "Adam, don't do this. I'll cry, and you've had enough of that."

"I'm starting to figure out how much it hurts. As Dad gets sicker and sicker, I'm feeling it."

The tears began to flow. Catherine gritted her teeth.

"Then you move to a new town and get hammered with reports of a murder and warnings that you're in danger, all while you're struggling to launch your studio. Then one of your students is nearly killed, you're scared to trust anyone, and to top it all off, a longtime friend—"

"I don't think she meant to hurt me." Catherine swiped tears away with her fingertips. "She was calling things like she saw them, and she was honestly worried for you."

"I owe you an apology for bringing up what she said. That was a selfish thing for me to do."

"No, I'm glad you told me. And . . . maybe she's right. Partially, at least. I *am* too self-focused. Look at me tonight, rattling on about Olivia, oblivious to how much that hurts you when—"

"Catherine, no, don't feel you can't—"

"And I *do* care too much what people think of me. I *did* hope all of Riley would love and admire me for my wonderful program."

"Did she say that to you?"

"I was trying to use my noble, charitable program to prove I wasn't a self-centered brat, and she made the point that my motives weren't exactly pure charity."

"I don't think—"

"No, she's right. I *did* want people to be grateful to me for coming here. I *did* want to be honored for it. I didn't realize it, but now that she's pointed it out, I can see it. It's true."

"If it is, so what? How many people do you know who've reached the point where they don't care at all about being appreciated or honored for their hard work and skill? You're putting a lot into this program. It doesn't make you self-centered if you were hoping people would appreciate that."

It was more than just wanting to be appreciated, but she didn't feel like analyzing her feelings in front of Adam. She was ashamed enough already. "I'm sorry about tonight. If I sneak out now, can we mentally delete this evening and start over another day?"

He smiled. He still looked tired and pale, but he no longer looked tense. "Let's start over now. Would you like a refill on the cider? Let's talk about something not related to Riley. Tell me about your dad."

CHAPTER 20

CATHERINE WAS SMILING AS SHE closed the garage door and walked into the studio. She felt better than she'd felt for . . . how long? She hadn't realized how much she was trapping inside until Adam's questions got her talking, crying, laughing, spilling out memories of her parents. She'd stayed so long she barely made it home in time. Lewis was due in five minutes.

It made her grin wider to think about how much she'd enjoyed being with Adam. He was kind. He was thoughtful. He was patient with her insensitive blunders. He had a fun, low-key sense of humor. For all the bad she'd encountered in Riley, it was hard to wish she hadn't come when she thought about Adam.

Get a grip, she lectured herself as she fixed her eye make-up in the master bathroom. *He's a good listener, and he's fun to be with, but it's a little early to send out wedding announcements.*

Talking with Adam had pulled her out of the crazy diversion into fear and violence that had dominated her time in Riley and had planted her feet back on the ground of real life. She'd panicked too quickly and had let herself become far too obsessed with Olivia's murder and the idea that she needed to take action regarding it. The police would solve the case—both the attack on Maren and Olivia's death. There was nothing Catherine could do or needed to do about it except pray for Maren—and she didn't need to live in terror either, Renee's warnings aside. Renee was a troubled, lonely woman still mourning Olivia. The fact that Maren had been wearing Catherine's raincoat didn't mean Catherine had been the intended target or that she'd be the next target. If someone wanted to attack Catherine, why not come to the studio? Why wait for her to leave home? Maren had either been a random victim or a victim of domestic violence.

Catherine would be careful, of course—no more walking alone at night, she'd keep the house alarm set at all times when she was home alone, and she'd keep her security guard on duty at night—but she wasn't going to live in fear. She would do what she came here to do—concentrate on making the music studio a wild success, blessing the lives of her students.

She headed briskly down the stairs. She also wanted to get to know Adam better. *And* she was going to figure out how to mend fences with Danielle so the friendship didn't end up poisoned by resentment—either hers or Danielle's. Danielle had been wrong to go behind her back in talking to Adam, and she had a somewhat skewed view of Catherine, but she *had* been right on some counts. Catherine *was* too self-centered. Much as it stung to hear Danielle say it, better to hurt now when she could fix the problem than hurt later when Catherine had driven Adam away or done other damage in her life. If she was too weak to take criticism and correct problems, she wasn't worthy to be a Clayton.

She reviewed her checklist of what she wanted to discuss with Lewis. She'd had the gardeners clean out the prefab storage shed in the backyard, and she'd put a desk in there so Lewis could use it as a temporary guard shack until she could arrange for a permanent structure, complete with heat and electricity. Between tall, muscular Lewis pacing the yard at regular intervals and her alarm system, she wouldn't worry at all tonight.

Everything would work out. The fear would end. She'd be happy in Riley. The students whose parents had withdrawn them from the program would return, given a little time, and new students would come as well. If only Maren . . . Catherine chewed her lip and looked at the flute case she'd set on her desk. Maren's flute—Detective Burgess had given it to her. She'd tried to get permission to visit Maren, but the hospital said no visitors were allowed. Catherine didn't know if that order had come from the police or Maren's husband or both. *Please let her recover.*

The phone rang. Recognizing the name on the caller ID as the surname of one of her trumpet students, she picked up the phone. "Hello, this is Catherine."

"This is Tessa Barrister, Ella Barrister's mother." The woman's voice sounded tremulous, and Catherine's heart sank. Had something bad happened to Ella? *Please no.*

"What can I do for you, Mrs. Barrister?"

"Ella won't . . . she won't be coming to your studio anymore. We're too busy. She has a lot of homework this year. She doesn't have time."

Catherine inhaled slowly and silently. "I'm sorry to hear that. Ella has great potential, and she loves the trumpet."

"School has to come first."

"Mrs. Barrister, I'm sorry to be intrusive, but is school the problem, or are you concerned about the sad incident that took place near the studio?"

"Ella is too *busy*. School has to come first."

Click.

Exhaling, Catherine hung up and looked at the blinking message light. Three new messages. Three more students dropping out? She wouldn't be running a studio anymore. She'd be sponsoring a ghost town.

Calm down. What happened to your optimism? It'll be okay. People are panicky now, but they'll return once they realize what happened to Maren isn't contagious.

Before she could listen to the messages, the doorbell rang. Glad to have an excuse to put off listening to bad news, Catherine went to let Lewis in.

The sight of handsome, burly Lewis on the porch made Catherine smile. Let some cowardly creep try to get past *him*.

"Hi, Lewis. Come on in."

"Um . . . thanks." The hesitation in his voice and the tentative way he stepped across her threshold made Catherine's satisfaction wilt. Why did he look so nervous?

Wonderful. I have a linebacker of a security guard who looks scared at the prospect of talking to his boss. I can't wait to see how he deals with actual trouble.

"Come sit down," Catherine said, hoping she was misreading Lewis. "There are a few things I want to go over, and then I'll take you on the tour."

Lewis sat on the couch, his posture stiff and his gaze not meeting hers. She *hadn't* misread him—he *was* nervous. Bleakly, Catherine thought of how Jan would feel when her son got fired before he even started work. But Lewis hadn't seemed nervous when she'd talked to him about the job. He'd seemed excited, confident, capable.

Maybe he doesn't know how to act one-on-one with you at your house. You're a single woman. He's a good-looking guy. You're not that much older than he is, and he probably feels this is a weird situation, working for you. Give him a chance to get comfortable.

"May I get you something to drink?" Catherine asked. "Hot chocolate on a cold autumn night?"

"No, thanks." He reached down and picked a damp fragment of leaf off his shoe. "Sister Clayton . . . um . . ."

"Catherine." She sat in her father's recliner. "Are you all right? You look nervous. I'm not *that* cruel of an employer."

He gave a fake chuckle. "Yeah, I know. Um . . . listen . . . people are saying weird stuff about your studio."

"I know people are apprehensive after Maren Gates and the vandalism," Catherine said, puzzled at the way Lewis was squirming. Why was he acting like this was new information? Why did he think she'd hired him in the first place? "Are you changing your mind about working here?"

"Um . . . I was . . . over at a friend's house today. When I told him I was working security for Bridgeside Studio, his mother overheard, and she . . . kinda freaked out."

Catherine tried to figure out why another mother's worry would shake Lewis when Jan had been fine with things. "I realize a job as a security guard is not risk free, but you've done this type of work before, and when we talked, you seemed confident you could handle any problems. If you don't want the job, then say so. I'll look elsewhere."

Lewis messed with the zipper on his jacket, tugging at it. "His mother told me there are . . . problems here."

The embarrassment in his voice was so stark that it was obvious he wasn't talking about Maren or anything else Catherine had already discussed with him. Dylan's ludicrous accusations of enabling women in cheating on their husbands crossed her mind. "What kind of problems?"

"That the . . . reason you can afford to give all these free lessons is because the studio is . . . funded by drug money."

"*What?*"

He spoke quickly, as though the faster he could spit the words out, the less awkward it would be. "She said someone—she didn't know who—had researched you and that you've done this before under a different name but had to leave town when the police started to figure out what was going on. The deal you have going is that in exchange for the funding, you'll get a certain number of kids addicted and a certain number of kids selling."

Catherine was so flabbergasted that she couldn't speak.

"It . . . sounded crazy. But she was . . . sure it was true."

Breathe deeply. Stay calm. "That is the most ridiculous thing I've heard in my life."

"Yeah," Lewis said. "It's . . . totally ridiculous. When Tyson . . . my friend . . . told his mom how much you were paying me, she said that was more proof—no way could anyone but a drug cartel pay that kind of wages to a security guy."

Catherine wished she could laugh, but she felt like her brain was going to shatter. So much for feeling generous when she'd offered Lewis twice what security guards normally made. Lewis didn't think the accusations were "totally ridiculous." He was upset. He wanted the job, but he was scared he'd been hired by a drug pusher.

"What else did she say?" Catherine struggled to keep her tone matter-of-fact.

"Just that her source was reliable and how could you fund this fancy studio and all those instruments and free lessons without illegal money? No real donors would support something like that in this economy. And why would you come to a cruddy place like Riley unless you had . . . other reasons?"

"Let me guess," Catherine said. "I'm the one who attacked Maren. I tried to kill her because she found out what was really going on here."

"It's dumb, isn't it?" Lewis was sitting tensely on the edge of the couch cushion. Catherine wondered if he was preparing himself to dive for cover in case she pulled a gun and told him he knew too much and she'd have to kill him.

"What is Tyson's mother's name?" she asked.

"Uh . . . she wouldn't want me to say. Not because I think you'd . . . I mean it's . . ."

"Never mind. I don't want you thinking I'll go burn her house down. I'm just trying to figure out where this rumor started."

"I didn't really believe her."

"Okay." *Breathe deeply. Your mind's already gone, but don't lose your temper too.* "Here's what you need to know. I have never and would never get involved with drugs in any way, and to suggest that I would give them to children is so insulting that I don't even know how to respond. I am here for one reason: to share my love of music with anyone who'd like to learn. As for the funding—*I* fund the studio." Forget nebulous talk of backers; Catherine was too angry to be anything but candid. "Myself. I fund it. My father is Jeremy Clayton. Tell your friend's mother to Google his name, and she'll see why I have enough money to run something like this. As for why I came to Riley, I wanted an area that could particularly benefit from the program, and I had a personal connection here. If your friend's mother would like to call me, I'd be happy to speak with her. I'd like that much better than hearing secondhand that she's spreading rumors about me." Her and who else? How widespread was this absurd rumor, and where had it come from? The parents who'd pulled their kids out—had they heard the rumor too? She'd thought they were scared that Maren's attacker might be lurking around the studio. Were they instead scared that Catherine *was* Maren's attacker?

"Sorry," Lewis said. "It's stupid."

Catherine clenched her jaw. Part of her wanted to yell at Lewis to get out; if he was uncertain enough of her to get shaken up by these crazy rumors, fine, go home, and she'd find another security guard.

She restrained her anger. Why *shouldn't* he be uncertain? He didn't know her. Terrible things *had* happened at or near the studio. "You can also tell your friend that parents are always welcome to remain with their child for every minute of every lesson here at the studio. Everything here is open. No secrets. Lewis, I understand if you don't want to work here. Even if you don't believe the rumors, some people will, and I'll understand if you don't want to be associated with Bridgeside."

Lewis shook his head. "No, I want the job." His voice sounded firmer, and Catherine could tell he was feeling better. She'd done a reasonable job of not acting like a drug-pushing demon.

"I'd appreciate it if you'd let me know if you get any hint of where these rumors started, because there's someone in Riley I need to talk to," she said.

Lewis nodded, but Catherine doubted she'd ever get a name out of him.

"Would you like some character recommendations?" she asked. "I could give you the name of my former bishop. Or my neighbors who knew me when I was a kid."

"That's okay."

"I'm sorry your friend's mom gave you a hard time. Not fun for you."

He shrugged. "Nothing's much fun these days."

Catherine thought of what Jan had told her about Lewis's friendship with Olivia and Jan's suspicion that Lewis had had a crush on her. Catherine vowed to be sensitive to his feelings when she made any reference to Olivia or the possibility that Olivia's killer was back. She would *not* be oblivious like she'd been with Adam earlier this evening.

"If you ever hear anything else strange about the studio or about me, please come immediately to me with the information," Catherine said. "I promise not to shoot the messenger."

"Okay."

The phone messages she hadn't listened to. Did any of those messages mention the rumors? "Excuse me," Catherine said. "I need to check something." She hurried into her study, grabbed the phone, and listened to her messages.

Three more cancellations from nervous-sounding parents.

CHAPTER 21

CATHERINE SPENT MORE TIME PACING than she did sleeping. Thank heavens Lewis had decided to stay on the job, but she worried he'd take flack for working for her. The rumors were so ludicrous that it was hard to believe anyone could take them seriously, but given the fear permeating Riley, the fact that Catherine was new and unknown, the attack on one of her students, and the protectiveness of parents where their children were concerned, maybe it wasn't surprising that people gave credence to the absurd.

After breakfast, she called Detective Nancy Burgess. If rumors had reached the police, the police obviously didn't think there was enough grounds to talk to Catherine about the gossip, but she wanted to get Burgess's take on the situation.

"Yes, we've had a few people call us," Burgess confirmed. "I'm sorry you've been the target of ugly rumors. People often react irrationally to fear."

"Does anyone offer any so-called evidence against me?"

"No. It's all 'a friend of a friend told me.'"

"You've checked me out, I assume?" Catherine asked.

"We checked you out before this," Burgess said dryly. "If it helps, we've told anyone who calls that the rumors are groundless."

"It helps. Thank you. Do you have any idea where the rumors started?"

"I don't. If anyone knows, they won't say."

"Probably because they're afraid my drug-running buddies will shoot them in their sleep if they squeal."

"Catherine, if anything new happens—any problems at all—please keep me informed. We're keeping an eye on your studio—you've probably noticed patrol cars in the neighborhood."

"I appreciate that. And I've hired a security guard to watch the place at night."

"Someone you're sure you trust?"

"Yes. Also . . . I forgot to tell you this before, but the coat Maren Gates was wearing when she was attacked belongs to me. It was raining that night, and she'd forgotten her coat. I don't know if that . . . makes a difference." Catherine felt her heartbeat accelerating as new fear squeezed past the temporary confidence she'd gained in talking to Adam.

"It was *your* raincoat?" Burgess asked.

"Yes."

A pause followed. Catherine swallowed and moistened her lips.

"That's a very distinctive coat," Burgess said.

"That's a nice word for it."

Another pause. Catherine paced across the kitchen and stopped in front of the sliding door.

"Have you worn the coat lately?" Burgess asked.

The question sent adrenaline prickling along Catherine's nerves. There was only one reason Burgess would ask that. "Yes. I've worn it a lot. All over Riley. Do you . . . think there's any significance to the fact that Maren was wearing my coat?"

"I don't know. But I'm concerned. We have some information we've never released concerning the attack."

Light-headed, Catherine gripped the handle to the sliding door, bracing herself. "What information?"

"Please keep this strictly confidential."

"I will."

"The wound on Maren's head is unusual in shape, made with a distinctive weapon. According to the medical report, the injury on Mrs. Gates matches the wounds found on Olivia Perry. There's a high probability that these two women were attacked with the same object."

Catherine's skin went clammy, and her knees felt weak. The weapon that killed Olivia? The elaborate wrought-iron vase that Trent and Adam had described?

"I'm not trying to frighten you, but we need to explore all possibilities. I know you've been associating with several people who knew Olivia. I'd like to talk to you about it in person as soon as possible. Would you be able to come to my office this morning?"

Catherine gazed at the sunlight highlighting the dewy flowerbeds edging the patio. It was a gorgeous morning. She'd love to be out walking, absorbing the beauty of autumn.

Walk if you want to. Walk to the police station, checking over your shoulder every ten seconds. Sound fun?

"Catherine?"

"I can be there in a half hour," Catherine said numbly.

* * *

By the time Catherine returned home at noon, she was drowning in physical and emotional exhaustion. Burgess had asked lengthy, detailed questions about Catherine's association with Adam, about Dylan, Renee, and Will, about everything Trent and Kelsey had ever said to her. So much for her word to Kelsey to not repeat Kelsey's report on Adam and Trent; Catherine didn't think that promise held when she was being questioned by police in a murder investigation. When Catherine had mentioned Esther Knight's being present—and not happy—when Will had arrived at the studio, Burgess had dug into everything Catherine knew about her; when she mentioned Lewis's name, Burgess had interrogated her about Lewis. By the end of the interview, Catherine had felt like a traitorous, finger-pointing gossip, even though she'd been careful to be as factual as possible and avoid drawing conclusions from anyone's behavior.

Catherine dragged herself into the house and crumpled on the couch in the family room. She'd particularly hated answering questions about Adam. Discussing him with Burgess had been extremely uncomfortable— not because it made her doubt him but because she suspected Burgess did, and Catherine didn't like discussing Adam in that context.

Now what? Burgess had said she had no idea if Catherine, not Maren, had been the intended victim, but given the number of times she'd urged Catherine to be careful, she was worried.

Wearily, Catherine checked her watch. She still had three hours before her first student was due. She kicked off her shoes and closed her eyes, hoping she could nap, but within a few minutes, she knew sleep was a lost cause. She couldn't endure lying here doing *nothing* while Olivia's killer . . . whoever he or she was . . .

When Catherine had admitted to Burgess that she'd made some efforts to figure out what had happened to Olivia, Burgess had sternly ordered Catherine to leave this to the police; if she had questions or theories, she should bring them to Burgess, not run the risk of asking a question of the wrong person and scaring the murderer into action.

Catherine had promised to avoid any private investigating, and she had no inclination to break that promise—especially not with the stakes so high. But there *was* something she could pursue, a way she could work to settle some of the turmoil in her life and keep herself from going crazy.

She could try to figure out who had started the rumors about her studio. If she could rip the rumors up by the roots, that would be best. If the rumor spreader wouldn't listen to reason, Catherine would call her lawyer. She didn't want to turn this into a legal battle, but she would not let someone destroy her reputation and her studio.

Feeling a surge of energy at the thought of taking action, Catherine sat up. She'd start by talking with people who'd heard the rumors to try to find a connection between them or follow the trail as far back as they'd let her until she zeroed in on a source. The rumors could only be a few days old at most, so it shouldn't be too hard to figure out where they'd started.

Half an hour later, she'd tried the home and cell phones of all seven parents who'd withdrawn their children from her program and hadn't gotten a single person to pick up the phone. She left messages but couldn't imagine they'd be returned. Fine. The parents would have to return the borrowed instruments— who would dare keep a violin or clarinet belonging to a drug pusher?—and she could talk to them then. Unless they dropped the instruments on the porch and dashed away before Catherine could catch them.

Her cell phone beeped. Hoping for any kind of heartening news, Catherine grabbed it. It was a text from Danielle: *Heard crazy rumors about your studio. Are you ok?*

Catherine stared at the text. Danielle probably would have called but didn't know if Catherine wanted to hear from her.

Did she want to hear from Danielle? Last night she'd been determined not to let hurt feelings and pride destroy her friendship with Danielle. This morning, she was so frustrated and tense that she wanted to scream at Danielle a lot more than she wanted to accept an olive-branch text.

Get over yourself. Don't you have bigger things to worry about? She's already apologized for talking to Adam instead of to you; you're not going to get her to apologize for the content of what she said. You can either decide it's not worth being friends with someone who—not totally without cause—thinks you're flawed but likes you anyway, or you can get over this and move on.

Get over it.

Trying not to feel grudging but feeling crabby and sulky anyway, Catherine texted Danielle back: *I'm ok. Just angry. Any idea who started the rumors?*

Restless, Catherine wandered around her backyard while she waited for Danielle's answer. It was a beautiful piece of property—trees glowing fiery red and yellow, flower beds bright with autumn flowers—but now it was tainted property in the eyes of Riley.

Her phone beeped. *No idea. I'll see what I can find out.*

Danielle would have better luck than Catherine in coaxing a frightened parent into talking to her. Feeling a little less cranky, Catherine texted: *Thanks. I appreciate it.*

No problem. Let me know if you need anything.

I will. Thanks.

Catherine tucked the phone into her pocket. Pretending in text messages that she wasn't still stinging over what Danielle had done was relatively easy; it would be harder when they were together. But if she was making the decision to forgive Danielle and move on, she'd fake a good attitude until she gained a real one.

She *did* appreciate Danielle's offer to help. But even if Danielle could persuade a skittish parent to confide in her, Catherine's determination to trace the rumors to the source might be a lost cause. The rumors *might* have been malicious, started by someone who wanted to drive the studio out of town, but more likely the rumors sprang from gossip and ignorance, with someone wondering how the studio was funded and speculating that Catherine was involved in something illegal. Rumors—fueled by fear over what had happened to Maren—had probably exploded from there.

Still, she couldn't sit and hope the rumors went away. She'd confront them as directly as she could.

From inside her open patio door, she heard the landline phone ring. Eagerly, she raced inside and grabbed it. Lewis.

"Hello, this is Catherine."

"It's Lewis. Listen, I tried to find out who told my friend's mom that trash about you, and she wouldn't give me a name. But she did let some information slip."

"What did she tell you?" Catherine asked, pleased that Lewis had pursued this.

"She said someone who knew about music had warned her, someone who could see your studio was a sham. That no real studio would run like yours does, and she'd known right off the bat you were doing something bad there, even before she learned about the drug money. That's all. I tried to get more out of her, but once she found out I'd taken the job, she wouldn't talk to me."

"I'm sorry she gave you a hard time."

"Not a big deal."

"Thank you *so* much for the information."

"See you tonight." Lewis hung up.

Catherine hung up the phone and rested her elbows on the breakfast bar, her thoughts racing. Someone who "knew about music." Maybe someone who hated the fact that her studio had come to town and wanted to think the worst of it—or at least pretend to think the worst of it?

How about a piano teacher?

An angry piano teacher who had confronted Catherine in a bakery and accused her of putting the other music teachers in town out of business?

It would make tons of sense if Frances Randolph was responsible for the rumors. Because she was a music teacher, scared parents would think she was a credible source when she savaged Catherine's professional reputation.

Her cell phone rang. She glanced at it and was glad to see Adam's number. She'd texted him a little while ago, asking him to call her when he had a chance.

"What's up?" he asked.

"You won't believe it. It's insane."

"At this point, I'll believe almost anything."

"Try this on. I'm a drug pusher. The studio is funded by a drug lord who supports it in exchange for my getting kids addicted to drugs and selling them."

Adam was silent for a moment. "Ohhh-kay. Know what else I heard?"

Catherine steeled herself. "What?"

"That every time the school board asks for your credentials, you get them singing barbershop so you can sneak away."

To Catherine's surprise, she laughed; she hadn't known she had laughter in her this morning. "I'm serious. That's the rumor flying around Riley— that I'm the pawn of a drug cartel." She told him about Lewis's report.

"Oh brother. That *is* insane. This town has lost its mind if anyone can believe that."

"People are so jumpy. I'm not surprised they're willing to believe something crazy. I felt so bad for Lewis—he was *so* nervous to tell me last night. I think he was about 95 percent sure the rumors were bunk, but 5 percent was enough to leave him sweating."

"Do you have any idea where the rumors started?"

"Maybe." She told him about her run-in with Frances Randolph.

"That's one way to run your competition out of town," Adam said. "The downside is that your competition might sue you for slander."

"I'd rather talk to her to see if we can handle this without lawyers. Naturally, it might not be her, so don't tell anyone I suspect her—there might be a whole group of music people who want to drive me out. She's just the only one who's confronted me so far."

"Catherine . . . be careful."

His admonition made her think of this morning's interview with Detective Burgess. Should she tell Adam about that? Not right now. Talking about it would crank up her stress level, and she couldn't share the most frightening fact she'd learned anyway—that the vase used to kill Olivia had likely been used to attack Maren. Better to stay focused on the rumors about her studio. "I don't think there's any danger in talking to Frances. What's she going to do? Pump up the gossip by telling people I'm a vicious space alien here to take over the planet?"

"Still, be careful. Anyone who'd spread rumors like this isn't someone who plays fair. If you're planning to talk to her, you should take a witness along."

"Good idea. But at this point, I have no idea if she even has anything to do with it. I need to think about it for a while. Don't worry. Whatever I decide to do, I'll be smart about it."

"You must think Riley is cursed," Adam said.

"Do me a favor. If you hear any rumors, see if you can subtly interrogate the gossiper to figure out where they heard such slanderous nonsense."

"I'm also willing to punch them in the face."

"You can do that too."

"Take care, Catherine."

"I do. I've never been so paranoid in my life."

* * *

The more she thought about it, the more she realized it wouldn't be smart to confront Frances yet. All Catherine had was a suspicion, and if she asked Frances if she had spread rumors about the studio, Frances would say no, and where would the conversation go from there? Catherine had no proof. She needed to talk to more people first to see if she could find a connection to Frances.

Tate Maxwell was coming for a cello lesson in the afternoon—a lesson that had been a group lesson before the two other kids in the group had dropped out yesterday. Catherine couldn't imagine the other parents hadn't alerted Tate's mother, so if she hadn't yanked Tate out, it meant she didn't believe the warnings. Maybe she could give Catherine some additional information about the source of the rumors. She'd been very friendly so far, talking about how she'd always wanted to learn an instrument and how excited she was for Tate.

Catherine hoped she was still excited.

When three thirty neared, Catherine found it hard not to pace and obsessively check the clock. What if Tate didn't come? What if the rumors had built to the point that no one came—not even the students who hadn't officially canceled? At three fifteen, she double-checked to make sure she'd put the placard out that instructed students to walk in rather than knock. At three twenty, she tuned the studio cello Tate would be using for his lesson so he didn't have to haul his practice cello on the bus that he and his mother rode to Bridgeside.

At three twenty-seven, she heard the front door open. Trying not to look overeager, she strolled into the main studio to greet Tate and Tonya Maxwell. Tate was a small-for-his-age fourth grader with huge blue eyes and cropped brown hair that stuck straight up.

"Hello, Tate," Catherine said. "I'm all ready for you. I'm afraid you're solo today."

"We know." Tonya, a tiny black-haired woman, clenched her jaw. "We know."

"Tate, go ahead and start on your exercises," Catherine said. "The cello is tuned for you. I need to talk to your mother for a minute."

Tate hurried toward the cello, grinning as though looking forward to showing off what he'd practiced.

Catherine led Tonya down the hall to her office.

"I can't believe this!" Tonya erupted as soon as Catherine closed the door. "Have you heard the crazy things people are saying? Did Hunter's and Cassidy's parents tell you why they quit?"

"They didn't tell me, but I heard the rumors from someone else. Thanks for not believing them."

"Ha! People watch too many movies. After what happened to Maren Gates, everyone has lost all common sense. I reminded them that you said parents can stay for lessons, but they kept insisting it wasn't safe and they couldn't take the chance. People are such idiots. Don't worry. These rumors will die out soon. Nothing that dumb can live for long."

Catherine wasn't sure the stupidity of a rumor would ensure its death, but it was nice to hope so. "Thanks for your support."

"I'm out there going to bat for you, let me tell you. Please don't let these idiots scare you away from Riley. We need you here."

"I'm not leaving. Tonya—when you heard about this, who told you?"

"Cassidy Jefferson's mom told me first."

"Did she say where she'd heard it?"

"Said she'd heard it from a friend . . . Sorry, I don't remember the name, but that friend heard it from some so-called expert, and Jeannie Jefferson made a big deal about how this info came from someone who knew what they were talking about."

Catherine needed to be careful not to hint at anything, lest she influence Tonya's words. "What type of expert?"

"Some music expert. I asked for the name, but she wouldn't give it. Said the source wanted to stay anonymous. Scared they'd be killed if they spoke up."

"You know Cassidy's family, right?"

"Yeah, our kids are in school together."

"Cassidy mentioned she used to take piano lessons. Do you happen to know who she took lessons from?"

"Sure, old Francie Randolph." Tonya's black brows arched. "Hang on—do you think Frances might be the one, the expert . . ."

"I have no idea." Catherine didn't want to start a rumor of her own, but the second mention of a musical expert plus a connection between a student's family and Frances Randolph was enough to seal Catherine's decision.

Tonight, she was going to visit Frances.

CHAPTER 22

CATHERINE FIGURED IT WAS BETTER not to call first. That would forewarn Frances, and her best hope for figuring out if Frances was the source of the rumors was to catch her off guard and tell Frances what she had learned. Frances would be smart enough not to admit anything, but if Catherine could surprise her, she might be able to read guilt in her face. That would be enough for Catherine to give her a clear warning that if she spread her nonsense any further, she'd hear from Catherine's lawyer.

Catherine parked in front of Frances's house and sat in her minivan, scanning the house. It was a redbrick house with a black iron railing around the porch. The yard was tiny, but in the glow of the streetlights, Catherine could see it was neatly mowed and edged, and the leaves had been recently raked. Light showed through cracks around the edges of the blinds, and an old Ford sat in the carport. Someone was home.

Catherine drew a deep breath and went to ring the doorbell.

The door opened. A short, balding man wearing a faded blue sweat suit and holding a cane gave Catherine a grumpy, alert look as though readying himself to interrupt her sales pitch.

Catherine decided not to introduce herself until she had to. "May I speak to Frances, please?"

"Who are you?"

"Another music teacher."

"C'mon in." He turned and limped down the hallway. "Francie! Door's for you!"

Frances emerged from the back of the house. She was wearing an apron and had a bowl in her hands. "Gracious, sit down, Hart. You're supposed to keep that knee elevated. You should have had William get the door."

Hart clomped down the hallway and disappeared, leaving Frances to approach Catherine. Catherine moved a little to the right so she was standing in the living room. She didn't want Frances to get a good look at her until they were face-to-face.

"Hello—" Frances froze and stared at Catherine, horror in her eyes.

"Hello, Mrs. Randolph. I think you remember me. Catherine Clayton from Bridgeside Music—"

"Hart!" Frances shrieked. "William! William, help me!"

"Mrs. Randolph, I just want to talk—"

"*William!*" She backed away from Catherine. "My nephew is here. My husband is here. If you try anything—"

Hart's limping footsteps thudded in the hallway, and heavier footsteps thumped overhead.

"Mrs. Randolph—"

"Stay away from me!" Frances flung the metal bowl in her hands at Catherine. Catherine dodged too late; the bowl smacked her in the chest, spraying flour all over her. "The police know about you! You'll never get away with this!"

"Francie, what in the world—" Hart goggled at Catherine.

A dark-haired young man galloped into the room, and Catherine gasped. Will Conti.

"She's the drug dealer! I told you about her!" Frances yelled. "Grab her, William! She's trying to kill me! Be careful! She's armed."

Angrily, Catherine brushed flour off her face and sweater. "I am *not* armed. I came to *talk* to Mrs. Randolph. I'm not going to hurt—"

"Grab her! Before she pulls a gun!"

Will charged toward Catherine.

"Don't you *dare* touch—" Before Catherine could speak the rest of the warning, Will caught her arm, whirled her around and propelled her toward the door.

"Don't worry, Aunt Fran," he yelled. "I'll get rid of her."

"Let *go* of—"

Will pushed her through the still-open door. "Close it and lock it," he hollered back. "I'll take care of her."

The door slammed. Catherine struggled to yank free of Will's grip, but his hands were too powerful.

"If you don't let go of me, I'll—"

"Keep cool." Will hauled her into the street. When they were on the other side of her minivan, with the van blocking them from the view of the house, Will released her. He slumped against the side of the van and started laughing.

"Dangerous . . . drug . . . dealer . . . come to . . . kill . . . You are one scary chick . . ."

Rubbing her sternum where the bowl had struck her, Catherine snapped, "This isn't funny."

". . . you . . . kidding? I'd pay money to . . . see that . . . did she throw her bowl at you?"

Catherine scowled and batted at the flour still clinging to her sleeves. "Frances Randolph is your aunt?"

"Yeah. My gut . . . I'm dying . . ." He wiped tears off his face. "Can we do that again?"

"If you touch me again, I'll break your jaw."

He grinned. "Didn't have a choice. I had to save my aunt's life. Could you try to run away? Then I could tackle you."

Catherine brushed flour off her chin. "You realize your aunt is in there calling the police."

"Nah, she won't call."

"She thinks I was trying to kill her!"

"She doesn't trust the police. Thinks you're bribing them." He burst out laughing again. "So are you going to charge her with assault with a mixing bowl? Assault and batter. Get it? Assault and batter! You know, like cake batter?"

Catherine fought the urge to kick him. "Is she crazy? I mean honestly, clinically crazy?"

"No." Still out of breath from laughing, Will struggled to stand up straight.

"Why does she think I'm a drug pusher?"

"Can we sit in your van to talk?"

"No. Answer my questions."

"Why the heck do you drive a mommy car like this?"

"I need the space for hauling instruments around."

"Borrrring."

"I didn't know Frances was your aunt."

"Yeah. Uncle Hart can't take care of the yard or house anymore, so I'm over here a lot." He smirked at her. "I have my pottery studio out back. Cozy. Private. We could sneak back there and I could give you a . . . tour."

Flirting again. Apparently he was no longer angry at her for turning him down. That thought gave Catherine a shuddery feeling—she'd been so flustered by Frances's attack and so startled to see Will that she'd momentarily forgotten he was on the list of people she didn't want to be alone with. "Can you tell me what's going on? Why is she saying these crazy things about me?

I know she wasn't happy about me coming to Riley, but why would she make up something this nuts?"

"How did you know she was the one telling people this stuff?"

"I'm psychic," Catherine said acidly.

"She didn't make it up. Someone sent her a letter about you."

"A letter!"

"She showed it to me. It was this anonymous thing saying how the writer was scared to tell anyone and didn't think anyone would believe them anyway, but they knew you'd done this music studio scam in another state—maybe more than once—and it was a front for drug pushers. You lure kids in, get them hooked and get them selling, and once they're in too deep to get out, you move on before the police can catch you."

A letter. Disconcerted, Catherine gathered her thoughts. "Why did the letter writer send it to your aunt?"

"Because she's a 'music professional' and an upstanding Riley citizen who cares about the safety of our kids. Or something like that. Made a big deal about begging her to spread the word but be careful—you're dangerous." Will winked at her. "Dangerous. I like that."

"What excuse did the letter writer give for not going straight to the police?"

"Said they didn't dare, that they were sure you were paying off the cops, and if they tried, they'd end up arrested on fake charges or dead. That the only way for us to be safe was to spread the word so no one dared go near your place and you'd have to shut down and leave."

"People *have* called the police," Catherine said. "The police told them the rumors are trash."

"I think they're true." Will stepped closer to her. The streetlights shone on his wavy dark hair and highlighted the white T-shirt clinging to his broad shoulders. "All true. You sure scare *me*. I'd love to have you scare me a little more."

Catherine stepped back. "Do you think your aunt wrote the letter herself and pretended someone sent it to her?"

"Uh . . . can't imagine her coming up with something this fun on her own. And she seemed all freaked out when she read the letter. Can't believe she'd be good at faking that. Nah, someone sent it to her."

"Do you have *any* idea who'd send her a letter like that?"

"How would I know?"

"Your aunt has no idea who wrote it?"

"It was anonymous. No signature. No return address. Mailed locally though."

"I want to see it."

Will laughed. "Sorry. She burned it."

"*Burned* it?"

"Yeah, I saw her do it. The letter said to destroy it after she read it because if anyone found it in her house, she'd be dead."

"Oh, *please.* Would you mind walking me back inside? I need to talk to your aunt."

"You nuts? She'll knock your head off with a frying pan."

"Does she know *you* think the rumors are crazy?"

"She's my aunt, sweetheart. She makes me cookies and roast beef dinners, and she let me build a kiln out back. You think I'm going to break her heart by telling her that her beloved nephew doesn't believe her?"

"Congratulations on your family loyalty, but I don't appreciate you supporting her in sabotaging my reputation."

"Hey, I never spread any rumors. Don't blame me."

"I need to talk to her. She *cannot* keep saying these things. This is slander, and it's illegal."

The mischievous humor disappeared from Will's expression. "You're not going to sue her, are you? She doesn't have a lot of cash. Come on, Catherine. You'd destroy her, and it would kill Uncle Hart. She's not being cruel on purpose. She just got scared by that letter."

Will looked so worried that Catherine grudgingly admired how much he cared about his aunt and uncle. "I don't *want* to sue her. I want her to *stop.*"

"You're not going to get her in trouble for the flying bowl, are you?"

"I'm not calling the police about a mixing bowl."

"Good." A gleam replaced the anxiety in his eyes. "You can try talking to her if you want to, but I'm not standing between you two. I like my body in one piece."

Catherine sighed. Will was right—there was no point in confronting Frances when she was this scared and angry. "Okay, fine. Please go tell her the letter writer was lying about me and attempting to defame me, and if she doesn't stop spreading these rumors, I will take legal action to—"

"Catherine—"

"—*but* if she stops now and retracts what she said, I won't call my lawyer. Please also tell her she is welcome to visit the studio at any time and—if parents give permission—to observe music lessons. You can also tell her I'll be needing to hire an accompanist soon, and if she's interested, she should let me know."

Will's jaw dropped. "You'd hire her?"

"I'm trying to run a music studio. I want to support the teachers in town, not be in competition with them." Catherine unlocked her van. "I'm going home. I need to wash flour out of my hair."

CHAPTER 23

DUE TO TOTAL EXHAUSTION, CATHERINE was able to sleep that night, but she awoke at five in the morning. Comforted by the thought of Lewis pacing her property, she felt momentarily safe as she lay in bed in the darkness, but anger and discouragement quickly replaced the calm. Who had sent that letter to Frances? Or had Will been lying? Or had Frances faked the letter?

She'd never imagined she could feel such a temptation to climb in her car and drive away from everything. Abandon her commitments, abandon her studio, abandon her remaining students—leave her real estate agent to deal with the issues of closing up the studio and selling her property. Just run away and forget she'd ever set foot in Riley.

Her father would never forgive her for that degree of cowardice and irresponsibility. And besides, now she understood far better why Adam had chosen to stay, not wanting to leave Riley until his innocence was established. If she fled now, she'd leave the permanent conclusion in many minds that she was the drug dealer those rumors had painted her to be. That taint would follow her for life. It would make its way onto the Internet and corrupt her reputation if she tried to establish a studio again—or even get a job as a musician. No matter how outrageously stupid the rumors were, they'd be enough to make people doubt her. Forever.

Of course, staying here and dying wasn't a terrific option either.

You're not going to die. Stop thinking like that. Catherine threw back the covers and went to take a shower.

At seven, a weary Lewis reported in. All had been quiet during the night. Catherine thanked him and told him she was planning to hire a second guard to assist on the night shift, as well as a guard to watch the studio during the day. With a killer possibly targeting her, she didn't want Lewis on his own at night.

The hour she spent alone in the studio before Esther arrived at eight seemed eternal.

"Morning." Esther tossed her sequined bag on the ground next to the desk. "You doing okay?"

"More or less," Catherine said.

Esther's eyes were bloodshot, and she looked as tired as Lewis had. From this morning's stint in front of the mirror, Catherine knew she didn't look any better. What a batch of zombies they all were these days.

"I want your help planning an open house," Catherine said as Esther sat down behind the desk.

"An open house?"

"Yes. I could use your help designing an ad to go in the local papers and a flyer to hang around town."

Esther gave her a quizzical look. "You want to party here?"

"Yes, I do. I want all of Riley to come visit the studio. I want to demystify and de-rumorize this place. I want people to feel free to stop by and see what I'm doing here."

Esther pursed her lips. "You think people will come?"

"We'll do everything possible to make them want to come. If they don't . . . we'll be eating leftover refreshments for months."

"People won't come. They're scared."

"*You're* here," Catherine said lightly. "You're not scared. Maybe we ought to post YouTube videos of you vouching for the reputation of the studio."

The dubious expression on Esther's face hardened with an emotion Catherine couldn't discern. "*That* wouldn't do you any good. People will look at me and think for sure we're pushing drugs."

"Give me a break."

Esther averted her gaze. She had Danielle's dark brown eyes—usually softer, more vulnerable eyes than Danielle's but now covered with the same tough, slightly fractured shield Danielle wore. "You only know me through Danielle, and I'm betting she told you what she wanted you to hear. Trust me, my endorsement would only hurt you. Having me here probably *already* hurts you."

"Esther . . . whatever problems you've had in the past don't matter anymore. You're doing a great job here."

Esther didn't speak, but Catherine could read the response in her face: *What makes you think the problems are past?*

Fighting burgeoning discomfort, Catherine couldn't think of what to say. She had no idea what problems troubled Esther's life. Danielle had never confided much about Esther's issues, though Catherine knew she worried a lot about her. But Esther *was* doing a great job at the studio. *Focus on that*, Catherine thought.

"Danielle wouldn't have recommended you if she didn't think this would be a good situation for both of us. You've been a great help to me. I think people *will* come to the open house. Anyone with half a brain will see that the rumors about Bridgeside are nonsense—once they set aside knee-jerk fear and start thinking."

Esther rapped her purple fingernails against the desk. "People won't think at all. Not right now."

"You don't have to agree with me. But I could use your help."

"You're the boss," Esther said curtly. "But you're wasting your time and money."

Catherine sat in one of the chairs opposite the reception desk. "You don't think there's any truth to these rumors, do you?"

Esther gave a harsh, incredulous laugh. "You're joking, right?"

"Just making sure. You . . . look so tense."

Esther played with a yellow enameled ring on her finger. "I'm tense because you want me to fight for a lost cause."

"A lost cause?"

"Come *on*. You think an open house is going to fix the reputation of this place? People think you're a drug pusher. You need to get out of Riley. Seriously, you need to go."

"Esther! I can't run away. I've made commitments. I have students—"

"Give it a few more days, and you *won't* have any students."

How could Esther urge her to fold? She'd thought Esther was stronger and more stubborn than this. Anyone who could lock horns with Danielle *must* be stubborn. "Not everyone believes this garbage about the studio. I can't run away and leave people to think—"

"The longer you stick around, the worse it'll be for you. What if Maren dies?"

"That would be awful, but—"

"People are *scared*, and they hate you. You think a couple of broken windows is the worst they'll do if they think you killed Maren—and are trying to destroy their kids? They'll burn your studio down."

"They wouldn't—"

"You could jump on a plane right now and go anywhere you want. You're *free*. Instead, you want to wait for a mob to come slash your throat. They'll do it, Catherine. People are crazy when they're scared. They do stupid things. Horrible things. You need to *get out!*"

The fury in Esther's voice jarred Catherine so badly that she couldn't decide if she wanted to head immediately for the airport or stand her ground and yell back at Esther. She made herself speak quietly. "*You* want me gone."

"I want you *safe*."

The tears filling Esther's eyes startled Catherine. She reached across the desk and touched Esther's arm. "Thank you," she said. "But you're overreacting."

Overreacting? You know Olivia's killer is back and struck near your studio—attacking a woman wearing your *raincoat—and you still think Esther is overreacting to be worried for you?*

"These rumors are new." Catherine shoved aside thoughts of her conversation with Burgess; that wasn't the issue now. "They have no roots. It shouldn't take too much work to yank them up."

From the disdainful expression on Esther's face—even as she wiped tears away—she didn't believe Catherine. Fair enough. Catherine wasn't sure she believed herself.

"If it's uncomfortable for you to work here, given the rumors, I'll understand," Catherine said. "Or if you need a break for a week or two until the talk dies out, I'll hold the job for you."

Esther looked away. "I don't want to quit."

"Me either." Catherine toyed with her turquoise and copper bracelets, rotating them around her wrist. "What does Danielle say about the rumors?"

"What do you *think* she says?" Esther snapped.

"That people are brainless to believe them." Catherine hoped this was true.

Esther didn't contradict her. "What she won't admit is that this scandal isn't doing *her* any good. Everyone knows she helped you launch this program, so if it's tainted, so is she."

Catherine grimaced. She hated the thought of Danielle's reputation getting damaged by her association with Catherine. "Does *she* think I should leave?"

"She's too stubborn to say anybody should quit at anything." Esther jerkily ran her fingers through her green-streaked hair, tousling the smooth style she'd worn to work. "But it's bad for Dani, having you here. It stresses her out. And she's stressed enough."

"The rumors will fade. Danielle wouldn't want me to bail out now."

"It's not just the rumors!" Esther's voice rose.

Annoyed, Catherine rose to her feet and said coolly, "Staying or going is my decision. I'd appreciate it if you wouldn't yell at me."

"What*ever.* I'm trying to help.*" The pain in her face eased a little of Catherine's anger at her rudeness.

"Maybe we should talk about something else," Catherine said.

Esther played with the paper in the printer tray, bending the corner of the top sheet. "Is . . . anybody else around here right now?"

"No. Just us."

"This shouldn't come from me, but since Dani will never tell you . . ." Her voice died.

Slowly, Catherine sat down and pulled her chair closer to the desk. "What won't she tell me?"

Esther crumpled the sheet of paper she was toying with and snapped, "She was in love with Robert Fields."

Catherine felt as though she'd been walking around with her eyes closed and had smacked into the wall. "In love with him! She never—I had no idea—"

"She's totally private that way. She didn't *tell* me, but I figured it out. She was crazy about him. She pretended it didn't bother her that he loved you, but it did."

"Oh my goodness." Catherine put her hands over her face. "Oh goodness."

"If that's your substitute for swearing, it's not very satisfying."

Catherine laughed hoarsely. She wanted to bang her head against the desk over and over to punish herself for being so clueless. "I'm an idiot."

"She's private. She didn't want you to know. She didn't want me to know either, but she can't hide everything."

So this was why Danielle still brought up Robert to Catherine four years after his death. This was why Danielle had put him on such a high pedestal that she couldn't comprehend why Catherine had broken up with him and thought the only explanation was Catherine's selfishness and commitment phobia. Catherine groaned. It must have torn Danielle apart to watch Catherine and Robert together.

"When you dumped him, he came to her," Esther said, "confided in her. I think she was the first person he told."

"She told you he talked to her?"

"Yeah, she thought I was too dumb to read between the lines and figure out how she felt about him. When she told me, she pretended it didn't matter to her that you'd dumped him, but I could tell she was over the moon. It was obvious she thought maybe . . . once he got over you . . . and they were already friends, and he was turning to her for support . . . but then a week later, he was dead."

Catherine felt sick. She wracked her brain to remember how Danielle had acted in the months after Robert died and was deeply ashamed that she couldn't remember. She didn't remember Danielle's being around much at all during that time or saying much when she was around. She didn't remember worrying about Danielle either. She'd assumed Danielle was fine. It had never occurred to her that Danielle was hurting beyond the shock of losing a friend. She must have been devastated, and Catherine hadn't even noticed. No wonder Danielle thought she was self-centered.

"I need to talk to her," Catherine said.

Esther shook her head. "*Don't* bring it up."

"I hate that I was so blind to how she felt."

"It's not your fault she fell in love with your guy. Dani thinks she's so strong and logical and organized, but . . ." Esther rolled her eyes.

Catherine sat silently, assimilating what Esther had told her. "She's still hurting. Four years after his death, she's still hurting. And she never said anything."

"You see why it stresses her out to have you around?"

"She encouraged me to come here."

"Because she's Danielle." Esther shoved back angrily from the desk and jumped to her feet. "She's logical. She's organized. She knows your music program is a good thing for Riley, so she wanted it."

"Then why—"

Esther dropped back into her chair, as though once on her feet, she hadn't been able to think why she'd risen. "Since she's Dani, she probably thought she was in *control* and she was over Robert and it wouldn't bother her anymore. But she's a wreck. I know she doesn't show you that side of her, but I see it. Trust me, she's a wreck. And look at everything else going on—everything's been a disaster for you here. You need to go. Pack up and go somewhere else while you can."

"Esther . . . it's not that straightforward."

Esther's gaze burned Catherine. "It *is* straightforward! You have the money to do anything you want. You don't even need to work. Just go somewhere else—*anywhere* else—and start *over*."

Too dazed to untangle her thoughts, Catherine didn't know how to respond. Esther looked so intense—angry—frightened. Esther thought she should leave Riley, that she'd never be able to undo the damage caused by the rumors. But Danielle wanted her here . . . or wanted her program here, yet she was still hurting over Robert . . . Was *that* the reason she'd tried to warn Adam away from Catherine? Not out of worry for Adam's happiness but out of bitterness at the way things had unfolded last time Catherine had been in love?

Beneath her outward friendship and support, how much did she resent Catherine? Could Danielle be attacking her reputation in other ways besides bad-mouthing her to Adam?

Could Danielle be the one who had sent that letter to Frances?

That's ridiculous! She wanted you here! She suggested you come to Riley! Just because Danielle reacted negatively when she thought Adam might be getting interested in Catherine didn't mean she would spread vicious rumors about Catherine's studio to try to drive her out of town. Danielle had her own issues, but she was *not* indecisive. She wouldn't urge Catherine to come to Riley then change her mind and play dirty trying to force her out.

"Thanks for being honest with me," Catherine said. "I . . . need to think about this a little longer." She wanted to change the subject and discuss the open house, but from the stress in Esther's face, she was not in the mood to discuss flyers or catering or decorations. Wanting to get away from Esther's anger and anxiety and sort out her own thoughts, Catherine stood. "If you could finish indexing that music this morning, that would be great. Let me know if you need anything. I'm going to practice for a while."

Esther nodded.

CHAPTER 24

"Esther thinks you should run?" Adam slid the takeout container of sesame chicken toward Catherine.

"She's scared the rumors will lead some whacked-out parent to do something violent." Catherine didn't add that Esther also wanted her gone because of the stress she was bringing into Danielle's life. That was too private. If Danielle hadn't even told Esther about Robert, then Danielle certainly didn't want it broadcast to anyone else.

"I'm scared for you too," Adam said. "I want to drive you straight to the airport and put you on the first available plane."

"You do?"

"After what happened to Maren so near your studio? Are you kidding? If there's even the smallest chance that you're in harm's way, I want you out of here."

Catherine knew he must be thinking about her raincoat that Maren had worn, but he didn't want to rattle Catherine further by even hinting that the coat was relevant.

"But I do understand your feelings about not buckling under pressure," he added.

"Believe me, part of me *does* want to buckle and get the heck out of here. I'm scared, and I'm frustrated, and Esther's probably right—soon, a bunch of people with pitchforks will burn the studio down with me in it . . . unless Olivia's killer gets to me first. But every time I think of leaving, I can't stand the thought of running like a coward, abandoning everything. My dad would be mortified, and *I'd* be mortified. If that's how I respond to stress, I don't think I can live with myself."

"There's nothing cowardly in removing yourself from danger."

"If you were in my place, would *you* close down the studio and leave?"

Frowning, Adam resumed eating, ignoring Catherine's question.

"You *wouldn't* go," Catherine interpreted.

"That doesn't mean you shouldn't go."

"I'm being careful," Catherine said. "Lewis has put me in contact with some people at the security firm he used to work for, and I have some leads on hiring more security for the studio. If the area I'll be passing through is at all isolated, I'll drive instead of walk, though it makes me claustrophobic to drive on little trips. Everything's locked and alarmed and so on. Even if . . . even if Olivia's killer is interested in me for some reason, he's not going to catch me by surprise. As far as the success of the studio, I have some plans for how to handle these wretched rumors." She told him about the open house.

"An open house is a good idea." Adam poured more water into his glass. "With people like Tonya Maxwell behind you, you'll be able to gather critical mass at an open house, and the goodwill will spread."

"I hope so." Would Danielle support the open house? Now that Catherine had a better understanding of Danielle's contradictory behavior, she needed to talk to her. Would Esther be upset if Catherine ignored her advice and spoke bluntly to Danielle?

"Do you know Esther Knight personally?" Catherine asked.

"Just a little. She knew Olivia from the gym—Esther used to go there."

Catherine had already learned of the connection with Leonardi's Fitness when Esther had been angry after Will had shown up at the studio. She'd never thought about the fact that Esther would have known Olivia.

"What did you want to know about Esther?" Adam asked.

"I'm not even sure why I asked the question." Catherine scooped more rice onto her plate. "I suppose I just wish I knew her better. Thanks for bringing lunch over so you could listen to the next installment of my nervous breakdown."

"Anytime."

While Catherine ate, her mind kept picking through the past, seeking overlooked hints that should have told her how Danielle felt about Robert and how crushed she'd been by his death. Even as she cursed herself for her obliviousness, she knew that, in fairness, part of the reason she hadn't noticed was because Danielle hadn't wanted her to notice. She hadn't even wanted Esther to notice.

Thoughts of the letter Frances had received slipped again into Catherine's contemplation of Danielle.

Stop it. It's ludicrous to suspect her, and you know it.

But a letter like that . . . a skillful letter, playing on both Frances's prejudice against Catherine and her pride in her position as a music teacher . . . It was a clever tactic, getting Frances to spread the rumors so the letter writer didn't have to do it.

Danielle had known about her clash with Frances. Catherine had told her about it.

"What's on your mind?" Adam asked. "I get the feeling you're not telling me something."

Catherine smiled feebly. "Are you saying I wasted my tuition money on that Poker Faces 101 class I took in college?"

"Ask for a refund. What's bothering you—beyond what you've already told me?"

Catherine sighed. "Esther told me something about Danielle that surprised me, something that explains why she . . . has mixed feelings toward me. I'm reeling. But I can't talk about it now."

"When you do want to talk about it, I'm ready to listen."

"Thank you." Catherine took her half-full plate to the sink. "I think I'd better talk to her first."

Adam stood. "I wish I could stay longer, but I—" He glanced at his watch. "Oops. I need to get back to work. I don't like leaving you here alone."

"I won't be. I have several lessons scheduled . . . if anyone shows up."

Adam picked up his plate and reached to pick up his water glass but bumped it against the container of hot and sour soup, spilling the remainder of the soup across the table. "Aaah! I'm sorry." He grabbed his napkin, but it wasn't enough to deal with the spill. Soup spread across the table and dripped onto the floor.

"Sorry about that. Throw me a towel, and I'll—"

"Let me take care of it." Catherine grabbed the dish towel. "You're already running late. Go on. Thanks for lunch."

"I'll call you. Sorry about the mess." Adam hurried out of the kitchen.

* * *

The afternoon and evening went far better than Catherine had anticipated. Not only did all of her scheduled students show up, but also five new people called her—three wanting to sign their children up for lessons and two offering to volunteer at the studio if Catherine needed help with anything. Catherine swiftly accepted the help, asking the volunteers if they'd assist with the open house she was planning. Both women identified themselves as friends of Tonya Maxwell. *Bless you, Tonya.*

But apprehension and confusion still churned as she waffled between calling Danielle immediately and waiting.

I should call. We need to talk.

But Esther will feel betrayed if I tell Danielle what she told me.

But things will only get worse if I wait.

But Esther was so sure that approaching her is a bad idea.

With her last student gone and the studio quiet, Catherine wandered upstairs into the unused bedroom where she'd left her cello. After everything that had happened, she didn't dare leave her cello in the main room of the studio where visitors—or vandals—had easy access to it.

If she'd ever needed a de-stressing practice session, she needed one now. Maybe an hour of bow against strings would smooth out her thoughts and allow her to make a decision about how to handle Danielle.

There isn't a way to "handle" her. You want to fix the problem, and maybe it's not fixable. You can apologize for not being discerning enough to sense that she was hurting, but how much will that mean to her, given that she didn't want you to know? You can't heal her wounds for her.

But maybe talking about it openly will relieve at least a fraction of her pain.

Even with the light on, the room felt too dark. Dark and chilly.

It's all in your head. Start playing, and you'll warm up. Catherine reached to unlatch the case. A folded piece of white paper was tucked into the handle.

She snatched the paper and unfolded it. It was a note, typed in black print.

Trent Perry is right about me. Too bad he'll never prove it. Let's see if he can prove I killed you.

CHAPTER 25

"IT WASN'T HIM," CATHERINE REPEATED, leaning toward Detective Burgess's desk. "He didn't leave the note."

Burgess tapped her finger against the plastic evidence bag holding the note. "We'll see what we can figure out. Thank you for bringing this to me immediately."

"It wasn't Adam. If he did kill Olivia, why would he advertise it?"

"Good question," Burgess said blandly. Catherine figured she knew what Burgess was thinking: if Adam was sick and cruel enough to kill Olivia, attack Maren, and spread fear all over Riley, he'd take pleasure in terrifying Catherine before he killed her. And Adam had had the opportunity to plant the note when he'd left Catherine mopping up soup in the kitchen while he supposedly headed out the front door. It would only have taken a few seconds for him to move silently up the stairs, plant the note, then exit the house. Catherine, with the water running as she cleaned up the spilled soup, wouldn't have noticed anything. A printed note on a plain piece of paper couldn't be traced to him, so he wasn't incriminating himself. He could simply deny knowing anything about it, and Burgess couldn't prove otherwise.

Adam hadn't left the note, but *someone* had crept up the stairs, searching for a place to leave the note, seen her cello in the empty bedroom, and decided it was the ideal spot.

Burgess had promised to send someone over to dust the cello case for prints, but Catherine knew it was futile—whoever had left the note couldn't have been stupid enough to touch the case with ungloved fingers.

"It wasn't him." Catherine tried not to sound desperate. She *couldn't* stop trusting Adam. If he was the killer, wouldn't she have sensed something off about him?

So you're too smart to be fooled. You're smarter than every other person in history who got taken in by a psychopath.

"Adam is not a psychopath," she said aloud.

Burgess's gaze was keen. "I didn't suggest he was. I'll need to speak with him, but I don't think it will shed any light on who left the note."

"Oh no, please don't—" Catherine swallowed the rest of her words. She couldn't beg Burgess not to talk to Adam. She couldn't even ask Burgess to make sure Adam knew that Catherine had not accused him. It wasn't Burgess's responsibility to carry messages for Catherine.

"Trent Perry left me a note once before," Catherine said. She'd already told Burgess of Trent's note in her purse. "Maybe he's twisted enough in his hatred of Adam to try to scare me like this—and drive me away from Adam."

"We'll speak with Mr. Perry, of course."

Fighting despair, Catherine looked at the list resting next to Burgess's hand, the list she'd written of everyone who'd been in her house since she'd last opened her cello case. Would Burgess interview all of them— including her young students—to learn if they had seen anything? Another frightening event at Bridgeside Studio. How many more students would this drive away?

"Be careful," Burgess said. "Be careful who you trust. The note might be a prank, with no connection to the murderer. But please don't gamble your life on it."

"I won't," Catherine said bleakly.

* * *

The Mozart horn concertos usually calmed Catherine. Intellectually, she knew even the mellow tones of a french horn and the clarity of Mozart wouldn't make a dent in her anxiety, but she kept the concertos playing on her home audio system while she sat at the dining room table and brainstormed ideas for the open house. She couldn't stand the thought of silence tonight.

Through one of the arched dining room doorways, she could see into the darkened main room of the studio. She was tempted to go turn on the lights but resisted. She'd already left the family room lights, kitchen lights, and hallway light burning; she didn't need to illuminate the whole house. How much of a child was she? Deciding to take a break, she walked through the doorway behind her into the well-lit kitchen and poured a glass of lemonade.

Back at the dining room table, she sipped from the glass, typed more notes, and periodically checked the clock. Just a few more minutes until Lewis would arrive at eleven. She hated the fact that being alone worried her now, even with her doors and windows locked and alarmed.

She'd tried twice to call Adam, but he hadn't answered. Was he at the police department talking to Detective Burgess? Or had Burgess already talked to him and he was avoiding Catherine's calls because he assumed she thought he'd left the note?

Trent Perry is right about me. The words made her shudder. She did *not* believe Adam was a killer, but someone wanted her to think he was.

Someone who hated the idea of Adam and her together?

She hadn't mentioned Danielle's name to Detective Burgess. Danielle hadn't been to the studio in a while, and Catherine had no reason to think she had shown up unannounced today. But she hadn't been watching the door every moment.

It was time to confront Danielle and have a candid discussion about Robert, Adam, Frances, the note Catherine had found, and any other issues that came to mind. Esther might be angry, but Catherine had never promised Esther she'd keep the information about Danielle confidential, and she couldn't endure more of these exaggerated suspicions jumping into her thoughts. It was too late to call Danielle tonight, but she'd call first thing tomorrow and set up a time to meet with her.

Glad to have reached a decision, Catherine opened a new tab on her browser and started searching for nearby caterers who might be able to handle open-house refreshments.

Refreshments. Food sounded like a good idea. She'd been so stressed out by tonight's trip to the police station that she hadn't eaten dinner. A grilled cheese sandwich sounded appealing. Catherine slid her chair back and turned toward the doorway that led to the kitchen.

The kitchen was dark.

Confused, Catherine stopped. She must have automatically switched the lights off when she'd exited the kitchen, habit overcoming paranoia. With the brightness of the dining room lights and her back to the kitchen doorway, she hadn't noticed she'd done it. *Good grief. Calm down. If you turned the lights off without thinking about it, that's a good sign. Don't be so jumpy.*

She took a step toward the kitchen and froze again. The kitchen was *completely* dark, which meant the adjoining family room was dark as well.

She *knew* she hadn't switched off the family room lights. At warp speed, her brain searched for explanations—burned-out lightbulbs, breaker problems—none of them made sense.

Through the house speakers, Mozart played—loud enough to mask stealthy footsteps or the click of light switches?

Terror crashed into her chest; she couldn't breathe. *I'm going to die.* She whirled around and snatched her phone from the table.

A dark figure burst through the doorway and hurtled toward her, a large, dark object in his hand.

A tall, wrought-iron vase.

With a scream, Catherine rushed toward the opposite doorway. The dining room lights went off.

Catherine sprinted into the main room, heavy footsteps following her. She couldn't see where she was going; her elbow knocked into a music stand, sending it clanging to the floor. She'd never make it to the front door before the intruder reached her. She cut to the right, heading for the hallway.

Something—the vase—slammed into her shoulder, hurtling her into the shelves of instruments. She fought to keep her balance, but the pain was so overwhelming that she stumbled and landed on her knees, dropping her phone. A thunk sounded behind her—the vase striking the shelves.

Catherine staggered to her feet and lurched into the hallway. The vase grazed her ribs and thudded into the wall. Something fell and shattered.

Hands held out front of her in the darkness, Catherine ran into the family room and veered toward the kitchen, moving in the direction of the sliding door. The blur of the intruder moved between her and the exit.

Catherine sped back toward the family room, feeling the rush of air as the vase whooshed past her. She collided with a lamp table, knocking it over with her on top of it, the edge of the table jabbing her in the gut. Winded, she scrambled away from the table, struggling to stand.

A thudding, splintering noise—the attacker was striking the fallen lamp table. Was he toying with her, or was he having trouble seeing her in the dark? All Catherine could see of him was a shadow.

She needed something she could defend herself with—the fireplace poker. Back on her feet, she lunged in the direction of the fireplace.

A swish of air behind her head—if the assailant had been a couple of inches closer . . .

Her shin collided with the edge of the hearth. Fumbling in the darkness, she reached desperately for the poker. This was hopeless—she was going to die—

Catherine's fingers found the poker. She whirled around, swinging it hard. It struck nothing. Where was . . .

The hiss of the sliding door moving in its track—the wail of an alarm filling the house . . .

The shadowy intruder exiting through the sliding door.

"*Catherine!*" A deep voice yelled her name. Lewis.

"Help me!" Catherine shrieked. "He ran out back!"

Through the din of the alarm, she heard Lewis hollering, but she couldn't tell what he was saying. She hurried toward the open door. She could see neither Lewis nor the intruder in the brightly lit yard.

Sirens joined the wail of the alarm.

Trembling and sick to her stomach, she collapsed onto the kitchen floor.

* * *

Catherine was giving half her attention to the paramedics and half to Detective Burgess when Lewis came panting into the family room, escorted by a police officer. He was holding a dark wrought-iron vase. Catherine stared at the twining leaves and vines of the vase.

"Got . . . away . . . Sorry . . ." Lewis handed the vase to a police officer and sprawled on the carpet, clutching his gut. One of the paramedics moved swiftly toward him.

"No . . . I'm . . . okay." Lewis flapped a muscular arm in the air, waving the paramedic away. "Just . . . gotta . . . catch my breath. But . . . I . . . got a look . . . at . . . Saw . . . face . . ."

Burgess left Catherine's side and strode toward Lewis. "You saw the face of the attacker?"

"Yeah . . . chased . . . almost caught . . . grabbed jacket . . . slowed 'em down—grabbed the hat . . . I mean mask, ski mask . . . ripped it off . . . got a glimpse . . . she broke away—"

"*She* broke away?" Burgess asked sharply.

"Yeah . . . it was a woman." Still panting, Lewis sat up. "Sorry . . . I tried to stop her, but she got away . . . finally lost her."

A woman. Catherine pressed her palms against the couch she was sitting on and breathed deeply, fighting dizziness.

"She dropped that." He pointed at the vase.

"Did you recognize her?" Burgess asked. "Do you know who it was?"

Lewis mopped sweat off his face with his sleeve. "Yeah, I . . . I . . . It's . . . not . . . I wish . . . didn't want to think . . . but . . . that . . . hair . . . green stripes in it . . . streaks, I mean, green streaks . . ."

Catherine sat paralyzed. *That can't be right.*

"Her assistant . . . Catherine's assistant," Lewis gasped out. "Esther Knight."

Burgess looked at Catherine.

Catherine's mouth was dry. "That doesn't make sense. Esther wouldn't . . ." Danielle's words about Esther's temper—the fury she'd seen in Esther today . . .

"Are . . . you okay?" Lewis asked. "Did you get hurt?"

"Just my shoulder."

"Sorry . . . should have . . . stopped her sooner. I was walking up to the house, and I heard a crash . . . a scream . . . pounded on the front door, but no one responded . . ."

With the cacophony of the intruder breaking things and her own distraction in trying to elude the blows, Catherine hadn't heard the pounding, but the intruder—*Esther?*—must have. That was why she'd raced out the sliding door.

"I ran around back . . . sounded like the noise was coming from the back of the house," Lewis continued. "I saw her running out the door."

Sweaty and icy cold, Catherine closed her eyes. Esther Knight had killed Olivia Perry.

CHAPTER 26

THE COMBINATION OF INTENSE FATIGUE and a sleeping pill knocked Catherine out for so long that when she opened her eyes in the Peraltas' guest bedroom, the numbers on the clock startled her. One o'clock in the afternoon! She pushed back the covers and rose gingerly to her feet.

Her left shoulder hurt so much that it was hard to lift her arm, and the right side of her rib cage was tender, but the rest of her was merely stiff. Catherine closed her eyes and added one more prayer to the hundreds of prayers of gratitude she'd already offered. If that vase had struck her in the skull—

It was a miracle she was alive, a miracle that her worst injury was a sore shoulder. If Esther had launched her attack even a few seconds earlier, Catherine would have been dead before Lewis could have interceded.

Esther.

She'd liked Esther. Trusted Esther. At one point or another, she'd suspected just about everyone else in Riley but never Esther.

Congratulations on your world-class people-reading skills.

Danielle . . . *Oh, Danielle.* She must be shattered. No matter how much she fought with Esther, caring for her had always been Danielle's top priority. Catherine couldn't even comprehend the pain Danielle must be feeling.

Even if Danielle didn't want to hear from her now, she had to try to talk to her. Forget Robert, forget crazy suspicions about who had sent the letter to Frances—forget everything. She could deal with all that later. Right now, Danielle needed to know she cared. If Danielle hung up on her or slammed the door in her face, so be it—at least, through her anger, she'd know Catherine wasn't oblivious to how much she was hurting.

For once.

Catherine shuffled to the bathroom. She showered, dressed in a fleece warm-up suit Jan had loaned her, and pulled her damp hair into a ponytail.

When she entered the kitchen, Jan was sitting at the table with . . . Ava?

"Ava!" Catherine exclaimed. "When did you—I didn't know you were—"

"I got here this morning." Ava jumped to her feet and came to embrace Catherine. "Adam called me last night."

"Adam called you?"

"Yes. He was afraid you wouldn't let me know you needed help, so he took it on himself to inform me. Bless the boy."

"I *was* going to call you today. You know I would have told you everything!"

Ava studied Catherine through her red-framed glasses. "And you were also going to tell me you were fine, didn't need anything, and don't trouble myself to come to Riley. Now you're stuck with me." She smiled, but tears welled in her eyes.

Catherine stepped forward for another hug, her own eyes wet. "Thank you for coming."

"My dear daughter," Ava murmured, pressing her cheek against Catherine's hair. "I'm sick about this. I should have ordered you on a plane the instant the first window got smashed. Instead, I kept telling you not to worry!"

"I'm a little old to order around," Catherine teased, her voice shaky. "It wouldn't have done any good."

"I could have tried!" Ava stepped back. "How are you feeling? Are you *sure* you're all right? I know you were at the emergency room last night, but you should see a doctor today—"

"I'm fine. Just sore."

"How sore? Are you in a lot of pain?"

"As long as I don't move my arm too much, I'm good. I took some ibuprofen."

"Sit down." Ava led Catherine toward the table. "You must be hungry."

"We're having lunch," Jan said. "But I can offer you breakfast if you'd prefer."

"I'm fine with whatever you're eating." Catherine sat down. "Have you . . . heard any news?"

Jan shook her head. "No. I keep checking, but I haven't heard that she's been arrested yet."

"She must have left town." Ava took off her glasses and reached for a napkin. "Poor Danielle. I feel so sorry for all of them. And to kill out of jealousy!"

"Jealousy?"

"We've been watching the news," Jan explained. "They were speculating that Esther killed Olivia out of jealousy over Will Conti. Did you know she'd been involved with him?"

"I figured there was a history between them from the way she acted when he showed up at the studio."

"They interviewed Will, and he said he'd dated Esther before Olivia, and Esther had never gotten over him." Jan rose to her feet and headed toward the cupboard. "He was really upset in the interview, said it was his fault Esther had gone after you—that Esther had seen him at your studio and knew he liked you, so she cracked again. I didn't know you and Will . . ."

"Good heavens, no, we weren't involved. Did the news say we were?"

"Not exactly. They just quoted him saying he liked you."

"He came to the studio pretending to be interested in music lessons," Catherine explained. "He flirted with me. I told him he wasn't my type. That was it. But, yes, Esther overheard it." If Will hadn't come to the studio that morning, Esther wouldn't have seen him with Catherine. She wouldn't have lashed out at Maren, thinking she was Catherine. Maren would be fine right now.

And Catherine had specifically *wanted* Esther there during Will's appointment to keep things appropriate. Esther had joked about being a chaperoning ninja, trained by Danielle.

"Are you okay, honey?" Ava squeezed her hand.

Catherine sighed. "Wishing I could go back in time." The way Esther had urged her to flee Riley, using the rumors and Danielle's feelings as an excuse . . . had Esther not *wanted* to kill again? Had she known she was losing control and the only way to keep Catherine alive was to get her out of Riley?

And Catherine had dug in her heels, blind to the storm building inside Esther.

What about the note purporting to be from Adam? Had Esther left the note yesterday afternoon in one final, frantic attempt to scare Catherine away from Riley—but her rage had already built to the point that she couldn't stop herself from attacking on the same night?

"Do they know if Esther was responsible for the vandalism?" Catherine asked.

"No word on that." Jan set a bowl and plate on the table. "Oh, I wanted to tell you—Adam stopped by this morning. He didn't want to wake you, but he left those for you." She pointed to a vase of pink roses on the counter. "Would you like some soup? Homemade chicken noodle. Leftovers from last night."

"I'd love some."

* * *

After lunch, Catherine returned to the guest room and called Danielle's cell phone. She couldn't imagine Danielle would be at work today. But then again, maybe she would be—forcing herself to keep her chin up and keep working despite the agony she was feeling over Esther and the humiliation of knowing all of Riley was buzzing about how Danielle Knight's sister was the murderer.

Why had Esther kept the vase—that heavy, unique vase, with its twisting vines and flowers? She'd probably never meant to kill Olivia. Grabbing and swinging Olivia's vase must have been a horrible impulse. But why hadn't she gotten rid of it afterward? Guilt? And using it again on Maren, then on . . . did some sick impulse keep driving her back to the same weapon?

Danielle didn't answer her phone—not to Catherine's surprise—so Catherine left a message. She'd try again later, and if she hadn't heard from Danielle by tonight, she'd visit in person.

At Catherine's insistence, Ava drove Catherine to the studio. The police had finished their work, and Burgess had given Catherine permission to go inside. Time to see how bad the damage was and get pictures and information for the insurance company.

"How did Esther get in?" Ava asked as they walked up the porch steps. "Did she have the code to the alarm system?"

"No one has it except me. The police think she must have returned after her shift while the studio was unlocked and students were coming and going. Since she worked here, no one would have thought anything of seeing her around. She could have stayed, hiding in the house—maybe in the basement."

Ava winced. "Terrifying."

Terrifying and hard to fathom. Had she been hiding for hours, wrestling against the impulse to attack Catherine until she couldn't restrain her hate any longer? How could Esther appear so sane and yet be so completely unhinged? Had Danielle suspected how sick her sister was? She must have known Esther had serious problems but not that they'd led her to murder.

Ava opened a notebook and got out her camera. "First, we document the damage."

As they moved through the house, with Ava writing notes and taking pictures, Catherine found herself feeling nauseated and shaky at all the smashed furnishings and dents in the walls. Esther had been swinging the vase like a maniac. How had Catherine escaped alive? Grimacing at the pain in her shoulder, she picked up a piece of the sculpture that had been on the table in the hall—a glass sculpture of a violin.

"At least it's insured." Ava eyed the fragment in Catherine's hand. "Your father bought that from a museum for some exorbitant price. I told him he was overpaying."

Catherine dropped the shard of glass and sighed. It had been a beautiful piece.

"You must have been running all over the place, or she had dreadful aim." Ava pointed at a hole in the wall opposite the broken sculpture. "Was she smashing everything she could reach?"

Catherine thought back, cold inside as she remembered rushing through the darkened house . . . falling . . . being certain the intruder was about to shatter her skull. "It wasn't a focused attack at all. She took a lot of random swings. Fortunately for me." Every dent in the wall was a dent she *hadn't* put in Catherine; every smashed sculpture or picture had helped keep Catherine intact.

Ava wrapped her arm around Catherine's waist. "I'm so sorry, honey. "

Catherine trailed her fingers over the splintered edge of the table in the hallway. "I liked Esther a lot. I knew she had issues, but I never imagined . . ."

"You must be in shock."

"Pretty much." Her phone rang in her pocket. "Excuse me. I don't dare ignore that. It might be the police." She pulled the phone out. "It's Adam."

"I'll give you some privacy." Ava headed into the family room.

* * *

Catherine was relaxing in the Peraltas' backyard in the late afternoon sunshine with Jan, Lewis, Ava, and Adam when her phone rang again. Hoping it was

Danielle, she grabbed it. The number seemed familiar, but she couldn't remember whose it was.

"Hello, this is Catherine."

A gruff voice spoke. "This is Dylan Gates. Maren's husband."

Oh no. How had Dylan gotten her cell number—oh, from Maren's phone. She braced herself for Dylan to launch a rant about how it was her fault Maren was hurt, how *she* was supposed to be the one in the hospital, that Esther never would have touched Maren if it hadn't been for Catherine.

Dylan said nothing. He was waiting for her to respond. Cautiously, Catherine asked, "How is Maren?"

"She . . . she . . ." His voice went raspier. "She's awake."

Joyfully, Catherine sprang to her feet. "That's wonderful! Is she . . . can she . . . talk to you?"

"Yeah . . . little bit. She's been . . . waking up for . . . really short stretches for a couple of days . . . she was out of it, couldn't talk to anyone, but this morning, she was finally awake for longer, and she was starting to remember stuff."

"That's a great sign!"

"Yeah . . . the doctor said it's good. She doesn't remember anything about the attack, but she . . . remembers you. That flute thing she's doing. The lessons."

"She talked about her lessons?"

"She's . . . worried . . . wanted you to . . . know she . . . that she wants to come back, that she's not . . . flaking out." He spoke faster. "She's out of it right now, doesn't know what she's saying, but she keeps talking about the flute, so I said I'd call you. Tell you she wants to come back. So I'm calling you, like I told her I would."

"Thank you," Catherine said in astonishment. Dylan was trying to comfort Maren by letting Catherine know she still wanted to take lessons? "Tell her I'll hold her spot for her for however long it takes her to recover."

"Okay."

"Would it be possible for me to visit Maren?"

"Not now. She's too weak." Dylan hung up.

Everyone had gone silent, watching Catherine. Catherine smiled and sank back onto her lounge chair.

"Good news about Maren?" Jan asked eagerly. "She's awake?"

"Yes. And talking!"

"That's wonderful!" Ava said, reaching over to hug Lewis, who was sitting next to her. Lewis's eyes widened, and Catherine wanted to giggle.

If Lewis was around Ava long enough, he'd find out that anyone sitting or standing next to her at happy moments was going to get squeezed.

"I can't believe I had a civil conversation with Dylan Gates." Catherine slid her phone into her pocket. "He said Maren was worried about her flute lessons, and he told her he'd call me about it. Maybe he's not 100 percent jerk after all."

"Maybe nearly losing his wife was a wake-up call on how he treats her," Adam said grimly.

"I hope so. He's obviously not planning to stand in the way of her taking lessons, so that's progress."

The surge of excitement over Maren's awakening soon ebbed into peaceful warmth, and Catherine, sleepy in the sunshine, found it increasingly difficult to track the conversation well enough to contribute. She let her eyes close, the conversation a comfortable background noise.

Adam's voice saying, "I need to get home," finally jolted her out of her doze. She opened her eyes.

"Stay for dinner, Adam," Jan invited.

"Thank you, but I need to check on my father."

Yawning, Catherine rose to her feet. "I'll walk you to the door."

The way Jan and Ava both smiled made Catherine blush. She should have just bluntly announced, "I'd like a moment alone with Adam."

At the front door, Adam stopped. "You going to be okay?"

"Yes." Catherine wrapped her arms around him. Adam had looked dazed all afternoon, and Catherine suspected he was adjusting to the fact that the police finally knew who had killed Olivia. Adam was no longer a suspect.

Was he also looking back, reviewing anything Olivia had ever said about Esther, wondering if he'd missed any warning signs? She hoped he wasn't blaming himself.

From the tension in Adam's arms as he embraced her and the overlong silent hug he gave her, Catherine knew he was also struggling with the fact that Catherine had nearly been a victim of the same killer.

"I wish I could keep an eye on you for a while," he muttered, drawing back at last.

"I wish you could keep an eye on me too. But your dad needs you. Call me later."

"I will."

He touched her hand. "Let me know how Danielle's doing and if there's anything I can do."

"I will. I hope to hear from her soon."

"You're a good friend to her."

"She needs *someone*. She doesn't have any family who'll support her. I can't imagine how isolated she must feel. And the things that went wrong between us don't seem to matter now. I hope I can give her at least a little support."

"I'll talk to you soon." Adam pressed her hand between both of his and headed out the door.

Catherine returned to the backyard. The bright sunlight was beginning to dim, and the temperature was dropping; she should have fetched her jacket from the guest room.

"Nice boy," Ava said sweetly.

"Don't get any ideas. We're just friends."

"Oh, for goodness sakes, child. If we have to pretend to believe *that*, we're going to whisper about you whenever you leave the room. Why not be candid so we can talk openly?"

Catherine laughed. "I *am* being candid. We're just friends . . . for now. I didn't say that can't change!" Her phone rang. She grabbed it and saw Danielle's name on the screen. Heart pounding, she lifted the phone to her ear. "Hi, Dani."

Jan and Ava both leaned toward her then drew back as though realizing they were attempting to eavesdrop. Lewis focused his gaze on the sandwich he was eating.

Danielle spoke quietly. "Are you all right?"

"Yes. Dani . . . I'm so sorry." She wanted to say more but couldn't think of anything that didn't sound trite. "I'm so sorry."

"Did she do a lot of damage?"

"It's a . . . bit of a mess, but we'll take care of it."

"And you?"

"I'm fine. Can I do anything for you? Can I help you in any way?"

"No."

"Have you . . . have you heard anything from her?"

"No."

Not surprising. The last person Esther would want to face was Danielle. "Would you like company? I could come over."

Danielle said nothing.

"I don't want to be pushy," Catherine said quickly. "But if you need anything, please call."

"It would . . . be all right if you wanted to come over." Danielle sounded tired. "The house is suffocating me."

"I'll be there in fifteen or twenty minutes."

"Thanks." Danielle hung up.

"I'm going to see Danielle," Catherine said. "Ava, can you drop me at the studio so I can get my car?"

Lewis sprang to his feet. "I'll take you," he said. "I dropped my flashlight somewhere in your neighborhood last night, and I want to find it before it gets dark."

"Don't worry about the flashlight," Catherine said. "I'll replace it."

"Thanks, but that'd be a waste. I'll find it."

"Whatever you want. Let me get ready." Catherine went to the guest room, changed into a pair of jeans and a sweatshirt that she'd shoved into a duffel bag when she and Ava were at the studio earlier, and met Lewis at the front door.

Lewis said nothing for the first part of the drive. His broad shoulders were squared, and he was sitting up so straight that Catherine wanted to say, "At ease, soldier."

"Thank you again for everything," Catherine opened the conversation. "I've never been able to say 'I owe you my life' to anyone before, so this is a new experience. I probably owe you a bonus too."

Lewis's jaw clenched. "I'm . . . sorry I didn't do a better job. Should have gotten in there faster . . . kicked the door down or something."

"Lewis, do you have any idea how solid that front door is? You would have broken your foot, and the door wouldn't have budged."

Lewis didn't answer. Last night must have been so traumatic for him, Catherine realized, an increasingly familiar sense of shame regrowing inside her. She hadn't been thinking about how awful it must have been for Lewis to interrupt Esther's attack.

You need to set some new goals for yourself, she told herself firmly. *Like, "Think about at least two other people every day before you start stewing over your own problems."*

Lewis wiped both hands on his jeans before swiftly gripping the steering wheel again. Sweaty hands. He looked so tense. Was he thinking about Olivia? They'd been good friends, according to Jan. Jan even thought Lewis had had a crush on her. And Lewis was the one who'd chased down her murderer . . . who'd picked up the weapon that had once been stained with her blood. Did he take any satisfaction in being the one who'd uncovered Esther's identity? Or did he feel guilty that she'd escaped him?

"I'm sure they'll find Esther soon," Catherine said, hoping she wasn't increasing Lewis's stress by talking about this.

He nodded curtly.

Be quiet, Catherine berated herself. *Can't you tell he doesn't want to talk about it?*

Lewis parked in front of the studio. "Can I look inside first? I might have dropped it in the house."

"Of course." Catherine almost added, "Make it fast. I don't want to keep Danielle waiting," but changed her mind. Lewis already seemed so edgy. If she made him feel he was inconveniencing her, he'd decline to check inside at all, and after everything he'd done for her, the least she could do was let him look for his flashlight.

Catherine unlocked the front door and deactivated the alarm. "I didn't see it when Ava and I were here today, but it might have rolled under the couch or somewhere else we didn't check."

"Okay." Lewis headed into the main room of the studio.

Catherine retrieved her mail, checked for phone messages, and tried not to appear impatient, but Lewis was going so *slowly*. It took him ten minutes before he reached the family room, where Catherine was sitting, pretending to play games on her phone. He trudged around and checked closely in places—like corners in plain view—where he should have been able to tell from across the room that there was no flashlight. He didn't talk while he searched, and he had such a tight expression on his face that Catherine knew he wouldn't welcome her chatting with him.

He paid a lot of attention to every dent in the walls and every broken piece of furniture, and Catherine wondered if he was mentally reconstructing the attack. A few times, she thought he was going to say something—he'd draw a breath and glance at her—but then he'd avert his eyes.

"Looks bad, doesn't it?" Ready to go crazy from the delay and the silence, Catherine finally spoke. "At least we swept up the glass—or Ava did; she wouldn't let me touch the broom. Wouldn't believe me when I told her I was fine and didn't need to rest."

Lewis grunted.

"I'm sorry to hurry you, but I need to get to Danielle's." She rose to her feet. She felt guilty rushing him—maybe studying the scene of the attack was helping him come to terms with what happened, but she couldn't keep Danielle waiting any longer. "If the flashlight was in the house, you would have found it."

"Sorry to hold you up."

"Not a problem. But we'd better go now."

"It's . . . crazy." Lewis touched a gash in the drywall. "Esther."

"I can't believe it either. How well did you know her?"

"Not well, but I knew *about* her. From Olivia. Olivia used to talk about her and her sister."

"Did—" Catherine stopped. Asking if Olivia had ever been afraid of Esther was cruel. If Olivia *had* said anything like that, Lewis must be consumed with guilt for not realizing Olivia had been in danger.

"I hope she . . . doesn't get blamed for anything she didn't do," Lewis muttered.

"I'm sure she'll get a fair trial. I just hope they find her quickly. Lewis, I really need to leave."

"Okay."

Catherine switched off the family room lights and headed toward the front door. The sound of Lewis's footsteps behind her unsettled her. She was tempted to look over her shoulder to verify that it *was* Lewis. She knew that impulse was irrational, but talking about Esther while standing in the damaged studio had given her the chills. All day, she'd been either too stunned to think clearly or too relieved that they knew the identity of the murderer to think a lot about the fact that Esther was still free and still dangerous.

"Thanks, Lewis." She opened the door. "Feel free to search the property for your flashlight. And if you want to take tonight off since I won't even be sleeping here—"

"No, I'll be here. I want to keep an eye on the place."

"Thank you. I'll go out through the garage, since I need to get my car. Have a good night."

Despite the fact that Catherine was holding the front door open for him and waiting for him to step outside, Lewis didn't move. He had such a remote expression on his face that Catherine's anxiety swelled. *Get a grip. You know who the killer is! You don't have to be scared of Lewis.*

"Good night," she said again. "I'm running late."

Finally, Lewis stepped across the threshold. Relieved, Catherine shut and locked the front door and headed for the garage.

She couldn't blame Lewis for being so thrown that he was acting strange. She should have insisted he take the night off—but maybe that wouldn't have helped. If she told him to go home, he'd probably lie in bed, unable to sleep, worrying about the unguarded studio. Lewis was so conscientious.

How distressing to be the one who had yanked Esther's mask off! And to be the only eyewitness—he must be feeling heavy pressure there. Is that why he was worried about her being blamed unfairly for something? Did he doubt he'd identified her correctly?

Could he be *wrong*? Could Esther be innocent?

Uh-huh. And somehow innocent Esther disappeared the instant the police started looking for her. Dream on. Lewis is just shaken at having been the one to ID her. You would be too.

As she drove across the bridge in her minivan, she glanced in the rearview mirror. Was that Lewis's car? She'd thought he wanted to stay and search the neighborhood. Maybe he was too tired to care about the flashlight anymore tonight. Catherine should have insisted that he let her replace it; Lewis shouldn't have to worry about—

Will you stop obsessing over Lewis and his flashlight? You need to think about how you can help Danielle.

Her eyes stung, but she blinked the tears away. If Catherine started bawling about Esther, Danielle would view that as pity, and it would annoy her, not comfort her. Danielle didn't do tears.

But Catherine knew she'd cry for Esther, whether or not she ever let Danielle see it.

CHAPTER 27

DANIELLE OPENED THE DOOR. SHE looked vulnerable, even childlike, to Catherine, dressed in a T-shirt, jeans, and tennis shoes, her cheeks pale and her eyes devoid of makeup. "Come in." She glanced at Catherine's minivan, parked in front of her house. "When will you get some class and get a nicer car?"

"It *is* a nice car," Catherine said. "It's almost new!"

"It's a *minivan*." Danielle closed the door. "You're a single woman in your twenties, not a forty-year-old soccer mom."

"Ever try to haul a pile of musical instruments around in a sports car?" Catherine wanted to hug Danielle and express her sympathy, but taking her cues from Danielle, she stuck with a light approach.

They sat on the couch. Arms folded, gaze focused on the opposite wall, Danielle asked, "Would you like something to drink?"

"You don't have to play hostess. I'm here to help *you*. Have you eaten dinner?"

"Yes. But if you haven't, we could go pick something up."

"I'm fine. Unless you want to get out of the house."

Danielle sighed and leaned forward to scrape at something on the coffee table with her thumbnail. A fleck of nail polish from Esther? "I do want to get of the house. I'd love to get as far out of the house as possible but not for fast food. We can skip it."

"Would you like to go for a walk?" Talking would be easier while moving side by side instead of sitting here not sure whether to look at each other.

"Walking as therapy," Danielle said. "Your specialty. Sounds fun, Cate. Let's walk around the neighborhood and keep count of how many neighbors rubberneck at us."

Catherine grimaced. Walking around Riley was definitely a bad idea.

"Sorry," Danielle said. "I'm not mocking your suggestion. Walking would be wonderful, but this stuffy house is better than dealing with . . . attention. *Slightly* better."

Where could they walk that would be more private? Catherine thought of the gorge, where she'd picnicked with Adam a few days ago. The tranquility of nature would be a vast improvement over inquisitive neighbors or a house filled with reminders of Esther.

"If you want to get out and avoid gawkers, we could go to Orenda Gorge," Catherine suggested. "Have you been there?"

"Yes. Nice place."

"Interested? We still have a couple of hours of daylight, and it only takes twenty minutes to get there."

"You can't possibly be up to hiking. You . . . must be sore."

"Not my legs. If you'd like to go, I'm game."

Danielle gave her a dubious look. "You don't have to suffer to entertain me."

"I'm *fine*. I'd love to go. If you'd enjoy getting out, then I'm happy to take you to the gorge."

"You're sure?"

"Absolutely."

"If you're sure, let's do it. It sounds better than sitting here. Thanks, Cate."

Danielle changed into sturdier shoes and put on an orange jacket; the bright color made her look paler.

As they headed for Catherine's minivan, her phone rang. "Sorry about that. I would have turned it off, but Detective Burgess asked that I stay available." She pulled her phone out of her pocket and checked the screen. Adam.

"You can go ahead and answer it if you want to." Danielle opened the passenger door. "I'm not Miss Manners."

"That's all right." This would not be a good time to chat with Adam. "Just let me send a quick text." She hit the button to decline the call and followed it with a rapid text letting Adam know she and Danielle were heading to the gorge. Given how edgy Adam was, she didn't want him worrying if he didn't hear from her for a while.

Catherine started the engine. "Ava arrived this morning."

"Nice of her to come check on you."

"Yes."

Silence. As they drove out of the neighborhood, Catherine tried to think of a topic of conversation that didn't involve Esther and didn't sound petty. She couldn't think of any. How could they *not* talk about Esther?

"How long do you think it will take to get the studio fully functioning again?" Danielle asked. "Does Ava already have people lined up to do repair work?"

Grateful for this suggested topic, Catherine went into detail on what she and Ava had discussed today. Danielle asked additional questions about the studio, and Catherine launched into her plans for the open house. Since it was apparent that Danielle found this a relatively safe topic, Catherine continued into reports on individual students, treading into dangerous territory only when she asked if Danielle had heard that Maren was awake. Danielle said yes and promptly asked her about another student; Catherine took the hint and didn't mention Maren again.

She was relieved when they pulled into the parking lot at Orenda Gorge. Maybe it would be easier to talk about Esther when they were walking. Or would the whole evening be like this, filled with discussions that avoided Esther's name?

Maybe Danielle was waiting for Catherine to bring up Esther, unable to do it herself but wanting desperately to vent her pain. As they started on a trail lined with autumn foliage, Catherine debated what to do. What would be the most comforting, the most helpful?

Be straightforward. If Danielle didn't want to talk about Esther, she could say so, but Catherine needed to give her the opportunity.

Catherine rallied her nerve. "I don't know what to say, Dani, but I want you to know that I care about Esther, and if I can help either of you, I will."

"Offering money for a lawyer?" Danielle's tone was matter-of-fact.

"If it would help."

"This man who ID'd her, your security guard. He's sure?"

Catherine's heart ached. Danielle was grabbing at a last straw, hoping Lewis had made a mistake. "He's sure."

"He's the only witness? Or did *you* see her?"

"Not such that I could identify her. When the lights were still on, I only got a glimpse—an impression of a dark mask, a dark jacket. After that, all I could see was . . . a blur. It went so fast, and the house was dark. I could hardly even see a *person*—just darkness and motion. But Dani . . . if he made a mistake, then where *is* Esther?"

Danielle said nothing.

Catherine couldn't blame her for hoping Lewis had made a mistake. If Lewis hadn't told Burgess that it was Esther, none of them would have suspected—

If Lewis hadn't told Burgess—

Catherine stopped walking. She'd only seen *one* shadowy figure and had heard Lewis yell from outside. She'd never seen two people together. Lewis had said he'd pounded on the front door, but she hadn't heard him. She'd thought the noise of Esther smashing things had drowned it out.

What if he'd lied about hammering on the door?

What if it had been Lewis swinging the vase? Catherine scoured her memories, trying to picture the dark figure attacking her. Esther was a tall woman, but Lewis must be twice as broad. Catherine should have been able to tell the difference even if she could hardly see the attacker. But in the darkness . . . her senses skewed by panic . . .

She didn't know. She couldn't picture the attacker at all, let alone how big he or she had been.

Danielle, a dozen yards up the trail, paused and turned toward Catherine. "What's wrong?"

Catherine pushed herself forward to where Danielle waited. Why would Lewis have wanted to hurt Olivia?

Jealousy? He was in love with her, but she rejected him?

You're jumping to conclusions. Even if he had a reason to kill Olivia, why would he try to kill you?

"I . . . think I'm losing my mind," Catherine said.

"What is it?"

"Have you seen Esther at all since last night? Or any evidence that she stopped by home to get money or clothes or whatever?"

"No. The last time I saw her was before I left for work yesterday morning. Why?"

Everyone assumed Esther had disappeared because she was guilty and on the run. But what if she'd disappeared because she was . . . dead?

Lewis *could* have killed Esther after she left the studio yesterday morning, sneaked into the house while the studio was open, and hid until nearly time for him to arrive at work. Then he could have staged the attack, pretended to interrupt it, pretended to chase the attacker, and returned to identify the assailant as Esther.

"I don't like how much this case relies on one man," Catherine said. Lewis, acting strange at the studio. Lewis's car behind her on the road. She hadn't looked back again to see if he'd followed her to Danielle's. What if he'd followed them to the gorge?

Why would he follow you? Why would he want to hurt you? He could have killed you anytime if that was his goal. And why would he feel the need to stage the attack to get Esther blamed for killing Olivia? No one suspected him; he wasn't in danger.

Danielle scrutinized her, her eyes keen. "You think Lewis Peralta lied?"

"I don't know. It seems crazy. *He'd* have to be crazy, completely insane." She explained her train of thought to Danielle.

Without commenting, Danielle turned and resumed walking up the trail. Catherine kept pace with her. She couldn't tell what Danielle was thinking. Her cheeks were flushed and her expression set. Catherine's suggestion must have stirred an agonizing mix of hope and horror. Maybe Esther was innocent of murder. But if she was innocent, she was probably dead.

"I need to call Detective Burgess," Catherine said.

"Do it."

Catherine pulled out her phone and found the number. If there was any validity to this wild theory, Burgess was likely already investigating it, but Catherine had better share her thoughts anyway.

Danielle kept hiking, her pace so rapid that Catherine wondered if she was using physical exertion to distract herself from emotional pain. It would have been easier for Catherine to make the call while she wasn't galloping up the hill, but she didn't want to ask Danielle to hold still.

Burgess answered on the third ring. Trying not to sound too out of breath, Catherine shared her thoughts about Lewis.

"Thank you for contacting me," Burgess said. "Where are you now?"

"Walking at Orenda Gorge with Danielle Knight. She—hasn't heard anything from Esther."

"You're at the gorge! Catherine, it's not a good idea for you to be in an isolated area. Come back to Riley immediately, but don't go home or to the Peraltas'. Check into a hotel. Then call and let me know where you are."

New worry hit Catherine. "My stepmother is at the Peraltas'. She arrived from Virginia this morning."

"I don't think she's in any danger, but let her know where you're staying and ask her to join you."

"All right."

When Catherine lowered the phone, Danielle glanced at her. "What did she say?"

Catherine stopped walking. "To go home and check into a hotel."

"A hotel?" Danielle halted and faced her.

"I'm staying with the Peraltas, which suddenly doesn't seem like a good idea. Hang on; I need to call Ava right now."

After asking Ava to go somewhere private so she could talk freely, Catherine explained the situation. Ava calmly reassured her that she would invent a graceful excuse for stepping out, find a hotel, and then text Catherine the location. Catherine could tell that Ava thought these fears about Lewis stemmed from a futile desire to prove Esther innocent for Danielle's sake, but Ava would wait until they were together to discuss it.

During the conversation, Catherine tried a couple of times to start heading down the hill, but Danielle didn't move with her, and Catherine gave up and stayed where she was. Danielle obviously wanted explanations before action.

"What did Detective Burgess think of your theory about Lewis?" Danielle asked as Catherine slid the phone into her pocket.

"She's hard to read. She might have thought I was nuts, or she might have already been investigating him. Dani, I'm sorry. I know that no matter what the truth is, it's not good."

Danielle nodded and started back up the hill.

"We need to go home," Catherine said, catching up with her. "Detective Burgess is right. I'm worried about where Lewis is. He told me he was going to hunt for his flashlight in my neighborhood, but I think I saw him driving away when I did."

"Are you afraid he might have followed you here?"

"I'm nervous. I'll feel better with more people around."

"He didn't follow us."

"How can you be sure?"

"Esther's missing," Danielle said shortly. "I'm always looking around, checking behind me, checking *everywhere* for a glimpse of her or her car. No one followed us. We're safer here than we would be in Riley."

"Still, I told Burgess I'd go back."

"Go if you want to, but I can't stand the thought of sitting around and staring out the windows. I'll hike a little longer."

"We came in the same car. I can't drive away without you."

"I'll find another way home."

"Don't be a martyr." Catherine tried not to sound curt. She knew Danielle was under a lot of strain, but if Detective Burgess had said go back, they should go back.

Danielle smiled a brief, tense grin. "Sorry. It's just good to work out some stress. Can we do fifteen more minutes?"

"Fine." Fifteen minutes wouldn't make a difference.

"Thanks, Cate." Danielle increased her pace.

CHAPTER 28

CATHERINE'S UNEASINESS AND HER DESIRE to return home grew more intense as they hiked farther. The sky would darken soon. It was already getting cold. Even if there was no way either Lewis or Esther could know they were here, Catherine didn't like feeling alone, not tonight.

She shouldn't have felt alone with Danielle, but Danielle wasn't talking. She was hiking silently, her expression remote. Catherine couldn't blame her—in Danielle's situation, Catherine wouldn't have felt chatty either. But given the state of Catherine's nerves, along with her bruised, aching shoulder and rib cage and her waning stamina, she was finding the walk onerous.

She checked her watch. Fifteen minutes *must* have passed by now—

Catherine's phone rang. She snatched it out of her pocket. The number on the screen had a Riley area code, but she didn't recognize it. "I don't know who this is. I'd better answer." She lifted the phone to her ear. "Hello, this is Catherine."

A choked female voice spoke. "It's Esther Knight. *Don't hang up!* I need to talk to you."

Nerves prickling with shock, Catherine halted momentarily in her tracks then stepped clumsily forward, glancing at Danielle. Danielle kept walking, her gaze on the scenery.

Esther's alive! Catherine wanted to grab Danielle and tell her, but if Esther knew Catherine was with Danielle, she might panic and hang up.

"Okay," Catherine said carefully. "Where are you?"

"I was *not* trying to kill you last night." Esther's whispery voice jumped to a louder volume as though she couldn't control herself enough to speak softly. "I was trying to scare you."

Catherine's emotions knotted into such a snarl that she had no idea what she was feeling. Esther *was* guilty. "Why would I believe you?"

"How big of a loser do you think I am? I hid for hours and got all the lights in your house turned out before you even clued in that I was there. Don't you think I could have bashed your skull in if I'd wanted to? I was just trying to freak you out, to scare you into leaving town. I wasn't trying to kill you."

Picturing the way the house had looked when she'd inventoried the damage with Ava gave Catherine a weird feeling. There *had* been so many random blows, so many things broken. Esther *could* have tried a lot harder to zero in on her. How many times had that vase actually struck Catherine? Twice, and neither had been a dangerous hit.

"Why would you do something that insane?" Catherine asked.

The phone connection crackled. "*I was trying to save your life.* The rumors weren't enough—"

"*You* started the rumors? You sent the letter to Frances Randolph?"

Danielle halted and stared at Catherine.

"Yeah, but it wasn't enough," Esther said. "So I thought that freaky note I left you—you found it, right? With your cello case?"

"Yes." Catherine touched Danielle's arm and mouthed, "Esther." Danielle's eyes widened, and she drew a sharp breath; Catherine shook her head and held her finger to her lips.

"I thought if you stopped trusting Adam—Dani told me you liked him—I thought if you stopped trusting him that would make you more willing to . . . If I left the note, then attacked you, the police would suspect him; *you* would suspect him—you'd go—" The phone crackled again, covering up Esther's voice. Catherine glanced at the screen to check the strength of the signal. It was strong. The problem must be on Esther's end.

Please don't let the call drop, Catherine prayed. "Why would you—"

More static. ". . . planned last night so Lewis . . ." Static. ". . . in time to make you think he'd saved . . ." More static.

"Esther? Are you still there?"

". . . didn't think he'd *catch* me. That clod is *fast*."

Catherine's heart hammered. Esther had known what time Lewis was scheduled to arrive. Catherine hadn't thought much about that—she'd assumed Esther, in her virulent hatred and insanity, had forgotten. But the timing had been so perfect . . .

". . . didn't want to do any permanent damage. But I had to scare you. I thought *that* would be enough . . . but now it's all messed up, and everyone thinks I'm the killer . . ." Static. ". . . did *not* kill Olivia Perry or Maren Gates."

"Then where did you get the vase?" Catherine asked. Realizing she was digging her fingernails into Danielle's arm, she lowered her hand. "Olivia's vase?"

Catherine thought Esther said, "It doesn't matter," but the connection had gone bad again, and she couldn't discern all the words.

"I'm not the one who used it to kill her," Esther said. "You have to *leave Riley. Now.* If you wait, you'll die."

"If you know who the killer is, why won't you tell me? If you want to save my life, tell me who the murderer is."

"I can't do that. Go and everything will be okay. Please . . . I don't want anyone else to die . . . You . . . you don't deserve . . ."

If Esther was telling the truth—if the killer wasn't Esther or Lewis—who was it? Who would Esther want to protect?

"It's Will Conti, isn't it," Catherine said. "You're protecting Will."

"*What?* Are you kidding me? That snake wouldn't . . ." Static.

"Esther? Can you hear me? Listen to me. You need to turn yourself in. You need to come in and explain—Esther?"

She'd hung up. Catherine wiped sweat off the glossy screen of her phone and met Danielle's gaze. "I was wrong about Lewis."

"She admitted she attacked you."

"She sounded . . . It was bizarre. I have no idea what's going on in her head." Catherine recapped the conversation.

When she finished, Danielle resumed her hike up the hill.

"Danielle!" Catherine followed her. "We need to leave! And I need to call Detective Burgess to tell her I heard from Esther."

The trail was drawing closer to the edge of the gorge. Through the trees, Catherine could see cliffs sloping downward to the river that foamed over jagged rocks. It was spectacular, but never had Catherine had less ability to appreciate nature. She felt more ready to explode with stress than to whip out a camera for a *National Geographic* moment.

"Danielle—"

"The place I want to stop is only a couple hundred yards farther, and then we'll turn back."

"Are you kidding me? We're going back *now.*"

Danielle ignored her.

Grinding her teeth, Catherine kept pace with her. She couldn't abandon Danielle at the gorge.

What was going on in Esther's head? Did she think she could explain away last night's attack and disassociate herself from the weapon that had killed Olivia? Did she think anyone would believe she'd been trying to—in a warped, roundabout way—help Catherine?

If Esther *was* scared for her, why would she take such a rash course in trying to urge Catherine out of harm's way? Why couldn't she tell Catherine—or the police—the name of the person who wanted Catherine dead? Who would Esther want to protect?

The answer to that question was so easy but so illogical that it gave Catherine the feeling she'd applied the wrong formula to the problem and come up with nonsense. Yes, Esther would want to protect Danielle, but Danielle couldn't possibly be a murderer. She'd loved Olivia. She didn't have a motive for killing her.

Catherine glanced at Danielle, hiking resolutely up the trail.

This was insane. Controlled, intelligent Danielle was the last person who'd attack anyone. But Catherine couldn't stay here any longer. She stopped walking.

"Dani, I'm going back. If you're not ready, that's fine. I'll call a taxi on my way down and have the driver wait for you at the bottom of the gorge for however long you want to stay. Send me the bill."

Danielle stopped and turned toward Catherine. She smiled. "Does hiking remind you of Robert?"

Catherine gaped at her. What did Robert have to do with this? "Esther told me how you felt about him. I had no idea, and I'm sorry. We can talk about it later."

"He loved *you*. I can understand that. But you didn't care about him at all. You used him."

Catherine wanted to scream at her. What did Robert matter right now? "I did care! I *loved* him. Our relationship just didn't have a future. Danielle, this is not the time—"

Danielle's eyes were ice. "He was handsome, he was fun, so you used him."

"I did not—"

"Then when he wanted a commitment, you pushed him aside. Broke his heart. That's why he was out hiking that day. Did you know that? Did you care about him enough to find out *why* he was in the mountains the day he died?"

"He enjoyed hiking and walking, even in winter. That's one thing we *did* have in common. I didn't think it was unusual—"

"He talked to me. Before he left."

"You never told me that."

"Why would you have cared?"

Catherine's mouth was so parched that it was hard to make her tongue work. She'd never seen—or even imagined—the seething hatred burning in Danielle's face. "You *know* I would have cared about what he did that day. The fact that I didn't see us getting married didn't mean I didn't care about him."

"How diplomatic."

"What did he tell you?" This was lunacy. She needed to get back to Riley. She needed to call Burgess about Esther. Instead, she was standing here discussing Robert Fields.

"He was planning to stay out all day, hike as far and as hard as he could, then camp. Said being near you was driving him crazy. He needed to get away."

"I never wanted to hurt him. I'm sorry I didn't know how you felt about him. We can talk about this after—"

"I talked to his cousin after he died. I asked him how it happened. He said Robert had been careless, which wasn't like him. He'd been hiking too fast downhill, not watching where he was going, talking about you the whole time." Danielle stepped toward Catherine so they were face-to-face.

Catherine wanted to shrink backward, but acting like a coward wouldn't help her handle Danielle.

"He died because of what you did to him," Danielle said. "You didn't even care enough to find out that it was your fault. You don't care about anything except your own pain. Does this hurt, Cate?" Moving so fast that Catherine barely saw her hand move, Danielle slapped her across the face.

The force behind the blow jerked Catherine's head to the side and made her stagger. Without time or presence of mind to think through what was happening, Catherine whirled around and sped down the trail.

Danielle crashed into her from behind, hurtling her forward. Throwing her hands out to brace herself, Catherine slammed full length into the trail. Pain exploded through her wrists and up her arms.

Danielle grabbed the back of her jacket and yanked her upward. Catherine made it to her knees, which hurt worse—she must have slammed her left knee into a rock when she fell. Gasping, fighting nausea, she twisted away from Danielle's hands and slumped against a tree at the side of the trail.

"It's too bad you didn't hit your head," Danielle said. "Like Robert."

Pain made Catherine feel she wouldn't be able to stand, let alone outfight Danielle. She chose her words with caution. "Dani . . . please. I didn't know how you felt. I didn't want to hurt you or Robert. Let's go home . . . Let's talk honestly, for once in our lives."

"You're not *that* dense. You know we're not going home. By now you know what Esther meant. Poor Esther . . . I was afraid she'd do something colossally stupid someday, but I didn't think it would be *this*. She likes you. You were nice to her; you treated her like she was worth something. Thanks, Cate. I do appreciate that. You're not all bad."

Terror jumbled with confusion and incredulity as Catherine stared up at Danielle. "You would kill me over Robert Fields?"

"No." Danielle's voice trembled. "I'm going to kill you for Olivia Perry."

CHAPTER 29

CATHERINE BENT HER LEGS, AND with her back against the tree trunk, pushed herself to her feet with the tree supporting her. Her wrists burned, but she could flex them, and all of her fingers worked. "That makes no sense. I never even knew Olivia. I wasn't here when she died."

The second slap shouldn't have surprised her, but she still didn't see it coming in time to deflect it. Face throbbing and neck aching, Catherine lunged to the side, ready to make a break for it, but Danielle caught her arm.

"If you run, I'll kill you now."

Catherine was regaining her wind and her strength, and she could match Danielle in a fair fight. She wasn't going to stand here and—

Something cold jabbed against her rib cage. Catherine looked down and saw the black metal of a gun.

She froze. "Danielle . . . please . . ."

"Let's walk. This way." Still gripping Catherine's arm, Danielle led her off the trail into the trees. Ahead, Catherine could see sheer cliffs and the river gushing over rocks far below. *Don't panic. Stay calm. You have a problem; how are you going to solve it?*

Her logical thoughts fragmented into panic, and she wanted to start screaming. *No. Don't lose control. Calm down.*

"Where did you get the gun?" she asked.

"It was my dad's. I took it away from him a long time ago—didn't want him leaving it around where someone might get hurt. I never wanted it . . . kept it in storage for years . . . but I decided I needed it tonight. I knew you'd bring us here. You're so easy to manipulate."

"How could you know—" Oh—she'd mentioned the gorge to Danielle a few days ago when talking about Adam. All Danielle had had to do was drop hints, guiding her until Catherine thought coming to this isolated place was her own idea. "Detective Burgess knows we're here. You heard me tell her I'm here with you. Ava knows. Adam knows too. I told him in that text I sent before we left your house. If I don't come home, they'll know that you . . . You won't get away with . . . it's impossible . . ."

"Seriously, Cate?" Danielle spun Catherine around and pushed her against a tree, holding the muzzle of the gun against her stomach. Danielle's face was so pale that it resembled marble. *Ghost-white marble. Marble headstones in a cemetery.* Ava would arrange for Catherine's name to be carved into a headstone. Ava would take her body to Virginia for burial next to her parents.

Catherine clenched her jaw to keep herself from screaming.

"Do you think I plan to go back after this?" From the way Danielle's voice bounced up and down, she sounded like she was both laughing and crying.

"If you think you can escape—"

"I'm not *escaping*." Her fingernails gouged Catherine's arm. "Do you think I'd run off and leave the cops thinking Esther is the murderer? Leave her to pay for what I did?"

For what I did . . . "How did Esther figure out that you . . . killed Olivia?"

"I'm not sure. Esther is perceptive. Smart. Figures things out about people. She might have suspected . . . after Olivia died . . . might have guessed why I was . . . so upset. But I don't think she knew . . . really wanted to know . . . until Maren."

"You attacked Maren. You thought she was me."

The rage in Danielle's face made Catherine certain Danielle would pull the trigger. Instead, she shoved the barrel of the gun so forcefully into Catherine's stomach that Catherine folded forward, gasping in agony.

"Your ugly lobster raincoat . . . Why did you let her *wear* it?"

Catherine struggled to stand upright. With her head lowered, she felt she was posing for Danielle to slam the gun into the back of her skull and fracture it like she had Maren's. And Olivia's. "Esther—used the—vase last night." Almost too sick with pain to speak, she forced the words out of her mouth. "Olivia's vase. How did she find it?"

"I'm not sure. I think after Maren, when she could tell I was so . . . that I was losing control, I think she went looking for anything incriminating, like paint. I'm guessing by then she knew I was the vandal."

Finally able to stand straight, Catherine leaned hard against the tree. Danielle had taken a step backward.

"I'd hidden the vase in a box in the garage," Danielle said. "I should have thrown it away, but when I'd try, I . . . couldn't. It seemed wrong to throw it away, throw away Olivia's vase like it was garbage. I needed to keep it until I used it *right*—used it for *you*. But Esther found it . . . She must have figured everything out. Must have panicked."

Catherine dizzily assembled the puzzle pieces. Esther knew about Robert and must have sensed Danielle's buried hatred for Catherine. When she'd found the vase, she'd recognized Danielle's crimes—and she'd guessed Catherine was next. She must have thought if she could drive Catherine away, Danielle's rage would cool and Catherine would be safe.

"Stupid kid." Danielle sounded exasperated. "She probably thought it was brilliant to use the vase then drop it on your lawn so you'd be sure Olivia's killer was after you and you'd leave town. Right now, she's probably cowering in a friend's basement, stunned at how all of Riley thinks *she's* the killer and wondering what to do next. Do you think I'd let her suffer for my crimes? I already mailed a signed confession to Detective Burgess and left another copy at my house. I confessed to your murder too, so it's complete."

Catherine's terror made it difficult for her to focus on Danielle's pale face. Danielle didn't care about being caught. She was going to kill Catherine then kill herself.

Stall. Keep talking to her.

But what good will that do? No one knows you need help. Catherine's hand brushed uselessly across the hard rectangle of the phone in her pocket. There was no way she could call for help without Danielle's seeing her reach for the phone.

Obviously following her thoughts, Danielle jammed her hand into Catherine's pocket and pulled out her phone. She set it on a rock and slammed the butt of the gun repeatedly against the screen.

Despair surged higher, even though Catherine knew the loss of the phone didn't make a difference. Even if she could have called for help, no one could have reached her in time.

"Why did you encourage me to come to Riley if you hate me like this?" Catherine asked. "Why did you want me here?"

"So I could kill you."

"You could have come to Virginia to kill me. Why did you want me here?"

Danielle said nothing, but from the confusion in her eyes, Catherine wondered if she even *knew* the answer to that question.

"What do I have to do with Olivia?" Catherine asked quickly, desperate to keep Danielle talking.

Tears trickled down Danielle's face. "It was all so idiotic. I'd had a bad few weeks . . . it was nearing the anniversary of Robert's death, and I'd needed to do *something* to bleed off pressure. Smashing that cutesy fountain . . . and a few windows . . . so juvenile, but you know, Cate, it *did* make me feel better. Every cute frog I smashed on that library fountain was you. Every window I smashed had your face in the glass. It was crude, but it helped."

"The new vandalism too? Was that you? The school and Olivia's apartment?"

"It wasn't easy having you come to Riley."

So Catherine's arrival had driven Danielle back to lashing out against glass or wood or concrete. Had she thought at first that the vandalism would be enough and she could avoid attacking Catherine?

"How does this involve Olivia?" Catherine asked.

"It was a mistake, a bad judgment call. I brought the folder to school—you remember the 'vent' folder, the one I kept in college?"

"The . . . folder where you wrote those hilarious revenge plans when you were mad at someone?"

"Yes. I'd been writing about you, about what you experienced when I 'killed' you—how you were the fountain, you were the windows, you were whatever I'd destroyed. All your pain, all the reasons you deserved to suffer."

"But—the things you wrote in that folder used to be funny! Clever!"

"The ones I let you read were funny. They weren't all funny."

"Did you plan to kill me all along?"

"It was a *fantasy*, Cate. You know the things I wrote were fantasies. I never thought I'd *really* hurt you. I had the folder in my briefcase at work. I was so *stupid* to take it to work, but I was so frustrated with everything."

"Frustrated with what kinds of things?"

"Esther was driving me crazy. She'd failed the classes she was taking—she'd stopped attending but hadn't told me. She was spending her life in front of the TV or sleeping, and she was drinking, turning into Dad. Work was a stress mill—the budget cuts were insane; how did they expect us to run a school with so little money? And *you're* posting pictures on Facebook from your trip to Hawaii with your father and Ava—so *glad* you had a marvelous time. I don't suppose it occurred to you that it was the two-year anniversary of Robert's death."

"It *did* occur to me," Catherine said fiercely. "I thought about him."

"Gave him five minutes between the beaches and luaus, did you? Don't even pretend you were sad."

The anger in Danielle's voice kept Catherine from defending her feelings toward Robert. No matter what she said about Robert, it would set Danielle off.

Danielle shifted the gun to her left hand, flexed the fingers of her right hand, then shifted the gun back.

"Why did you take the folder to school with you?" Catherine asked.

"When things got that bad, I felt better keeping it with me so I could look at it or add to it when I needed to."

"Did . . . Olivia see it?"

"I was getting something else out of my briefcase, and I knocked the whole case to the floor. Papers spilled everywhere, next to Olivia's desk. She went to help me pick them up, and I ordered her off. Later, in my office, I went through the folder. I knew exactly what I had in there. It was all new work. I burn the old papers. I don't need them anymore. I was missing one page, a page about you."

Catherine focused on the gun in Danielle's hand and fought an urge to run. "Did you find it?"

"No. Renee was out sick that day, so I came up with an excuse to get Olivia out of the office for a few minutes, and I searched everywhere the paper could have fallen. It wasn't there. I panicked—what if Olivia had found it? Had she read it? Had she told anyone? I sneaked her phone out of her purse. She hadn't called or texted anyone, so that was good at least. Maybe she hadn't found the paper—but maybe she *had* and didn't know what to do about it yet."

Catherine drew shallow breaths, trying not to increase the pain in her gut. "Did you confront her?"

"I turned off her phone and hid it in my purse. It was near the end of the day, and Olivia acted normal toward me—so normal that I got hopeful. The paper must have drifted into some random spot where I hadn't thought to look. She didn't seem to notice her phone was gone— naturally, she didn't chat on it at work. I don't put up with that." Danielle spoke rapidly, with an eager look in her eyes as though she *wanted* to tell Catherine this story. It must be a relief for her to confess the truth. "But I was still terrified. Do you know what it would mean if she'd seen that paper?"

Catherine thought at first it was a rhetorical question, but from the way Danielle paused, she wanted an answer. "If she'd . . . told anyone, they might have known you were the vandal."

"*Might* have known? And even if I could have convinced them it was only a fantasy, that I wasn't the person who went around town smashing things, that wouldn't have saved me. A school principal writing down her sick fantasies of murdering her old friend and carrying those papers with her to school? It was my handwriting—I couldn't pretend it wasn't mine. Even if I wasn't arrested, I would have been fired in a heartbeat, and no school district would have ever hired me again. It would have destroyed me and destroyed Esther. Who would take care of Esther if I lost my job? Lost my job, lost my house, lost everything? She'd self-destruct. She'd *die*, Cate."

"What did you do?"

"I didn't know *what* to do. A few minutes after Olivia left for the day, she came back, saying she couldn't find her phone. She cracked a joke about how she was always losing it, searched, got frustrated, and finally left, saying she needed to get over to the library. A couple of times a month, she did this after-school reading program, where she'd read to the kids. They loved her . . ."

Tears streamed down Danielle's face. Catherine shifted slightly forward so she wasn't leaning against the tree. If Danielle lowered her guard, Catherine wanted to be ready to jump at her to try to knock the gun out of her hand.

"When she said she was going to the library, I said that had reminded me I had some things I needed to pick up there and maybe I'd see her."

"You wanted to follow her to the library to keep an eye on her?"

"Yes, of course. I wandered around, took a few books off the shelves. Passed the children's section a few times, wanting to make sure she was still there, still in a group . . ."

"You mean that she couldn't have gone off to tell anyone. *If* she knew anything."

"Yes. I made sure she didn't see me more than once. I didn't want her to think I was stalking her. When she did see me, she was so normal, so cheerful, that by the time the reading session was done, I'd convinced myself she hadn't seen the paper. It was there in the office. I'd missed it. I went back to the school to search, sure I'd find it."

It was unreal—the gun pointing at her, the rushing noise of the river far below, the agony of guilt in Danielle's eyes. Maybe Catherine *had* lost her mind. Maybe she was imagining this.

"I didn't find the paper," Danielle said. "It wasn't there. I had to talk to Olivia directly. I had to figure out if she knew. Maybe I could bribe her to keep her mouth shut."

"You didn't plan to kill her."

"No. But thank goodness I was careful. I didn't want anyone to see me, to ask her why I'd been there. It was dark by now . . . I wore a big coat, a hood that covered my face. When I got to her apartment, I saw her through the sliding door that led onto her front patio. She was sitting on the couch with a computer on her lap. There was a piece of paper on the couch next to her, but from where I was standing, I couldn't tell if it was mine." She nudged Catherine in the ribs with the muzzle of the gun. "You want me to stop talking, don't you? You don't want to hear the rest of this."

Light-headed at the cold touch of metal, Catherine said, "I do want to hear it. I think you need to say it. What happened when you confronted Olivia?"

Danielle drew the gun back a few inches. "I rang the bell. She jumped—closed the computer, grabbed her paper, and shoved both under the couch. I don't think she realized the blinds were open a little and I could see what she was doing. I held her phone up so when she looked through the peephole, she'd see it and think I'd found it and had come to return it.

"She opened the door and thanked me sweetly for the phone. I asked if I could come in for a moment, that I had a question for her. She said sure." Danielle grinned. Catherine had never imagined that a smile could expose so much pain. "I suppose she still couldn't imagine that Principal Knight would ever hurt her. She asked me if I'd like some cookies. *Cookies!* She offered me cookies!" Danielle started laughing. "She said her boyfriend had made them for her a few days ago, and they were delicious, but he'd just dumped her, so she didn't want to eat them now. To get her out of the room, I said I'd love some cookies and asked her for a glass of milk as well. Cookies and milk! Can you believe it?"

Catherine's heart pounded, and sweat trickled down her back. Danielle was getting hysterical. Should she try to steer the subject away from Olivia? That wouldn't work. What was she supposed to do—ignore the terrifying scenario Danielle was unfolding and comment on the sunset?

"She went into the kitchen." Danielle wiped tears off her face. "I slid her laptop and the paper out from under the couch. The paper *was* mine. On the computer, she had three tabs open. One was the contact information for the school board. The other was a Google search—she'd been Googling *your* name, wanting to know who this Catherine Clayton was whom I was threatening to murder. The third tab was her e-mail, but she hadn't sent anything yet. She must have been trying to figure out what to do."

Catherine felt sicker, imagining Olivia in the kitchen putting cookies on a plate, confident that as long as she pretended to know nothing, Danielle would never hurt her.

"I panicked," Danielle whispered. "I realized trying to bribe her was useless. There were too many identifying details about you in that paper— your money, the fact that you were a musician, other details that would let her find you. Olivia would figure out you could offer her far more money than I could. Helping *you* out by alerting you that I had some psychotic vendetta against you would pay a lot more than helping *me* by keeping my secrets—if she'd even been influenced by money, which she probably wouldn't have been. Olivia loved the kids at Flinders. Loved them. After reading that paper, she must have thought I was simmering with dangerous, violent impulses. A vandal and a potential murderer. That's not someone you'd want around kids. She wouldn't know what I'd written about you was just venting, that I'd never really hurt you. And neither would the superintendent."

Catherine bit her tongue, not daring to point out the ridiculously obvious fact that Danielle *was* dangerous.

"It was so hard to think. All I could feel was panic . . . fury . . . terror at the thought of her telling anyone, ruining me, destroying everything I'd worked for, even sending me to prison on petty, humiliating charges of vandalism. Destroying Esther. If Olivia told anyone, it was the end for Esther. She came back in with a plate of cookies. I picked up that big wrought-iron vase she had sitting on the table behind the couch, and I . . . killed her."

The gun barrel tipped a little downward, no longer aiming straight at Catherine. Danielle's hand must be getting tired. If Catherine jumped at her, catching her by surprise . . .

"I don't even remember when I took the first swing." Danielle's voice went quiet. "Before I could stop myself, she was dead. On the floor. Blood all over her hair."

Catherine didn't dare speak. Danielle edged closer to her, her finger spasmodically touching and pulling away from the trigger of the gun. "I killed a woman. Killed Olivia, sweet Olivia. She was *dead*. And it came back to *you*. I never wanted to kill anyone, but you . . ."

Danielle lifted the gun and flipped it around. Seeing the blow coming, Catherine lurched to the side, but the butt of the gun still struck her cheek. Fireworks went off in her skull, and she landed on her knees.

"I never wanted to hurt her!" Danielle shrieked.

From the fury in Danielle's voice, Catherine knew another blow was coming. She was *not* going to kneel here and die passively one blow at a time. Still on her knees, she threw herself toward Danielle, crashing into her legs. Danielle fell backward.

The gun went off, but wherever the bullet went, it didn't hit Catherine. She grabbed frantically for Danielle's hand, reaching for the gun. Danielle jerked it out of the way, but Catherine followed it, clawing and grasping, and Danielle couldn't steady her arm enough to aim. To Catherine's surprise, Danielle flung the gun away from her. Catherine tried to scramble toward it, but Danielle caught her by the hair.

Dragging Catherine with her, Danielle staggered to her feet. Catherine struck at her, but every blow sent shocks of pain up her arms, and dizziness made it hard to see. She felt herself being hauled over rocks, between trees.

The sound of water coursing below them—the gorge . . . Danielle was going to push her over the edge. If she didn't die from slamming against the rocks, she'd drown in the torrents of water.

Catherine struggled wildly. Danielle lost her grip, and Catherine landed face down on the ground, her elbow crashing into a rock. Rocks, sticks, something to use as a weapon—Catherine grabbed for a chunk of loose granite. When she felt Danielle grab her from behind, she twisted and slammed the rock into whatever part of Danielle she could reach.

The rock struck Danielle in the arm. She screamed and released Catherine. Catherine swung the rock again, but Danielle sprang out of range.

"This is *crazy*!" Catherine yelled. "You never *wanted* to kill anyone. You can stop this *now*! We don't have to die!"

"I want to kill *you*." Danielle picked up a rock and hurled it at Catherine. Flinging herself out of the rock's path, Catherine lost her grip on the rock she'd been wielding. Danielle sprang forward, grabbed Catherine by the arm, and hauled her over the ground with what felt to Catherine like superhuman strength. They were near the edge of the gorge, the ground beginning to slope downward.

Catherine thrashed, yanking her arm out of Danielle's grip. Lithe and fast, Danielle whirled around and sprang on top of Catherine. She locked her arms around Catherine and rolled, propelling both of them toward the edge of the gorge. Catherine struggled, clawing for a root or bush she could hold on to, but there were few trees this close to the edge, and the brush she tried to grab slipped through her fingers. She felt herself and Danielle skidding closer to the edge. In a few more feet, they'd fall.

"Dani, *no!*" Catherine clamped her hands around a root sticking out of the ground. Her body twisted as Danielle tried to drag her onward. Grabbing the root with her other hand, Catherine kicked as savagely as she could. "Dani . . . listen . . . to me. If you die . . . Esther will be alone. Don't *do* this, don't leave her."

She felt Danielle pause, her arms still clamped around Catherine.

"Don't leave her," Catherine repeated. "She needs you."

Danielle's breathing was loud and rough, her body a motionless weight on top of Catherine. "I can't help her anymore. How could I support her from prison?"

"She doesn't want money. She wants her *sister.*"

Danielle didn't move. Praying fervently, Catherine gripped the root as hard as she could.

Danielle shifted, her muscles tensing. "I can't *help* her," she yelled in Catherine's ear. "*You* caused this." She hammered her fist on one of Catherine's hands, pounding against her knuckles. With a yell of pain, Catherine released the root with that hand, swung her arm back, and slammed her elbow into Danielle's throat. Danielle recoiled, her grip on Catherine loosening. Keeping one hand on the root, Catherine contorted her body, squirming around so she was almost face-to-face with Danielle. Her fist caught Danielle on the side of the skull. Kicking, jerking her entire body in an effort to dislodge Danielle, Catherine struck again. Her vision was too blurry; she couldn't see where the blow had landed, but when she threw herself to the side, she felt Danielle's weight slide off of her.

On her back, she kicked at whatever part of Danielle she could connect with. She heard a grating, sliding noise—Danielle, skidding along the loose rocks on the edge of the cliff. Danielle's hand clamped around Catherine's ankle, yanking her so powerfully that Catherine lost her grip on the root.

Screaming, her body sliding toward the chasm, Catherine kicked as hard as she could. Her shoe hit something, and the grip on her ankle loosened. She kicked again, and the pressure of Danielle's fingers lifted.

Catherine drew her legs up under her and crawled frantically up the slope, reaching for the root. She grabbed it with one hand and pulled herself to a sitting position, turning to face Danielle's next attack.

Danielle was gone.

Blinking in the waning twilight, Catherine scanned the edge of the gorge. No sign of Danielle. She crawled upward, back to level ground, and rose, trembling, to look into the gorge.

Water gushed past boulders. Downstream, momentarily caught against a rock, was a flash of orange. It shifted in the water, then broke loose, rounded the boulder, and continued along the rapids.

It couldn't have been anything but Danielle's orange jacket.

* * *

Catherine shuffled down the trail. She had to get help, had to tell someone . . . The pain made her sick; she had to stop, bruised rib muscles convulsing as she vomited by the side of the trail. It was dark . . . too dark . . . It shouldn't be this late . . . Why was she on the ground? She could feel the mud on her cheek, taste it on her tongue. Salty, wet . . . Not dirt. Blood. She was bleeding. *Get up. Find help.*

It was cold; she shivered. It shouldn't be this cold. It had been a sunny day, the leaves brilliant crimson and yellow against a blue sky. Clear water, rushing through the gorge. An orange jacket. A broken body caught against a boulder.

The ground was cold. *Get up.*

She urged her body up and stumbled forward. Tree branches slapped her face.

Was someone calling her name? She was hallucinating. No . . . she heard it again, a male voice. Blearily, she tried to discern where it was coming from.

"*Catherine!*"

Down the trail. She should shout back, but everything hurt so much that the thought of straining her muscles in order to yell made her cringe. She stumbled into the middle of the trail and sat on the dirt.

Hot tears, chilling against her face. Her fingertips digging into the dirt of the trail. Pain in her hands, her wrists, her arms.

Shout back. Tell them you're here. Catherine closed her eyes, drew as deep of a breath as she could manage, and cried out, "Here!"

The effort brought a surge of agony. She sprawled backward on the dirt and waited.

"*Catherine!*" Footsteps, voices—two voices. Light—painful, searing light. The light dipped, moving off of her face. Shadows knelt next to her.

Catherine blinked, struggling to focus. Adam. And Lewis.

"*Catherine.*" Fear resonated through Adam's voice.

"I'm . . . okay."

"What happened?" Adam touched her cheek. "Where is Danielle?"

"I'm sorry. I'm sorry." Lewis's voice cracked. "She attacked you, didn't she?"

The ground beneath her back was hard and bumpy. "Help me sit up," she mumbled.

Hands slid behind her and gently lifted her to a sitting position. "Where's Danielle?" Adam repeated.

"She's . . . dead. She . . . tried to kill me. We fought. She fell into the gorge. Why are you . . . here?"

"We need to get you to the hospital," Adam said. "We'll carry you down the hill."

"I can walk."

"Forget that," Lewis said. "Just put your arms around our necks, if you can."

Holding her breath, Catherine managed to drape a heavy arm around each man's neck. Together, they lifted her and started down the trail.

"How did you . . . know I needed help?" she asked.

"Lewis called me," Adam said. "He was worried about you going off with Danielle."

"How could you have . . . known . . . she was dangerous? None of us knew."

"I didn't know," Lewis said. "But things just seemed wrong."

"What do you mean?"

"Olivia used to talk about Esther and Danielle Knight a lot, and it didn't seem . . . I mean, think of everything that's happened, and no one ever got caught. Then all of a sudden, there's this crazy, wild attack, and I see Esther. *That* one seemed like Esther, but the others . . . attacks with no mistakes, no clues left? Not so much. I didn't think it could *all* be Esther. I wondered if Danielle was involved. I'm a total idiot . . . I should have said something to you tonight, but I couldn't figure out what to say. I kept telling myself you knew Danielle a lot better than I did, and if you weren't worried, why should I be?"

Catherine thought dully that one reason she hadn't noticed Danielle acting strangely tonight was that she'd been preoccupied with false worries about Lewis.

"But after you left, I couldn't stop worrying, so I called Adam, and he knew where you two were going, so we came . . . Sorry . . . If I hadn't been so slow, you wouldn't have gotten hurt like this."

"It's not your fault. It's mine."

Adam spoke softly. "Did Danielle kill Olivia?"

Catherine closed her eyes, new tears streaming down her face. "Yes."

CHAPTER 30

AVA KEPT TRACK OF ALL the flowers and get-well cards that arrived at the studio, making a list for Catherine. Catherine sat in her father's old recliner, looked at the flowers, and made tiny goals for herself.

Comb my hair.

Change the channel on the TV.

Put on a different sweatshirt.

It would have been far easier to do nothing until Ava took her by the hand and directed her, but every time she wanted to lapse into a fog, she felt as though her father were watching her, eyebrows raised. *This is how you cope? By sitting in a stupor and letting Ava tell you when it's time for bed?*

She didn't want to think about Danielle. Every time she imagined Danielle's face, memories stabbed to the core, impaling all of her thoughts and emotions until she couldn't feel anything but pain. The police had recovered Danielle's body a couple of miles from where she'd fallen in. After the news reports of her attack on Catherine, her confession, and her suicide had hit the news, Esther had shown up at the police station and turned herself in.

Renee sent Catherine daisies and carnations. Will sent two dozen red roses in one of his handmade pottery vases. Jan showed up to clean the house; when Ava insisted she didn't need to bother and that Catherine had a housekeeping service, Jan brought several nights' worth of dinners instead. Lewis came early to work every night to walk the property, even though Catherine couldn't imagine any threat remained. He apologized repeatedly for not arriving at Orenda Gorge in time to prevent Danielle's attack, even as Catherine tried to convince him that if he *had* shown up earlier, Danielle likely would have shot all of them. At that point, she had nothing more to lose.

She heard nothing from the Perrys until four days after the attack when Ava brought her a potted orchid someone had left on the porch. The card was signed *Kelsey and Trent,* but Catherine suspected it was solely Kelsey's doing. Trent's feelings toward her were probably too mixed to make him want to send flowers or good wishes.

Adam brought roses as well, peach roses tipped with sunset reds and oranges. Catherine added a new goal to her list: rise from the recliner at least three times a day, walk into the dining room to where Ava had set the roses on the table, and take a few seconds to touch the soft petals and breathe their fragrance. She would *not* forget to appreciate beauty. She would *not* forget to be grateful that she was alive to see and touch these flowers.

But sometimes, it was hard to make herself stand up.

Catherine was en route to the recliner after an evening visit to the roses when the doorbell rang. She hesitated. Should she answer the door?

Too big of a goal for now. It might be a friend, or it might be a reporter or someone else she didn't want to see. Ava could run interference for her. Catherine sank into her chair.

A few moments later, Ava walked into the room. "Adam and his father are here," she said. "Do you feel up to a visit?"

Startled and pleased, Catherine rose to her feet. Dale had come here?

Ava escorted Adam and Dale into the family room. Dale looked even more haggard than he had the last time Catherine had seen him, but he smiled at her.

"Forgive me for barging in, but I've been so worried about you that I forced Adam to drive me over here."

"You shouldn't have. I could have come to you." Catherine moved clumsily forward to greet Dale. Adam remained close behind him, one hand reaching forward as though he feared his father might fall.

Dale took both of Catherine's hands, pulled her to him, and kissed her on the cheek.

"My dear, I'm so sorry for what you've endured and pray the nightmare is over for you."

"Thank you. I'm sorry that . . ." Catherine tried to think of what to say. She felt a compulsion to apologize for the grief, stress, and suspicion Adam had endured when Olivia had died—a murder resulting from Danielle's hatred of Catherine—but couldn't think how to arrange the apology in logical sentences.

"What do you have to be sorry for?" Dale asked. His eyes were kind. Fatherly.

Catherine gave the apology another try. "I . . . I'm sorry that . . . if I hadn't been so oblivious to . . . what was going on in Danielle's head . . ."

"Catherine, your friend's acts of evil were her choice. You tried your best and have nothing to apologize for. I'm just grateful that you are alive, Maren Gates is alive, and my son's reputation is completely clear at last."

"Please, sit down," Catherine said. "You shouldn't overexert yourself."

"I'm happy to overexert myself in a good cause. And I won't be staying. I just wanted to see you." He rested his hand on her shoulder. "I know you're hurting, physically and emotionally. But don't make it harder by condemning yourself for things beyond your control. You couldn't have fixed Danielle."

Calm, firm words. Echoes of her own father. Catherine fought an impulse to grab Dale's hand and hold on. "I . . . wish . . . I could have done *something*."

"So does everyone who knew her and cared about her," Dale said. "She was a remarkable woman, from what I hear. I'll be heading home now, if this lovely lady will give me a ride." Dale nodded at Ava. "That will allow my son a little more time here. I think he wanted a longer visit, if that's all right with you, Catherine."

"Let me get my jacket," Ava said so smoothly that Catherine realized Dale had arranged this with her beforehand.

"Take it easy on yourself." Dale embraced her lightly. Catherine wanted to cling to him, but she knew she couldn't ask him to stay. From the way Adam was hovering, he must fear Dale was tapping into the last of his strength and would collapse at any time.

Tears filled her eyes. "Thank you for coming."

"Come visit me soon."

"I will."

Ava returned, coat on and car keys in hand.

"If I could borrow your arm, Ava, I'd appreciate it," Dale said. "I'm not too steady on my feet—do *not* walk me to the car, Adam; you're annoying me. You stay with Catherine. She needs you, and I need to be rid of you for a while, so this way, everyone gets what they want. Ava will escort me where I need to go."

With a rueful grin of surrender, Adam let Ava escort Dale out of the room.

Catherine wiped her eyes, hoping she could keep more tears from flowing. It didn't work; they poured down her face. "It was sweet of him to come see me," she said. "How's he doing?"

"He's weak, but when he wants something, I can't stop him. When I told him I was coming to see you tonight, he insisted he come along. He's been extremely worried about you and wanted to see you himself." Adam paused then asked, "How are *you* doing? You look better. *Much* better."

"I do?" Wiping away tears, Catherine pictured the glimpse of herself she'd seen recently in the bathroom mirror. "I cringe to think how I must have looked before."

"You're joking again. You're smiling." Adam touched her damp cheek. "You looked like you were in shock, but now you seem . . . awake again."

"Half awake, maybe. It's still hard to focus on anything for long. Or decide anything."

Adam led her to the couch, and they sat down together. After a silent moment, he asked, "What kind of decisions do you find hard?"

"Like . . . whether or not to change out of my pajamas. Deciding to get up out of my chair and actually do something—*anything*. It doesn't help that I can't play the cello right now." She lifted her battered hands. "I could *really* use that stress relief."

"How long until you can get back to it?"

"Not long, I hope. I'm fervently grateful there's no permanent damage." She lowered her hands. "You know what's odd? Danielle accused me of having an 'all about me' attitude—and guess what?" Fresh tears filled her eyes. "The murders—or rather the murder and attempted murder—in Riley really were about me. Nice irony, huh?"

Adam intertwined his fingers with hers, his touch so gentle that she knew he was being careful of her injuries. "The murders were about Danielle, not about you. You were her excuse. I wonder if . . . Well, I'm not a psychiatrist, but after she killed Olivia, I think she *needed* to hate you more than ever for her own sanity. If she could blame you, she didn't have to accept responsibility for what she'd done."

Tentatively, Catherine examined this idea. "I *have* wondered why she made the effort to stay in touch with me if she despised me. I even asked her why she invited me to Riley, and she said it was so she could kill me . . . but there were a lot easier ways to get to me than to go through all the work of helping me get established here. Maybe she needed me close to keep the hate fresh." She sighed. "I guess it's impossible to know what she was thinking. Esther would have a better grasp on what motivated her."

"Have you been able to talk to Esther?"

"No, but I did send the message that if I can do anything to help her, I will."

"That's generous after the things she did to you."

"Adam, she went about it in a rash way, but she *was* trying to help me. And if she hadn't called me while I was hiking with Danielle, I would have been completely off guard. Danielle would have been able to walk me right to the edge of the gorge. I'd be dead now."

Agony showed in Adam's eyes. "Catherine . . ."

Catherine tightened her fingers around his as much as she could without aggravating her scraped, bruised knuckles. "I wonder why she repaid the money," she said, wanting to turn the subject away from what had happened in Orenda Gorge. As soon as she spoke the words, she realized she'd never told Adam about the money she'd given Danielle anonymously in grad school. *Oops.* She didn't want to explain now, but hiding the story from Adam as though she were ashamed of it was silly.

"What money?" Adam asked.

Catherine explained. "Why would she have repaid me if she was planning to kill me?"

"Interesting question. Maybe it's hard to kill someone when you feel indebted—even grateful—to them. Maybe she was . . . trying to clear the way for what she planned to do."

Catherine thought of Danielle's saying brusquely, *The account is closed now. I'm out of debt.*

Done with that painful topic, Catherine said, "Tonya Maxwell called today. Ava screens my calls—I haven't been up to talking to people—and Tonya asked her what I was planning to do. If I was planning to stay or if I was closing up shop."

"What did Ava tell her?"

"That no decisions have been made yet. How's that for vague and businesslike? Ava's been so good to me. If I'd had to field that call, I would have been a deer in the headlights . . . wouldn't have even been able to answer Tonya. Did I mention I'm having trouble with decisions?"

"That's a huge decision. You don't have to make it right away. Take some time to rest."

"I'm scared to stay . . . scared of what challenges there might be . . . scared of memories that hurt so much that all I can do is bawl—um, here's a live demonstration." Catherine pointed to her tear-filled eyes. "I'm scared that the public image of the studio will always be shadowed by everything that's happened."

"I doubt . . ." Adam trailed off. Catherine knew he had too much experience with damaging rumors to glibly dismiss the issues she might face due to gossip.

"My name is all over the news," she said. "Or so I hear; I'm avoiding the news right now. I feel . . . what's the word . . . Did I mention it's hard to think? Like I'm—can't think of the word. An anticelebrity?"

"Infamous?" Adam suggested.

"Yes. *Infamous.* Tabloid fodder. Half of Riley must be wondering what kind of devil I am to torment Danielle Knight to the point of murderous insanity. How do I deal with that? How can I run the studio with that hanging over me?"

Adam had a thoughtful look in his eyes. "First of all, I can't imagine that more than a handful of kooks think you did anything wrong. I haven't heard any buzz in that direction."

"I can't believe *everyone* thinks I'm a saint."

"Okay. Realistically, there might be a few cruel people out there who have a warped view of your role in what happened. I know what it feels like to have people believe false rumors about you. You want to stand on rooftops and shout out your innocence. You want every person who ever doubted you to admit that they're wrong. It doesn't work that way. Which reminds me—Trent Perry came to visit me."

"He did? I hope he crawled!"

Adam chuckled. "He gave a very stiff, formal apology. We shook hands. He took off."

"He could have done a lot better," Catherine said. "But progress is good. I hope the Perry's are more at peace."

"Everyone still has a lot of healing to do. Catherine . . . if you decide to leave, you don't have to feel guilty about that. You have more than enough legitimate reasons for packing up. You're not obligated to tie yourself to Riley if it hurts too much to stay."

"I'm going to hurt no matter where I am. I've been trying to think about it today. Not very successfully, but trying. Honestly, Adam, there *is* part of me that wants to run away from Riley—run away from people whispering about me and wondering about me. If I *did* come here for the praise and honor and all those limelight perks, then I *should* go, because my reputation is destined to be a mixed bag for a long time. Danielle was right—I *did* care about that too much. But I won't let myself care too much anymore. I'm here for my students and future students—to bring joy to *them*. People like Maren Gates . . . Tate Maxwell . . ."

"You sound like you *have* made a decision."

"Maybe I have." She gestured at the flower-filled room. "When I think of walking away from this, I feel awful." She turned so she could look Adam in the eyes. "And I want more time to get to know you."

He smiled crookedly. "I'm honored to be a factor in your decision. Since you've already told me you want to stay, I'll go ahead and confess I was hoping that would be your decision. But even if you feel you need to leave, I'll make sure we see each other. I want whatever is best for you."

"Thank you." She felt clearer in her mind than she had since the battle with Danielle. "Thank you for everything."

"Let me help you with whatever you need." Adam leaned closer. "I can do handyman repairs, gardening, whatever. Guard duty. Floor mopping. Open-house refreshments—if you want to go ahead with that."

"I do, but I'll wait a few months. A party feels wrong right now."

"I understand."

They looked at each other, wordless. Catherine felt her cheeks turning pink and her pulse accelerating.

"When you're . . . ready to plan the party, say the word, and I'll do whatever you need," Adam said.

"Okay." All Catherine could think of was how much she wished Adam would kiss her. He leaned a little closer, but she could sense his nervousness, see the hesitation in his eyes. He was afraid he was pushing things too fast at a time when Catherine wasn't ready for it.

Catherine put her hand on the back of Adam's neck, pulled him toward her, and kissed him.

When they drew apart, Adam grinned, his neck flushed. "Was I playing it too slowly?"

"Yes. Start at the beginning and speed up the tempo."

He held her face between his hands, his fingers light. "Looks like I need to practice."

"You do," Catherine whispered. "I'm a tough teacher. Try it again."

ABOUT THE AUTHOR

STEPHANIE BLACK HAS LOVED BOOKS since she was old enough to grab the pages and has enjoyed creating make-believe adventures since she and her sisters were inventing long Barbie games filled with intrigue and danger or running around pretending to be detectives. She is a four-time Whitney Award winner for best mystery/suspense, most recently for *Rearview Mirror* (2011).

Stephanie was born in Utah and has lived in various places, including Arizona, Massachusetts, New York, and Limerick, Ireland. She currently lives in Northern California and enjoys spending time with her husband, Brian, and their five children. She is a fan of chocolate, cheesecake, and her husband's homemade bread.

Stephanie enjoys hearing from readers. You can contact her via email at info@covenant-lds.com or by mail, care of Covenant Communications, P.O. Box 416, American Fork, UT 84003-0416. Visit her website at www.stephanieblack.net and her blog, Black Ink, at www.stephanieblackink.blogspot.com.